13.95
.95

DIVINA TRACE

ROBERT ANTONI

DIVINA TRACE

A NOVEL

The Overlook Press
Woodstock • New York

For María Rosario de Medina Antoni
1891–1986

First published in 1992 by
The Overlook Press
Lewis Hollow Road
Woodstock, New York 12498

*Portions of this novel have appeared in the anthology Hot Type and in
Ploughshares, Conjunctions and the Paris Review.*

Library of Congress Cataloging-in-Publication Data

Antoni, Robert. 1956–
   Divina Trace / Robert Antoni.
      p.   cm.
   I. Title
PS3551.N77D5   1992
813'.54 – dc20   91-26626
   ISBN 0-87951-445-0 (cloth)   CIP
   ISBN 0-87951-485-X (paper)

DOMINGO FAMILY

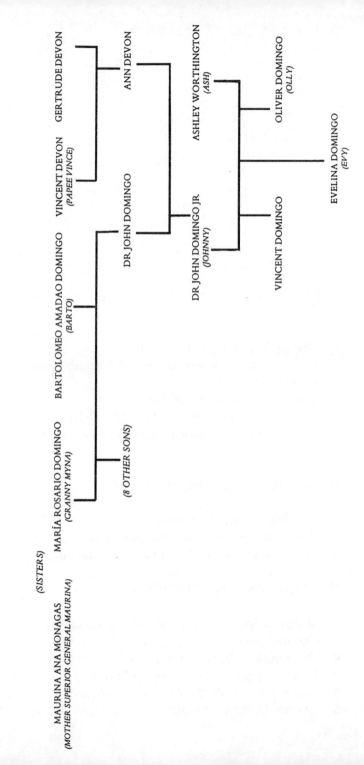

MAURINA ANA MONAGAS
(MOTHER SUPERIOR GENERAL MAURINA)

(SISTERS)

MARÍA ROSARIO DOMINGO
(GRANNY MYNA)

BARTOLOMEO AMADAO DOMINGO
(BARTO)

(8 OTHER SONS)

DR JOHN DOMINGO

GERTRUDE DEVON

VINCENT DEVON
(PAPEE VINCE)

ANN DEVON

DR JOHN DOMINGO JR
(JOHNNY)

ASHLEY WORTHINGTON
(ASH)

VINCENT DOMINGO

OLIVER DOMINGO
(OLLY)

EVELINA DOMINGO
(EVY)

I

FROGCHILD ON THE DAY OF CORPUS CHRISTI

1

Granny Myna
Tells of the Child

THE BOTTLE was big and obzockee. I was having a hard time toting it. It was the day before my thirteenth birthday, seventy-seven years ago: tomorrow I will be ninety years of age. I am still a practising physician, and as I sit here in this library, at this desk of my father's, of my father's father – lugged as a trunk of purpleheart wood by six Warrahoon Indians out of the misty jungles of Venezuela, floated down the Orinoco and towed across the Caribbean behind three rowing pirogues, my grandfather calling the cadence stroke by stroke in a language nearly forgotten – I can still hear him, sitting behind this desk, looking out of this window at this moon above the same black, glistening sea. I can still hear him. I know my grandfather's voice, even though he died ages before I was born. Even though I could not remember who told the story or when I'd heard it, nor did I know what those words meant or whether they were words at all, as I carried the huge glassbottle my steps suddenly fell into the rhythm of his voice: *Na-me-na-na-ha! Na-me-na-na-ha! Na-me-na-na-ha!*

I was bareback, wearing only my baggy school short-pants and my old jesusboots, so skinny my navel stuck out in a tight knot. I held the bottle against my chest. My arms were wrapped around it, my fingers cupped into the hollow of the bottom, the top butting up my chin with every step. I couldn't look down, so I didn't have to see what I knew was inside. It was a very old bottle, the kind used to preserve fruit, made of thick glass with wire clamps to hold down its glass lid. I was sweating. My stomach kept sticking to the bottle. My bung navel rubbed against the glass, sometimes pinching and sending a shock down my legs to my toes. I sucked in my belly as I walked.

The sun was already rising behind me, rising with the dust stirred up by my hurrying feet. I was thinking: *Maraval must be ten mile from Domingo Cemetery at least. How you could foot it there and back in time?* Thinking: *Ten mile from Domingo Cemetery to Maraval Swamp fa the least. Daddy ga box you ears fa true if you don't get back in time. This bottle heavy like a boulderstone. And these arms only crying to drop off. But how you could stop to put it down?*

There were no people yet on the trace, only some potcakes curled up among the weeds pushing out in the middle, and a few old billies on their way to pasture, lengths of twisted rotten cord dragging behind them. They were as tall as I was, and they came at me snuffling, pressing their bearded faces into mine, staring at me through silver eyes from another world. I kicked them away, thinking: *How she could be dead if she eyes aren't closed? But if she isn't dead, and you are home in you bed dreaming all this, then how you could be tired toting this bottle?* Thinking: *You know they ga start with the funeral first thing as she was so hurry hurry. So you best just keep on walking, and don't even bother templating bout stopping to put it down to waste no time, and anyway you don't want to have to look at he face neither.*

There were small villages along Divina Trace, the footpath which began behind the convent, weaving its way through tenements in the outskirts of St Maggy, and passing behind the graveyard. Then it stretched out through cocoa and coconut estates in the country, cane-

fields, finally ending with the Church of Magdalena
Divina at the edge of Maraval Swamp. Now, outside of
town, the trace curved through bush – with the shanties
and roukou-scrubbed mudhuts half-hidden behind giant
tufts of bamboo, schools of yardfowl scurrying in dust-
waves as I approached, the odours of cooking coalpots,
stench of rubbish – unless the trace traversed one of the
estates. Then it ran straight, mossy grey cocoa trees on
either side, with nutmeg or brilliant orange immortelle in
between to shade them from the sun. Otherwise the trace
passed among thick groves of coconut palms, their fronds
rustling in the breeze high above, or it would be closed in
by purple walls of cane, the air sweet-smelling, charred if
the field had been scorched to scare out the scorpions for
harvest. There were hills from which the mountains could
be seen at one horizon, hot black sea at the other.

I'd been to Maraval Swamp many times before, but I
didn't want to believe it was ten miles away. I kept
thinking: *Maybe it's not so far as that? You know it is ten mile
at least. How many times you been to the church with Mother
Maurina and the whole of St Maggy Provisional to see the
walking statue and hear bout the Black Virgin? How many times
you been to the swamp with Papee Vince and the whole of form
three science to collect specimens fa dissections? With daddy and
all five troups of seascouts to catch jumping frogs fa the summer
jamboree?* Thinking: *You know it is ten mile fa the least. How
many times you been with you jacks to catch guanas to pope them
off on the Indians by Suparee fa fifty cent fa each? Running and
grabbing them up quick by they tails and swinging them round
and round until they heads kaponkle, and they drop boodoops
sweet in the crocasssack! And the time you get a dollar fa that big
big one, and you eat so many julie-mangoes fa that dollar you
belly wanted to bust froopoops! How them coolies and Warrahoons could eat them things?* But Granny Myna say Barto used
to eat guana all the time in Venezuela when they was first
married, and they had the cattle ranch in Estado Monagas where

*daddy was born. And the time Barto try to bring one inside and
she chase him out with he own cutlass, because one thing Granny
Myna wouldn't stand in the house is no kind of creature curse to
walk on he belly, and it is from eating that nastiness that kill
Barto young so. But daddy say a Warrahoon bring him a stew
guana to the hospital once, and he couldn't tell the difference from
fricassee chicken.*

I didn't want to think about the contents of the bottle,
about the ten miles ahead, and I didn't want to think about
getting back too late for the funeral. I'd been up the whole
night, and I was already tired carrying the bottle. I'd only
just left the cemetery. I hadn't been able to fall asleep that
night, turning in my bed thinking about old Granny
Myna. She'd told me a story once about a frog she'd seen
suck out the eye of a woman in Wallafield, and I could not
dissolve from my mind the image of this woman struggling with the huge, white frog. It was one of those flying
frogs, and the woman had been sitting good as ever
beneath a tamarind tree. As soon as she looked up the frog
flew out and stuck *frapps* to her face. Granny Myna told
me it took two big men to pull off this frog, and when he
came off the eye came out too. She said that if Barto had
not been there to pick up the eye from out the mud, to spit
on it and rub off the mud and push it back in, the woman
would have walked away from that frog without an eye.

It was not unusual for me to awaken in the middle of the
night and begin thinking of Granny Myna and one of her
stories, but I remember this time I could not put her and
the frog out of my mind. My grandmother was ninety-
six, always talking about dying, yet Granny Myna had
never known a sick day in her life, and I was convinced
she'd live forever. I couldn't fall asleep, so I woke up my
younger brother to ask him about the woman from
Wallafield. He cussed me and rolled over again. I remember I lay there listening to the oscillating fan, its noise
growing louder with each pass, until it seemed to be

screaming in my ears. I threw off the sheet and jumped out of bed. I pulled on my shorts, buckled on my jesusboots, and walked quietly down the hall. Papee Vince, my grandfather on my mother's side, had his room at the end. I hurried past and on down the stairs. Granny Myna's door was open, so I stuck my head in. She was sitting up in her bed waiting. I went and sat beside her. She looked at me for a long time, reached across me to put her gold rosary down on the bedstand, and she began to talk.

HE WAS BORN a man, but above he cojones he was a frog. It happen so, because Magdalena Domingo was a whore, and a black bitch, and on top of that she was a bad woman. Magdalena make this practice of going every Sunday to Maraval Swamp, because I used to follow her and sometimes she would meet there with Barto beneath the samaan tree, she go to Maraval Swamp because she like to watch the crapos singando. Magdalena just love to see the frogs fucking, and is that she must have been looking the moment she conceive the child, because Barto used the same principle to create a zebra from two donkeys by putting them to do they business in a room he have paint with stripes. So too again everybody take you daddy for another St John, because above my bed I have the picture hanging with him still smiling happy on the dishplate that I used to look up at it in all my moments of passion, and that is why you daddy have that same crease right here in the middle of he forehead, and how else could it be you daddy is the only Domingo with those eyes always watching you just like St John? You see how Papa God does do He work? In the same way Magdalena make that child with the face of a frog to mimic she own, and with the cojones of *every* man on this island of Corpus Christi!

When Dr Brito Salizar see this child coming out, he only

want to push it back inside Magdalena pussy and hide it from the rest of the world. Dr Brito know nothing good could come from this child that is the living sin of all the earth. Because it take Magdalena only one look in the face of this frogchild to kill sheself dead: she press the pillow and hold up she breath until she suffocate. By the time Dr Brito have realize and cut the pillow from out she lock up jaws she was already dead. Feathers was gusting back and forth in that little hospital room like a blizzard. Dr Brito blow into the air before him to clear way the floating feathers, he cross heself, and Dr Brito open he mouth wide to bend over to bite off the cordstring from the belly of this crapochild to join the world of the living with the world of the dead for the whole of eternity!

That night there was such a great rain that the Caronee have overflow sheself, and the next morning there was cocodrilles in the streets and the basements of all the houses. So when Barto arrive now dress in mud up to he cojones, and holding this shoebox in he hands, I grab on to he moustache and I put one cursing on him to say he is *never* coming inside the house with that crapochild! But Barto is a man that nobody couldn't tell him nothing once he have make up he head, and he don't pay no attention a-tall never mind my bawling to break down the roof. I tell him Papa God will kill him and all of us too if he try to bring that crapochild inside, but Barto can't even hear, because he walk straight through the front door and he put this shoebox down in the middle of the diningroom table. And if I would have give Barto only half a chance, he would have lay this frogchild right down next to Amadao who is sleeping in my bedroom in the crib, born no even six months before.

Well Evelina, she is the servant living with me even in those days, just a little negrita running round the estate when she mummy dead and I take her up, Evelina only have to hear about this crapochild coming inside the house, and she start to beat she breast and shout one set of Creole-obeah bubball on the child, and she run quick to she room to bury sheself beneath the bed. Reggie and Paco, they is the last of the nine boys before Amadao sleeping in the cradle, Reggie and Paco come running to Barto to question him where do he find this chuffchuff frog, and could they please take him in the yard to find out how good can he jump. But Barto only have to make one cuteye on these boys for them to know he is no skylarking, and little Reggie and Paco take off running and we don't see them again until late in the night. As for me now, after a time I have quiet down little bit and Barto turn to me, because of course at this time I am still nursing Amadao, and he want to know now if I am ready to feed he Manuelito, which is the name Barto pronounce on the child official with salt and water. Sweet heart of Jesus! I look Barto straight in he eyes, and I tell him if he only bring that crapochild anywhere near by me, I will squeeze he cojones so hard they will give off milk like two balls of cheese, and he could feed *that* to he pendejo frogchild!

But nothing couldn't stop Barto. Like he want to take on Papa God self. Because next thing I see he have pick up he revolver again to protect against the cocodrilles, and he go outside to the shed for the big cow that we have there by the name of Rosey. And this Rosey have been with us so many years that she have come tame tame, that the boys used to ride her all about the place like a horse, and we have to be very careful no to leave a plantain or anything so on the table, because soon as you turn round she would push she head in through the window and carry it way. So here is me now only standing up like a mokojumbie watching at Barto leading this cow through the mud that is high as Rosey belly, and Barto carry her straight through the entrance hall into the diningroom up on top the table. Oui Papayo! Well now I know I am soon to go viekeevie!

Barto leave Rosey there just so, and he gone to the sea for a bucket of water to wipe off the mud from Rosey pechugas. But when Barto pick up this frogchild out the shoebox, and I have a good look at this frogchild face for the first time, I take off with one set of bawling again because you never see no creature on the skin of Papa God earth so ugly as that! Even Rosey have to jump when she see this crapochild, and Barto have to hold her down to keep her from bolting out the door. But nothing couldn't stop Barto once he have make up he head, because next thing I see he is untying the cowboy kerchief from round he neck, and he fix it to hide poor Rosey eyes. In no time a-tall she have calm down again, and Barto is holding this crapochild below her with the tottot in the big frogmouth, and he is sucking down milk that is spilling all over the ugly frogface, and he is talking one set of froglanguage like *oy-juga oy-juga oy-juga!*

That night I am in my bed trying my best to sleep with all this confusion going on in the house, and Barto come inside the room, because Barto used to keep he own bedroom upstairs, in the one you mummy and daddy use now, he come inside the room just here at the end of this bed pointing he revolver at me with he eyes only spitting fire, demanding to know what have I do with he Manueli-to. Sweet heart of Jesus! I answer him that this frogchild have make he brain viekeevie now for true, because is no me a-tall to touch that crapochild no even until the ends of the earth, and if he have disappear I don't know nothing as the last I see him he is still sleeping happy in he shoebox cradle in the middle of the diningroom table. But Barto have reach into a state now over this crapochild, so I decide to go and wake up Evelina and the two of us begin to ransack the house, looking in all the drawers and beneath the beds and all about for this child, that we can't find him nowhere a-tall and we don't know what we will do. Just then I hear Evelina scream someplace outside, and

I take off running to find her there by the pond for all the ducks to come and bathe theyself, there standing up with she eyes open wide wide like she have just see a jabjab, only watching at Reggie and Paco and this frogchild swimming!

Next morning the whole of St Maggy have reach at my doorstep to see this crapochild. The Caranee have no even begin to go down yet, and the mud in the streets is still high as you knees, but nothing couldn't slow down these people. In all the windows they is jam up standing one on top the next waiting half the day for only a glimpse of this frogchild, and the little baboo boy see the crowd to come running pushing he bicyclecar through the mud with all the bottles of sweetsyrup spilling out, and he begin to shave ice like he catch a vaps, selling one set of snowball to all these people only looking through the glass licking licking with all they tongues green and purple and yellow like this is one big pappyshow going on now with this cow and this crapochild inside the house! Everybody is laughing and bawling and blowing out they cheeks making one set of frogfaces to imitate this child, and soon I begin to hear somebody mamaguying me about how *I* is the mother of this crapochild, when they know good enough the child belong to Barto and that black jamet Magdalena and I don't have nothing to do with him a-tall, and how they use to see *me* with Barto all the time by Maraval watching the frogs fucking. Sweet heart of Jesus! I run quick to that shoebox cradle and I grab up this crapochild, and I go to Barto on my knees to beg him please for the mercy of Papa God please to carry him way!

Barto look down on me a moment, and I see that I have finally touch him. Because he reach down and he take way this crapochild that is wrap up now in a white coverlet that you can no even see the half belonging to a man. Barto carry the child to the big closet of glass that we have there in the parlour to keep all the guns. He take out the biggest

one, this is the rifle all bathe in silver and mother-of-pearl
that we have there since the days of General Monagas, and
Barto carry the child and the gun both up to the garret. He
climb out on top the roof and he walk straight to the very
edge. Barto did no even open he mouth to speak a word.
He stand up there just so in he leather clothes that I have
rub all over with sweetoil until they are glowing, and he is
holding this frogchild with he legs spread wide and the
spurs on he cowboy boots and he eyes only flaming, and
he reach out slow with he arm straight and General
Monagas big rifle pointing up at heaven to fire so *boodoom!*
and all these people take off running swimming in the mud
like each one get jook with a big jooker *up* they backside!

PEOPLE HAD BEGUN to appear on the road, most
walking in the direction of town. They were dressed in
their best clothes for church, or they were already costumed as some saint or Bible character, some figure from
the Hindu holy books. That day was a big one for Corpus
Christi: it was the religious feastday after which the island
had been named. Most of us went to Mass in the morning.
In the afternoon there were parades through the streets of
St Maggy, the fêtes continuing until midnight. Because at
the stroke of twelve all the music stopped, and we
returned to church to begin the Easter Vigil. There were
never any motorcars on the trace other than the occasional
truck or jitney belonging to one of the estates. Bicycles
and donkeycarts went by, some already decorated with
crêpe paper and papier-mâché.

Everyone who passed looked at me toting the huge
bottle. I was sweating, covered in dust, thinking: *Supposing somebody see this frogbaby now and push out a scream?
Supposing somebody question you where you get him from?
What you ga say? You dig him up in Domingo Cemetery? You*

catch him in Maraval Swamp? Then I began to think: *But
nobody seeing this frogbaby a-tall! You sure you have anything
in this glassbottle? Maybe it's only fill with seawater? Maybe
this frogbaby is only some monster you dream up? Some jujubee
Granny Myna push inside you head?*

Just then a boy about my own age – costumed as Moses
in a white turban, and dragging a big tablet of pasteboard
commandments behind him – grabbed his father's sleeve
and pointed at me: 'See that, Daddy? Look the frog that
boy hold up inside he glassbottle. He big as a monkey! He
live you know, Daddy. He *swimming!*'

MAGDALENA JUST LOVE to go to Maraval to see the
crapos singando, because she used to walk all the way
from St Maggy Convent every Sunday parading through
the streets dress up in she white clothes of a nun before the
face of Papa God, when beneath she is nothing but a black
whore. And it is those frogs fucking Magdalena must have
been looking to make the impression of that frogface the
moment she conceive the child, because a crapo is the only
creature on the skin of Papa God earth that can hold on and
singando passionate for three days and three nights without even a pause for a breath of air, and how else could he
come out a man perfect so with the big business hanging
and the rest a frog? Of course Dr Brito realize straight way
this child is a crapo above the cojones, and he say that he
have hear of more frogchildren even though he never have
the privilege before to see one heself, but I know that is
impossible because this world could never be big enough
for two. The other schoolboy-doctor in the hospital then,
he is the first to come from England with a big degree
stamp by the Queen that was Elizabeth the segundo one,
but how can anybody with sense listen to a doctor who
learn everything from a book without even seeing a sick
person? this little schoolboy-doctor say the child isn't no

frog a-tall, but he have a kind of a thing in the blood or the genes or something so. He bring out the big black book that is so big he can hardly tote it, and he point to the picture of this thing now that is name after the first two girlchildren to be born with this disease, and he mark it down on a piece of paper for me to believe it: ANNA-AND-CECILY. The little schoolboy-doctor say this thing means to be born without a brain, and that is what cause the child to *look* like a frog. But it is you Uncle Olly, he is the scientist of bones and rocks and a very brilliant oldman, Uncle Olly prove without any questions that the child *is* a frog, and he *do* have a brain, even though it is no bigger than the size of a prune.

The frogchild didn't have no skull a-tall, but only the soft soft covering on the head like the skin of a zabuca. So all Uncle Olly have to do is cut a little cut with the scissors, and squeeze on the both sides, and the little brain pop out like a chenet out the shell. Of course the first thing Uncle Olly do is run quick to Maraval for a big crapo grande, and he take out the brain of this frogbull to compare it with that of the child. Well the two was so much the same in size and shape and weight and every-thing so, that soon as Uncle Olly go outside for a quick weewee and come back, he forget who belong to who.

I only wish to Papa God Uncle Olly could have satisfy heself with that brain! But when it come to he science nothing couldn't satisfy you Uncle Olly. By the time he have finish with that brain he was all excited, and he decide now he want to preserve this crapochild for more dissec-tions. It is Uncle Olly then who put the child in the bottle of seawater, but the same night Barto discover him floating downstairs on the shelf in Olly laboratory, and that, is the beginning of the end.

A MAN in an oxcart going in my direction stopped beside

me: 'Eh-eh whiteboy, tell me what you say!'

I stood staring up at this oldman who'd wrapped himself and his entire oxcart in aluminium foil. He nodded his nose at the bottle: 'Where you going toting dat glassbottle fa health? Dat ting big as you own self! Why you don't climb up here rest you load, let me carry you little bit down de road?'

'Who you is?' I asked. 'Robot?'

The oldman chupsed: he sucked his teeth in exasperation. 'I is de archangel St Michael, dis my chariot going to battle. And you best get you little backside up here fa sin, you ga dead up youself toting dat big glasstin.' He chupsed again. '*Robot!*'

I gave the bottle a heave onto the shelf where the oldman rested his feet. He leaned over and studied it for several long seconds. He sat up again, his costume crinkling, and we looked at each other.

'Come boy!' he said, and I climbed up onto the bench next to him, the bottle between us. The oldman nudged his nose over his shoulder: 'Plenty more tinpaper back dere fa you, you know. Why you don't costume youself proper, we to play mas fa so!'

'You don't think one robot is enough, oldman?'

He chupsed, and he gave the worn rope he had for reins a tug. We left slowly, pitching from side to side as we went, the solution sloshing in the bottle at our feet. The oxen was a huge coolie-buffalo, with widespread s-shaped horns and a sticky mist rising from its bluegray hump. After awhile the oldman looked at me again, his face beaded with perspiration. His white stubble of beard, grey eyes and lashes looked silver against his umber-burntblack skin: it all seemed to match his aluminium outfit.

'Where you going toting dis bottle on Corpus Christi Day?' he asked. 'Corpus Christi is the day fa play is play!'

I was looking up at his cone-shaped hat, the cuffed brim riding on the bridge of his nose, like the oversized cap of a yankee-sailor.

'What wrong with you, boy? You don't talk?'

'You not hot inside all that costume?'

He chupsed. 'Where you going with dis glassbottle, boy?'

'You ever see a frogbaby before, oldman?'

He sucked his teeth again. 'Ninety-some years I been walking dis earth, me mummy tell me. Still plenty tings I never see.'

A breeze came up and the oldman held on to his hat. I shielded my eyes against the dust raised from the road.

'Oldman, you think somebody could die with their eyes open?'

He turned to look at me: 'Everybody born with dey eyes close down, and everybody die with dey eyes open up round. Papa God mistake is He do de whole business back-to-front. And dat boy, is de beginning of all dis confusion and quarrelment. Now tell where you going toting dis glassbottle.'

'Maraval.'

'Quite so to Maraval footing? Good ting I stop, boy. You would have dead up youself polapeezoy, time you arrive by de swamp with dis big glasstin.'

He reached behind and handed me the roll of aluminum foil. 'Corpus Christi not de day to tote no heavy load. Dress up youself proper let we play! We ga meet up de band down de road, do one set of monekeybusiness before we pray!'

I told him I had to go to Maraval Swamp.

He chupsed. 'Suit youself den, whiteson. Time as we bounce up with de flock of Seraphim, you would have almost reach you destination.'

I put the roll of foil down as we continued, the ox walking at its slow, steady pace, the cart pitching on its unsteady wheels.

I NEVER HOLD nothing against Magdalena. Papa God is she judge, and if she is a whore she must answer to Him. Who am I to say she is wrong to be Barto mistress, and how can I hold that crapochild against her, or Barto, or anybody else when he is a creature of Papa God, touch by He own hand, make of He own flesh, breathing of He own air? And so I pick him up. Even though he is the most hateful thing to me in all the world, he is still the son of my husband, and I must go to this child. I am there with Evelina in the kitchen in the middle of preparing dinner when I feel something touch my heart. I don't even finish putting the remainder of the dasheen leaves in the pot of boiling water to make the callaloo, but I leave it there just so and I go to this frogchild. I pick him up with so much tears in my eyes I can hardly see, with so much trembling in my hand I can hardly hold it steady enough to push my tottot in he mouth, but I do it. For the love of Papa God I do it! I feed him with the milk of my *own* breast!

I never hold nothing against Magdalena. I try my best never to listen to what people say, and let me tell you people can say some words to push like a knife in you chest. But I never hold nothing against Magdalena. I am kind to her, and when I meet her in the cathedral with all the other nuns I make a special point to wish her a pleasant todobien, because who am I to say Barto must give he affections to me alone when he have enough love in he heart for all the world? No husband have ever honour he wife more, and offer her more love and devotion than that man give to me. Barto raise me up on a pedestal, you hear? On a *pedestal!*

But something happen when that child begin to suck at my breast. Something happen, and I don't know what it is. Like some poison pass from out he mouth to go inside my blood, because next thing I know I am running back to the kitchen for that big basin of boiling water that is waiting for me to finish the callaloo, and I push him in.

Evelina scream but I can't even hear her, because before I can know what my hands are doing they are bury up to they elbows in this boiling water, and how to this day I can no even feel it I couldn't tell you, because here am I drowning this child in the basin of boiling water with the dasheen leaves swirling swirling like the green flames of hell!

Soon as I can realize myself I pull him from out the water, but by now he is already dead. I can no think what to do. I can only plead with Evelina for the mercy of Papa God please to take him way. I beg her to carry him back to Maraval where he belong, but Evelina refuse to come anywhere near this crapochild no matter if he is living or if he is dead. After a time though she have accept to carry him way from me, and I swear her to go straight to Maraval and pitch him in, and I go outside in the street to look behind Evelina walking with this crapochild hold upside down by he legs like a cockfowl going to sell at Victoria Market. I watch behind Evelina until I can no see her any more, and I go back in the house to try my best to finish seeing about the callaloo. I only wish to Papa God I could have remain in that street! Because I put loud goatmouth on myself saying about that crapofowl, as no sooner have I go back inside the house when Evelina turn round to come all the way back, only to sell this crapochild to Uncle Olly for a scrunting five coconut dollars. Uncle Olly have decide now he want to make some of he science on the child, and that night Barto find him floating on the shelf downstairs in Olly laboratory. Sweet Heart of Jesus! I thought Barto would kill me. I have never see him so upset as when he come to me with this bottle, and he demand me to tell him what happen to the child. When I have finish, and I am kneeling down on the ground pleading with him standing above me with he eyes only flaming, he tell me that I will suffer for this the whole of my life and death, because I can never even look forward to lying in the ground in peace beside my husband, as between us will be this crapochild to remind me on myself and torment me until the ends of eternity. And with that Barto leave toting the bottle into the night.

But I can never suffer any more. After ninety-six years I have no more strength left to go on. My eyes have dry up, and there is no more tears left to pass, and Papa God have forgive me. He have forgive me, and tomorrow I will be with Him in heaven. Papa God have forgive me, and Barto must forgive me now after all these years of crying in the dark, and I am ready. I am ready to lie down my bones in peace, peace that I have earn with sweating blood cold in the hot night, but I will never know peace so long as I have to be bury next to that crapochild. *Never!* But you will take him way, Johnny. You will go for me tonight to Domingo Cemetery, and you will dig him up, and you will carry him way. Now I am ready to die. Go and call you mummy and daddy.

WE COULD HEAR the Divina Church band beating steeldrums in the distance long before we met them. The sun remained hidden behind the dark clouds, but the oldman continued to sweat in his aluminium outfit. A breeze came up and blew away his hat, so I took up the roll of foil and stood on the bench to make him another, a tall spike shooting up at the top – helmet fit for an archangel. There must have been fifty people in the band, and as many children, all costumed as angels. The oldman steered his oxcart to the side of the road and we watched the parade go by, the angels waving to us as they passed. Most went on foot, but there were bicycles and three or four donkeycarts. The children were running back and forth, screaming, flapping their wings. Each of the angels carried a musical instrument of some sort – steeldrums, horns, quatros – but most of the instruments consisted of nothing more than a pair of toktok sticks, a rumbottle and spoon, or a dried calabash with a handful of poinciana seeds shaking inside. The oldman began to sing, his lips flapping over his nearly toothless gums, spittle flying. He took hold of my hands and shook them up and down with the music, his aluminium arms crackling: 'Time to jubilate whiteson, open you mouthgate!'

I began to sing too:

Sal-ve Re-gina,
Regina Magda-lena!
Be-ne-dicimas te,
Glo-ri-ficamas te,
A-do-ramas te,
Regina Magda-lena!

When the band had passed I got down from the cart and the oldman handed me the bottle. He turned the oxcart around and waved, his costume flashing molten metal for an instant as it caught the light, shouting something which I could not make out over the music. I watched the oldman disappear into the cloud of dust which followed his band of angels. I looked after him for a long time, until the dust had settled and the steeldrums had been reduced to a rumble in the distance. I looked around and realized I was suddenly alone. There was no one left on the trace. It was quiet. I turned and continued walking, calm now, unhurried.

GRANNY MYNA stared at me in silence. I couldn't move, couldn't get up from the bed. She reached and took both my hands in hers: 'Go Johnny. Tell you mummy and daddy I am ready.'

I ran upstairs and called them, my brother, Evelina and Papee Vince waking with the commotion. We crowded around Granny Myna sitting up in the small bed, her back against the pillow against the headboard: my father in his drawers sitting next to her listening to her heart through his stethoscope, my mother holding my baby sister with one arm, my younger brother holding her other hand, Papee Vince in the chair leaning forward over his big belly, old Evelina mumbling some obeah incantation, and me thinking: *This is not you standing here seeing this because you are upstairs in you bed sleeping. Why you don't go see if you find youself and then you would know it is only you dreaming?*

My father pulled the stethoscope from his ears and left it hanging from his neck. He looked around, got up and went to the small table covered with Granny Myna's religious objects: a statue of St Michael, of St Christopher, a photograph of the Pope, of Barto, a plastic bottle shaped like the Virgin filled with holywater from Lourdes, some artificial roses, multicoloured beads, all decorated on a doily she had crocheted in pink, white and babyblue. My father took up a candle and put it in Granny Myna's hand, closing her fingers around it. He lit a match, but before he could touch it to the candle Mother Superior Maurina, Granny Myna's sister, entered the room. We all turned to look at her. No one had called her, and as far as we knew she and Granny Myna had not talked in more than fifty years, since before Mother Maurina had run away to the convent. She had never set foot in our house.

My father lit another match and touched it to the candle. He told us quietly to kneel down. My grandmother studied the flame for a few seconds, took a deep breath, blew it out: 'Stand up! Pray for me to *die* if you have to pray!'

My father chupsed. 'Mummy –'

'Tomorrow is the sixteen of April, Holy Thursday: Corpus Christi Day. It is the *happiest* day in heaven, and I am going to be there. I don't want no funeral confusion. Barto have the stone and everything there ready waiting

for me. Just dig the hole and push me in the ground *first*
thing in the morning!'

We didn't know what to do. My father sucked his teeth.
He looked at my mother, got up again and sat next to my
grandmother, listening to her heart through his stethoscope. Granny Myna's hands lay on her lap, her fists
clenched. Her lips were pressed firmly together over her
gums, her pointed chin protruding, trembling slightly.
Her eyes were wide, unblinking – fixed on me. I watched
her jaw drop slowly, her lips go purple and open a little,
her skin turn to soft wax. I kept thinking: *Her eyes aren't
closed so she isn't dead. Her eyes aren't closed so she isn't dead.
Her eyes aren't –* My father turned. Before he could look up
I was already running.

I ran halfway to Domingo Cemetery before I turned
around and went back for the shovel, thinking: *If the bottle
isn't there she isn't dead. Just make up you head not to dream up
that bottle too.* The graveyard smelled of wet earth, rotting
leaves, tinged by the too-sweet smell of eucalyptus. A
small coral wall ran all around. The huge trees rustled in
the breeze, the undersides of their leaves flashing silver in
the moonlight. I went straight to Granny Myna's intended
grave, everything but her deathdate chiselled into the
headstone. I dropped the shovel and squinted to see the
line of graves. On one side of the plot where my grandmother would be buried was Uncle Olly's grave, Manuelito's on the other. Beside Manuelito was Barto's grave,
and beside him, Magdalena María Domingo. I moved
closer: MANUELITO DOMINGO, NACI XVI ET MORI XIX APRILIS,
ANNO DOMINI NOSTRI, MDCCCXCIX.

I picked up the shovel again, thinking. *If it isn't there she
isn't dead because you refuse to dream up the bottle. You can go
back home and laugh at youself sleeping.* But I hadn't sent the
shovel into the ground three times when I hit something
solid. I threw the shovel aside and got down on my knees
to dig with both hands. After a moment I realized I'd

found the bottle.

I tried to pull it out but my hands slipped: I fell backwards as though I'd been shoved, my head thudding against Manuelito's headstone, and someone threw a clump of wet earth in my face – like I'd been slapped. I spit out the dirt and tried to wipe my eyes. There was no one there.

I got up slowly, brushed myself off. I knelt, digging carefully, all the way around the bottle. I placed a foot on either side of the hole and lifted it out. I rolled the bottle into a clear space and got down on my knees again, rubbing my hands over the glass, spitting, removing the dirt. I bent closer, still couldn't see. I stood. Straining, I lifted the bottle over my head, the moon lighting it up.

BY THE TIME I neared the end of Divina Trace the breeze had come up. Several dark clouds eclipsed the sun. The eight or ten houses of Suparee Village were deserted, not even a fowl or a potcake in the street. At the end of the trace the Church of Magdalena Divina was small, grey against a grey sky. The thick wooden doors were wide open. It was empty, cold inside. I walked slowly up the centre aisle, my jesusboots squeaking on the polished stone, slapping against the soles of my feet, each step echoing through the church. There was a gold baptismal font off to one side of the altar. On the other side there was a small chapel, devotion candles flickering in their red glass holders, the smells of Creole incense and sweetoil growing stronger as I approached.

I stood in front of the chapel, but I could see nothing in the darkness within except the bright red flames. I put the bottle down on one of the pews and climbed the steps, a line of calabash shells filled with sweetoil on either side. I knelt at the chapel railing. She began to take shape slowly out of the darkness, reflections of the tiny red flames rising on her face, flashing through the clouds of rising incense: her gentle eyes, comforting lips, the crimson mark on her forehead, her burnt-sienna skin, long wig of black hair. Her faded gown was covered with jewelled pendants, her outstretched arms thick with silver spiked churries and bangles, a solid gold rosary hanging from her neck – offerings for prayers answered – Magdalena Divina, Mother of Miracles, Black Virgin of Maraval! I closed my eyes: *Hail Mary full of grace the lord is with thee blessèd art thou amongst women blessèd is the fruit of you womb Jesus. Holy Mary mother of God pray fa we sinners now at the hour of we death amen.* I dipped my finger into the basin of holywater, crossed myself. I picked up the bottle again, walked quickly across the altar, left through the sanctuary.

Behind the church there was an immense samaan tree, spread symmetrically over a plot of green grass. Beyond it Maraval Swamp was greenish-black, mangrove growing along the edge and in the shallows, their thick moss-covered banyans arching out of the water like charmed snakes. I walked along the line of mangrove – picking my way through the tall reeds, the mud sucking at my jesusboots – until I found a gap where I could walk out into the water. I put the bottle down and it sank an inch into the mud. I flipped open the wire clamps at the top and lifted off the lid. I'd expected some pungent odour: there was none, only the stagnant smell of the morass. I tried my best not to look into the bottle, but I couldn't avoid seeing two bulging eyes at the top of a flat head: the lid slipped from my hands landing *clap* in the mud.

I took a deep breath and picked up the bottle again, slippery now with the mud on the glass and on my hands. I walked slowly, the cold liquid in the bottle spilling down my chest, and at the same moment I put my foot in the water several things happened almost simultaneously: the frogs which were making a big noise ceased their croaking, and there was absolute silence; the light became immediately dimmer; and a gust blew, stripping blueblack tonguelike leaves from the mangrove limbs, their banyans quivering in the wind. I continued carefully into the water until it reached my waist, the bottle half-submerged, and stopped – shin-deep in the mud. Slowly, I tilted the bottle, feeling its weight slip away and the solid splash before me in the water. I wanted nothing more now than to turn quickly and run: I couldn't budge my feet. Standing there, holding the finally empty bottle, seeing myself again with my baggy navyblue school shortpants billowing around my hips, feeling my feet again in my jesusboots beneath the mud, looking down again through the dark water again, thinking, not understanding, believing: *He is alive. Swimming.* I watched his long angular legs fold, snap taut, and propel him smoothly through the water; snap, glide; snap, glide; and the frogchild disappeared into a clump of quiet mangrove banyans.

2

Papee Vince Speaks Of Barto's Relationship With Magdalena

THE BOTTLE was big and obzockee. I was having a hard time toting it, but I did not want to put the bottle down because I did not want to have to look at his face. I never saw it. From the time I left Domingo Cemetery, until I arrived at Maraval Swamp ten miles away, I'd put the bottle down only twice: on the shelf next to the oldman's feet to climb up into the oxcart, on the pew to kneel before the Black Virgin. I'd seen only his eyes for an instant at the top of his flat head. For a single instant, as I removed the lid and he looked at me over the lip of the bottle, I at him, but to speak of that is to speak of nothing more than the figment of a child's imagination. And when I say that I see the same eyes now, seventy-seven years later, as I sit here in this library, at this desk of purpleheart in this Windsor chair – this absurd miniature Warrahoon-Windsor chair, carved from the same trunk of wood according to the diagram Barto had found in the *Oxford Dictionary*, but the little Warrahoon had sized the chair to fit himself and not my grandfather, with its legs too short, its arms pressing uncomfortably into my sides, its saddle-seat shaped as though it were intended for the buttocks of a large boy – when I tell you that as I sit here I can still see the frogchild's eyes, staring up at me, I at him, I speak of nothing more than the phantom of an oldman's dotish fancy. I never saw his face. For all I know he had the face of every other child.

That is what I wanted to believe. I had tried for two years. For two years after Granny Myna's death I had tried to forget Magdalena and the frogchild, to dissolve from my memory that distant Corpus Christi morning as though I were dismissing a bad dream. But it was a nightmare which would not leave me alone, despite my efforts to distract myself, and I did whatever I could. I broke biche on the school days of our excursions to Divina Church. I did homework instead of playing mas on Corpus Christi Day. To avoid sitting idle in church, I took the other acolytes' turns, and I did it so many times they started calling me El Papa.

Those were days of football and cricket, of unending hours of schoolwork which began after six o'clock Mass each morning, continuing until they rang the bell for me to run myself to exhaustion on the football field again. The muddier I got, the more exhausted, the happier I felt. And when I left the football field or the cricket oval half an hour after the sun went down, I made sure I had only enough energy left to pedal my bicycle home, to eat dinner and sit through the two hours of homework before my father climbed the stairs to check our sums, and tell my brother and me we could go to bed. Even before my mother came in a minute later to kiss us and out the light, I was usually already asleep. Only the nightmares interrupted the routine.

Each time I awoke in the middle of the night, breathless, sweating – looking quickly to see that my younger brother was still in his bed beside mine, that the oscillating fan was still blowing – I would throw off the sheet to feel the fan sweep my naked body, hear its fanbreath move slowly across my wet skin, slowly back again, and I would tell myself that the face which haunted me in my dreams was not the face of the frogchild, because I had never seen it.

That is what I told myself again: it was Wednesday, April 22, five days after my fifteenth birthday. I had dreamt I was back on the trace toting the bottle, and my arms had grown so tired in my dream I'd had to put the bottle down. Again I told myself that the face which frightened me out of my sleep was not the face of the frogchild. And I began to think that if no man could look at the face of God, as Granny Myna had told me, then maybe the same was true of the devil? *If to look on God face is enough to kill you, then surely to look on the devil own ga do you worse. That face in you dream could never be the frogbaby own. Aren't you still live? Aren't you still breathing?*

Because the time Jesus came to visit Granny Myna in her bedroom in the house on Rust Street, she had not seen his face either. She'd been lucky enough to see his toes first. Granny Myna was sitting up in her bed rolling her beads, and when she felt the breath of cool air touched by the faint smell of roses, and opened her eyes, there were his feet at the end of the bed with the toes that were long and white and creamy like icecream. He had spoken to her in Spanish, and he had held her, but she had not seen his face because his toes were so beautiful she could not look up from them wherever he went in the room. That is the way Papa God does do He business, she had told me, and I wondered if maybe the devil did *his* business the same way.

I woke up my brother to question him about it.

'What?' he asked.

'Remember the time Granny Myna saw Jesus toes in the Rust Street house?'

He chupsed. 'Carry you ass!' he said, and he rolled over and went back to sleep.

I lay there trying to decide if I should go see if Papee Vince were still awake. Sometimes he'd be up reading, and I'd go sit next to him on his bed. Papee Vince would tell me stories about the old Domingo Estate, or about the short potbellied Warrahoons who made bows which were longer than they were, and who shot arrows clean through the three-inch-thick planking of his bungalows, high at the top of oil derricks in the Orinoco Delta. He told me stories about shrunken heads which the Warrahoons fed every day, and spoke to as though they were family, and put cigars in their mouths every evening to smoke. Sometimes Papee Vince asked me about football matches, and sometimes I asked him about the Warrahoons. He'd taught form three science for several years, and sometimes I asked him questions to prepare for exams. But I never asked Papee Vince about Magdalena and the frogchild. I never asked anyone.

I jumped out of bed, pulled on a shorts, and tiptoed down the hall to his room. Papee Vince wasn't in his bed, so I climbed through the trapdoor in the ceiling to see if he was up on the porch above his bedroom. How my old grandfather made it up that ladder without pelting down I'll never know. He spent all his evenings up there, reading or looking at the sea, until we called him down to dinner. After dinner Papee Vince would read until he felt tired enough to sleep, or he'd climb up on to the porch again to sit and look at the lights, at the moon shining on the water. Sometimes my grandfather would sit up there the whole night, and my mother would send Evelina with a coffee for him in the morning. The porch was six or eight feet square, set partially into the roof, a short railing around it. They were built at the top of practically every roof in St Maggy – *cobos' roosts* we called them – because in the old days the wives climbed up there, and they must have looked like buzzards waiting for their husbands' ships to return from sea. For years only the mailboat and a few local fishing smacks have ventured into our harbour.

It was a full moon night and Papee Vince was sitting in his hammock, wearing his baggy boxer drawers and a merino-vestshirt. He'd strung the hammock diagonally across the porch, and he'd padded it with newspapers which had turned yellow and musty-smelling. My grandfather suffered from the gout, and he was too heavy to lie comfortably in his hammock. Papee Vince sat with a leg on either side, his big belly in his lap, both soft swollen feet on the floor to steady him. I ducked under one end of the hammock and sat on the railing; there was scarcely enough room on the roost for both of us. My grandfather had an absorbed look on his face. Neither of us spoke for a while. I looked at the lights of St Maggy shining below, at the moon on the dark water, and when the breeze blew I smelled the foul odour of Maraval Swamp in the distance. Papee Vince unfixed the wire curves of his glasses from around his ears. He folded them carefully and put them down on the railing. The wire had oxidized into a brilliant bluegreen, leaving permanent stains on the bridge of his nose, in partial circles around his eyes, and behind his ears. My grandfather breathed heavily. When he began to speak his voice was slow, dignified. And each time he excused himself and paused. I would listen anxiously to the waves beating against the rocks, to the loud insects, the chickens scratching at the hard ground beneath the tamarind tree in our back yard, as Papee Vince managed the ordeal of sitting up to spit in an old Carnation sweetmilk tin.

YOU SEE SON, yardfowl has no business fighting cockfight, and by that, is meant to say this: I am no bloody physician now to loop the loop fa you. Neither am I any one of those fetusologist fellows, or who ever the hell kind of people they have to make a study of these things in particular, such that I ga have the knowledge sufficient to look you in the face and say, well yes, such and such, and so and so. I am a simple man. I have lived a simple life. But don't let the one bamboozle you, son. Because let me tell you this: a little whiteepokee-penny-a-pound such as I was at thirteen years of age when I ran from England, and skipped ship at the first port which so happened to be this island, does not work he way up to the position of manager of a cultivation the size of the old Domingo Estate (fifteen-hundred-and-some-odd acres of cocoa, cane and coconuts, sixty-some half-naked half-wild East Indians and Creoles and Warrahoons, and they thousand-and-one children, with the nearest field-doctor twelve miles away in Wallafield) a little whiteepokee such as I was does not experience all that, without learning a little something of the art of Medical Science. Neither does a man work the oilfields of the Delta Orinoco there in Venezuela, fa thirty-five bloody years, hidden somewhere up in the bush behind God's back, living among such species of savage as can be found in *that* place – and neither does a man watch a man lop off and desiccate another man's head, pepper and eat another man's flesh – and not learn a little something of the mysteries of life.

Right. One thing, from the start, from the very beginning. Because son, some of the things I ga tell you now, some of the things you are about to hear fa the first time, may seem, in one way or another, disrespectful to those defenceless old souls with whom they concern. I can only assure you of this: I would be the last man on this green earth to abuse the memory of you Granny Myna. She was the patroness of we family (my own wife, like Barto, having died at a relatively young age) and I would be the last to send her rolling in she grave. As fa Barto, he was my great old friend and employer fa twenty-two years. Other than Granny Myna, and this woman, I knew him better than anyone, dead or alive. I have nothing but the utmost respect fa you grandfather. And let me tell you something else son, while we here: I am no cokeeeye slymongoose, to sit in this hammock professing to decipher fact from fiction fa you. Yardfowl don't pass collection plate when he preach to guineahen. Because son, these days story selling like tanyafritter. It filling you belly fast as windball. In the end, as with everything else on this good earth, you must decide fa youself.

Enough. The facts are these: seven-months-birth. Naturally, the child not sufficiently well formed. So much to be expected. But let me tell you something, son: this child is plenty more than forceripe. I myself have delivered seven-months-babies in Mayaguaro, and I had my own beautiful box of instruments made by the Johnson and Johnson people, given to me in the old estate days by you grandfather – and I was so happy with that box of instruments that the first day I got them I took out an abscess the size of a tomato from some poor woman's breast that had been humbugging her fa donkey's ages – but let me tell you something, son: not *one* of those children remotely resembled this child. Not a one. I have even delivered a five-months-baby once. That child had lain dead in he poor mummy's belly fa three days. Even *he* was not the cacapoule this child is. Not by a chups.

To begin with, he skin green green like green. He head flat, with he two eyes bulging out at the top. They are, I should say, three to four times the size of normal, human eyes. He nose is nothing more than a couple of holes, say about the size of the holes you might jook out in a paper with a writing pencil. He ears are normal. He lips are thickish, as is he tongue, which protrudes, like it too big to fit up inside he mouth. He has no chin, no neck a-tall. He shoulders begin directly beneath he ears, and he chest looking somewhat deficient, particularly in comparison with he rather elongated trunk. Five to six inches of he umbilical cord remain attached to he belly, but nothing peculiar in that, particularly if Salizar responsible fa delivering the child. And we have every good reason to believe he is. Because do you think fa one second any bushdoctor like Brito Salizar ga tie the navelstring with a fishing-twine, and cut it short, and do the thing proper?

Not fa cobo-jawbone he wouldn't. He ga leave it hanging there just so, and when it drop off in its own good time he ga bury it beneath a breadfruit tree or a mango-julie to keep the jumbies away, or whatever else Warrahoon-Creole nonsense those bushdoctor-obeahmen like to do.

No son, there is nothing odd about an umbilical cord. But what does seem to me rather curious, very peculiar, is this: here is a child who comes out he mummy's belly with both fists clenched tight round he navelstring. Now naturally, you ga want to ask youself: What in bloody hell is this forceripe little fucker trying to do? Because the child's fists remained clenched just so, fa the entire three days he lived, and no one could pry them loose. Well now: I don't know what you want to make of this navelstring business son, but I have considered it a good many years, and I think I have arrived at the explanation. Let we suppose now that this child *did* refuse to let go he umbilical cord, as they say he did, then it seems to me he is struggling instrinctively with the memory of he mummy: either he fighting to hold *on* to her, or to *rip* heself free.

But wait awhile. Wait awhile, son. We haven't yet arrived at one of the most curious aspects of this child. As I understand it, and I have had it confirmed by several individuals who actually saw the child, particularly you own grandfather – because of course, *I* never saw this child, so I can only repeat fa you what I myself have been told – and as Barto assures me, in addition to the bulk of the remaining evidence which substantiates, in the very least, a birth of an enigmatic nature, that not only was this child born with the face of a crapo, he came into the world bearing the bloody tool and the stones of a full-grown man.

Of course, these days story telling quicker than you can beg water to boil pigtail, and the mother of this crapochild may, in fact, have been a saint, a whore, or both. I couldn't tell you. What I can tell you is this: she was,

without question, the most beautiful woman this island
has ever seen, and she had every manjack basodee basodee
over her. To be sure, it would take nothing short of a
grand old cock of you own grandfather's making to turn
the table, but wait awhile. We coming to that one. Now:
just where this woman came from, and who brought her
here, if, indeed, she came from anywhere other than right
there in Village Suparee, just there by Swamp Maraval
(which would at least explain why she made all those
pilgrimages out to that stinking morass, even why the
statue always walked about by there, if you choose to
believe it ever really walked about a-tall) wherever the ass
this woman came from, and whoever brought her here,
that, I couldn't tell you neither. I would like to take a good
lag on the ass of any son-of-a-bitch who could tell you he
could. Because before precisely 6 a.m., on that Easter
Sunday morning of the 19th of April, when she appeared
from out the smoke kneeling at the top of St Maggy
Cathedral steps, she white capra soaked down in red
blood, no one had never *heard* of Magdalena Domingo. To
this day, there is not much about her of which we can be
sure.

Right. Good. Easter Sunday fête begins at dawn, following the three days of Easter Vigil, following Corpus
Christi Day, as you know well enough, when all the little
boys set off they firecrackers, and roman-rockets, and
whatever not in front the cathedral to wake up everybody.
Well: as fate is always inclined to favour slight coinci-
dences, soft anachronisms, you grandfather happened to
be there. You see, Barto was the self-appointed Captain of
the Corpus Christi *Navy* in those days (because in those
old days we actually had this navy, if you want to go so far
as to call it that) we had this navy which you grandfather
convinced everybody we needed fa some odd reason or the
other, and which he himself fitted out with three pirogues,
and half-a-dozen Warrahoons dressed up in white sailor-

boy costumes sent toute-baghai from England. The truth,
however, is that Barto accomplished little more with this
pappyshow navy than to prepare the first official map of
Corpus Christi, and to lead an unofficial expedition to
Venezuela fa which he is credited, in many of the history
books, as having discovered the source of the River
Orinoco. Barto's only legitimate duty, as captain of this
navy, was to fill the position of master of the St Maggy
boyscouts (the seascouts, as they are called) which was
only fitting as he had a home busting with badjohns heself.
At all events, as I have said, Barto happened to be there on
that Easter Sunday morning, both to watch over the boys,
and to supervise in the setting off of all these firecracker-
rockets.

Well they had only just gone off. The little wajanks
were still running about the place, bawling and screaming
and howling like a pack of cocomonkeys, when all of a
sudden that old clock at the top of Government House
cross the square begins to strike fa six o'clock. Son, every
one of them went quiet in one. How, I couldn't tell you.
How that blasted old clock that is striking all day every
day to beat back bloody dawn could distract anybody,
much less a band of catacoo little boys, and a half-dozen
sleepwalkers now rolling out they grave. But son, fish
never bite before back scratch you, and cock never crow
before Saturday morning, and wife never sing sweet
before doodoo bawl fa sweetman. Is just so the thing
happened. That old clock begins to strike, and it is as if the
earth decides to hold up she breath. Just as the smoke from
those firecrackers begins to rise from the cathedral steps,
Magdalena appears, kneeling at the top, she hands folded,
with all of we staring up at her in silence like she is some
kind of jablesse, because she cheeks and she capra are
covered with tears of blood.

Well: some say they knew from that moment she was a
saint. But son, frizzlefowl love to dress sheself up like

guineahen. In truth, were it not fa all these tears of blood,
were it not fa she very sudden appearance (and I suppose
she'd been kneeling there quiet the whole time, but with
all that fireworks confusion no one had noticed her) were
it not fa all these tears of blood, you wouldn't twink you
eyes twice at this timid little girl. Because the truth is that
at first glance this Magdalena looks no different from all
the little half-coolie, half-Creole, half-Warrahoon, half-so-
and-so little callaloos running round in Suparee, and
Grande Sangre, and Wallafield. Only after you examine
her close, do you become aware of that subtle quality
wherein rests she extraordinary, quiet beauty.

Because on the day she first appears, Magdalena is
fifteen years of age. She is dressed in the same simple white
capra of light muslin (the long strip of cloth wrapped
clockwise round and round the body, passed between the
legs and up over the left shoulder) just as all the East
Indians wear, the Hindus and Muslims and so. She is quite
small, with fine, delicate features, extremely large dark
eyes, the scarlet tilak tatooed there on she forehead. She
skin is a rich sienna-brown. She hair is straight, thick, and
intensely black, and it must have reached down almost by
she knees, because it was gathered all on the steps round
her. And to my recollection they never cut off, even
though she pledged and *re*pledged she vows to the nuns –
as if they had to give her a bushbath quick quick every
time that blasted Chief of Police pounced on her – because
son, you know those old goatface nuns good enough, and
you know they don't give the little girls a chance to
promise chastity, and poverty, and whatever else not,
before they shave them down like a clean-neck-fowl. No
son, fa some odd reason they never cut it off, and she must
have had some way of hiding all that hair beneath she
nuncostume, but it seems to me you could hide a ramgoat
beneath that amount of veils, and kerchiefs, and the
pasteboard headdress and so. Because one year after she

first appeared, on the day of she death – the day she gave birth to the child, and suffocated sheself soon as she saw the child's face – on the day of she death she hair was every bit as long as it was on that Easter Sunday morning when she first appeared, she white capra soaked down in red blood.

Of course, the first thing we all thought was that she'd been mortally wounded. Fa months afterward many even said that she had, and some still do to this day. That Gomez, the Chief of Police, in the midst of all that fireworks confusion, had shot her. Because there was little Gomez, dressed in he military police uniform, halfway up the steps, he short legs straddled over three of them, pistol high in the air. There is little Gomez daring anyone to touch her, and he ga shoot *them* too. But the truth is that Gomez had thought the same thing. He'd looked at all the blood and assumed, naturally, that she'd been mortally wounded. He'd actually raised he gun in she *protection*. So there the three of them stood: Gomez, halfway up the steps, pistol high in the air; Magdalena, kneeling at the top facing the cathedral – or Barto, who is to say which? – she hands folded; with him standing there in the open cathedral doorway, dressed in he white naval uniform, the gold braids, the epaulettes, the Captain's hat, standing there as always with he arms folded loosely in front of him, he eyes bright above he curled, waxed moustache. And it is as if these three figures, set against the cathedral in the background (if we can hold them there quiet a quick moment) it is as if these three figures standing there are a tableau telling the whole story, before the story has even begun. Because it is as if the two of them are already basodee in love with her, and she is already a sanctified saint, and there is little Gomez, already fighting over her as he would not only with Barto, and this same Mother Superior General Maurina, and the whole of Corpus Christi, with the oldman upstairs as well.

But he wasn't fighting yet. He simply stood there,
staring, he pistol in the air. We all stood here, looking up
at her in silence, watching she capra growing redder and
redder by the second. Until someone calls out to her. She
turns to look at him, but she does not answer. Well: by
now half of Corpus Christi has gathered there round the
cathedral steps. By now there is plenty racket going on,
murmuring and sighing and ohmeloassing and so. All of a
sudden *out* busts Mother Superior Maurina from St Maggy
Convent adjacent, running fullpelt with all she veils flying
wild in the wind, and she pushes through the crowd,
marching boldface right past this Chief of Police, straight
up the steps to Magdalena. Mother Maurina grabs her up –
so now it is two of them swimming in blood – and before
any of we can even take in what has happened, Magdalena
and Mother Maurina have disappeared behind the bolted
doors of St Maggy Convent, leaving all of we to stare
behind cokeeeye, and Gomez, the Chief of Police, with he
pistol *still* in the air.

BEFORE I can even remember, from the age of six or
seven, I had been marched off with the other children to
the Church of Magdalena Divina. I know, because I can
remember walking along watching the younger ones
walking up ahead – themselves no older than six or seven –
and wondering if their first memories of those yearly
excursions would be like mine: sitting there crowded into
the little church listening to Mother Maurina, thinking:
*But this crackpot oldwoman already tell you all this foolishness
already. So why you don't beg Sister Ann to go in the bush fa
weewee, and then you could run by the swamp fa quick looksee if
you find youself a fat guana?*
    Mother Maurina did not recognize me as her grand-
nephew, and I did not think of her as my own grandaunt. I
knew only that she and Granny Myna had quarrelled long

ago – some confusion, with Barto promising himself to both of them at the same time – but in the end my grandfather had married Granny Myna, and Mother Maurina ran away to the convent. She'd had nothing to do with any of us since. And I was happy not to have to acknowledge my relationship to the Mother Superior General, particularly before my friends, particularly on the days of those excursions.

They were days we all looked forward to, except for the part in the church. Classes were cancelled after lunch, when the nuns lined us up for the walk to Maraval; and we were given snowballs when the ordeal in the church was finished, and the nuns lined us up again for the long walk back to school. Because whether we liked to admit it or not, and whether we were in stage one or form six, there was always something a little frightening about the aspect of the Black Virgin in her dark chapel, no matter how peaceful she looked. And there was something even more frightening in Mother Maurina's frantic exantaying about her.

We used to tell stories among ourselves, about how the Black Virgin was Mother Maurina's own illegitimate child by an old coolie-yardman in the convent we called Toeteelo (named for his huge toetee, which we would hide behind the oleander hedge to get a look at each time he went to the big silkcotton to weewee); and how Mother Maurina had raised Magdalena in a convent closet, then made up all the Black Virgin business when she found her daughter pregnant for her own father (the same Toeteelo); and finally, how Mother Maurina had brought her story to life by building the mechanical walking statue. But we never imagined that the stories we concocted bore even the slightest resemblance to reality. Furthermore, we all knew that Magdalena Divina belonged to a time much older than Mother Maurina and Toeteelo. Even the crumbling walls of St Maggy Convent seemed too young to have contained her. She seemed as old as Corpus Christi itself.

Or perhaps we never believed in the mythical woman who preceded the statue at all. Perhaps – even without knowing it – we believed the flesh-and-blood Magdalena was only part of the legend fabricated and disseminated by Mother Maurina herself, by Monsignor O'Connor, by the others who wanted so badly to legitimize the cures, the unexplained events, all the miracles. Perhaps we believed it was their attempt to claim the statue as our own: to establish Magdalena as the patron saint of Corpus Christi. Their way of preventing the higher orders from coming and tying down and crating up our miraculous walking madonna, from carrying her away in the Vatican's own ship.

Because we were told about little more than the miracles; we never heard much about the flesh-and-blood Magdalena. We heard only that she'd been a sister in St Maggy Convent for a short time, that she'd been devout, that she had died – we assumed, from natural causes – at a very young age, and that she'd been promptly forgotten until her statue surfaced to take up her story again many years later. Nothing more.

So when Granny Myna told me about a Magdalena who'd lived during her own lifetime, who'd been mistress to my own grandfather – who had given him an illegitimate child – I could not, even in my wildest fantasy, have considered this woman to be Magdalena Divina. Yet there is something I am quite sure of now, though I was not conscious of it then. Then, at thirteen years of age, as I sat listening to my grandmother on her deathbed: that the Magdalena I pictured in my mind as Granny Myna told me her story – the dreamlike woman I envisioned along with the grandfather I resurrected from the photograph before me on Granny Myna's altar – this woman was the statue of the Black Virgin brought to life in my imagination. And there is something more: that on the Corpus

Christi Day when I carried the frogchild to Maraval Swamp, I made no conscious decision to enter the church, to kneel and pray to Magdalena Divina, even in two quick breaths. I realize now that that was exactly where I was going – just as surely as I was going to Maraval Swamp without being told explicitly to do so – that that was the only thing I could have done: it was the thing conditioned in me to do. Even then, as I searched out the Black Virgin in the darkness of her chapel, I did not make the connection. Such a possibility was far too remote, impossible. Not until that frogchild swam away, not until he disappeared – as I stood looking down through the dark water, watching the cloud of mud settling slowly to the bottom where he had disappeared between those mangrove banyans – did I realize suddenly who his mother was. Yet I tried to deny it for two years. For two years after Granny Myna's death I told myself that if there were such a thing as a frogchild, then his mother could never have been Magdalena Divina.

And as I sat there on the railing of that cobo roost, suspended, balanced awkwardly with my feet hanging a few inches above the floor, I wanted to deny it again, thinking: *Why is this chuffchuff oldman telling you this if you didn't ask him? Why this bobolups oldman is so determined to tell you this thing you don't want to hear? And if you don't want to hear it, why you don't get up and carry youself? This Papee Vince ga put one boofootoo on you now with all this badtalk. One boofootoo on you head now with all this badtalk. Get youself from here! Like you bamsee stick up on this porchrail. Like you eyes can't close, and you neck can't turn, and you foot can't walk. How long you ga let this frogbaby and this Black Virgin blank you so?*

OF COURSE, I wasn't there. At that time I was still down in Mayaguaro breaking my back with all those

Warrahoons, and East Indians, and Creoles – packing the
sweathouses and dryingsheds with cocoa beans, scorching
canefields, bicycling up and down those coconut trees –
and if any somebody would have come to tell me this
Black Virgin had just appeared in front the cathedral
crying tears of *blood*, I'd most certainly have told them to
carry they ass. I'd tell them the same blasted thing today.
No son, I am no boseyback manicouman to sit here in this
hammock, and try to convince you this woman appeared
as they say she did. I wasn't there to see it. Nonetheless,
the stubborn truth remains – and it is a reality which has
taken me eighty-seven years to affirm, so of course I could
never expect you to submit to it now – the truth remains
that there are certain things in this world which defy
explanation. Explanation, that is, in the terms which we
recognize: the explicit terms of science and logic. What's
more – more unsettling fa you son, but all the more
encouraging fa dead up oldman like me – what's more is
that such things are encountered every day. Son, wasn't it
just day before yesterday, fa instance, you daddy took me
fa some exercise walking to King's Wharf, and there we
met an old patient of his by the name of Lakshman
Ramchad, fa the price of a shilling would douse he hands
in two buckets of water and hold up an electric eel in each,
the light bulb lighting up in he mouth? Well then? All I can
do fa you son is to repeat what I myself have been told: one
minute this woman appears with these tears rolling down
she cheeks, and the next minute she disappears again with
Mother Maurina behind the bolted doors of St Maggy
Convent. Quick as that. And she was quite forgotten by
the time she was next seen, one Sunday morning, seven
weeks later. Because fa those seven intervening weeks
nothing more was heard about her. Gomez had even
raided the convent a couple of times trying to find her –
raiding in the middle of the night under the pretence of
fabricated official business, inspecting the rooms one by

one looking fa fabricated official bandits, and putting
goatmouth loud on he bloody self each time he said that
the first place any policeman worth he salt looks fa thief is
in the nuns' bedrooms – but eventually, even Gomez had
forgotten her.

Then, suddenly, one Sunday morning seven weeks after
that first Easter Sunday morning when she first appeared,
she was seen again, walking by sheself along the road to
Swamp Maraval. She wasn't a nun yet. Clearly, she'd been
living in the convent the whole time, but she wouldn't
pledge she vows until the following morning, still barefoot as she walked the dusty trace to Swamp Maraval.
Beautiful as ever. What she wanted at that swamp, and
why she made a pilgrimage there every Sunday morning
until the day of she death, I couldn't tell you. Not oysters,
or chipchips, though I don't have to tell you how they
grow there in abundance. (In fact, when Sir Walter
Raleigh told them back in England that on the island of
Corpus Christi, where he was convinced he'd discovered
El Dorado, oysters grew on trees, they took him fa
madman. Of course, any of we who have been to Maraval
know to the contrary: you only have to dive down and
look on the banyans of any one of those mangrove trees,
growing out there where the water is brackish, and you
will see more colossal big oysters smiling up happy at you
than the sweetest of sweetdreams.) But son, I should
imagine Magdalena would prefer to buy she oysters fa five
pence at Victoria Street Market, than to dive them up in
that miserable morass. None the less, that was where she
went often enough, and that was where she was going that
Sunday morning when, again, by some coincidence of
fate, or happenstance, Barto happened to be waiting with
all five troops of he seascouts. You see, he'd brought these
scoutboys, just as he did every year the first Sunday in
June – there like a band of cannibal Caribs, screaming,
stripped down to the skins they were born in, swimming

back and forth and in and out of those mangrove banyans
– only looking to catch crapos fa they summer seascout
jamboree. Because you know well enough, the St Maggy
boys always take the prize fa the crapo-jumping competition, as there are no crapos in the world to compare with
the ones they grow there in Maraval. But I suppose now,
in retrospect, all Barto and those boys managed to accomplish on that Sunday morning was to delay the inevitable.
Because sure as the skin of you backside belongs to you,
Gomez would get at her that night.

He was already pounding down the road, he big black
steed already frothing at the mouth, before Magdalena had
even reached by the swamp. How Gomez knew she was
walking, on that particular morning, that particular road, I
couldn't tell you. All I know is that somehow or other,
like everything else, he found out. And he found out
quick. Because before Magdalena even had chance to get a
few good sniffs of that swamp, Gomez caught up to her.
So by the time Magdalena reaches Maraval *she* is running
fullpelt – and you know those little callaloos can bust a run
– with that same Chief of Police on the back of that horse
running fullpelt behind her. Of course, Barto only tells
those boys to let loose they crapos, and this horse comes to
a quick fullstop. Because son, whether or not an elephant
is afraid of a mouse, or a coolie-buffalo is afraid of a
jackspaniard-wasp, I couldn't say. But one thing I *can* tell
you from my own experience, horses sure as hell don't like
crapos, particularly a thousand-and-one *duck*-sized crapos
jumping up five feet in the air.

Gomez couldn't get he horse to budge a bloody inch.
Rearing up, bellowing horsecries, with he horseyes
opened up so wide they looked like they wanted to jump
out. And by the time this little Chief of Police realizes
what has hit him, he is flat on he backside there in a cloud
of dust and leaping crapos, watching at he horse pelting
now in the direction from which he had come. By the time

Gomez has a chance to twink he eyes twice and look up, there is Barto staring down at him from out the muzzle of that big rifle (the same fancified one hanging downstairs in the parlour, given to Barto in the old days by you great-granduncle the General Francisco Monagas, twice president and liberator of the slaves in Venezuela) and this little Gomez has no choice but to take off running behind he horse.

Well: Magdalena is swallowed up by this tribe of shouting, crapo-hunting scoutboys. In no time a-tall *she* is stripped down naked too (in fact, she is little more than an adolescent sheself, and only a couple of years older than the oldest of them) there is she swimming in the waist-deep swampwater, with the band of shouting scoutboys splashing like boynymphs in the water round her. Off in search of more crapos. And Barto, there watching from the cool shade of the huge samaan tree, looking like some bloody mythological figure heself – lying there on he back in he merino vestshirt, he head propped up against the samaan trunk, white jacket and Captain's hat hanging from the tree above him, blowing in the breeze with the thousand-and-one boyscout shortpants, the jerseys, the washykongs, the twenty-foot-long strip of white muslin – there watching over Magdalena and the boys, smoking he thin Cuban cigar through the gold cigarette holder. With that same Chief of Police, not far distant, back again on the back of he horse, watching too, grinding he teeth.

That night he two policeman used they bootoos to bust down the door of the convent with a few quick blows. Gomez left one there posted beneath she window, the other following him up the stairs, straight to Magdalena's bedroom. Because by now he'd already found out where it was. He didn't give the nuns chance to wake up. And they hadn't even finished the first session of a novena before he walked out with he two policeman the following morning. By that time there was already a small crowd gathered

there in Sir Walter Raleigh Square in front the convent, all
looking up at Magdalena's window, all staring up at the
empty balcony outside she bedroom. Gomez marched
straight through them, he and he two policeman, like they
didn't even exist, like nothing whatsoever had happened,
and they crossed the square to sit at one of the outdoor
tables of the parlour to take a coffee.

I don't know, son. I don't know the way those nuns and
priests think, nor will I ever. Because they said absolutely
nothing. Mother Maurina could have had that blasted
Chief of Police strung up by he stones right here in the
same square that same *afternoon* if she'd put the authority
of the Church behind it. But she said nothing. Instead, and
without even asking Magdalena – because the order was
issued even before Gomez and he two policemen cleared
out – instead she sent fa Barto: she commissioned him to
find he backside there in the chapel of that convent, fast as
he legs could carry him. You see, Mother Maurina had
decided Barto would be the one to represent Magdalena's
father (as Magdalena sheself didn't know who she father
was, but why the ass she chose Barto above every other
cock in the henhouse I couldn't tell you not fa sorrel
sweetdrink) because fa some odd reason Mother Maurina
had decided *he* would be the one to give her away.
Understand son, the pledging ceremonies fa these nuns are
exactly like weddings – exactly, with the big white
weddingdress flowing down, the lace veil on she face, the
ring on she finger and everything so – but you must
imagine Christ as the groom.

Because that was all those nuns could think to do. To
get Magdalena into she gown and down those stairs into
the chapel – not even wasting enough time to throw little
iodine on she bruises when they finish burning the sheets –
down the stairs into the chapel and consecrated good and
proper. I couldn't say, son. Why the ass they were in such
a hurry is a mystery to me. I suppose, in they own

perverse way, they believed those vows might purify her again. I have no idea. All I can tell you is this: when that organ music begins to play, when those nuns begin to sing, and Magdalena takes up Barto's arm to walk up the isle of that chapel, she hand is still trembling from the night before. She wrists and ankles have not even been bandaged where the pressure of those bindings which held she limbs tied tight to those bedpost stanchions the whole night have lacerated them, and the contusion above she right eye is swollen to such an extent she can scarcely see out of it. Not until Barto puts the ring on she finger, does she stop shaking.

By this time half of Corpus Christi has gathered there in the square. We are all staring up at Magdalena's window, all telling the story of this Chief of Police who has – by the time the Government House clock strikes fa eleven o'clock on that Monday morning – led the entire police forces of Corpus Christi in a gang-rape of Magdalena. And by the time the clock strikes fa twelve noon, we'd made up we minds to lynch him, still sitting there with he two policemen drinking coffee on the other side of the square. And we would have too – beat the shittings out of him right there in the square – had Mother Maurina not appeared on the balcony outside Magdalen's bedroom, and sent we packing like a band of schoolchildren. Like the Pope she appears, announcing the consecration of a new sister to St Maggy Convent: *Magdalena María Domingo*. 'Go home!' she says. 'You lunch cold already!' And we all went home.

When, however, this same Mother Superior General Maurina announces that the new novitiate, Magdalena, is leaving the convent to marry sheself to the same Chief of Police who had raped her not even two months before – the same Monsignor O'Connor who'd pronounced her a sister of the Corpus Christi Carmelites the morning after she'd been raped, to pronounce her married in the same chapel to the same man who had raped her not two months before – everything blows up again. Understand son, it had long been common knowledge – a common joke animated by every prostitute in Corpus Christi fa years – that this Chief of Police shot blanks. Some said he couldn't even shoot a-tall. That is to say, he is *sterile, impotent*: a *tantieman*, a *mammapoule*. So no one ever stopped to consider the possibility that Magdalena might be pregnant, and needed a husband, which, indeed, she was *not*.

On the designated day the crowd gathers once more in Sir Walter Raleigh Square in front the convent. It is a Saturday morning, and everyone has come to see fa theyselves. We didn't come with rice. We came with glassbottle, stone and cutlass. But before any of we can manage even to work weselves up to a mild pitch, Mother Maurina appears on Magdalena's balcony again to send we home. She doesn't appear like the Pope this time. She appears like Christ, Magdalena next to her there on the balcony, daring any of we to pelt the first stone. So by the time this Chief of Police arrives, most of we have taken she advice and gone home fa breakfast.

The ceremony lasted only a couple minutes, and the marriage lasted not much longer. Because within a few weeks Magdalena was back in the convent again. Just what went on between sheself and Gomez, no one knows. Some said she never left the convent a-tall – that old Mother Maurina was going viekeevie now fa true with all she marriage talk – but the fact is she *did* live with Gomez as he wife a period of exactly thirty-eight days. Because Barto and I sat there one evening on the gallery of my bungalow, and we fired back a couple tasas of punching rum, and we counted it out. (Thirty-eight days exactly, which I was able to substantiate many years later by digging up the duplicate marriage certificate deposited there in the Re-cords Room of Government House, and checking the date

– Saturday 1 August – and counting down the thirty-eight days to the feastday of La Divina Pastora of Venezuela – Monday 7 September – which was the day Magdalena assured Barto she returned to the convent.)

Well son, I don't know what you want to make of all this commess. I can tell you it sent my head tootoolbay a good long time. But again, I continued to turn it over until I arrived at the logical explanation. Because of course, you have to ask youself: Is this Magdalena an ordained nun, a married woman, or a consecrated whore? And the answer, it seems to me, is obvious enough: she is all three. Consider it fa second, son. Though we all knew fa years that this Chief of Police was a mammapoule, that he was sterile, perhaps the nuns did not? All I am trying to suggest to you here son is this: during those same two months or so between Magdalena's rape, and she subsequent marriage to she abductor, the same Chief of Police, Magdalena not only had time enough to make up she mind she was pregnant, she had time to convince Mother Maurina too. That Mother Superior Maurina not only *arranged* fa the marriage, she *dictated* it. When, however, Magdalena discovers she is not pregnant a-tall, she takes off running from this Chief of Police fast as potcake can run from bigstick.

MY GRANDFATHER would pause, and my arms would feel suddenly tired. I would feel the strain in my back, my shoulders, the fatigue in my legs again. Because as I sat there, balanced on the railing of that cobo roost, listening to my old grandfather, it was as though it was Corpus Christi Day again, and I was back on the trace toting the huge glassbottle. It was as though I could feel the lid butting up my chin, the glass rubbing against my belly and pinching my bung navel. As though I could feel the shock running cold down my legs to my toes. But it was Papee

Vince's voice which I carried in my dream now. Papee
Vince's voice which I listened to without asking for or
wanting to hear. It was Papee Vince's voice which I could
not put down.

And as I sat there, watching my old grandfather strain to
sit up in his newspaper-padded hammock, as I watched
him reach to the railing beside me for his old, ragged-
edged, Carnation sweetmilk tin, once filled with the
condensed milk of colossal cows living somewhere on the
other side of the sea – *contented* cows the label said – as I
watched Papee Vince reach to the railing beside me for his
old sweetmilk tin, and spit carefully into it, I was thinking:
*Why is this chuffchuff oldman so tie-up with this Magdalena
woman? Look at him sitting there. Why is he tie-up so with this
woman that don't have nothing to do with him? Then again,
how the same woman could tie you up too?*

WELL SON, now begins the history of Magdalena's
relationship with you grandfather. It would last until the
day of she death, seven months later. Just what sort of
relationship it was remains, I suppose, relatively obscure.
Because the fact is that fa the whole of those seven months
Magdalena resided as a nun in St Maggy Convent. Now:
how it is that you grandfather came to confide in me all of
this business is obvious enough. Understand, fa twenty-
two years I was employed by him there on the old
Domingo Estate, with Barto riding out from St Maggy
two or three times every month, with both of we invariably ending up each evening sitting there on the gallery of
my bungalow, knocking back we tassas of punching rum,
talking we oldtalk. Because it was not long after I married
Gertrude, you grandmother, that we went to live on the
estate, and it was twenty-two years later – not long after
Gertrude's death – that I came out here to St Maggy, to
Barto, and asked to be relieved of my duties as manager of

the cultivation. What I could not have known, as that precise moment – though perhaps I should have expected something of the sort, fate again, advocating coincidence – was that only the week before, both Magdalena and she child had died. At all events, Barto sold the estate the following day. That same morning he saw me aboard my ship destined fa the Delta Orinoco, where I was to remain fa thirty-five years. But it was on the night before I departed, on a moonlit night just like this one, that Barto brought me up here where we could be alone. Right here, on this cobo roost, on this very night so many years ago, here where you and I sit at this very moment. He told me about the events which had taken place during the previous week: about Magdalena's death, about the birth and death of she child. About the events which would, on the same afternoon of the same day on which my ship set sail fa Tucupita, up the River Orinoco, in so far as any of we can tell, bring Barto to take he own life.

Right. It happened that first Sunday morning quite by caprice. With a vaps: Barto sat there eating he eggs and blackpudding, and he felt the sudden urge to see her again. Just like that. He decided to go to Maraval on the chance that she might do the same, that perhaps he would find her there. This, I suppose, must have been a few weeks after she'd left Gomez and returned to the convent. He found her, of course. What's more, she told Barto she'd often hoped to see him there again, which may well be the reason she continually returned to the swamp. They spent the day there together, sitting beneath the same samaan tree where Barto had sat watching her catching crapos with the scoutboys only three or four months before, he, telling he oldstories and smoking he thin Cuban cigars, and she, sitting there beside him listening quietly. Because the truth is that Magdalena never said much. In fact, she was so extremely quiet that some even went about the place calling her a dumb deaf-mute, and some still do to this day. But son, this Magdalena wasn't no kind of dumb deaf-mute a-tall. Quite to the contrary. True, she never said much, not even to Barto. But on the few occasions she did open her mouth, I can tell you she spoke a kind of soft, smooth eloquence easy as guava icecream.

Good. It was a pleasant, though uneventful morning that first Sunday morning, the first of many such Sundays mornings spent sitting there beneath the same samaan tree. And it was late one Sunday night (after the usual day at Maraval, after Barto had gotten to know Magdalena quite well) that he awoke from he sleep in a cold sweat. He sleep had not been disturbed by thoughts of Magdalena. Of this he was certain. Nor did Barto contemplate her an instant as he dressed heself. He'd decided to go fa walk along King's Wharf, to take in the cool seabreeze. What was peculiar, and Barto seemed surprised heself as he spoke, was that he felt pressed. Hurried to get to the docks. So much so that when he closed the front door behind him, and sat on the step to lace up he shoes (you see, Barto slept upstairs, in the bedroom you mummy and daddy use now, and he did not want to make a load of racket on the stairs to wake up Granny Myna and Evelina sleeping below) he felt so hurried that he left the shoes there. He did not want to waste the time to lace them up. Just so: he took off in he bare feet. And when he returned home on Wednesday morning, three days later, the shoes had disappeared. (No doubt Granny Myna had found them there the following morning and pitched them in the sea, a beautiful pair of hardbacks stretched from the skin of a macajuel Barto heself had wrestled up the Orinoco, because he never saw those shoes again.)

But he had taken off in the wrong direction. Still, he had not contemplated Magdalena. He had thought only *King's Wharf*, and now he did not think even that. Neither did he think of Sir Walter Raleigh Square, though that was where he was going. Going in a hurry. And what he did there was quite peculiar. The whole sequence of events seems peculiar, and as Barto related them to me, they seemed connected by that strange sense of reality which connects nonsensical events in dreams. It was a full moon night, and the square was empty. Barto stood beneath the statue, looking up, and he saw that there were pigeons sleeping, perched all over it: on Raleigh's shoulders, along he upraised sword, on the plume of he hat. Barto found the pigeons repulsive. Why, he couldn't say heself. Only that the sight of them there, hunched up, molting and musty-smelling, the sight of they stool splattered over the statue, was to him suddenly repulsive. He began to rap on Raleigh's shin with he knuckles. It was like knocking a melon: soft, hollow thuds. One or two of the pigeons ruffled up he feathers, moved over a bit, hunched up again. Barto had another idea: he went to one of the almond trees and began collecting up rockstones. The earth beneath the tree had been trampled smooth, so much so that he had to scrape them out. Barto returned to the statue and began pelting the rockstones, one by one, at the pigeons roosting on Raleigh's shoulders. He went to the tree again, in a boyish kind of vexation, and he was not satisfied until he had driven every pigeon away. He was in a sweat now, and he sat on the step round the base of the statue, feeling in he vest pocket fa the cigar which was not there.

At that moment the Government House clock began to strike fa midnight, startling him, and he turned quickly to look at it across the square. Something stopped him, startling him again: it was the figure of a woman, there, naked in the moonlight of one of the balconies of St Maggy Convent, and only then did he contemplate Magdalena. In the distance he made out the face that was not looking down at him, but up, at the huge moon. And as that clock beat twelve times, Barto took twelve deep breaths. She disappeared. Not turning: stepping backward into the darkness of she room.

Barto left he clothes bundled up in the fork of one of those almond trees. He was perspiring heavily now, and in the moonlight he white white skin seemed to be glowing. Stepping in the chinks between the coral stones, gripping the ivy, he climbed up the wall onto she balcony. They made love fa three days and three nights: continuously. Without pause. And to Barto's own astonishment, he erection did not subside fa three days and three nights either. Not until he climbed down from the wall again with the first light of Wednesday morning. I couldn't tell you, son. I would be the first to admit to you that you grandfather was above the ordinary. Whether or not he could sustain this erection fa such a prolonged period of time, is, of course, questionable. But son, what you or I choose to believe seems of little consequence: because by the time Barto climbed down from that balcony on Wednesday morning – by the time he took down he clothes still there bundled up in the fork of that almond tree, and began to dress heself – Magdalena was convinced he was *angelic*. And he, was convinced of no less of her.

Gomez returned to the convent that morning. The same Wednesday morning. How he knew Barto had been there – and under what particular *circumstances* he'd been there – that, I couldn't tell you. No one else knew. The nuns theyselves didn't know. But again, like everything else, somehow or other Gomez found out. He was insulted, I suppose, but that would be putting it mild. Because not only had Magdalena left him just a few weeks before, now she'd *cuckolded* him. Remember: all this time Magdalena is legally he wife. In addition, you must understand that this Chief of Police suffers from a tremendous inferiority complex. Not only is he of inferior stature (and I would say he stood no more than fifty-four inches tall, weighing no more than eight stone) not only is he of inferior stature, but the whole bloody island takes him fa tantieman. In a backyard where bantycock never *smells* the henhouse. The result, of which, is a zandolee lizard swelled up too big fa he hole, a megalomaniac of grandiferous proportions. Let me tell you, Barto had scarcely climbed down the wall of that convent, when Gomez arrived with he jooker aflame. Literally. He came to defend he manhood. To prove he prowess. He came, to give he wife licks, fleet, cuttail. But as usual, cobo came to shit on he head.

You see, having spent all those years out there in Mayaguaro, living among those Warrahoons and such, I have had plenty of opportunities to learn about this thing. Which is not to say I indulged myself. But again, like anyone else, you do have a certain scientific, medical curiosity, and you would like to satisfy youself. But you take the proper precautions. You don't go like Gomez, mixing up you own medicine any which way, in whatever concentrations such that you overdose youself, so much so that after five days – the last two spent in the hospital with you toetee packed up in ice – you flagpole is *still* standing tall like a standpipe, and not a thing in this world can bring him down.

Right. Good. You want to know about this thing: roupala montana, or as we have come to call it, bois bandé (with an acute accent on the *e*). It means, in the Creole, stiff, or hard wood. Correct. Now: it is a common forest tree, a climax forest tree, which has been utilized by the natives – I suppose you could say fa medicinal purposes – fa years. (In fact, when Raleigh reported that a Corpus Christi native had given him a potion which enabled him, in the privacy of he ship's quarters, to sustain an erection fa twenty-seven hours at a stretch, they thought he'd lost he head. What Raleigh did *not* know, is that the Warrahoons had been using bois bandé fa donkey's ages, batting it back every night before they go to bed like we drink Ovaltine in warm milk.) To prepare it, you use the bark – like mauby, or chincona, from which quinine is made – boiling it down in much the same way. But you know how bitter mauby is? A little piece of the bark big as you fingernail like this goes in to make up a whole jorum? Well this bois bandé is every bit as potent. And of course, you take a dose now, and when the effect subsides after a few hours, if you still haven't satisfied youself to exhaustion, of course you take another.

Gomez must have eaten down the whole bloody tree. Because what began as kicksin, finished in LBW. Leg-before-wicket. Penalty box. Let me tell you, Gomez got heself into some *serious* trouble. Because son, as you can well imagine, like any other over-strained muscle, after a time this thing gets to be bloody painful. Not to mention the fact that you killing to make a weewee. Let me tell you, when that Chief of Police cleared out the convent on Friday afternoon, after the three days – with that Mother Maurina doing nothing again, except of course assembling in the chapel fa another novena – when that Chief of Police cleared out, he went *straight* to St Maggy Hospital. He was in that much pain. Of course, Salizar could do nothing but pack him up in ice and throw a sheet over him. With all the little whitecap-nuns, every time they go down the hall lifting up the sheet fa little peep, because of course, everybody outside wants to know how the Chief of Police's flagpole is going. To be sure, this bushdoctor Salizar is straight out the jungle of Venezuela, and he knows bois bandé as well as any of we: there is no antidote. No counteractant except time. Son, Gomez bawled down the place fa three days. Half of Corpus Christi is gathered there in front of the hospital – with that crackerjack Uncle Olly thinking up the idea of a *lottery* now to guess the precise minute this Chief of Police's flagpole is expiring, there with he megaphone selling tickets like bush, and making heself a bloody fortune — when Salizar decides he ga to try an old Warrahon cure-all: a mixture of peppersauce, limejuice and rocksalt.

Son, they tell me it worked like a charm. But by the time Salizar finished rubbing down Gomez's toetee with this commess, he had to remain in the hospital packed in ice fa another three days.

Of course, before he had even arrived in the hospital – before he had even cleared out of the convent – Mother Maurina had sent fa Barto again: she'd commissioned him to return to the convent fa another of those wedding-nunpledging ceremonies. Except this time Magdalena was in worse condition. Again Mother Maurina did not waste time tending to she bruises. She didn't even waste the time to feed her. Understand: Magdalena had gone without food now fa six days, from Sunday midday to Friday afternoon, though admittedly, the first three were of she own volition. Again, all that Mother Superior General could think to do is to pelt her down the stairs into the chapel to repledge she vows. And when Monsignor O'Connor directs Barto, fa the second time, in the name of Christ, to push the ring on she finger, Magdalena has to take it off she still trembling hand and give it to him fa him to do it.

Enough. I am finished now with those three: Gomez, and Monsignor O'Connor, and this same Mother Superior General Maurina. Finished. Nothing more was heard from any of them. Not until after Magdalena's death anyway, seven months later. They came fighting down Barto fa the body – some bubball, with the three of them digging up, and reburying, and mismolesting all the poor old jumbies sleeping peaceful enough in Domingo Cemetery – which apparently, Gomez settled good and proper by dropping down dead suddenly heself. Because I suppose the other two, Mother Maurina and Monsignor O'Connor, were frightened the same would happen to them.

Magdalena's final seven months were quiet. Very quiet, in comparison to the months which preceded. It was

during those seven months which Magdalena secretly met
with Barto every Sunday beneath the big samaan, those
seven months during which she secretly carried he child.
No one else knew about the pregnancy. In fact, few knew
anything about Magdalena's relationship with Barto a-tall.
The truth is by this time Corpus Christi seemed to have
lost interest in she affairs altogether – overwhelmed and
desensitized, I suppose, in they astonishment – and fa the
last seven months Magdalena was quite forgotten. Even
the spectacle of this beautiful, sienna-skinned woman,
walking alone by sheself each Sunday morning along the
trace to Swamp Maraval, dressed in she white nuncostume
with the rosary consisting of beads the size of marbles tied
up round she waist, the dust a continuous cloud rising
round she bare feet – so that she seemed almost to be
walking in air – even the spectacle of this beautiful,
dark-skinned woman was no longer a spectacle, but a
common weekly occurrence. No one noticed. That is, of
course, until the birth of the child. The child I have already
described fa you. The unthinkable, preternatural, prog-
idiferous child which would throw us all into a world
beyond the mysterious, into the unfathomable. The child
which would bring Magdalena to take she own life. Which
would, inevitably, bring Barto to do the same.

    What sort of child he was, I would not venture to guess.
Some called him the jabjab heself, son of Manfrog, the
folktale devil-sprite who waits in a tree to rape young
virgins at dusk. Others saw nothing peculiar in the child
a-tall. Some even said that the child was beautiful, perfect:
that the child was the reflection of he viewer. Some argued
the hex of an obeah spell. Others, the curse of Magdalena's
obsession with Swamp Maraval, with frogs fucking: that
he was, as Salizar suggested, a crapochild. Still others,
prompted by the young physician who'd just come to St
Maggy Hospital then, said he was the result of a congenital
abnormality which caused him to appear like a frog: a

condition (which the young physician printed out on a piece of paper fa me to read it) a congenital condition resulting from a failure of the brain and the encasing skull to develop as normal, known in the correct clinical language as AN-EN-CEPHALY. This, of course, would seem most plausible – except fa the fact, acknowledged by the bright young physician heself – that these congenital monsters are generally stillborn, whereas this child lived strong as ever fa three days. Even with half of Corpus Christi fighting down each other for the privilege to kill him. Son, we can resign weselves to only this: there is no logical explanation. We will never know.

IT WAS Papee Vince's voice which carried me in my dream now. Papee Vince's voice from which I could not escape. And as I sat there, suspended, balanced awkwardly on the railing with my feet hanging a few inches above the ground, I could just barely point my toes and touch it. Could just barely touch the tip of my big toe to the finger of reality, and know that I was alive within the confines of my dream. And as I sat there, listening to my old grandfather, sitting there in his hammock stretched between me and that trapdoor which led down the ladder, I was thinking: *This oldman have you hold-up on this cobo roost like that same frogbaby hold-up inside he glassbottle. Just like that same frogbaby hold-up inside he glassbottle, with you toting youself now in this baddream to this place you don't want to go. So why you don't dream youself onto that railing on the other side of Papee Vince? Why you don't dream youself cross there, and then you only have to run down the ladder to get youself way from this Papee Vince, and Granny Myna, and Magdalena and this frogbaby fagood faever?*

THAT IS WHAT Barto said to me. Sitting here, on this

very cobo roost, beneath this same moon above the same
black sea. That is what Magdalena had said to him: you
will never understand. Believe. And this will be the sign:
that the child will appear like no other. Because she told
him these things on the Sunday before she death, sitting
there beneath the same samaan tree. That she sheself
would live long enough to see the child's face. Because the
child was to be the sign fa her too: she took one look in he
face and held she breath until she suffocated. She told
Barto that the child would live fa three days, until Easter
Sunday – one year exactly from the day Magdalena first
appeared in Corpus Christi – and on that Easter Sunday
Barto was to bury the child in Domingo Cemetery, there
beside her. And she left him with this last promise: three
days later she would be with him again.

But Barto must have sat there listening to her the same
way I sat here listening to him, the same way you are
sitting here now listening to me: incredulous. Confounded. And on the following morning, as I sat there on the
deck of that ship, she bowed pointed at the open mouth of
the River Orinoco, Corpus Christi sinking slowly behind
in the turbulence of she wake, I still did not understand
what Barto had told me. And when you grandfather
gathered Granny Myna, you father and he brothers, Uncle
Olly and Evelina round him sitting there at the big
diningroom table, and he pulled the cork from a bottle of
rum and passed it round smiling, saying he would be
leaving them that same afternoon, they were sure he was
going on another of he expeditions up the Orinoco. But it
was I who had left on the expedition this time, I who had
replaced Barto. Because he simply disappeared. He remains have never been found.

You father was the one who deciphered it, three or four
weeks later. He went to Domingo Cemetery and discovered a row of four new black marble headstones. No one
had seen them before. Headstones belonging to Mag-

dalena and the child, and two others, one intended fa
Granny Myna, the other fa Barto heself. How they got
there no one knows to this day. We can only assume that
sometime prior to he disappearance, Barto heself gave
instructions for them to be placed there. Sometime prior
to he *death*, if that is what you choose to believe. Because
three of those four headstones were dated: Magdalena's,
on Corpus Christi Day, 16 April; the child's, Easter
Sunday, 19 April; and you grandfather's, 22 April.
Wednesday, 22 April: the same day I set sail fa the Delta
Orinoco, the same day you grandfather gathered the
family downstairs round the big diningroom table.

They buried an empty casket. Empty, except for three
or four good-sized chockstones. You father, the eldest,
decided that would be best fa Granny Myna. He would
not have her live out the rest of she life faced with the
uncertainty of she husband's death. You must understand
son, that in those old days people felt very strongly about
such matters. I know myself, in fact, that you grandmother
actually lived fa the day she would be buried in peace next
to Barto. Such feelings suggest a depth of love which
perhaps you and I cannot comprehend, but a depth of love
none the less. You father told Granny Myna that the body
had been found, decomposed and piranha-disfigured, that
it was not fit fa her to see. Perhaps you will think of this
deception of you father's as wrong, as dishonest, but you
must try to see the compassion with which these things
were done. It is a compassion I much admire in you father.

He was the one who wrote and explained all of this to
me, in a letter which found me in Cutacas, after I had lived
there nearly a year. In the same letter he spoke of plans fa
marrying you mother. Plans which had long been enacted
by the time I read of them, lying there in my hammock in
a bungalow high at the top of one of those derricks. It was
as if fate was speaking to me again, saying that I had better
get used to that jungle. That I would be there awhile. Son,

I remained fa thirty-five years. Thirty-five years living in a world no description can begin to describe. But don't you understand son, that it would take thirty-five years of telling myself over and over again that if this man, Barto, you grandfather, could believe, could believe fervently enough to take he own life at she word, then you can say it too: *Yes. I believe.*

WITH THAT my grandfather began to sit up in his hammock. He trembled fixing the wire curves of his glasses around his ears. My grandfather stood, holding on to the rope of the hammock to steady himself. He turned and started down the ladder, descending into the darkness. I pushed myself off the railing, and as I landed on my feet my legs almost folded beneath me. They had gone to sleep sitting there on the railing. They were numb. I couldn't budge my feet. Standing there, seeing myself again looking down through the black rectangular hole of that trapdoor, watching my grandfather disappearing slowly into the darkness of his room below, hearing the water on the rocks and the chickens scratching and the cool breeze on my wet skin in the tamarind tree of my own backyard, smelling the musty odour of old newspapers and the foul smell of the swamp blowing from the distance, feeling my feet numb and unyielding again in my old jesusboots beneath the mud, watching him swimming again disappearing again into darkness not even the huge unfading moon overhead can penetrate, thinking: *There is no end to any of this. There is only beginning, and between, and beginning again.*

3

Evelina Gives an
Obeah Spell

I AWOKE to a premonition of death: old Evelina's dark
wrinkled face looking down at me, her hand clasped over
my mouth so I could not breathe. She made a sign to keep
quiet, another to come, and for a terrifying instant I
remembered I had not said my prayers before sleep. Then
she disappeared. I sat up in my bed, breathing deeply,
looking for signs of reality in the darkness: the oscillating
fan swept the room. My younger brother was still in his
bed beside mine. On top the bureau were my new
washykongs, one of my shortpants and a jersey. I couldn't
figure out what my new washykongs were doing on top
the bureau. Then I realized Evelina had taken them out and
left them there for me to put on. I'd go with her
sometimes to catch crabs at night, to collect some noctur-
nal flower or lichen for her bushmedicine, or if someone
were sick, we'd go to the cathedral to light a candle and
say a rosary for La Divina Pastora. Sometimes, when I
couldn't sleep, I'd go to Evelina's room and she'd tell me
stories about the old Domingo Estate, stories about the
forest and Papa Bois and La Gahoo, or stories about the
French Creoles and Africa and obeah. But never before
had Evelina come to awaken me at such an hour, and
never before had I seen such a serious look on her face. I
threw off the sheet and jumped out of bed. I pulled on my

shorts and the jersey, but I hesitated with my new
washykongs: they were for special occasions, and I could
think of few special occasions occurring in the middle of
the night.

I found Evelina down the hall, waiting beneath the light
at the top of the stairs, outside Papee Vince's old bedroom.
It was my sister's bedroom now. For the second time I was
frightened by the appearance of this woman who'd raised
me since birth. She looked a hundred years old – and must
have been nearly that – dressed in a faded longdress with a
kerchief tied around her head, another over her shoulders,
barefoot, a dozen silver bangles rattling like old bones on
her wrists. She turned and started down the stairs. I
followed her to the bottom, walking on my toes to keep
the crêpesoles of my washykongs from squeaking. Evelina
led me down the hall, past the livingroom and around the
big diningroom table, through the kitchen and into her
bedroom. In the corner was her small altar, now with
creole incense and several candles burning, lighting up
some glossy lithographs of her saints, a crucifix, and her
statues: one of St John the Baptist, whom she also called
Shango, Maker of Thunder and Lightning, his tool leaning
up against the statue, a bullpistle whip; of St Michael, large
feathery wings growing out of his back – Ogoun, the
Warrior – his two-edged sword beside the statue; and St
Anne, or Oshoun, Goddess of Water, with her rusted
penknife which she used to write messages from the dead
in the dirt. Evelina's beliefs were a mixture of Granny
Myna's Catholicism and her mother's obeah, itself a
mixture of the same Catholicism and a Yoruba religion.
Scattered among the statues were some artificial flowers,
plastic beads, and a few smooth, round thunderstones.
Evelina took up two rumbottles from behind the statues.
One was filled with rum and corked. The other was
half-filled with rank pitchoil, a charred rag sticking out of
the top, several red-and-black jumbie beads soaking at the

bottom: she called it a bouteille d'feu in her patois, and she'd told me the beads were to make its flame jumbie-repellant. Evelina got down on her knees and reached beneath her bed, taking out a cutlass and a small bundle wrapped in a flowered kerchief, the corners tied in two big knots, suspended from the cutlass blade like the handle of a handbag.

She led me through the kitchen and out the screen door at the back. Evelina shooed the fowls off the stoop, sitting on the step with her bundle on the ground at her feet. I sat beside her, just as I had sat a thousand times to watch her shell pigeonpeas, or patiently pluck a chicken clean – its head dangling at the end of its long thin neck – then in a sudden gesture stretch it out and bite it off at the shoulders. Evelina untied the knots of her kerchief and spread it out. With the light above the back door I saw what looked like a small pile of rubbish: a shard of mirror, a jumble of cord, a piece of dried bush, of old cloth, a tiny package wrapped in newsprint. Evelina took up a large box of kitchen matches. She lit the torchlight, dropping the matches into her skirt between her knees, adjusting the wick with a few quick tugs of her long fingers in the flame, her bangles rattling. She gave me the bottle of rum, took up the cutlass and the flambeau, and she led me over to the huge tamarind tree in our back yard.

There was no moon. Evelina spread out the kerchief again and stood holding the torchlight above her head, studying the ground beneath the tree. She located the spot she wanted, went and knelt in front of it, and she began scraping at the hard ground with the blade of her cutlass. The fowls started to gather around her, looking to see what she was doing. I took a few steps behind them and they ran off in a burst of cackle. Evelina dug up a small square tin, covered in a powder of bright orange rust. She dusted it off carefully, and I read, stamped in the lid: TINNED IN GREAT BRITAIN. She went to the kerchief and took up the piece of old cloth, which I saw now had been sewn into a pouch. Evelina opened the pouch and dropped in the sardine tin. She picked up the jumble of twine, pulled out a piece about two feet long, and cut it off with the cutlass. She used the cutlass to strip off a branch of the dried bush, dropping it into the pouch with the sardine tin. Evelina tied the middle of the cord around the open end of the pouch. She threaded on the piece of mirror through a hole in the glass, let it slip down next to the pouch, and she tied the two ends of the cord together. I was thinking: *A shard of mirror or a donkeyeye seed fa to parry maljoe, oui.* Evelina hung the cord around her neck.

She turned and looked at me for the second time since she'd awakened me, standing there holding the bottle of rum. She made a sign for me to follow, and we went and stood in front of the hole where she'd dug up the sardine tin, facing the tree. Evelina reached up and picked a long brown pod. She cracked it between her teeth, took out a meaty seed to suck – square-shaped, its four stringy umbilical cords attached at the corners – and she gave me another, so acid it tied up my mouth. Evelina took the bottle of rum from me and uncorked it. She threw her head back and mumbled something in her African language, took a sip, and she poured some of the rum over her fingers, wiping them across her face, behind her ears, and at the back of her neck. She gave me the bottle, and I stood staring at her. She nodded. I took a deep breath, a sip – almost choking on the tamarind seed – and wiped my eyes with the back of my hand. I looked at her again. Evelina chupsed. She took the bottle and poured some over her fingers, anointing me too. She poured some of the rum into the hole, got down on her knees again to fill it in, smoothening the ground over with the blade of her cutlass. Evelina began sprinkling rum on the ground, walking in a big circle around the tree. By the time she'd finished I'd made up my mind to spit out the tamarind seed, but just as I went to do so she looked at me again: I continued sucking. Evelina gave me the bottle of rum to carry, took up her kerchief and the torchlight, and she led me around the house, out the front gate. She went to the middle of the road and carved a cross in the dirt with her cutlass, delineating it with a pinch of flour which she took out of the tiny newsprint package. I was thinking: *She told me about that one too: A cross in de street fa to keep Soucouyant from walking behind you.*

Evelina wrapped up the flour again and retied her bundle. She walked ahead with the torchlight, me carrying the bottle of rum, following in the trail of her smoke, hurrying to keep up. The tamarind seed was so sour it numbed my teeth, and each time they rubbed together I felt the electric shock in my mouth. I was afraid to spit it out, and I knew that I could not – even if I had wanted to – any more than I could have put down that obzockee glassbottle three years before. I continued sucking, re-signing myself to that tamarind seed in the same way I had come, finally, to acknowledge the place assigned to Magdalena and her frogchild in my own fate. And in a sense, my acceptance of them made it easier for me to ignore them. Because I still broke biche on the school days of our excursions to Divina Church, and my friends still called me El Papa. But in some irresolute way I had come to accept my fate, a fate I knew was taking a turn with me again. The date was too significant to be otherwise: it was Wednesday, April 15, the eve of Corpus Christi, and two nights before my sixteenth birthday. Already I knew where Evelina was taking me. Already I knew I could not turn back. This ritual, whatever it was, had been set into motion. It was as if the smell of that rum which still lingered on my forehead – the feel of it still cool and sticky behind my ears – were the memory of that distant Corpus Christi morning which would not allow me to dismiss Magdalena and her frogchild, because it left me with no

choice now but to follow behind this old woman who had
raised me.

So I was not surprised when we passed between the
short coral gates of Domingo Cemetery, the air confused
by the odours of dank earth and over-sweet eucalyptus,
that Evelina led me straight to the frogchild's grave. It was
as though I had known we were going there from the time
we left the house. Evelina spat out her tamarind seed on
the grave. She didn't have to look at me: I was happy to
spit out mine too. She put her bundle down, brushed away
some of the wet leaves, and she set the torchlight in the
dirt in front of the gravestone, the flame reflecting on its
polished surface, on those of the tombstones around us.
Evelina turned and sat on the headstone, gesturing for me
to sit on the one opposite, about three feet away, the
flambeau between us. I put the bottle of rum down and sat
on the headstone, and when I looked up I shuddered: there
in front of me was the line of my family's gravestones. For
an instant I was thirteen years of age again, standing there
in my baggy school shortpants and my old jesusboots,
reading the names written on those headstones for the first
time: Manuelito Domingo, Barto and Granny Myna on
either side, Magdalena and Uncle Olly on either side of
them. For a confused instant I was afraid I'd be late for
Granny Myna's funeral again. Then I remembered the
boxing my father had given me when I arrived home at
dusk that evening. We'd buried Papee Vince next to Uncle
Olly only two months before Evelina brought me to the
cemetery, but his headstone had not been completed yet,
and in its place stood a nondescript wooden cross. I
shuddered again, perceiving several other things, almost at
the same time: that as I sat there my legs were not long
enough to reach the ground, my feet hanging in my new
washykongs just an inch above it; that we'd forgotten to
chisel in Granny Myna's deathdate to complete her headstone; that the headstone of that crapochild I had carried

away *alive* marked the centre of my family plot.

Evelina took the cord with the shard of mirror and the pouch from around her neck, held it above her head, looking up, speaking loudly:

Ogoun, beh weh ja go,
Ogoun, ay ree lay.
Ogoun, beh weh ja go,
Eshu, bah rook nay!

She repeated it three times. Then she leaned forward and hung the cord around my neck.

YES DOODOO, now de burden of dis curse must fall pon you. Because old Evelina not here to push she foot but few more step long de road again, and you is de firstborn Domingo manchild, beget by de firstborn Domingo manchild, beget by dis wajank-diab who is Satan self, who defile Papa God own sweet saint of heaven to beget dis diab-crapochild and bring down he curse pon you, pon all Domingos, pon dis whole island of Corpus Christi, pon all de earth. It happen so, because she make de mistake to let night catch she sitting dere with he neath de same samaan side de swamp, because we follow he dere with you granny cursing from de time she leave de house, and we watching whole day from behind booze-mahoo bush. Soon as night fall de diab change he shape not to Soucouyant, or Mokojumbie, or even de manquenk La Gahoo, but he change heself to de worst *all* Satan shape – and dat is Manfrog, Papamoi! – because soon as she look up he jump out and he stick pon she and jook is jook he jooking she with she nundress all tear up. You granny crying behind de mahoo bush with me doing me best to console she, but before we finish de prayer to St Jude she jump up bawling out, *Singate pendejo, Barto!* dat me have to hold she down pon de ground and knock she back of she head with a chockstone to try to bring she back to she senses, and keep she from swimming out to pull dey loose. But nothing couldn't stop you granny once she temper fly, and now is three dey tumbling in de mud, but of course dat Manfrog done stick with frogstick strong like pembois-laglee, so no matter how hard Granny Myna pull she could never pull dey part. Out from nowhere come storm like me never see storm before, oui. Lightning flashing, and rain pelting, and wind blowing, and Manfrog jooking with he throat swell up big big and red and he eyes flashing green like break cocacola glassbottle through de night, with you granny clamp on he back trying to pull dey loose. All in a sudden Manfrog let go cry of consumption dat is no language of dis world – because it silence all de element of de storm in one, Papamoi! – and just as de earth stop to hold she breath he unstick rolling over leaving she lying dere in de mud with all she mummy expose bleeding before de face of Papa God, looking like if she dead.

Storm commence, and Granny Myna commence to struggling with Manfrog, and me run to Magdalena see if she dead fa true. She kaponkle but she breathing good enough, so me carry she up by de grass neath de big samaan. Me wrap she up in de kerchief from round me shoulder to cover she proper, and me run to de bush fa some aloe and sweet granadilla leaf to stick pon she chest and she temple. In no time a-tall Magdalena recover sheself, oui. But dis child is Papa God own sweet saint céleste, and she stand up fast as paragrass to go by de water again kneeling down in de mud to pray de big chapelet from round she waist. Granny Myna still struggling Manfrog out in de swamp with de storm raging worse den ever, and sometimes dey disappearing neath de water half-hour at a stretch without a breath of air – but you know even as a man dis cacashat-wajank love nothing

better dan to wrestle big mappapire and macajuel up de
Orinoco, oui fute! – but when you granny temper fly she
want to fight up St Michael self. All me can think to do is
go down in the mud side Magdalena to pray chapelet with
she, and when me look good me see she crying now with
de whole sea a sea of blood every time de lightning
flashing with she tears. Granny Myna wrestle Manfrog
whole night, oui. Not until most daybreak do she let go,
with Magdalena and me running to lift she out de water
high as we waist, and de mud high as we knees, standing
dere with de new light of dawn showing we Manfrog
swimming neath de water push-slide, push-slide before he
disappear in a mudcloud tween de mangrove banyan.

When dis child come out with he head of a crapo and he
forceripe business of a man hanging down tween he legs
like a calabash green guts, Magdalena only turn she eyes to
look in he face when she turn to boulderstone. *Black*
boulderstone. Black as de gravestone you bamsee resting
pon right now, black as Bazil backside, because dis is how
dis diab-crapochild pronounce he birth to all de world, and
how else could we have dis statue perfect so in every
feature down to the Warrahoon middletoe cut out from
both she foot, up to de red coolie-mark pon she forehead,
when she is a *white* woman? White white and beautiful and
fair as morning sweet self – never mind what foolishness
you hear bout she being a callaloo mix up with coolie and
Creole and Warrahoon and every kind of blood with
blood, Papamoi! – because me used to see she every
Sunday morning me go with Granny Myna to watch dey
sitting neath de big samaan, and praying to La Divina
Pastora every Wednesday midday me go to dust out de
cathedral and put in fresh bouganvilla flower fa all de saint,
and dis Magdalena is a clearskin woman. You poor daddy
didn't know what to do, oui. Time as he look up from dis
crapochild she already a statue of black boulderstone, so
heavy she throw down de bed exploding de mattress with

all de white snowflake of copra-stuffing flying bout dat
little hospital room like blizzard. You daddy cross heself
and he take deep breath to blow way de snowstorm of
copra stuffing from in front he face, but when he bend
over to bite off de navelstring from de belly of dis
crapochild he see de child holding on tight with both fists
clench round it dat he done pull it out from he mummy
heself, and he not letting you daddy nor nobody else even
near dat cordstring to work no science with it a-tall. Just
den de two police of Gomez use dey bootoo to bust down
de hospital door, and before you daddy even get chance to
turn round Mother Maurina grab way de child, and
Monsignor O'Connor and he three acolytes grab up de
statue – with dat Chief of Police locking on de cufflinks
same time, oui fute! – parading you daddy like chicken-
thief barefoot through de crowd waiting outside with de
green doctor kerchief still tie up round he face, and de
blizzard of copra stuffing following behind in de rush of
dey wake, straight down de street to de jail.

Next morning dat scoundrel Barto arrive carrying he
diab-crapochild in a saltfish-crate. Granny Myna start to
bawl, but before Barto can push he foot through de door
she take off running to save sheself, and she spend whole
morning hiding in de bamboo cross de street. How dis
man get he crapochild way from dat Mother Maurina me
couldn't tell you, because de same Mother Superior
Maurina went bout de place saying one set of foolishness
bout how dis crapochild is an angel from heaven just like
he mummy. But doodoo, you know good enough how
vex is dis Mother Maurina with Barto ever since he send
she to convent heavy with child marrying up Granny
Myna instead, so me say dat Mother Maurina thief dis
crapochild only to make *sure* Barto bring he home, not
only to kill Barto heself, but *all* of we on top. Me can think
only to burn down de house top *dey* head first, oui. Me run
quick to dat coalpot still burning from dose fritters just fry

fa de children breakfast before dem go school, and me shoo-way de fowls to put live coal in de straw each one dem roosts hanging pon de wall above de washbasin in de back. Me run quick to Granny Myna room to grab up Amadao, and me carry he out de parlour room side door waiting by de duck pond case we have to jump in. But dis house not coming down a-tall a-tall, and when me look again in de kitchen me find all de henfowl back sitting pon dey eggs good as ever, and all de coals back in dey pot, with dis diab-cacashat-shitong sitting at table now eating one de *same* tanya fritter studying he diab-crapochild. Before me can think what to do next me running to take up dat boutielle d'feu from de chapelle inside me bedroom, and me climb de stairs to soak down Barto *own* big bed with all dat pitchoil. Me watching now until de flames stand up to lick de roof – because me not giving he no chance to out it dis time, Papamoi! – and me run with Amadao down de stairs out de back door waiting in de shed pon de big zebra-donkey case we have to bolt. But when me look again dis diab is back lying in he bed with de saltfish-crate side he, and now he reading newspaper smoking *cigar* pon dat mattress just soak down with all dat pitchoil. Well now me head viekeevie like a St Ann crazyhouse bobolee, and me run downstairs in de basement to Uncle Olly laboratory. Me lay Amadao pon de dissecting table tween de microscope and dat big instrument Olly invent to light up a lightbulb by taking out electricity from a crapo leg or a guana tail, and me take up de big petri basin shape like a giant calabash make from glass. Me grab up two-three of dose big bottle mark with Bazil skullface, and me mix dem up in de basin sprinkling dis commess in a big circle going right round de room. Soon as me touch de bunsen to it dat laboratory flaming to beat all bushfire, oui. Me don't even stop to look round now – because me tell you dis laboratory fill wall to ceiling only with shelf and bookcase of bottle and basin and test tube fill only with every kind of exploding chemical know to dis big world of manmen and monkeys, coeur sacre Jesu priez-moi! – and me fly up de stairs with Amadeo out de front door down de street leaving dis house to explode behind me like de firecrackers on Easter Sunday morning. Of course me run half-way Tunapuna before me realize dis house not exploding a-tall, and when me reach back me find Uncle Olly standing up outside on he soapbox-crate with he big megaphone selling tickets to dis crowd of people only line up to look through de glass at dis big pappyshow going on inside, and when me reach in de house me find Granny Myna dere waiting and she done bring Rosey inside with she to feed dis diab-crapochild. Me give she back Amadao as if to say *she* could live in dis house with dat diab and he diab-crapochild if she want – but me not having *nothing* to do with no madhouse belonging to Satan and he child both, Papamoi! – and me run quick to bury meself neath de bed.

NOW I DID NOT know what to think. Who to believe. Now I was dismayed again. It was not so much the obeah, or the Manfrog story, because Evelina had told me stories of Manfrog before, and I'd been exposed to her obeah rituals for as long as I could remember. All that made me uneasy enough – especially sitting there in the middle of that cemetery – but I could dismiss it for the time being without too much trouble. I could even accept Evelina's designation of my grandfather as a diab: Granny Myna herself had seemed unsure whether she wanted him canonized or burnt in hell. And though I'd never heard Mother Maurina had been pregnant with Barto's own child when he dismissed her to the convent and married Granny Myna in her place, I knew well enough from the way my family spoke of the whole affair – or avoided speaking of it – that his insult had been equally outrageous. Now: that this grandfather I had never known had been devil enough to rape Magdalena Divina; that she herself had been a white woman; that that frogchild had been ugly enough to turn her to a statue of black boulderstone the first time she looked in his face – all that was something else again. But as I sat there on the edge of that gravestone listening to old Evelina, smelling the thick vapours of oversweet eucalyptus suffocating slowly beneath the thin harsh odour of burning pitchoil – as I felt the trickles of sweat trailing slowly down my spine, vertebra-by-vertebra beneath my old football jersey until they collected at the base of my backbone, took off running along the backs of my legs to collect again in my new washykongs the crêpesoles of which were soaked, sopping with my own perspiration – as I sat there listening to this old obeahwoman, I was thinking of something else: *How daddy could be the doctor who deliver Magdalena frogchild? How daddy could be the doctor who deliver him? Then who is this Brito Salizar? How Granny Myna and Papee Vince could both be confused? And if they not confused, then how they both could give me the same boldface lie?*

Because when I had come, finally and reluctantly enough, to accept Magdalena and her frogchild as a legitimate part of my own history, I'd consoled myself by fixing them way back in the past – a past which only remotely belonged to me. And as my relatives who knew them, or of them, died, Magdalena and her frogchild drifted even farther away. So when Evelina told me that it had been my father in that delivery room – saying it so matter-of-factly that at first it did not even register – that seemed more incredible to me than all the rest put together. Because somehow I'd envisioned my father as a child himself at the time the frogchild was born. And when Granny Myna mentioned Amadao in the crib the morning Barto brought the frogchild home (or Paco and Reggie swimming with him in the pond) I know in my imagination I substituted my father for one of them. But

Evelina

Amadao was the youngest and my father the eldest by twenty-three years. So if Granny Myna had not been confused about the children – and I knew in that capacity she was never confused, as my grandmother remembered everything according to how it coincided with the ages and stages of her nine sons – then my father may well have been the doctor in that delivery room. Furthermore: if my father had been there when Barto died as Papee Vince had told me, and if *he* had not been confused – and I knew Papee Vince was seldom confused about anything – then my father may well have been there to bury Magdalena three days before. Then he may well have been there to deliver her child three days before that.

So maybe they both had lied? But why? Now I wanted to know. Now I had to stop Evelina and start asking questions: 'Evelina,' I said, 'how you could tell me it was daddy deliver Magdalena frogbaby? How *daddy* could be the doctor deliver him?'

Evelina paused. She looked at me again. 'Doodoo, what you asking? Me not saying is you daddy kill Magdalena. Me not telling you is he bring de child to be born looking so.' She chupsed. 'Me would never say nothing like dat bout you daddy. Is dat diab and he diab-crapochild kill Magdalena, oui.'

I shook my head. 'But Evelina, daddy wasn't in St Maggy Hospital then. Daddy was in England in Oxford studying in school. Is *Brito Salizar* deliver that frogchild!'

'No doodoo,' she said. 'You daddy were cross dere in dat England fa true. But he reach back to Corpus Christi in time to deliver Magdalena fa dis crapochild. Because dat same old Warrahoon Salizar is de main body, long with dis Gomez Chief of Police, to push you daddy in de middle de whole confusion, with all Corpus Christi pelting de blame pon he.' Evelina chupsed again. 'Neither you daddy nor no man pon de face of sweet Papa God earth could save Magdalena from dis diab-crapochild. You daddy say so heself. Say he *prefer* dat jailcage to we madhouse with dis crapochild inside. And doodoo, me could tell you *me* would have prefer dat jail to dis house too – but den *all* we would be dead like Magdalena, Papamoi! – because den me wouldn't have been dere to take way dis crapochild from Granny Myna, and work dis science pon he me handing down to you now.'

So Granny Myna and Papee Vince both had lied: they did not want me to know my father had gone to prison for Magdalena's murder. Then my father was the schoolboy-doctor Granny Myna had said something about, the one who'd just arrived from England with his big degree stamped by the Queen and his big black books. Then he was the young physician who'd just come to St Maggy Hospital, as Papee Vince had said. And if they did not want me to know badly enough to lie about the whole thing, then probably they thought he was guilty of killing Magdalena too. Because how could they ever expect me to believe Magdalena had committed suicide by holding up her breath? And how could I possibly believe this crackpot oldwoman, that that frogchild had killed Magdalena with a single look by turning her into a statue of black boulderstone? Now I was dismayed again, thinking: *Is daddy murder Magdalena Divina! Is you own daddy kill the Black Virgin of Maraval, patron saint of Corpus Christi!* Now I did not want to hear anything else. Now I could not help but listen.

BECAUSE DIS NOT de first time me see man take Manfrog shape to do Satan business. And dis not de first time me see crapochild neither. Everybody know de stories of Manfrog, and everybody know girlchild must never walk neath a big samaan, particular when night falling. Because in Blanchisseuse up beyond Wallafield already born two of dese crapochild, and one in Grande

Sangre so ugly he tie up de whole village and all who look in he face dat not even dose of castoroil nor green mammyseepot could loose dem fa near bout three weeks, and even today half Grande Sangre still bobolee from dat straining to make a caca. De difference is dat all dose crapochild born *dead*, but Satan don't make no mistake a-tall when he take possession of dis man Barto to defile Papa God own sweet saint céleste. Because dis diab-crapochild is born to bring death to all de world, and dere is no man nor saint powerful enough to kill he, not before he reap combruction pon all Papa God earth. So when Granny Myna pull he from out de pot of water boiling with de dasheen leaves squirrelling fa de callaloo, and she tell me dat he dead fa true so me could carry he back to Maraval where he belong, me could only push a chups at she and ask she if she take me fa poisson d'eau doux to believe some little heat not hot enough to burn she wrist ga harm dis diab-crapochild? Granny Myna say is not de heat boil he, is de water drown he like if me don't know crapo could breathe water easy as air. Me tell she isn't *nothing* pon de face of sweet Papa God earth could kill dis diab-crapochild – and de best we could do is work some science pon he fa we own protection, Papamoi! – but Granny Myna say she don't know nothing bout no Creole-obeah bubball, so me ga have to do it, and is just den me realize she speak de truth.

First thing is find some way make he let loose he navelstring. Because dis crapochild know good enough long as dat navelcord tie to he belly he don't belong neither to dis world nor de next, and dere is no man nor saint dead fa thousand years could stop he combruction. Is fa dat same reason you never touch a popo navelstring before it drop off, and den you bury it quick neath a breadfruit tree if he a man, or a mango-julie if she a girl, dat de popo could grow up to eat dat fruit to live old and strong. But if de popo die before he navelstring drop you cut it off quick and bury it neath a tamarind tree, because dat is de only way to keep dat popo from coming back to do you mauvais-fortune. But no matter *how* me molest dis diab-crapochild, he not letting go he navelstring not fa nothing. Me lay he down pon me bed still kicking up and fighting and squirming bout, and me struggling hard not to look in he nasty crapoface nor pon dat big business hanging down tween he leg like three forceripe groseegorro gumagalla-greenfigs, and me commence to pull and tug and tear at he arm and me try unwind he fingers. Me even rub down he two hands with some of dat black greegree oil mummy used to say does make all you muscle go limp, and turn you bones all to jelly, but is *me* own hand get jellify stead of dat crapochild own, with de bottle dropping out spilling down pon me foot turning to jelly too, throwing me *boodoomboops* pon de ground. Well now me head viekeevie again, and soon as me able to stand me grab up St John bullpistle whip to pelt one set of lash pon dis diab-crapochild – commanding he let loose he navelstring in de name of de great Shango, Papamoi! – but no matter what me do he, dis crapochild not letting go a-tall a-tall. Me can think only to jook up he foot with de cutlass, oui. Me grab it out from neath de bed, and me hold on to dat crapochild frogleg to jook de cutlass clean through de bottom of both he foot, because me thinking fa sure dat pain ga make he let loose he navelstring. But dis crapo-child only squirming pon de bed with de blood dripping down de colour of boil dasheen bush, and he only bawling at me some oy-juga oy-juga frogcurse with de green froth bubbling forth from out he mouth, and *still* he not letting loose. Doodoo, me raise up dat cutlass hot above me head – and me close me eyes to pray quick prayer to St Michael begging he thrust it deep inside he chest through he heart, Papamoi! – but when me open me eyes again me see de cutlass only jook out small jook in he side, and is *now* he green dasheen blood begin to flow like water. Spitting up in de air, gushing out pon de bed, soaking down dat whole bedroom with boil dasheen blood. Me tear up de sheet from off de bed to tie up dis crapochild jookwound, me press pembois-compress pon he side, but no matter *how* me try to keep dis blood from spilling is de more it continue to flow. Me cover head to foot only swimming in dis green crapoblood, and me tasting it in me mouth de taste of burn mollasses fa de fricassee, smelling it in me nose de smell of Brazil backside. Me forget all de science me was ga work pon dis crapochild in one, oui. Me can think only to run Maraval fast as me foot could carry me pitch he in, and me grab he up by he legs toting he upside-down like me carrying cockfowl to sell at Victoria Market. Me head so set now only pon pitching dis crapochild inside de swamp, seem like me walk dat whole ten mile to Maraval in two-three steps. In no time a-tall me dere standing up in de water sunk in de mud high as me knees, and me let go dis diab-crapochild to take off swimming just like he diab crapofather, push-slide in de direction of dose mangrove banyan.

Me breathing easy now fa de first time in three long day. Soon as dat crapochild disappear me close me eyes standing dere just so in de mud of dat swampwater, and me pray quick prayer to Papa God thanking He fa delivering me from de evil of dis crapochild without templation fagood faever amen. But me speak too quick and me put goatmouth loud pon meself same time fa true, because soon as me open me eyes again to turn round to climb out from de mud of dat swampwater, before me even stop to look up, here is he again lying neath de same samaan tree, and he only looking up at me out he big green crapoeye, only mocking me jooking out he long green crapotongue. Doodoo, me run to dat crapochild grab he up quick quick by he legs again, and me swing he round and round me head to catapelt he far out in dat swamp far as me arm could pelt, and me take off running not even stopping fa

second to catch me breath before me reach halfway St
Maggy. Me not praying no prayer yet fa no goatmouth dis
time, but even so soon as me step in de bush fa quick
weewee and me stoop down, dere is he again lying in de
shade a lantana-feverbush tree, and me only thankful he
give me chance to squat. Again me carry he back to
Maraval pitch he in one more time again, and me start
back St Maggy not even raising me eyes from me foot fa
fear of finding he sitting neath some next tree side de road,
and when me reach to de house me run straight to me
room to throw meself exhausted in me bed, but soon as
me raise me eyes just here on top dat same bundle of green
dasheen bloodstain sheet, is dis diab-crapochild. Me so
tired now me too tired even to curse. Is now me realize de
only *one* way possible to get hold of dis crapochild
navelstring, and me take up de cutlass to chop off both he
thumb. Now me can take hold he navelstring easy
enough, and me cut it off quick to coil it up inside dis
sardine-tinbox together with both he thumbfinger. Is now me
can take up dat rumbottle finally from behind dis chapelle –
because you know St Michael is a saint does like he rum
good enough, Papamoi! – and he will never fail to come to
you side long as you give he some, so me pour little in a
tasa and me rest it front he statue. In no time a-tall St
Michael drink it down, oui. Me take swallow and dress
meself with some de same rum pon me forehead and
behind me ears to let he know is me calling, and me fall
down pon me knees raising up dis sardine-tinbox with dat
crapochild navelcord coil up inside, and me pray de prayer
to St Michael begging he thrust dis Eshu back in hell, and
protect me against all he snare and malice. Of course me
pray it to Ogoun in de old Yoruba language de way
mummy first give it to me when me was a young girlchild
living pon de old estate, but you can pray it in de same old
Roman church-tongue easy enough. Because dat Yoruba
prayer me already give you is de same prayer we does pray

together with Monsignor every day fa service, and you does know it good as any other, because just like Papa God and Satan both, de saints could speak *all* de language.

THE TORCHLIGHT had sputtered a few times before it went out, and then it was only her voice in the dark: the too-sweet, dank, insect-silent, eucalyptus dark, interrupted only by the occasional distant cock crowing somewhere in St Maggy. By the soft barking of a solitary dog. By the occasional breeze which would come to blow cool across my wet skin, to rustle the leaves overhead and the paper-thin strips of bark hanging in long corkscrew-curls from the trunks around us. It was only Evelina's voice in the dark. But it was also Granny Myna's voice, and Papee Vince's voice: a collection of voices merging and separating, and occasionally falling into rhythm with my own quick breathing. With the rhythmic rise and fall of my small chest against this scientific obeahpouch containing – as I knew now – the actual relics of this frogchild: an actual devil-monstrance hanging from the cord around my neck.

And now, as Evelina repeated the prayer, her voice became even the voice of Monsignor O'Connor. And it was just before Consecration, and I was the acolyte walking around the altar beside him: my right had pressed firmly against my breast, my left holding his chasuble sleeve up off of his shoulder, as he swung the censer smoking passionately now with the crystalline chalky incense I had just sprinkled on from the little gold cup with the gummed-up spoon – smelling the smoke as plainly now as if the torchlight had relighted itself – as we walked around the altar together praying old Evelina's ancient African obeahprayer:

Sancte Míchael Archángele,
Defénde nos in próelio.

Contra nequítiam et insídias,
Diáboli esto praesí dium.

And now it was my voice too:

Princeps milítiae caeléstis!
Sátanam aliósque spíritus malígnos,
Qui ad perditiónem animárum pervágantur in mundo,
Divína virtúte in inférnum detrúde!

BECAUSE TO SHOW you how quick St Michael does
do he business, no sooner do me finish dat prayer when dis
crapochild quiet down heself. He take in he big crapotongue jooking out de whole while, and he close up he big
crapomouth and he big crapoeyes fa de first time in three
long day. And no sooner do me turn round from burying
dis sardine-tinbox, when just dere is Uncle Olly standing
neath de same tamarind holding up dis diab-crapochild
now heself, send by St Michael not only to deliver me
from de burden of toting he all de way back to Maraval
pitch he in again, but to make me present of five of dose fat
shiny English pound-dollars on top. Uncle Olly say now
dat he want to make some of he science pon dis crapochild,
but dis is not obeah-science he sciencing a-tall – it is de
science of medicine and magic, Papamoi! – and me tell he
to do what ever science does make he old heart glad, just
so long as he carry dis crapochild back to Maraval when he
finish and pitch he in. And me couldn't tell you what
amount of science Uncle Olly do pon dis crapochild – me
only know dis is how he squinge off he eyebrows and
loose he earflaps fa life when dat big crapoleg-lightbulb
explode, oui ma-doo mon-pere! – but doodoo, me could
tell you one thing sure sure: Uncle Olly never reach
Maraval with dis diab-crapochild. Here again is St Michael
doing he business, and he even show de strength of good

over evil when he choose Satan own wicked hand in de
hand of Barto to do he work, because what me didn't even
realize den, is de only one way to stop dis diab-crapochild
is to bury he good and proper neath de ground. Late dat
night Barto find he crapochild swimming in de bottle pon
de shelf in Uncle Olly laboratory. But he never stop to
look good to see he swimming inside de glassbottle, or St
Michael throw gravedust in he eyes when he raise it up to
study it neath de light, because straight way Barto take he
crapochild fa dead dat he thought neither flood nor fire nor
hand of man nor Papa God could destroy he, and he bring
de bottle to Granny Myna demanding to know how it
happen. You granny must be thinking dis is de only way
to get dat crapochild out de house and bury good and
proper longlast neath the ground, right here in dis same
cemetery tween sheself and Barto where he belong happy
enough, because Granny Myna look at Barto with she eyes
only spitting fire, and she give he dat boldface lie how it is
Evelina kill he diab-crapochild. She tell he dis is de curse
Papa God bring down pon he head fa coming with dis
crapochild inside de house, and she pelt both he and he
bottle out de door into de night. But doodoo, dere is *no*
man pon de face of sweet Papa God earth strong enough to
kill dis diab-crapochild. No man a-tall. Because you listen
good to me now. Listen good good to me here now,
because dis thing me preparing to tell you now, in de end,
is more important and more difficult to hear den all de rest
together. But doodoo, if you could hear de rest, den you
could hear dis one easy enough: dat crapochild is still
living nearth dis ground. He *living*. Swimming strong as
ever in dat seawater inside he glassbottle. And he only
waiting fa he chance to come out. He only waiting fa he
chance to reap combruction pon you, pon all Domingos,
pon dis whole island of Corpus Christi, pon *all* de earth.
But doodoo, he never coming out. Not so long as he
remain bury neath dis ground. Not so long as you come

every year pon dis selfsame night dat is de night of he
birth, and you work dis science pon he me handing down
to you now. Den dis crapochild could never harm you.
Den dis curse of you birth could be lifted longlast from off
you head.

EVELINA'S VOICE CEASED, thrusting me again into
the world of my dream. Abandoning me again to the
confusion of my unending nightmare. Now that her voice
had at last ceased, now that her story had at last reached
the end I had so long awaited, now I could not bear the
dark silence. Now I felt afraid. Sitting here before this
frogchild's own headstone, struggling to breathe the dense
moisture-saturated air with this frogchild's own obeah-
monstrance weighing down heavy on my breast, my
shoulders. Sitting here in the middle of this cemetery
having heard so much already, unafraid, undaunted. Now
at last confronted by the quiet stillness I had so long
awaited, feeling suddenly afraid, terrified. Praying it again
quickly now in my own desperate tongue. Two short
breaths whispered quickly into the dark night: *St Michael
the Archangel defend we in the battle guard we gainst the malice
and snares of the devil! Thrust into hell Satan and all the evil
spirits who roam through the world seeking the ruination of souls!*
Evelina's match struck with a loud hiss. Her bangles
rattled as she adjusted the torchlight, its flame reflecting in
flashes from the polished tombstones around us. Evelina
took up her bundle and the flambeau. She turned and
started towards the gate, lighting up a single row of
gravestones at a time as she passed, the occasional eucalyptus trunk with its bark peeling in translucent curls of
innumerable shades of purple, the undersides of its leaves
flashing silver above the torchlight. I shoved off the
headstone into the mud of my sweat-soaked washykongs.
Standing there, smelling the harsh odour of burning

pitchoil floating above the thick syrupy smell of over-sweet eucalyptus, the musty odour of rotting leaves and old newspapers and stagnant still water, feeling a trickle of sweat trailing slowly down my spine vertebra-by-vertebra beneath my old football jersey, my baggy navyblue school shortpants billowing around my hips, my feet in the mud of my new washykongs in my old jesusboots, watching him swimming again, believing again, now, still: *Alive.* As I bent to pull my laces and took off running, barefoot, running behind old Evelina her torchlight flickering ahead in the dark.

4

Dr Domingo Describes
the Child's Delivery

I HAD ALWAYS known I would grow up to be a
physician. As the eldest son of a doctor, as his namesake, I
was always told that this would be so. When Granny
Myna boasted that she was the only mother ever to
produce *nine* – even Amadao, who is the famous doctor of
chickens with that big chicken-hospital in Wallafield – I
always promised her I'd follow in my uncles' footsteps.
When Papee Vince spoke so admirably of the art of
Medical Science, I always assured him I'd pursue that
profession. But it was not until a few days after the night
Evelina brought me to the cemetery – not until a few days
after her death, because my mother found her dead in her
bed early the following morning – that I made the
conscious decision to become a doctor. It was not until
after the occurrence of several events crowded into those
few days – so that I seemed to have lived three years, in the
space of three or four days – that I actually made up my
mind.

My mother found Evelina sitting up in her bed, wearing
the elaborate white lace dress she'd been sewing for some
time, which Evelina had told us was to be her burial
gown. She'd tied a white lace kerchief around her head,
another over her shoulders, and she wore a scapular of St
Christopher around her neck, the saint of travellers before

they took him off the Calendar. She had on a pair of white lace gloves, her mother-of-pearl rosary in her folded hands – along with *my* small mother-of-pearl-covered Confirmation Bible – a present my father had brought back from the Vatican years before, which he'd told me had been blessed personally by the Pope. How Evelina got it I had no idea (because I was sure I'd traded it away to Tony d'Nizo the year before for a handful of special marbles we called deadeyes) but as I knelt with the rest of the family around Evelina's bed early that morning, half-asleep, mumbling a decade of the rosary, I was not about to take my Bible back. Neither was I about to contemplate the night before – which I was still not sure had been a dream or reality – and I remember that all I could think about was Evelina's poor feet, jammed up in those hard high-heeled shoes: it was the first time I'd seen her wearing anything more than go-forwards.

Evelina's bedroom was crowded with smells: Limacol and Creole incense, talcum powder and sweet oleander – the bed and the floor littered with white petals. Three candles burned still on her altar, one before each of her three saints. It was Corpus Christi Day: the day before my sixteenth birthday. After Granny Myna's death three years before, my parents took Evelina's preparations as sign enough: they decided to bury her that same morning. In those days there were no autopsies other than the ones required by the Chief of Police; and there was no embalming besides the customary ritual enshrouding, accomplished usually by a collection of grandmothers and old aunts, and this Evelina had already taken care of herself. Monsignor O'Connor was busier during Holy Week than at any other time – but Evelina was a favourite of his, having assisted him in the cathedral for years – and he'd certainly take the time out to bury her, as soon as the early Mass let out.

So there was not much problem hastening Evelina to the

burial ground. The problem was deciding which one. The old Domingo Estate had long been overgrown by bush, and with it the estate cemetery where Evelina's mother was buried; and because she was not a Domingo or Domingo relation, Evelina could not legally be buried in our cemetery in town. We did not feel right about putting her in any of the others. My father solved the problem. As head physician of the St Maggy Hospital he had access to the Records Room in Government House, and he went there that morning and discovered, just as he'd suspected, that Evelina had no birthpapers. My father sat down and made one out on the spot – and her deathpapers at the same time, stating that she had succumbed to natural causes – filing them both under the name EVELINA DOMINGO. On his way home he realized that the birthdate he'd given her recorded her as dying at age 113.

Meanwhile I was to go to the rectory to get Monsignor. There was no answer at the door. I let myself in and found him asleep in his morris-chair, snoring loudly, still wearing his tunic from the six o'clock Mass, his stole still hanging loosely from his neck. The whole rectory smelled of incense. I shook him gently and he opened his eyes, but he only looked at me for a long time without speaking, as if trying to separate me from his dreams. Finally Monsignor nodded hello, and he motioned to give me a hug; but when I complied he held me there on his lap, which was awkward as I was almost the same size. I could feel him trembling beneath me. I told him Evelina had died, that my father wanted to bury her that morning. He did not answer, and for a moment I thought he might be asleep again: 'Daddy say he want to bury her soon soon, before all the Corpus Christi confusion commence!'

He still did not answer, and I could feel him growing warm beneath me, his trembling becoming violent. Now I wondered if I'd awakened him too abruptly, if he was about to have another of his epileptic fits. *Because they say*

*you must never wake up old people less you soak they feet in a
basin of warm water first. But if they wearing hardbacks then
how you could soak they feet? This oldman ga pelt one malkadee
here fa you now you know! One set of jooking up and rolling
bout like the jabjab catch he! You ga remain here so to see all
that?*

I decided I'd better repeat myself and get out in a hurry.
I ran home and found my father waiting, and as soon as I'd
caught my breath I told him that Monsignor was coming
right behind me. To my amazement he was, surprisingly
well-recovered, loaded down with all the paraphernalia
needed to anoint the body and perform the interment.

The result of all this was that even before the bands
started up that morning in St Maggy, even before the first
masmen appeared in the streets, I found myself dressed in
my cassock, marching with Monsignor and my family,
back to Domingo Cemetery. But I was not so uneasy this
time, even after I discovered that one of the three little
Warrahoons carrying the coffin with my father in front of
us (the same three who'd just finished digging the grave)
was wearing my new washykongs. On the contrary, this
time I was being made to face my fears promptly – before
they were given much chance to work themselves up in
my imagination – and I could cope with them more
calmly. I could deal with them more intelligently. So as
we walked along the road to the cemetery – even as the
smoke rising from the censer I carried began to remind me
of Evelina's torchlight – I was able to convince myself that
since the frogchild had not destroyed me in three years,
there was little chance he'd do so that morning. *And even if
daddy had killed Magdalena Divina, Papa God's own sweet
saint of heaven – whether by accident or outright carelessness – no
lightning bolts had flashed to strike him down. No boulderstones
had dropped out the sky on top he head.* Furthermore, I was
not so frightened by death as I had been three years before.
Now, with Evelina, with this third encounter, I could

accept death as a natural event. At sixteen I could explain it in simple biological terms. At the same time I could acknowledge its mystery – its connection with all of our fates, that is – as one of the things Papee Vince had told me was real enough, and meaningful, but which could never be fully understood. Because even if we took our own lives – as Magdalena had, as Barto had, maybe even as Granny Myna and Evelina had – then that was the fulfilment of our fates too. Of all our fates coming together, if only for an instant. And in that sense, death was something like birth. By the age of sixteen I had come to acknowledge some connection between Magdalena and her frogchild and my own destiny. And that morning, as I passed between the short coral gates of Domingo Cemetery, I accepted the mystery of that connection too.

It was a clear day and the sun was out. The real heat would not begin for another hour. My father and the Indians laid Evelina's coffin across two ropes, stretched from a bamboo cradle over the hole. The Warrahoons were concerned that the coffin lay just right across the ropes, and they fussed over it for a minute before they disappeared into the bush behind the cemetery. I stood between Monsignor and my younger brother on one side of the coffin, facing my parents and my younger sister standing on the other side. Monsignor opened his Bible:

De profundis clamavi ad te, Domine:
Domine, exaudi vocem meam.
Fiant aures tuae intendentes,
In vocem deprecationis meae.
Sustinuit anima mea in verbo ejus:
Speravit anima mea in Domino.

He continued to read in the Latin which I could scarcely understand, but which was familiar and comforting to me, reading in a voice which was old, and broken, and comforting to me too. And as I smelled the familiar incense rising in clouds around me, the now-familiar damp eucalyptus air – standing in the cemetery surrounded by the five people I truly loved in the world, by the three others I knew were there too, because I was sure I could feel their presence – I closed my eyes for a moment to picture Evelina sitting before me on the tombstone. And as I listened to old Monsignor, as I heard Evelina praying her old African prayer, I whispered a word of my own in my own language, in my own way: *Yes*. And at that moment I felt a flood of emotions which I cannot honestly describe, a rush of ideas which I cannot truly recount, only to tell you that if there *is* such a thing as personal revelation, then that is the closest I have ever come to one in my life. Only to tell you that even as I sit here behind this desk of purpleheart, in this imitation Warrahoon-Windsor chair, seventy-four years later – even as I look through this window at this moon above the same black, glistening sea – I can still feel a slight surging in my chest. I can still feel a faint longing in my heart.

Monsignor closed his Bible. He sprinkled holywater on the coffin with the shaker my brother carried in the little gold bucket. He took the censer and we walked around the coffin together, me holding up his chasuble sleeve, Monsignor slinging puffs of smoke into the air. He gave me the censer and turned around, facing the rear of the cemetery, and the rest of us looked at each other in confusion. After a long minute he clapped his trembling hands together, three slow claps, and immediately one of the little Warrahoons came pelting from out the bush, hurdling the cemetery wall in one, taking a running swipe with his cutlass at a rope tied to the bamboo-cradle. The coffin began descending slowly and smoothly into the ground – through some mysterious physics of rotating bamboo poles and shifting ropes – and only after it thudded softly at the bottom, could we look up at the little smiling Warrahoon.

That was the only Corpus Christi Day I have ever fêted. The rest of the family had been busy making costumes for the band of Lost Israelites, and they gathered in the kitchen to help me assemble one quickly for myself. We cut three holes in a crocusssack and plastered a dozen little papier-mâché johnny cakes all over it – which were supposed to represent manna dropped from heaven – all of which my brother and I pulled off to pelt at each other in the first two minutes; I kept teasing him for being the hump of a camel between my mother and my little sister:

Sanc-tus, Do-mi-nus,
Sanctus Dominus Deus!
Sanc-tus, Do-mi-nus,
Hosanna in ex-cel-sis!

I thought of the frogchild only once the whole day, shuddering when the band passed in front of our house and my father made his appearance: he looked like a grown-up version of the little boy costumed as Moses who'd seen me toting the bottle three years before. But that day I shouted out all the anxieties stored up in me during those three years. And when the Government House clock struck finally for midnight – and we stopped our singing and shaking our shackshacks, blowing our whistles and beating our rumbottles – I was hoarse, and exhausted, but I did not sit down for a second. I ran straight home to shower and change my clothes, to go with the others to the cathedral and begin the Easter Vigil. Even after we'd removed the Eucharist from the church, and we'd followed Monsignor decked out in full costume toting the huge starburst-monstrance – across the square and into the chapel in Corpus Christi Convent, each with a candle in our hands and our heads bowed singing the Agnus Dei – even after we'd returned to the cathedral to strip the altar and cover the crosses and statues with their sacks of purple velvet, and Monsignor and I had consumed the last of the hosts in the tabernacle, extinguished the candle beside it in its red glass holder, outed all the lights, I was still not ready to go home to my bed. I returned to the chapel to sit with the reposed Eucharist. Only when the sun rose finally on that Good Friday morning – the morning of my sixteenth birthday – and I found myself kneeling in a chapel which was empty now except for two old nuns kneeling behind me, the huge starburst-monstrance shining before me with the clouds of incense rising slowly around it, the candle flames reflecting on its polished surface, did I go home to throw myself exhausted into my bed.

But I slept for only a few hours, because that afternoon I returned to the Cathedral to celebrate the Lord's Passion. The rest of the family stayed home this time, my father speaking for the others when he said he'd had enough church-business to last until Easter Sunday. Apparently I had not, because when Passion was finished I asked Monsignor if he needed an acolyte for the Veneration of the Cross. It was a spiritual marathon, a three-day jamboree of faith: most of Saturday I spent in the chapel with the reposed Eucharist, or assisting Monsignor in the cathedral with the various liturgies – of Light, of Baptism, with the Blessing of Water. All of Sunday was taken up with the Easter celebrations. And when Monday morning rolled around – and the streets had been watered and the garbage collected and St Maggy was itself again – I'd still not had enough: I got up early to serve the six o'clock Mass before school.

I put on the light in sacristy and dressed in my cassock. I poured the wine and water into their little crystal cruets – sucking the stoppers so as to know which was which – and I lit and blew on the small cake of coal for the censer, until the star pressed into the top was outlined in glowing red. I'd just finished dressing the chalice when I heard Monsignor behind me. I turned to look at him. He reached to hug me, so I returned the gesture, but when I had my arms around him he lifted my chin and brought his mouth down on mine so hard our teeth collided, and my first thought was that my lip must be bleeding. It was not. And I did not shove away or even turn my face. I could not: standing there, again, as always, as though I were dreaming. Lost again in the thickskinned numbed world of my dream as though I were perceiving reality from a distance, through lukewarm water, powerless to respond one way or another. Wondering if this was really me standing there, if *this* was really what Tony and Tim were talking about the time I thought they were talking about something else, something which had to do with the picture-magazines Tony stole from his older brother – because you could talk about such things as masturbation but you could never get *caught* talking about them (which was almost as bad as getting caught doing them) *like the time Timmy catch you and Tony in the cave looking at the magazines and smoking cigarettes, and Tony bust him in he ear so hard it swell up in a purple bubble like the back of a Portuguese man-of-war, and you wrestle him down on the ground and wouldn't let him up until he smoke down a whole cigarette and swore he'd been there with you and Tony the whole afternoon –* standing there thinking all this and wondering at the same time if my lip was bleeding, and deciding finally that it was not, otherwise I wouldn't be tasting incense in my mouth but blood.

I cannot tell you how it ended or how long it lasted: for me it could have been three days. All I know is that somehow I managed to serve Mass as usual, and when it was over I managed to clean up as usual, and when I was finished I managed to say goodbye to Monsignor as usual. But I never hugged him again, and he never tried to hug me.

After several hours my daze began to clear, and as I sat

at my schooldesk I began to feel angry. By the time I got home that afternoon I was furious: *Fucking old shitong mammapoule! Fucking tantieman!* Maybe it was simply a matter of bad timing: of my age and my Caribbean upbringing – of my staunch Roman Catholic upbringing – that this thing had to happen at a time when my emotions had been running strong for three days. Maybe it was simply the excuse I needed: the easy excuse I'd unconsciously been searching for for so long. I do not know. I cannot say. All I remember is that that night as I lay there in my bed, sweating, listening to the oscillating fan breathing louder and louder, I could think of only one thing. I can think of only one thing now: *To ass with the Catholic Church and all the saints! To ass with God!*

That night I made up my mind to become a physician. It was as if the world were suddenly divided, as if I could choose between science and religion and disregard the other. It was as though I'd found the answer to all my problems. As though they were already behind me. I wanted to tell someone, to pledge myself to it, but with all the old people gone there was no one left to talk to: my brother would only cuss me, my sister was too young, and if I woke up my parents and told them about Monsignor my father would only say I'd made up the whole thing, then he'd box my ears like the day of Granny Myna's funeral. I decided to go to the library and look through his medical books. But I had a problem: the only way to get there was through my parents' bedroom. Then I had an idea. If I climbed up the ladder in my sister's room onto the roost, I could cross the roof and hang down over the side above the library. And if I could get my feet on the ledge beneath the window, I could push it open and crawl in over the desk. If I missed I'd fall two-and-a-half storeys.

I threw off the sheet and jumped out of bed. I pulled on a shortpants and tiptoed down the hall to my sister's room. But I wasn't halfway up the ladder before she awoke and rolled over: 'What you doing, Johnny?'

I thought for a second: 'I going on the roost to pray.'

Considering my behaviour during the previous few days it was the perfect excuse, because she gave me an exasperated look, chupsed, and rolled over again. I pushed open the trapdoor and climbed up onto the roost. Getting into the library was easier than I could have hoped, fate contributing the lagniappe of an already open window: I tumbled in, literally landing on my face in the middle of the desk.

I lay there quietly for a moment, my cheek pressed into the polished wood – watching a cloud of vapour appear and disappear with each quick breath – waiting to find out if anyone had heard my noisy entry. No one had, and I got up slowly and shut the door. There was a tall bookcase on one side of the desk with all my father's medical journals. I selected my favourite, the one with the pictures of naked women: *British Obstetric and Gynaecological Practice*, by Sir Eardley Holland.

I sat in the chair and pulled it up under the desk. I opened the journal and began paging through. In no time at all I was lost in the journal, looking at the pictures and the long, strange-sounding words: *Anencephaly is due to a defective development of the medullary canal in the early embryo. It is commonly associated with spina bifida and occasionally with inencephaly, umbilical hernia, hare lip and cleft palate. The bony vault of the skull and the scalp are defective, but the facial portion is normal. The eyes bulge and the forehead is deficient, the eyelids are thick and oedematous and the tongue* . . . I turned the page:

protrudes. The neck is short and the head appears to sit upon the shoulders (Fig. 9.XXII).

An anencephalic fœtus is always associated with excess of liquor amnii and presents clinically as a case of hydramnios. This excess

FIG. 9.XXII.   Anencephalic fœtus.

may be due to transudation through the exposed choroid plexus and meninges. It is interesting, however, that no lanugo hair is found in the intestine, which suggests that the swallowing reflex is abolished and that liquor is no longer absorbed from the fœtal intestine and returned to the maternal circulation. Probably both explanations are correct : there is an increased formation of liquor and an inability to absorb it.

There was his face for the first time. *His face*. Right there in front of me. But I was *not* seeing it for the first time – which I realized instantly – because it was the same face which had already haunted me for three years. The very same face which had already haunted me for three years without ever having seen it – as though *my* imagination had conceived him, and carried him, and borne him into the world and given him life. The very same face which had haunted me for three years and will never disappear now, because there he *is*. And after seventy-four years I do not even need to open my eyes to find him. After seventy-four years I can sit here at the same desk in the same Windsor chair with my eyes closed, and I can reach now to the same shelf for the same worn-out old journal, and I can find the page by touch, by feel. Because it is as though my imagination has conceived the book too.

I made some sort of noise – not a scream but a loud gasp – loud enough to wake up my parents this time for sure. I clapped the book shut and shoved it into its slot on the shelf. I did not have time to consider what the frogchild was doing in my father's journal, or even turn to look towards the door: my father was there in a second, and I did not have to open my eyes to see *his* face either – the vertical scar running down the middle of his forehead which Granny Myna called the mark of St John, purple and pulsating now that he was angry. I sat there with my lids shut tight, waiting for his zobell to ring across the back of my head. To my surprise it never came, and when I did turn around to find him standing there in his baggy boxer drawers and a merino-vestshirt, his arms folded loosely in front of him, he was not even looking down at me, but out the window. His silence made me angry again. Suddenly *he* seemed like the source of all my problems – not the Church or even Monsignor O'Connor – and I sat there for a long minute until I could not hold myself back: 'Is you murder Magdalena Divina!'

He stood staring out the window – silent, as though he had not heard.

Now I let my emotions fly: 'Is you kill she dead and you make he come out a frog because I seen him with my own eyes! And they lock you up fa that too because Evelina tell me with Granny Myna and Papee Vince so shame they must lie bout the whole thing, and Brito Salizar and cordstring-Warrahoon and holding up she breath till she turn to the statue of black boulderstone! And is lucky fa you they no God in heaven to strike you down – nor saints in hell to pelt obeahcurse pon you head – because then you would be dead long time fa true!'

I continued bawling nonsense, waking the whole house, daring my father to pelt the zobell which would surely silence me. He stood with his arms folded. Mute. Staring out the window until long after I'd caught my breath. Finally he looked down at me:

'When is the last time you carry on fa me so, boy?'

I shrugged my shoulders.

'Think.'

'Me does remember good enough.'

'And what I did you?'

'You *beat* me!'

'Well I not ga beat you tonight.'

I understood I'd prefer the beating. My father turned his eyes from me again, looking out the window, and I sat through several more uncomfortable minutes of silence. Then he did something peculiar: after he shut the door he walked up behind me, turning me firmly in the chair – so now *I* was forced to look out the window – and he left his hands there on my shoulders. His grip relaxed a little. I could not turn my head (there was the inside of an elbow practically jammed up against each of my temples) and every time I tried to tilt my head back to look upside-down at his face, the back of the chair would butt me in the same spot. I had no choice but to stare out of the window. It was as though he would not permit anything to distract me from what I was about to hear, to keep me from taking in what he was about to say. As though to leave me without any choice but to sit here and listen.

I HAD NO business beating you that night, na. I was wrong, and I have cuss myself fa that ever since. I just couldn't prevent it. Realize: I had this idea in my head that somehow I'd buried Magdalena and she child in the ground with mummy. Somehow they belonged to her, and to daddy, but they did not belong to me, and now I could write them off fa good. Finish. Ca-go. But boy, when you reach back that night of you thirteenth birthday from wherever the ass you'd been since the night before – before you even open you mouth to say Magdalena's name – I only had to look you in the face to see the truth that I ain't buried nothing in the ground a-tall. Because boy, when you start in about how this crapochild swim way, about how Magdalena come to you by the water to give you she story sheself and take up she child again – or whatever else it is you tried to tell me because after a time the words couldn't come out fast enough – I had to put licks on you not because I thought you were talking bubball, not because I thought you were making excuse fa missing mummy's funeral, but because I believed you. Every word. I believed you and I did not want to hear it.

I couldn't understand what you were saying, and boy, you couldn't understand youself neither. Somehow I believed you still, and I had to stop you. Because as I sat here in this same chair on that same night listening to you, I had the distinct notion that I was my own father listening to *me*. Somehow in some baddream I had already dug up this same glassbottle – and I'd toted it the same distance and farther still – because just like you I have been toting this obsockee glassbottle all my life. Just like you this same

woman has appeared to me too – every night in my
dreams fa long as I can remember – even though at age
thirteen I'd never heard the name Magdalena Divina. Even
though I never saw her with my own eyes before I was
twenty-three years of age. Because boy, what the ass
difference does it make that you never saw her or this
crapochild a-tall? Is you reality any less real than my own?
All this confusion begins before we open we eyes, before
the first stories begin to tell, so how can we *ever* expect to
understand it? But boy, now is me talking bubball. Now is
me talking circles, and before I finish I ga give you one
more: it is not even you sitting here listening to me now,
na. Not yet. Sometime down the road yes, but fa the time
being it is some other youngboy sitting here listening to
some other middle-age man: fa the time being it is me
sitting here listening talking to me.

I'd only now reach back from away. I had my MB and
not a lick of practical experience, but my certificate called
me a Grade C Medical Officer of Her Majesty the Queen –
which was a big big thing fa this island in those days –
because I was the first doctor to come back to the island
with any kind of piece of paper a-tall. Fa three hours they
queued up to see it. To listen to they hearts through the
stethoscope, look up inside each other's ears through the
otoscope, to pose me fa pictures with the mirror on my
head and the mask tied up round my face. The truth is I
didn't know my own backside from a hole in the ground.
I'm sure I knew plenty less medicine than that old bushdoctor Salizar I'd come to replace. Even he recognized it,
though it was a little too late fa my version of the story by
then. Because boy, by the time daddy finally put a bullet
from General Monagas big rifle *hot* in the tail of that
cacashat Chief of Police to end the whole confusion, the
three of us had already been locked up in the jail six days.
That was where *I* first heard the story – though I could tell
my own version well enough by then – sitting there on the

cold concrete flooring of that jailcage with oldman Salizar and this same crackpot Mother Maurina. Because according to the versions each of them gave me, Salizar had been through one pregnancy with this woman already, and Mother Maurina had already been through *two*. Oldman Salizar even offered to return to the hospital and remain with me a couple months to make sure the same confusion didn't happen again, as if this world could ever be big enough fa another story like this.

Of course, the hospital was there long before I had reach back, because daddy built it before I'd even left to go way. Already he'd made up he mind he was sending every manjack of us cross the sea to study medicine. Like everything else daddy asked no one, and no one bothered to ask him what it was, even after the building was finished. They called it Barto's Church of the Jabjab – with the bedroom behind and the big, purpleheart caduces of the cross with the snakes climbing up it in front – and they waited fa daddy to arrive from Caracas with he three pirogues loaded down with whores. Instead he brought oldman Salizar from somewhere up the Orinoco, the pirogues loaded down instead with bundles of old bush, dried up crapos and zandolies and so, which were the ingredients fa all the medicines. To finish the picture daddy and Mother Maurina send cross two or three of she schoolgirl-nuns from the convent – because of course *she* had to pushfoot sheself in the picture too – and he dressed them up in some fancified nurse-costumes sent toute-baghai quite from Paris. Of course, all this pappy-show suited Corpus Christi fine. But pappyshow is one thing, and *dead* saints who give birth to *live* crapochildren is something else. Realize: it isn't only that *I* am not ready fa Corpus Christi. At the same time Corpus Christi isn't ready fa *me*.

Boy, let me give you a little story before we begin, showing you just what kind of place this place you living

in is like. It must have been already two or three years after
I'd arrived back from England. The little nurse comes
running in to tell me, 'Doctor, dey a woman sitting down
outside dere, whole *front* of she dress soak down in blood!'
So of course, I tell her we'd better get her in here right
away. We put her to lie down quiet on the table, and now I
ask the woman what is the problem. 'Doctor,' she says,
'no big problem. Nine children I bear at home, and dis
never happen before.' 'Well,' I ask again, 'what is the
problem?' She says the birthsack wouldn't come. So I raise
up the dress, and sure enough, there is the cordstring tied
up against she thigh with the dirtiest old dirty piece of rag
you could imagine (she'd left the baby at home to jump up
and come walking all the way from Tunapuna having just
finished delivering a child) so of course, I only have to
push a little bit here, little bit there, and *pssst!* the afterbirth
comes out. But I am intrigued by this thing now. I have never
seen nothing like this before. So after we clean her up little
bit, and we put her to sit up again, I ask how she cut the
cordstring. 'Man,' she says, 'use a scissors, na!' 'But did
you boil the scissors?' I ask. 'Did you *sterilize* it?' 'Na, na,
na!' she says. 'But soon as I reach *home* I ga boil it!'

So here am I now only my second or third day in the
hospital, when all of a sudden the two little nuns I have
there fa nurses take off running like somebody push a fire
up they backsides. What going on here? I look in the
waitingroom and I find out: there sitting down on the
bench is that Mother Superior General Maurina, and I
don't have to tell you *I* only want to bolt from this hospital
now too. (Because you know this Mother Maurina good
as anybody else, and you know all that confusion went on
between sheself and daddy, with him sending her away to
convent haveen with child and marrying up mummy in
she place.) But boy, now it is as if my feet stick up to the
ground with laglee. As if my neck stiff like a standpipe,
because I can't move my eyes from looking at this woman

sitting on the bench beside Mother Maurina. I couldn't say what it is about her, na. All I can tell you is that when she raise up she face to meet me, and I look into those big soft eyes of hers fa the first time, I feel something cool and lovely like creamsoda inside. So when this Mother Maurina tells me boldface just so that this nun is seven months *haveen*, I am not hearing her neither: I am still floating somewhere in my sea of creamsoda.

But boy, when I put her to lie down there quiet on the table – with this Mother Maurina of course breathing down my neck the whole time – and I lift up all that amount of nundress to take a look, I feel a jolt on my backside like a jookerfish jook me. Man, she belly big like a barrel! All I could think is this Magdalena *must* have made a mistake in she calculations, because judging from the size of she belly, this baby done reached full term. Of course, this is the first question I ask her, but of course before Magdalena even has a chance to open she mouth, Mother Maurina starts to bawl. She wants to know if you have a problem hearing schoolboy? I tell her not so a-tall, that sometimes a woman menstruates irregular, especially if she is young, especially during a time of emotional distress. She tells me she not talking no *menstruation* schoolboy, which don't have nothing to do with this girlchild neither, 'I am talking *conception* which occurred el dia domingo viente de Septiembre of La Divina Pastora feastday under my own *supervision*, and do you have any more shitong-schoolboy questions to ask?'

Well that one shuts me up in one. Now I am not only frightened to open my mouth, frightened of this crackpot Mother Maurina, but the longer I look at the huge size of Magdalena's belly, the more frightened I am about delivering this child. All I could think is that if Magdalena did *not* make a mistake calculating the seven months, then this baby coming forceripe fa sure. And prematurity responsible fa two-thirds of all neonatal deaths. Of course, what I have here is an extreme case of hydramnios (which is to say an excess of amniotic fluid in the womb) but of course, I ain't know a fart about no hydramnios at the time. All I know fa now is this woman's belly is bloato like she want to *bust*, like she ga spit out this child at me any second. And I ain't know a fart about delivering baby. Boy, I do the only thing I can think of: I excuse myself to go in the bush fa a weewee, and I run to the parlour next door to fire a rum.

By the time I reach back I am ready to perform my first delivery. Of course Magdalena hasn't even pass a birthpain yet. But my hands already scrubbed down, and I have on my first new pair of fresh rubbergloves, with the mask already tied up round my face. Realize: I am only a little schoolboy trying he best to play doctor. But this ain't no schoolboy monkeygame I playing a-tall. Because soon as I put on the stethoscope to listen fa this child's pulsebeat, I feel the next jolt on my backside. Man, this baby dead like a duck! I ain't hearing no pulsebeat a-tall. None. Ba-tai. Of course, a foetal heartbeat is difficult to detect anyway, especially with all that fluid distending the womb like this. On top of that, a diagnosis of foetal death *in utero* is more difficult still – even with x-ray which we didn't have available in the hospital then – but my mind is made up already what I have here to deliver is a *dead* baby. And as soon as I rest my hands on Magdalena's abdomen to examine her little bit, next jolt again: this child is not only coming stillborn, he is coming in a *breech* too. Instead of finding the head down inside the pelvis, with the child in what we call the r.o.a. position (right-occiput-anterior, or upside-down and curled up on he right side) what I find is the two legs. Realize: a breech delivery is always dangerous, especially fa the primiparous patient. So much so that fa some physicians it is an indication fa caesarean section. So here am I now a schoolboy-doctor with *no* experience in delivery, with a girlchild mother with *no* experience in childbirth, with a baby that is coming not only forceripe, and stillborn, but in a *breech* presentation too. Boy, all I could think is that this woman is in trouble. On top of that, *you* backside in trouble – and you don't know nothing yet about daddy and this Chief of Police – because you know enough about Mother Maurina and the Catholic Church, which is to say you know better than to fuck round with none of *that*. Boy, I excuse myself fa another weewee, and I take off running fa that parlour mask, mirror, gloves, everything, because all I can think is to fire a next rum.

By the time I reach back I am not only ready to perform my first delivery, I am in a *hurry* to do it. If this child *is* coming forceripe, I am glad fa that: premature labour is usually shorter and less painful. If he done dead up, if he coming in a breech, I am glad fa that *too*. I ga hold on to he legs and pull he out the quickest way I can. Of course, I could induce labour easy enough by breaking the sack, by amniotomy, but before I go in from below I decide to make another careful examination of she abdomen. Soon as I feel round a little bit I locate the head (just there in the fundus at the top of the womb where I expect to find it) but I ain't know what the ass kind of head it is. To me it feels like Magdalena has swallowed a dishplate. Something inside there flat and round (which is actually the bony orbital ridges) with this pyrex-dishplate protruding straight out from the child's shoulders as best as I can feel, like if they ain't no neck to this cacashat shitong baby a-tall. Boy, I am still feeling round trying to understand what the ass this woman is carrying inside she belly, when I press my finger on a soffee spot at the top of this dishplate. Man, this child live like spaniardhive! All of a sudden he pelts one kick so hard I jump back like the jookerfish jook me again, and even Magdalena is bound to open she mouth fa the first time: 'Amor Matris!' she says, and I am whispering something the same but a little stronger.

Now I don't want this child to be alive not fa nothing. Whatever the ass kind of monster he is with this dishplate head, *I* don't want to deliver him breathing. Boy, I press again and the child pelts the kick again. Again and again. (What I could never have known is that this is the spot where the hypoplastic cranial vault is thinnest, so of course he bound to feel something with me pressing down on he rudimentary brain like this.) And here am I now pushing my finger inside there again and again like a little boy who has just discovered he bamseehole fa the first time, with poor Magdalena jumping up with the kick of every press on this pyrex–dishplate, and all I know now is whatever the ass this woman has swimming inside she belly, *I* don't want to see him *a-tall*. Boy, I do the only thing I can think of: I excuse myself to run in the bush fa another weewee.

I HAD NOT HEARD a word my father had said: I was thinking about the picture. The picture of that frogchild which was not even my frogchild, because how could my frogchild ever end up in a journal belonging to Sir Eardley Holland quite in England? Then I remembered that disease Granny Myna and Papee Vince had told me something about, that *anencephaly* disease, and I realized Sir Eardley's frogchild must be a picture of a child born with that disease. *Because what else would a frogchild like my own be doing in the middle of a medical journal? And what else is a medical journal but a picturebook Bible of diseases? That frogchild of you own isn't even a frogchild a-tall. He isn't even a frogchild a-tall, but only a child born with that disease to make him* look *like a frog, with he flat head, and he big eyes bulging out, and he big tongue jooking forth like he trying to catch a fly. That disease which doesn't have nothing to do with frogs neither, because how else could they have them all the way in England where daddy says it's so cold they have only one guana and one macajuel and* one crapo in the whole country, and they live together in a special glasscage marked CORPUS CHRISTI in the zoo.

That anencephaly disease which daddy had written down on a piece of paper so Granny Myna could see it – and he'd even showed her the same picture in the book so she could believe it – but Granny Myna refused to believe even what she'd seen with she own eyes. The same disease daddy had told Papee Vince was a congenital abnormality – caused by a failure of the brain to develop proper – in which case it would remain the size of a prune which was exactly what Uncle Olly had dissected out. Even so, Uncle Olly and Granny Myna refused to belive him. Even Papee Vince refused to believe him. But you believe him! You believe him, because daddy's language of medical science understands everything clean clean. So the best way to forget that frogchild and this Magdalena and the whole confusion fagood faever, is to become a doctor like daddy and learn to speak that language.

BY THE TIME I reach back I am ready to face this Mother Superior Maurina. I put the two of them together to sit down calm and quiet in the waiting room again, and I make my first big mistake: I look at this Mother Maurina hard hard, and I give her the boldface lie that the child Magdalena is carrying is already dead. I am thinking that this way she will let me start Magdalena into labour now, without an argument – and I can get the whole confusion over with one time and finish – and even if this dishplate-child does come out breathing, I ga strangulate him quick and pelt him quick in the sea. Of course, Magdalena remains sitting there serene as ever, she eyes turned to the flooring – *she* knows I am lying good enough – but of course Mother Maurina flies up in a rage like I put her to sit down on a live coalpot. She jumps up to dress me down with one set of bawling about how you don't know what the ass you talking about schoolboy, 'because this is a special child promise to born and to live faever and there is no man walking the face of sweet Papa God earth strong enough to raise up a hand against him, even if it is over the *dead* body of me and Magdalena too!' And now she putting loud goatmouth on the poor woman without knowing what she saying.

I let her bawl sheself out na, and when she sits down again I tell her that if Papa God has a spoon in this pepperpot a-tall, it is only to bring about the termination of this child. 'Because due to Magdalena's young age, due to she small pelvis, due to she inexperience in childbirth – together with whatever else other complications are associated with the child *heself* – then if this baby *was* to grow to full maturity, if he *was* to deliver as normal, he delivery would certainly become a serious threat to Magdalena's life. Because *she* is the consideration here, not this cacashat child which is clearly characterized by some grotesque foetal deformity which I couldn't tell you not fa chups what it might be. But *I* would never want to deliver him *alive* not fa nothing!' Of course, this one sends her into a rage again, and she jumps up to tell me, 'You could push all you big schoolboy doctor-words up you little white *culo*, as it is obvious to me you don't know a *caca* what you talking about!' (because you know how she likes to cuss) and she grabs up poor Magdalena to pelt with her out the door.

Well boy, I have to sit down on the bench in that waitingroom now myself to try to recover from this thing, because the whole business done hit me over the head like bigstick. I am wondering if maybe this isn't the best thing that could happen? If maybe this Mother Maurina wouldn't deliver the child *sheself* in the convent now (which is what she told me later in the jail she wanted to do all along) and I wouldn't have to get myself involved a-tall? Boy, all I could think is that whatever ga happen it ga happen soon, because judging from the size of Magdalena's belly, this child is coming forceripe fa sure. Of course, she size is due primarily to the hydramnios, which is due primarily to the anencephaly, but of course I ain't know a fart about none of that at the time. Neither do I have the presence of mind to try to look up this child in the book (which I was to find out soon enough I had done already anyway without knowing it) and boy, there ain't no writing in the book to tell me nothing about this child a-tall. As the story tells itself however, like most anencephalic monsters this child *did* come forceripe (as some are known to go a month or two or even up to nine post-term, the small flat head being I suppose a bad dilator) and Magdalena *did* in fact go into labour the same night. And that same night I made my first delivery – though by way of a caesarean performed on a dead woman – but as I sat there on the bench trying to recover myself from this confusion which had not even begun to begin yet, all I could think is I hope I don't have to see this Magdalena ever again.

Boy, I am still sitting there on the bench, still in a daze – my own eyes focused now on the flooring – when all of a sudden I realize there is someone standing there in front of me. I look up to find that it is Magdalena who has come back already. She is looking at me again, with that same lovely creamsoda feeling again, and she does something now which always seems to me peculiar when I try to remember it. But boy, at that moment in those eyes it felt like the most natural gesture in the world: she bends to kiss me. Full. Long and slow and full in the mouth so that anyone who'd have walked through the door would have said that she is my own mistress now and not daddy's. When the truth is she ain't no one's mistress a-tall. No one's except maybe *His* – and that one I can tell you fa fact with my knowledge of Medical Science to support me – if there is any *He* looking down from up there a-tall. But boy, there are some things in this story which speak louder than he hardest of facts, and unfortunately these are the things I can never give you. Just as I cannot say how long that kiss lasted or how it ended, because fa me it could have been three days. All I can tell you is that when she was finished, and I discovered myself again, alone, sitting there on that beach in this empty waitingroom, I had the feeling as if an angel had just passed through. She had come with the flapping of gentle feathers to light calm and peaceful on my breast.

I WAS THINKING: *Fucking old shitong mammapoule! Fucking tantieman! It* was *Monsignor that Tony and Tim were talking about that time fa sure. Because why else would both of them quit from serving Mass all of a sudden so? And they never pushed they foot in the church again after that day neither. Ever since that day you caught them talking secret by the cave, and they wanted to put blows on you fa taking them by surprise, and you thought it was about the magazines. But it wasn't those picture-magazines they were talking about a-tall: they were talking about that mammapoule Monsignor O'Connor. And that same afternoon you cleaned them both out of deadeyes and some kyows and a metal tor from each, and Tony turn round to say, 'Obvious he been practising with Monsignor!' and then the two of them couldn't stop from laughing. Like if it is the funniest thing anybody ever said. And when you ask him, 'What the fuck is so funny? and if you don't stop laughing I ga bust you in you mouth!' and Tony answer, 'Why you don't go ask Monsignor?' and that started up the laughing all over again. And they never talk to you from that day neither. Even after you leave the whole set there fa them to find – every marble you ever had in two old paint-buckets because you thought it might even be Papa God who was vex with you fa trading way that Bible – but how can He* exist with *him a priest and you two best friends in the world never speak to you ever again?*

THAT KISS leave me feeling so peaceful, so calm, I didn't stop to worry over Magdalena again the whole remainder of the day. I never even remember to ask mummy and daddy and Uncle Olly about her when I reach home that evening fa dinner – which was no doubt fa the best – because soon as I pronounced she name mummy would have no doubt dump the whole pot of callaloo upside-down on top my head. And when I woke up in a sweat in the middle of the same night, I'm sure it wasn't Magdalena I'd been dreaming about. Even though I have tried fa years to convince myself it was – that somehow, in some absurd way the whole of Corpus Christi had dreamt the same simultaneous nightmare that night – that somehow we *all* woke up the following morning lying there on the cold concrete flooring of that jailcage, wondering what we hands were doing red with blood and green shit to the elbows. But it wasn't Magdalena I was dreaming about. And she didn't cross my mind as I dressed myself: I'd decided to go fa walk along the wharf, to take in some cool sea breeze, and fa some odd reason I am in a hurry to get there. So much so that when I sit down on the frontstep to tie up my shoes (because I used to sleep in you bedroom in those days, and I didn't want to wake up mummy and Evelina and little Amadao sleeping below) that I couldn't even be bothered. I leave them there just so, and I take off in my bare feet. And when I reach back to the house six days later, mummy tells me she mistake them fa daddy's and pitch them in the sea.

But instead of going to the wharf, fa some odd reason I take off in the opposite direction. What the ass I am thinking about I couldn't tell you, only that I'm sure it wasn't Magdalena yet. Not yet. Not until that clock begins to strike fa midnight – and I look up suddenly from the ground where I am siting there on the step round the base of that statue – do I contemplate her fa the first time since she'd closed the waitingroom door behind her that

same afternoon. Again she is standing there in front of me.
Again she does something peculiar, and again I am only
too glad there is no one there to watch: she hoists up she
nundress to expose sheself to me naked to the waist, right
there in the middle of Sir Walter Raleigh Square. With she
free hand she reaches to take up mine, and she places it
there gentle on she belly. She is standing above me with
the moon shining full in she face – with me breathing the
twelve breaths of that clock in those creamsoda eyes again
– when all of a sudden the world goes silent, and I feel she
womb contract in a long birthpain. A smile passes gentle
cross she lips, as if to tell me she time has come, and I
realize *my* time has come now too.

I walk her towards the hospital, making a stop along the
way to wake up oldman Salizar. Because one thing I know
fa sure, *he* has been delivering baby fa donkey's ages. He
wife come to the door. I tell her to call Salizar quick, but
all she can answer is, 'Na-me-na-na-ha! Na-me-na-na-ha!'
which I know from going with daddy to the old estate
means she doesn't understand a *fart*. Just as I am about to
push past her and grab up the oldman myself, Magdalena
busts out talking one set of Warrahoon like bush. (Of
course this comes to me as a surprise, as it is only later in
the jail that Salizar explained to me how Warrahoon was
Magdalena's first language, and how she'd actually told he
wife some nonsense about, 'Mummy, close up the windows quick because it ga pelt with rain tonight!') Of
course, *I* was sure now that Salizar would be coming right
behind us, so I hurried Magdalena off towards the hospital. By the time I put her to lie down in the bed she
birthpains coming regular. I scrub down my hands quick
in the washbasin at the back, and when I turn round now I
find all she nunclothes pile up in a pile on the ground, and
she lying in the bed naked naked. Boy, I am a doctor yes,
and I am twenty-three years of age, but the truth is that
this is the first time I have ever seen a live woman in such a

state of loveliness. The truth is I wanted to turn round again. And boy, I would have too if my feet wasn't stick up to the ground with laglee.

All of a sudden Magdalena sits up to pass another birthpain, and I realize I don't even have time to feel embarrassed. I lay her down again, and now I am sweating bolts wondering where the ass is Salizar. I decide to make an examination from below to find out how much the cervix has dilated – one or two or three fingers – which is the only true criterion fa the onset of labour. That was my second big mistake. Boy, I only push she legs open a little bit, and I want to close them up quick quick again. Man, she pussy hard like a wall! I am feeling something inside there fa sure, but I don't want to believe what the ass it is: like the churchveil still intact. Of course, I have on these gloves that they used to make from some rubber hard like a bicycle-tyre in those days, but as soon as I bend down to focus the mirror on my forehead to take a good look, that is exactly what I find. Ba-tam-bam. Clear as day. Of course, the churchveil *could* remain unruptured through a minimum of activity, and maybe this woman's own is a little thicker than normal, and maybe she boyfriend is a tantie like Uncle Olly with he toetee the size of a whistle. (Of course, they ain't no churchveil in the world could withstand the bruising of a history like the one oldman Salizar and that Mother Maurina gave me later – unless of course it make from castiron – but fortunately enough I haven't heard none of that nonsense yet.) Because boy, the *longer* I look at this churchveil, the *surer* I am that there is something peculiar about it. *More* peculiar even than the fact that it is there a-tall. All of a sudden I realize what it is, and boy, is now I feel the jookerfish: this churchveil is imperforate. I can't find no opening in it a-tall. Because of course, it must have a natural perforation fa the menstrual fluids to pass. But no matter how hard I look, I am not seeing it nowhere. Boy, I don't have to tell you the implications of this thing. I don't have to tell you which ideas are flying through my head now. Because of course, even though an imperforate hymen is very irregular, it is at least a possibility fa a girlchild Magdalena's age: *not* fa woman who haveen. Boy, all I can think is if this churchveil of Magdalena's *is* still intact, if it *is* truly imperforate, then I don't want to think about *how*, and I don't want to think about *why*, and I don't want to see it *a-tall*, so I close up she legs quick quick and I take off running to find oldman Salizar.

Which was my third big mistake: I take off in the opposite direction. Now my head viekeevie like a St Ann's crazyhouse bobolee – and I must have looked like one too, running round in the middle of the night with the mask on my face and the mirror still on my forehead – because now I can't remember where the ass Salizar lives, and all the houses looking to me the same. I pound down two or three different doors, and I get cuss two or three different times. Now I want to go back, but I can't find the hospital. How long it took me to find it again I couldn't tell you, but it must have been a good while, because by the time I reach back Magdalena is already dead. Of course, you can argue with me that there are any number of things could have killed her – that it is impossible to commit suicide by holding up you breath – and of course I will be the first to agree with you. But boy, the fact is that somehow this woman managed to do it. The fact is that when I found her she jaws were locked up so tight on that pillow – with the casing swallowed half-way down she throat-tube – that I had to cut it out before I could try to resuscitate her. Realize: there is no drive of the human animal stronger than a mother's instinct to protect she child. Realize: I had told Magdalena clearly enough that I was concerned about *her, not* the survial of this baby. But now that Magdalena was dead, I had nothing but she baby to consider.

Feathers were gusting back and forth in that little

hospital room like a blizzard. I knew the foetus could not survive very long in the womb of a dead mother, so I could be fairly certain *he* was dead too. That is what I am hoping. I have one quick, sure way to find out, and that is exactly what I do: I press my finger on the spot, and sure enough I feel the kick. All I can think now is that if Magdalena can offer sheself up fa this child, at least I am bound to attempt a delivery. I cross myself and I blow way the floating feathers from in front my face, I take up the scalpel, and I make a classical vertical incision from top to bottom. All of a sudden this stench hits me in the face so stink it almost knocks me down. One set of meconium packed up inside the womb – which is to say shit – which must have come with the foetal distress of all that poking and kicking. Boy, I hold up my breath and I reach inside there with both hands, and I pull out this child all soaked down in green stool – and when I look in that crapoface with those big eyes bulging and the big tongue jooking out at me – I get so frighten I drop him *boodoops* on the ground and I bolt fa the door.

On my way out I almost knock down oldman Salizar. Someone had woken him up saying there was some confusion going on in the hospital, and when he wife told him that I had been by earlier with Magdalena, he could figure out easy enough what it was all about. So he was not surprised to find her lying there in the bed. But I'm sure he was shocked to see what condition she was in: stone dead, covered in a slime of blood and green shit, with this crapochild bawling way like he trying to bring down the roof, practically *hanging* from the side of the bed by he cordstring. Oldman Salizar turns round quick, and he runs back in the waitingroom to slam the door shut and throw the bolt. (Later in the jail he told me that there was already a crowd gathered in front of the hospital, and he'd seen Gomez and he two policemen coming in a soldier-march too.) Salizar takes charge of the situation. He grabs up this crapochild who by now has taken hold of he cordstring in both hands – like if he afraid it ga pull out from he belly – and Salizar bends over quick to bite it off. He cleans up the child and quiets him down, and he wraps him up in a white coverlet so that now you can't even see the half belonging to a man. Salizar takes down a big cottonwool box from the shelf, he spreads out a layer on the bottom, and he puts this crapochild to lie down inside like if the box is a cradle. Then he gives him to me to hold.

But boy, if I didn't look way from that crapoface, I would have dropped him on the ground again. I am watching Salizar clean up Magdalena and dress her back in she clothes (he told me later he'd realized it was only a matter of time before Gomez busted down the door, and he wanted to clean her up and get me out through the window first) when all of a sudden I realize that I have seen this crapoface someplace before. I look down again at him and now I am sure, but I can't remember where the ass it was. Like if sometime somehow I have already dreamed this whole baddream already – because how else could this crapoface look so familiar? – when all of a sudden I realize where it was, and I run quick to the examiningroom with this crapochild. I put the cottonwool box down on the table and I reach to the shelf fa the book, and as soon as I start to flip through the pages I find him again. Ba-tam-bam. Now I remember lying there in that cold bed, in that cold mother-ass country, reading about this thing and studying the picture, and I remember saying to the little Canadian fellow I had fa my roommate: 'Shreve, look here at this picture, na. This child ain't no man a-tall. He ain't no man a-tall! This child is a *crapo!*' Shreve only chups and roll over again. But boy, when I finish my reading fa the night – and I close the book and I out the light and I drop asleep – I couldn't stop from seeing this child again neither. Only now in my nightmare he isn't lying there quiet so in the picture. Now in my nightmare he is *swimming*.

NOW I COULD not help but listen. Now I could not help but hear my father's voice. The same voice speaking to me above the same loud insects, above the same water beating against the same rocks. And I remember sitting here in this Warrahoon-Windsor chair, and wondering even then how it is that these insects cannot drown out this voice? How it is that these waves cannot outlive this story? And I remember thinking even then that the reason is because this story does not belong to this voice. To these voices. *This story belongs to that moon. To that black sky and that black sea. This story belongs to the same foul smell of the swamp when the wind blows.*

And I remember sitting here wondering even then whose hands were these weighing down on my shoulders? *Because if this voice is coming to you from outside there, then these hands you feeling on you shoulders could belong to anyone. And maybe if you could bend you head back without butting it up, you might find that it is not daddy but Papee Vince standing there behind you. Maybe even Evelina or maybe Granny Myna. Because if you could bend you head back without butting it up on the back of this chair, you might find that it is Barto standing behind you. Maybe even Magdalena Divina sheself.* And now, as I sit here in the same Windsor chair, looking out of the same window seventy-four years later, I can only wonder again whose hands are these still weighing down heavy on my shoulders? Whose arms are these still jammed up hard against my temples? Now that I can look back easily enough and see that there is no one standing behind me. Now that my father has been dead in the ground longer than sixty years.

BUT BOY, soon as I start to read about this thing again, I realize that this child of Magdalena's ain't no ordinary anencephalic monster a-tall. Not altogether so. What he is exactly I couldn't tell you, but you can't write him off so

easy. Because of course, he had the physical appearance of
a child born with this malformation. All other aspects of
the pregnancy would substantiate it: the hydramnios, the
breech presentation, the twitching on palpation of the
foetal head, the spontaneous premature labour. But boy,
this is a fatal condition. Of all the many deformities
known to occur among the human species, anencephaly is
the master monstrosity. These foetuses are invariably
stillborn, and if they survive delivery a-tall, it is only to
suck a breath or two before they expire. But boy, this
child lived through a delivery which would have killed
even the strongest of healthy infants (because there is no
way of knowing how long Magdalena had been dead by
the time I got to her, or how long I'd spent trying to
resuscitate her before I pulled him out) but I can tell you fa
fact that no normal child could survive half that amount of
time in the womb of he dead mother, much less an
anencephalic monster. On top of that, he lived through
three days of the most brutal kind of abuse – with mummy
and Evelina and the whole of Corpus Christi fighting
down each other to drown him, or burn him alive, or jook
him dead with the cutlass – and there is no way of
knowing how long he would have survived if Uncle Olly
hadn't gone so far as to dissect him up. Realize: this is a
congenital abnormality which affects the bony formation
of the skull, resulting in cerebral hemispheres which are
either rudimentary, or absent. So how could this child live
any time a-tall without a functioning brain? And boy, I am
not about to repeat fa you all that bubball you have heard
already: that this crapochild was intelligent. That he could
answer with nods of he head questions addressed to him in
three and four different languages. That by the end of
those three days he had learned to speak them too. All that
is of course nonsense. What I will tell you is this: this
crapochild may have looked like an anencephalic monster,
but he had the functioning brain of an ordinary, healthy

infant. And that is only the beginning. Anencephalics are born with they eyes open, but they are born blind: the optic nerves are absent. This child could see. He eyes always looked you straight in the face, and they would follow you hard hard wherever you went in the room. The sucking reflex in anencephalics is abolished – which is the reason fa the gross hydramnios – but as soon as you push you finger inside *this* child's mouth, he would suck down on it so hard you had to strain to pull it out.

That was how Salizar found me: standing there at the examining table reading in the book with this crapochild sucking way at my finger, looking like if I'd just made some profound discovery. I pull out my finger *plop*, and push it in again fa him to see, *plop*, but Salizar only gives me a face like I gone viekeevie now fa true. Just then pounding starts on the door. Salizar grabs way the child, and he drags me back in the bedroom now to climb out quick through the window. But boy, I don't know how I didn't kill up that poor oldman that night too, na. Because by the the time he has the pane open and he foot halfway through the window, he looks back again to find Magdalena with the nundress he had just put on her up over she head, and me between she legs my nose press up against she pussy, looking at that imperforate hymen again.

That was how this Chief of Police and Mother Maurina found me, with Salizar supposedly climbing *in* through the window trying to get heself *inside* too. Because it was obvious enough who was responsible fa Magdalena's death, who had delivered this crapochild: here my hands were red with blood and green shit to the elbows. And of course, everybody outside knew already that I was the one who killed Magdalena with all my fancified instruments and my medicine tablets and my big black books – because of course that is what happens soon as you let these modern educated doctors come from England and America and all about the place to tell us we business – and how else could this child come out half-a-man and half-a-crapo?

Even so Salizar tried he best to get me out of trouble by taking on the blame heself, because Gomez was so vex over Magdalena's death and the condition of he son, he was ready to put a bullet in me any second. But oldman Salizar only managed to get heself in trouble too. He went about the place saying how this crapochild heself killed Magdalena with only a single look from he nasty crapo-face, and soon as they saw the child fa theyselves they couldn't help but believe him. Salizar insisted so many times *he* was the doctor who'd made the delivery, that by the next morning Gomez had no choice but to lock him up in the jail too. That was when I first heard the story, sitting there on the cold concrete flooring of that jailcage, even though I could tell you my own story good enough by now. (Because apparently it was Salizar who made the diagnosis of Magdalena's pregnancy fa Gomez – dropping a few drops of water on she belly and watching to see how the water dance – and it was he who diagnosed a disappearance of the same child only a few weeks later. It was Salizar who sent her packing from Gomez back to the convent again.) And after we'd been sitting there in the jail a few days, and the fight starts up over Magdalena's body, with daddy and this Chief of Police, Mother Maurina and Monsignor O'Connor and the whole of Corpus Christi fighting down each other fa Magdalena's corpse – and Gomez locks up Mother Maurina in the jail on top of us too, then I heard the story of Magdalena's three-day jooking-sessions in the convent with daddy.

But boy, you have heard all of that already, and you will hear it all again before you finish. I could never tell you what to believe, because the truth is that I don't know what kind of relationship my father had with this woman myself. Whatever it was brought him to murder that Chief of Police, whatever it was brought him to put a bullet in he own head soon as he finished telling us goodbye, sitting

together round the big diningroom table that same afternoon, I couldn't say. All I can tell you is this: some things
speak louder than the hardest of facts, and from the first
moment I looked in Magdalena's eyes I knew she belonged
to no man of *this* world. That is what *I* have to help me
believe. What I have to give you is the medical fact:
Magdalena died a virgin. Where exactly this child came
from, and what exactly he was, there is no way of
knowing. I will give you the book, and you can read it up
and study the picture fa youself, but I can tell you one
thing from now: there is no answer written anywhere here
inside this book. Because there is only one man who took
Magdalena's virginity, and he took it a half-hour after she
was already dead, and he took it with this index finger of
this right hand, and he took it at the precise moment
Gomez and Mother Maurina busted down that hospital
door.

WITH THAT my father took his left hand off of my
shoulder too, and he reached to the shelf and pulled out his
medical journal. He flipped carefully through the pages,
and he left it open here on the desk before me. I heard the
door close softly behind him, and I closed my eyes at the
same moment. I wanted to feel for the book and shut it
quickly too, but I knew that was impossible. Because now
that I was finally free to get up out of this chair, now I felt
more trapped than ever. Now that I could push myself out
from under this desk – and I could run from this library
and this book and Magdalena and her frogchild easily
enough, finally – now I couldn't budge from my seat.
Sitting here listening to the loud insects again, to the water
on the rocks and the wind in the trees again, with no other
sound but my own silent voice as palpable as words
written on a page: *It is only a book in front of you. A book.*
But when I opened my eyes the book disappeared as

though it were a figment of my imagination. And I stood there again, holding the empty bottle, smelling the stagnant smell of the swamp, feeling my feet in the mud of my new washykongs in my old jesusboots, looking down again through the dark water again, alive, thinking: *No. It is more than a book because there he is swimming. And now he will never reach those mangrove banyans again to disappear.*

5

Mother Superior Maurina Speaks of Magdalena's Death

I WAS ALMOST eighteen when my mother took me to the Chinese tailor to be measured for my first pair of longpants. Actually there were two suits, both charcoal-grey: a light one for summer, and a heavy woollen one for winter, because we heard fantastic stories about how much it snowed in America, and snow was something which few of us could even imagine. But more than the snow, it was the longpants which had me excited. My father offered me a pair of his fancy, wingtipped hardbacks, which I accepted even though they were too small and made me walk broko. I'd hoped to go to Medical School at Oxford, but my marks were not good enough. My father wrote requesting the entrance examination regardless – a new thing since his day – but instead of returning my results, they wrote a letter asking if English were my mother tongue. He decided to send me to America. There we were assured there was no such thing as an entrance exam, and you could get anything you wanted, provided you paid the money. Accordingly my father managed to get hold of two one-hundred dollar bills of yankee money, which my mother folded and safety-pinned into the inside breast pocket of my summer jacket.

I was to report to the university in New York by the first of May, so it was almost by chance my departure happened to fall on Friday, April 16, the morning of my eighteenth birthday. Almost, because I'd delayed my departure a week so that the dates would coincide. That day seemed appropriate for whatever turn my life was about to take – I'd be leaving the island for the first time, and who knows when I'd return, if ever – but the real reason was that I wanted to be home for one last Corpus Christi Day. It was a challenge I set for myself. In my own absurd way, it was a challenge I set for God. Because I'd refused to go near the church for almost two years. For two years I had refused even to go to midnight Mass on Christmas Eve. First I was afraid my father would beat me. He said nothing, and I soon came to realize I'd grown beyond the age of beating. This realization only made me more proudfoot. My mother tried to talk to me about it once, and when I saw how upset she was I promised I'd go with the family the following morning: before we reached halfway to the cathedral I turned around and went to the only parlour open on a Sunday. My friends had long stopped calling me El Papa. Now I was the Freshwater Yankee.

My family tried their best to get me to join the band that Corpus Christi Day – this year they were playing mas with the Shepherds of Bethlehem – but I told them I still had packing to do. We all knew there was hardly more than the two suits, and the rest my mother had packed into my small grip a week before. Even so, when the band passed in front of our house the four of them burst in, and before I knew what happened my family had dragged me out into the street: I had no choice but to follow the band for a few blocks. They were singing at the tops of their voices – a hundred shepherds' crooks held high in the air, all bobbing up and down together with the music – and my father kept poking me with his own until I began to sing too:

Ky-ri-e e-le-i-son,
Chr-i-ste e-le-i-son!
Ky-ri-e e-le-i-son,
Chr-i-ste e-le-i-son!

Secretly I hoped the song would never come to an end. Because I can tell you the hardest thing I have ever done in my life, was to turn my back on the four of them that afternoon. I went to walk the wharf for a while, and I saw that the mailboat which would carry me to Caracas the following morning was already tied up. The dock was deserted – everyone in town celebrating – and I walked to the end and sat with my legs hanging over the side, just as I'd sat in the same spot a thousand times before. It was stale oldtide and my feet hung in the hot water. From there the singing in St Maggy was reduced to a rumble in the distance, and as I looked out at the sea I remembered myself again years before: standing there holding the bottle, watching the oldman in his aluminium outfit, his oxcart disappearing into the cloud of dust which followed his band of angels. He was waving, saying something which I could not make out over the music of the band. No doubt he was telling me goodbye. No doubt that oldman had died ages ago. But as I saw him again for the first time in so many years, I realized he might not be saying goodbye, but he might be offering me one last chance. Because now I could see plainly that he was not waving, but signalling me back to the cart. Now I could hear him clearly enough: 'Put down that glassbottle, whiteson! Run boy, run!'

And I thought that if I could do it all over again – if my life were only a story and I could begin the whole thing over again at the beginning – that is exactly what I'd do: I'd drop that obzockee glassbottle like if I'd caught a vaps. I'd take off running fa that oxcart as fast as my legs could carry me. And I'd grab on and I'd climb up and I'd take

hold of that toothless oldman's hands again, and now I'd
be singing too. Now I'd be riding on top that bisquankey
old oxcart wrapped up in all that tinpaper like a robot, like
an angel – a spoon in my hand beating up a rumbottle
pa-ding, pa-ding-ping – and now I'd be headed back to
town. Now I'd be headed back home. Not waiting to
climb aboard this mailboat with Corpus Christi already
sinking in its wake behind me, already headed for whatever was waiting at the end of this sea to swallow me up,
maybe forever.

I sat there for a long time. Eventually I got up and
started back, and by the time I reached town I felt almost
as though I'd already left. Suddenly everything looked
strange, distant: the broken-down houses, the rubbish, the
dirt roads, the old Creole woman selling newspaper-
packages of channa beneath a patched umbrella. They no
longer belonged to me, no longer belonged to any emotion which I could call my own. The people dancing like
children in the streets looked suddenly absurd, embarrass-
ing, and I could only wonder what it was they had to sing
about? What it was they had to feel so happy about?
Choking in the dust sticking to their sweating, glittered
faces. Streaming down their cheeks like tears of mud, of
bluegrey blood.

I stopped and turned around, and I looked up at the tall
belltower of St Maggy Cathedral, standing above the
whole town. I stood there in the middle of the street,
ignoring the band passing on either side, staring up at the
big bell I had rung so many times when I was younger. It
would actually lift me off the ground when I got it ringing
hard enough – completely off the ground – and I saw
myself again for an instant: a little boy alone at the bottom
of that tall belltower – laughing, screaming – pulling
harder and harder on that bellcord with the bell ringing
louder and louder, until I thought my head would burst!
And when I turned around again I knew that they were

fools: I had come so close to growing up a fool too.

On my way home I stopped at a parlour. Instead of the usual rum, the old coolie I knew so well made a pappy-show out of pouring me a whiskey: 'Birthpaper bun!' he said. 'Canejuice finish with boydays!'

We called him Oldtalk because he spoke only in clichés. I tasted the whiskey – like a coffee without the sugar. The coolie laughed. I drank it down as best I could, but when I went to pay he waved me off, saying he expected to get it back someday in medicine tablets: 'De kind dey does have in America to make you shit halfdollars!'

I promised him some and went home to lie down in my bed.

And I must have fallen asleep for several hours, because by the time I awoke the others had already been to the cathedral and come back: I found my brother aleep in his bed, his cassock from the Vigil service dumped in a heap on the floor. They had not even attempted to wake me. I threw off the sheet and lay there listening to the oscillating fan, feeling its fanvoice move slowly across my wet skin, and not before I recognized my new suit spread out across the bureau – my father's hardbacks beside it so polished they were shining in the dark – did I realize I'd be leaving in only a few hours. I sat up quickly in my bed. Suddenly I felt excited, and the more I thought about those longpants hidden beneath the jacket, the more excited I became: I had not put them on since I left the tailor's shop. Now I could not hold myself back. Now I *had* to put on those long-pants, and when I looked over at my brother sleeping soundly in his . bed, I could not resist that temptation either.

I reached over and gave him a hard flick behind his ear: 'What time you think it is, boy?'

He took a swat at my hand, chupsing: 'Time fa you to carry you ass by the yankees!' He rolled over and went back to sleep.

I jumped out of bed and started to dress: drawers, vestshirt, socks, pants, shirt, suspenders, jacket – everything – even the clip-on bowtie. More clothes than I had ever put on at any time in my life, and I still had the hardbacks to go! I took up the shoes and left quietly, hurrying past my sister's room and on down the stairs. Just as I sat on the frontstep I heard the Government House clock in the distance strike four times: I had two hours before I had to board the mailboat. Where I was going at that hour and in such a hurry I had no idea, but as I tied my laces I decided one thing for sure: *No matter how loud these hardbacks squeeze you you not leaving them here, because you not taking no chance on Granny Myna coming out from she grave to pelt them in the sea.* The fowls soon appeared, pecking at my ankles, confused as to what was going on. It was as if they couldn't recognize me all dressed up. I took a step behind them and they ran off in a burst of cackle.

The streets were strewn with litter from the Corpus Christi celebrations. Everything was quiet. Even the potcakes were still asleep, curled up in groups of two or three in the middle of the road. As soon as I approached they got to their feet – stretching on their front legs in a kind of potcake genuflection – and they came at me in slow, stealthy movements. It was as though they couldn't identify me in the suit either. I kicked them away, thinking: *Maybe you done reach in America and this is only a dream, because how else could these potcakes you known all you life not recognise you, just because you dress up dandan? This* must *be a dream, because nothing in real life feel so sweet as these pants breezing up silkysilk against you legs, and nothing could squeeze so hard as these hardbacks.*

I'd had the idea that I would go to the square and sit beneath the statue awhile, that maybe Magdalena would appear there to me too; at least I wanted to give her one last chance. But as I started to cross the square something stopped me, and I squinted past the big, wide-open doors of St Maggy Convent, into the chapel where the Eucharist was always transferred until Easter Sunday. That the doors were open was not unusual for Good Friday morning. What was peculiar was that the chapel was empty. Because the Eucharist was never to be left alone during those hours, not until after sunrise (a practice enforced, I told myself, ever since the apostles booted-off on Jesus in the garden). This the nuns took very seriously. Because even though we all made an effort to spend a half-hour or so with the reposed Eucharist at some point during the night – and often there were as many as fifteen or twenty of us crowded into the little chapel – the sisters took shifts regardless to make sure there was always someone there. But whichever nun's turn it was must have run in the back for a weewee, because sure enough when I crossed the vestibule and stuck my head into the chapel breezeway – my hardbacks squeaking on the polished stone, echoing through the convent – there was the starburst-monstrance surrounded by the candles flickering in their red glass holders, the incense smoking away, but the chapel was empty. I stood there for a second: *What the ass? It isn't as if this is a true church. It isn't as if you ga have to sit there longer than two minutes.* And before I'd considered the possible consequences, I'd slid into the end of the last pew, the one nearest the breezeway. But it was longer than two minutes, and eventually I chupsed out loud: *What the ass you doing sitting here, when Magdalena might be waiting fa you beneath the statue? Maybe with she nundress hoisted up above she waist?*

Just then the Government House clock began to strike, startling me, and I turned quickly to look out at the clock across the square: four-thirty. I was sweating, suddenly transfixed, and I remember counting the bells and saying to myself: *Soon as the fifth one comes you jumping up and running from this chapel.* But I was still counting when the tenth bell rang, thinking: *Fine. On fifteen you ga run.* But when the fifteenth bell rang and the clock went silent I was still sitting there, still transfixed, turned halfway in the pew, because now there was someone standing in the breezeway in front of me: Mother Superior Maurina walked towards me, got down on her knees, and she did something very peculiar: she bent over to kiss both my feet. She straightened up again, reached into one of her sleeves, and she removed a folded piece of paper – brittle-looking, tattered, yellowed – and held it out to me. I couldn't move. Couldn't raise my arm to reach for the piece of paper. I could only stare at this ancient ghost kneeling in front of me in her white habit, her greyish, blind-people eyes, her skin so thin and transparent I could see the yellow bones beneath, a medusa of tiny purple veins crawling slowly across each of her cheeks.

She nodded her head slightly and I took the piece of paper. She stood and turned away, and immediately I breathed a sigh of relief; but instead of leaving the chapel, she sat in the pew directly in front of me. I turned to face the back of her head. Before I could unfold the paper she was already talking.

HE WAS BORN with the cojones of a man, but he was the son of Papa God. It happen so, because Magdalena Divina was a saint, un ángel blanco caminando esta tierra negra, and the proof of that is she die a freshvirgin. Magdalena have this special veil of the church to protect her, that no wajank could never push heself inside no matter how hard he try, because I used to curse Papa God for doing that, and if He is a man He should have know better. He didn't have no business making this child so beautiful, and then turning round to stop her up with that thing, because it wasn't Magdalena looks that drive men so tootoolbay, and it wasn't she purity or even she innocence, all that they could have bear, it was only the idea that she belong to Him alone and they could never drink of she virtue thyself. Like if He sit down and study He head for the quickest way no to save her, but to *kill* her alive, because what begin as the cool frustration of that mammapoule Chief of Police, finish in the hot boiling frenzy of *every* man on this island of Corpus Christi. That Sunday morning they are there waiting for her hiding in the mangrove byside the swamp. Soon as Magdalena reach Maraval the three that is up in the tree jump out on top her, and the rest come splashing from out the mangrove already strip down naked bawling paint up in sweat like a tribe of cannibal Caribs running to hold a manquenk, and they pin her down beneath the tree to do they nastiness. One by one fighting down each other to try they turn until in they outrage they begin to beat her, *badam-bam-bam-bam* with my heart jumping up at the lick of every blow coming down like the cat-of-the-nine-tails to sting my own flesh, and my own sweet Magdalena lying there on the grass with she eyes close tight and she face shining in blood and she lips whispering a silent Ave Maria. Ay Dios mío cabron! It is as if my veins taste a poison. As if St Michael take hold of my bones with all he strength, because before I know what my hands are doing I have run out from that bush I am hiding behind and I grab on to those cojones of that wajank that is swimming in the grease on top her, and I squeeze them so hard they burst in the air like two naranjas de sangre españolas spraying us all down in red blood, and when those bassabassas see this thing every manjack take off running clasping he cojones for dearest life like each one get jook by a big jooker *up* they backside. Ay Dios mío shitong! All I can do is fall down on my knees to take up Magdalena in my arms, and I raise up my eyes to heaven to tell Papa God I only wish it was *He* cojones I could hold. But that same veil of the church was there to protect Magdalena even until the day of she death, even though it is only an accident of fate *it*

didn't kill her first, because just like every other man Papa
God have that same jigger in He backside when it come to
claiming he own freshvirgin, and just as I am told I open
she legs to show it you daddy that all the world can know,
now that she is dead in the bed with the child already cut
from she belly by a scissors, mea culpa! now that Monsignor is there already with the Chief and he three policemen
pounding down the door of this hospital with they
bootoos and Brito Salizar is climbing in the window with
he cottonwool box and all those fregando feathers of copra
is gusting back and forth again like a blizzard, mea culpa,
mea maxima culpa! because *he*, was Papa God own sweet
instrument of intercession. Su intermediare céleste de ce
monde humain, because didn't she run to me first thing
soon as Barto climb out the window of this convent on
that third morning only minutes before that tantie Gomez
return now she husband with he basket full to the brim
with secreye bananas and gumagalla green plantains to
molest her for the second time? and she pull me by the
hand the two of us running together to she room with she
eyes smiling heavy of exhaustion and she knees still
trembling with sweet passion, and she lie down on the bed
lifting up she nundress as if to beg me, Mummy please,
please Mummy look to feel in my pussy this churchveil
that I can still see with my fingers is true that I can *believe*
it? And didn't he love me too byside the river flowing
beneath the big immortelle that is bursting with flowers of
red and orange and yellow like if it is flaming in the sky
above us, that I can know *already* he can never belong to
this world of manmen? With the petals falling soft flaming
slow through the air on the ground in that immortelle bed
of fire, and the water running clear byside us with the
steam rising cool from we shoulders beneath the vines of
gentle blue moss hanging wet to brush along we backs
press warm against the soft black earth smelling of He
own sweet suffering, and sin, and the crown of thorns

crawling cross the rocks, that I can know my life is over already even as a child of fifteen because how can breath and blood and bones sustain me to live through *this* ever again? Gratias agimus tibi propter magnam gloriam tuam! Because Papa God mistake is He do the whole business backward. He should have make *Heself* good as He make this man Barto. That is when we was living in Venezuela in the cattle ranch there in Estado Monagas, and Barto have come from Corsica one day to go in the jungle with the Warrahoons to collect sap from the trees of rubber. There is only me and little Myna in the house then with mummy and Uncle Olly and all those cowboys, because daddy was a Captain of boats and he have die very young in the sea leaving only the ranch to preserve us. So when Barto return now from up the Orinoco dress in mud high as he cojones, and toting this big barrel of rubber on he back like a morocoy, I must tell him first thing that we can no marry again as he have promise, because now Papa God have punish me and make me haveen then the only thing for me to do is declare myself a whore and run to the convent in Caracas no to bring him this disgrace, and I beg him on my knees please to take up little Myna instead. He is standing above me looking down that I can see I have truly touch him, because he reach to he side to take out that big sword he use to wear on he belt then, all bathe in gold and mother-of-pearl on the handle that it was a present to him from you great-granduncle el Presidente General Francisco Monagas, and he raise it up slow pointing up at heaven with he eyes flashing and the long blade dripping of fire in the sun to pronounce for the *whole* of Baranjas to hear who have come running to the courtyard to see this thing, that he will suffer no shame before any man, and he will marry me just as he have pledge heself even if it mean to walk up to the altar parading this child like St Christopher on he shoulder, and with that he push the sword in the ground between he feet.

Oui fute Papamoi virtilite! All I can do is bend over quick
to wipe off the mud from he feet with my hair and my
tears and I press my lips to those same hardbacks *you*
wearing on you feet right now, the very same ones that
have come to you through you daddy that I knew them
walking cross the square even before I could recognize you
in he face, but that same night I am lying in my bed and I
become so afraid of myself now thinking about this man,
because who am I to say Barto must give he affections to
me alone when I know he have enough love in he heart for
all the world? that I jump through the window and I run to
that convent in Caracas fast as my feet can carry me. Now
I am satisfy my life is fulfill and the only thing remaining is
to offer myself up to Papa God and bear Him He child,
that at least He have give me this much to console me for
all my long life to come of penitence and suffering, but
that is a mistake of course and I should have know better
because Papa God *never* like to see nobody too happy,
because soon as they push the ring of a nun on my finger
and shave me down like a clean-neck-fowl He take He
child away. Ay Dios mío singon! Just so I wake up the
next morning to find the child gone from out my belly
disappear, and all I can do is fall down on my knees to raise
up my hands in the air, and I tell Papa God I only wish
firebug on He stones for doing me this swindle. But just as I
have reach to the depths of my despair and I decide the only
thing remaining in life is to jump through the window and
run to Baranjas to kill that little bitch Myna, I receive a
letter from Barto through the mail telling me no to worry.
He say that ESTA NIÑA QUE LLEVABAS EN TU
MATRIZ NO ERA DE MÍ, ERA DE DIOS, Y ERA
UNA SANTA DIVINA DESTINADA A SALVAR Y
DESTRUIR A TODO EL MUNDO CON SU FRUTO
SAGRADO DIABÓLICO, and he tell me that it is Papa
God QUE LO DESAPARECÍA as if I don't already know
PERO LO DARÁ OTRA VEZ EN UN TIEMPO MEJOR,

and he will send a sign for me to come when such and such a time have reach. But I am no understanding this thing too good a-tall like if it is write in a different language, so all I can do is sit down again to wait for the next letter to come when it is time for Barto to give me back the child. And it is so long that I don't hear nothing a-tall and I give up on that immortelle tree again, when all of a sudden ten years later I am busy in the middle of the jungle in Tucupita baptizing all those Indians like flies sticking on flypaper, when out from nowhere Barto appear to me one night in my dream standing byside the hammock all dress up dandan in the big Captain white-hat like daddy used to wear in the ship, and the white sailorboy-costume with the gold buttons shining and the frogs coil up and the silver tassels dancing, and the big gold-rope crawling round he shoulder like a fat macajuel snake. Oui fute Papamoi fantaisie! First I am frighten thinking that he must have come now to tell me that he is *dead*, because this is the first time he ever appear to me in a dream like this and why else would he be dress up pappyshow so? but straight way he lift up the skirt of that mosquito net and he answer shaking he head no that he is no dead yet, and soon enough my legs have open already of theyself trembling now to receive him hot inside me but Barto is shaking he head again, no, no, no, it is no yet time for that monkeybusiness neither, that he would have write a letter if he could but where he living in Corpus Christi they don't have no mail and no telegraph yet, so he have have to come in person to deliver this message that now is the time for me to come. But I am no understanding this thing a-tall a-tall because for some strange reason Barto is speaking *English* now, and this is a funny language sounding like the songs children compose to run skipping down the road that I have never hear a word of it yet at this time in my life, but soon as I arrive in Baranjas I understand exactly what he is trying to say because all the cows are gone now replace by the big

towers of pipe to suck oil. Now they tell me how Barto
have sell that ranch a long time ago to steal he fortune and
buy from the Queen of England the whole of this country
he call in my dream by the name of *Corpus Christi*, but
when I ask them where it is they can only spit a spit on the
ground and lift up they leg to push a fart *pffft* in the air as if
to say it is an island lost somewhere in the sea, so I decide
the only thing for me to do is to try to find it. By the time I
reach Corpus Christi the convent is already finish a year
without a nun inside. This is the first time they call a
building by the name of the Church of the Jabjab, and they
said Barto is going into competition now with Papa God
in He cathedral on the other side of the square. But that
same morning before I can even have a chance to catch my
breath Barto have already assemble the big crowd of
people only blowing on they fingers and clapping they
hands together, and he raise up he hand to quiet the
orchestra playing *um-pa-pa um-pa-pa* introducing me talking through the big pasteboard funnel like if I am the
Countess of Chackachkari or some big grand-saffe
tootooloo, so what else can I do of course but turn round
quick to throw open the doors of this convent proclaiming
myself by the title of *Mother Superior General Maurina
Queen of the Corpus Christi Carmelites*? Oui fute Papamoi
tutumulte! First thing I have to do is send to Venezuela for
some of my sisters to come and join me, and Barto send to
Paris for one set of fancify nun-costumes to come toute-
baghai with the big wings flapping on the headdress so big
that you have to turn to the side to be able to pass through
the door, and no sooner do we appear in the street wearing
these wings when we have a cockroach-cocktail-party
outside of every little callaloo girlchild from Grande
Sangre to Wallafield and Blanchisseuse line up fighting
down each other with stick and stone and glassbottle to see
who is the first to pledge sheself to the nuns. I am so busy
now to do all the things I have to do that straight way I

condemn the wearing of those wings on penalty of death except official parades, because that is the only thing to save weself from drowning in this big pepperpot of younggirls, and I am so confuse now I don't even have time to remember that promise Barto give me so long ago when all of a sudden one night I am lying in my bed dead of exhaustion rolling my beads, when out from nowhere come this breeze through the window to touch me cool cool and smelling sweet like roses, and when I raise up my eyes there at the end of the bed are those toes that are long and white and creamy like icecream. Now I can know I am no dreaming this time that he have come to me longlast in flesh and in blood that I don't even bother to waste no time to pinch myself, because let me tell you *nothing* in you imagination could live up to those toes, and all I can do is close my eyes quick no to see my death in he face this time sure certain, that before I can know what my thighs have open already of theyself again now to feel him burning hot inside me a pillar of fire pressing up from below beating against my breast that I can no even suck a breath of air to know I am still alive, with my head falling back melting slow behind me now until it is no longer even connecting my neck to my body with my feet in the cool water flowing clear against the warm black earth petals drifting soft flaming slow again in the air of that blue sky of schoolchildren running screaming in the mornings of they uniforms of navy pleated skirts and shortpants, of tall white socks and starch white shirts black and brown and red and yellow running together for three days and three nights without even a pause, without even a moment to breathe between the poundings of that clock in my heart with my eyes close still to smell the old fisherwoman calling alone from the saltfish square of she cocoreete *pong-fa-pong-a-fiepong!* for three evenings of three red hot sunsets of Him melting slow cool again a dry leaf forever on my tongue, benedictus qui venit in nomine Domini *oy*

oy Mari qui recours a vous *oy* Madre dulce Santa María
María José Jesú *oy yo-yuga yo-yuga!*

I COULDN'T MOVE. Couldn't turn to look out at the
clock across the square. I could only sit there sweating,
staring straight ahead – incredulous, confounded. Counting the five bells of that clock ringing now, because now
there were hands holding my shoulders again. Now there
were arms pressing against my temples, and I had no
choice but to sit staring at the back of this white
nunhabit-headdress-voice without even a face. A source.
As though the story were forming itself now not out of the
dregs of human time and memory, but out of the incense-
filled air itself. The ancient, decrepit, candle-flickering air
of that chapel breathed and rebreathing now not only by
this ancient nun, by this boy of eighteen; not only by
Magdalena and Barto himself, but by all of us sitting here
together listening, interrupting each other occasionally
sometimes two and three of us speaking together at the
same time. Each telling our separate version of the same
unending story.

Thinking: *But this woman is basodee over Barto! Then what
the ass is everybody talking so confuffled about? Because this
Mother Maurina not bite-up with Barto a-tall, she in love with
him. Assassatap! Tarangeebangee! So tabanka she could practically thank him fa making her haveen before the marriage – then
turning round to give him up to Granny Myna like if she offering
up a novena – only to save him from marrying a woman not a
freshvirgin haveen sheself now by* he *own making!* Thinking:
*But boy, don't even bother yourself to template none of that
nonsene. Don't even worry you head to think bout that mailboat
already ready to leave in only a quick hour. Because boy, tell me
instead how the ass these shoes could squeeze you so? How the
ass you feet could possibly be overbig fa these hardbacks, when
they used to belong to* him? *Because it was not you feet she*

kneeled down to kiss a-tall, but only these same shoes somehow
squeezing you now because somehow they used to belong to him.
To Barto!

And now: as I sit here at this desk of purpleheart, in this
imitation Warrahoon-Windsor chair, an oldman ninety
years of age, as I look through this window at this moon
above the same black glistening sea – now, as I sit here in
this pew sweating in my new suit, my new clip-on bowtie
the pinchers of a rockcrab biting up at my throat, Mother
Maurina's brittle piece of paper a flay of old dried fishskin
ready to disintegrate in my wet, oldman's fingers – as I
count the five bells of that clock ringing across the square,
something very bizarre is occurring before my eyes:
Mother Maurina's wings are slowly unfolding out from
her headdress. Not smoothly: in increments. Mechdical-
ly. Segment by segment, notch by notch, ten degrees from
the horizontal at a time like the landing flaps of a small
aeroplane. Slowly up and out from the sides of her white
pasteboard-headdress with the pointed fifth segment
folded, bent at an angle downward, so that now at the end
of those five bells they are fully extended, outstretched,
sprawling: the silver wings of a seagull. The sensory
apparatus of some strange beetle. The aluminium-white
antennae of this angelic robot sitting before me ready now
to receive and transmit some personal message from some
master-robot by the name of *God*. Before my eyes. In my
own ears.

NOW I AM HAPPY again for the second time in my life
that the only thing remaining for me to do is to praise Papa
God and bear Him He child, but I should have know
better than any of that cacashat because nine months later
soon as I have reach byside myself with longing waiting
for this child to be born on the morning of Corpus Christi
Day announce so long ago by the prophet in St James

living above Kentucky before I can even have a chance to enjoy for a moment all these beautiful sweetdreams I am having, when Barto appear to me again dress up again in daddy big Captain white-hat with the curls standing up on he wax moustache and smoking he little Cuban cigar through the special gold thimble for the tobacco no even to touch he lips, and he lift up the mosquito net to tell me how you will never even know the privilege of raising up you child yourself, and you will never be able to give that white-lie you have prepare already that she is one of those children leave in a saltfish-crate by the front door of the convent for the nuns to raise her up, and you will never even know that sweet pleasure of a mother looking she child in the face, because Papa God have decide that you must give her way to a family of callaloo-monkeys living in the bush. Aye Dios mío singon! Barto is standing above me looking down at me with he eyes burning slow like the coals in a coalpot, that I can see how sad he is to have to announce to me these things, because he tell me straight way that you must try and no despair too much as you will only be without her thirteen short years, and at the end of those thirteen years she will return to you asking to pledge sheself to the nuns but not knowing of course who she is or where she come from and not speaking no Español or Français or English or even Latin, but only the Hindi and Creole and Warrahoon, and these are three funny languages sounding the first like an oldman blowing struggling to make a caca, and the second groaning stretching he toetee shaking to squeeze out a weewee, and the third is holding he breath fighting to force a fart *pfffft* that I have never hear a word yet of any of them at this time in my life, but he say that you will recognize her straight way even though you never lie you eyes on her during all those thirteen long years she is living desperate in Suparee in the bush, and you can never reveal to her who is she mummy and who is she daddy because how can you speak even a

word to her in any kind of language that she can understand a-tall? and all this is now decree on you head forever
and time immaterial according to the inconscribable wisdom of Papa God Heself. Ay Dios mío cagon! I am so
viekeevie now to hear this thing that I wake up myself in
one and I jump up on the bed to send a spit at him flying to
deliver for me to Papa God and tell Him how He can push
all He big fancy Bible-words up he big fat culo, but Barto
have already dissolve way heself leaving behind him only
the smell of that cigar and my own big moko dripping
down in a string from the ceiling, when straight way I feel
the first pain of this child in my belly that I have to lie
down quick in the bed again for her no to drop out
blooppoops on top she head, because now is the time for her
to come. Of course my mind is make up already I am no
giving way this child no for *nothing* in the world, especially I am no handing her over to no monkey-callaloos to
raise her up eating dirt like a putu in the bush, but I should
have know better than to think any of that because of
course Papa God hear me straight way and He put one
accouchement on me now to bear this child, hours and
hours the birthpains continue with Sister Alicia and Sister
Robin Clark who are the only two of my closest sisters to
know about this child running back and forth with they
basins of hot water spilling and they kerchieves of Limacol
flying all about the room so nervous that before we can
even get a chance to realize what have hit us when already
the whole big bottle of brandy is already drink down, and
Sister Robin Clark have to hold down Sister Alicia to
knock her over she head kaponkle with the empty brandy
bottle to bring she to she senses because all she want to do
now is climb up on top my belly and sit and plounce in the
air *vups vups vups* to see if maybe she could squeeze out this
child through my pussy that she doesn't want to open up
sheself a-tall to allow this child to come out, and such a
pain now to send my brain viekeevie like if the band

beating outside in the square for this Corpus Christi Day
are beating inside my head, that now I begin to loose
myself and I bawl out to Papa God that into You hands I
condemn this child that You can do with her whatever the
ass You want just to let me die now quick and this pain
that is eating my guts inside to stop and finish, but that is a
mistake of course because just then Sister Alicia bawl out
to mire Robin Clark que la niña está viniendo! when I
loose my head for true because now I am hearing like if
one of those bands beating outside in the street have invade
the convent to come marching on the stairs to send the
whole convent trembling to the basement with the pounding of those steeldrums and they whistles blowing and
they shackshacks shaking when all of a sudden the door
burst open and into the room come marching the complete
band of angels dragging they cloud of dust behind them
singing surrounding the bed one with a sheep and some
straw in he hands and the next is pulling a goat on a string
each with they wings flapping and they halos of coathan-
gers bouncing on top they heads just as Sister Robin Clark
reach between my legs to pull out this child and she bend
down quick to bite off the cordstring to hand her over to
the oldman dress up head-to-toe in tinpaper shining
beautiful as the angel Gabriel himself, and he lift her up
slow still steaming from out my womb up above he head
singing *Gloria! Gloria in excelsis Deo, Gloria!* as the earth
stop to hold she breath now for Gabriel to throw back he
head and announce she name: *Magdelena Divina.* Ay Dios
mío singon! Before I can even have a chance now to realize
how happy I am for only an instant when all those lovely
angels of heaven have already disappear theyself leaving
behind them only the cloud of dust to choke us, and no
sooner do I look in the face of this negrita cocoachild
already sucking at my breast when some poison pass from
out she mouth to penetrate my blood, and Sister Robin
Clark and Sister Alicia have to hold on each to a leg quick

and pull her way, because this child is so ugly I only want
to pitch her out the window. Ugly is ugly this cocoachild
is ugly like a putu, like a sucked mango seed, with the little
brown head the shape of an old mildew cocoapod and the
funny black fuzz stick up on the top that every time they
even try to bring her near by me I start to scream and bawl
and spit one set of curses on them to pelt her quick in the
sea, that now they have have to think up something
straight way to do with this child and they even give her to
Barto to carry her home heself, but that same afternoon
Barto have to return the child again as soon as he discover
the little bitch Myna boiling her like the googleeye-fish in
the big pot of sopa pescado, because this cocoachild is *so*
ugly they couldn't find *nobody* to take her up a-tall that in
the end Papa God have get He wish as my sisters didn't
have no choice but to drop her *blooppoops* on the doorstep
of one of those families of callaloos living in Suparee, that
those people are always happy to take up any kind of
cocoamonkey and love them no matter how ugly it is, and
my sisters turn round quick to bolt before those callaloos
can have a chance to change they mind. But of course all
this is only another one of those swindles of Papa God that
I should have know better, because when those thirteen
long years are finish at last and Magdalena appears again
from out the smoke standing at the top of St Maggy
Cathedral steps with the stamp of a Hindu on she forehead
and she temples and she underarms all dripping down in
red blood, she is the most *beautiful* woman this island have
ever see and I know her straight way because just like all
the saints she is mark by the passion of Christ that she can
no pass water through she skin like a soursop squeezing in
cheesecloth but only the sweet sweat of sacred passionate
blood, and I push through the crowd running boldface up
the cathedral steps fullpelt past that mammapoule Chief of
Police already looking for somebody to shoot soon as
there is blood fresh in the air to smell, and I fall down on

my knees at Magdalena feet standing above me looking down with the sun shining full in she face when all of a sudden that whole big crowd of people laughing and bawling with they schoolboy-bombs exploding drop to a quick dead-quiet, with all of them staring up at her cokeeeye with they mouths hanging open like they seeing a diablesse standing before them, all watching up at her untying the capra from off she shoulder passing it out between she legs unwinding it slow to expose sheself naked to the waist with my heart beating the six breaths of that clock in those eyes again, as she reach out slow to take up my hand pressing it gentle against she belly that I can feel for the first time this child promise from Papa God so many ages ago that he is already beating inside. Salve Regina Mater misericordiae vita dulcedo et spes nostra salve! That same night I am lying in my bed rolling my beads trying to make myself *miserable* as possible to see if maybe this time I can make Papa God the bigassfool, but of course I should have know better than any of that because no sooner have I finish thrashing in the sheets a little bit and pounding my breast putting loud goatmouth on myself now with all those mea culpas before I have gather enough courage to close my eyes and drop asleep, when straight way Barto appear sitting byside me in the bed holding my hand gentle telling me again just as always how much Papa God does love you and Magdalena both, but by now I have learn to speak English perfect as the Queen so there is no chance for no more confusion to believe none of *that* cacashat, and I tell him please to carry you ass with all those fakeyfake condolences because I don't want no shit stinking up my doorstep thank you so please hurry and come to the point, and now Barto change he tune of course to tell me again how Papa God have decide the time is no yet ripe for this child, and He already take him way. Ay Dios mío cabron! I am so viekeevie again to hear this thing that before Barto can have a chance to dissolve way heself I bite down on he hand so hard I take off he thumbfinger in one and I spit it back at him like a fat slug twitching in a pool of blood in the bed that when I wake up the following morning to discover myself again swimming in all those bloodstain sheets of misery that is my life in this world, all I can do is jump up out my bed and run to Magdalena to take her up silent tender in my arms and try my best to console her, because of course there is no way for me to communicate to her in sign-language how Papa God have promise to send her He child again as there is no even a single word that I can say to her in no kind of language that don't make sense to her a-tall, but Magdalena is only smiling up at me peaceful as ever like if somehow as always she know everything calm and perfect already, so I decide the only thing for we to do is sit down right now to teach weself to speak. I run cross to the school for that big firstform textbook with the red paste-board cover the size of a gravestone and the letters tall as you finger because where it come from in America everything is big so, and I open it up half resting on Magdalena lap and half on my own with the two of us sitting happy together side-by-side, and I turn to the first page pronouncing it slow: SEE SPOT RUN! Now I point to the picture of the little potcake running happy at the bottom, and I pronounce it again: *potcake, perro, chien, canis!* And Magdalena smile now pointing to the picture sheself: *potcake, kutta, kanga, wa-roon!* I turn to the next page pronouncing it slow again: SUPERMAN WAS BORN ON THE PLANET KRIPTON! And I point to the picture flying cross the top: *Papa God, Dios, Dieu, Deus!* And Magdalena smile again pointing to the picture sheself: *Papa God, Shiva, Rama, Ogoun!* They are the *happiest* days of my life that I thought those quiet peaceful mornings of Magdalena and the big red yankee-schoolbook would have go on forever, that before we can even realize what have hit us when already we have teach

weself three or four different languages fluid as two
parrots in a stinkingtoe tree even though of course we still
can't say nothing worth a fart to each other despite that we
have translate Superman into every tongue know to the
world beside Sanskrit, but of course I begin to suspect
some swindle soon as that mammapoule Gomez arrive in
the middle of the night with he five policemen to bust
down the door with two quick blows of they bootoos, and
he climb the stairs leading them marching soldierfile
straight to Magdalena room because somehow just like
everything else he know already exactly where it is, and he
leave one there post in front she door with the others each
to hold down an arm or a leg for him to do he nastiness
with he strawbasket full to the brim overflowing with
silkfigs and little sweet sicrieyeas and mokos and imported
yankee chicitas and gromichellies and mataburos and long
green skinnywinny gumagallas and big black boiseyboy
hardplantains and every kind of banana that you could
imagine to push up inside there and such and such and so
and so, because of course it is a well establish fact publish
by every jamet-jagabat from Blanchisseuse to End of the
World Rock and farther that this Chief of Police is a tantee
with he toetee the size of a whistle that he can't even stand
up to do nothing a-tall like a squingy little zandolee lizard
sleeping in the shade between he legs, like the limp green
guts of a calibash hanging down, and he only like to push
up he fingers inside there and sniff them little bit and lick
them and play he schoolboy monkeygames with he bananas and he plantains and so, but when this Chief of Police
turn round again to bolt out the convent before the first
five minutes are finish I feel a jolt on my backside like the
jookerfish jook me, because now I know something very
serious is wrong. Of course I am assemble here below in
this chapel with all my sisters sitting holding hands
together *Domenee-ka-nee-ka-nee-ka oh my Domenee-ka-neek!*
that in truth we can no help weself from giggling little bit

to picture this scene that is going on upstairs even though
of course we feel bad enough for this trial Magdalena must
endure and I can only hope the mammapoule don't get
carried way with none of he hard plantains that can be a
very dangerous thing and no joke a-tall because let me tell
you I have see it happen with my nuns before, but when he
turn round again marching out from the convent quick so
before the first five minutes are finish I put a fast stop to all
that neeka-neeka business and I order them instead down
on they knees to pronounce a hard *novena*, and I take off
running up the stairs to find Magdalena kneeling on the
ground to gather up all this big basket of frustration that is
scatter cross the room, but when I ask her in signlanguage
as if to say what the ass is wrong child? she only smile up
at me calm as ever standing to take up my hand leading me
over quiet to she bed, and she unwind the capra lying
down with she legs open up to press my hand gentle the
both of us feeling together like two blind dumb-deafmutes
reading out loud in a book of braille, that I can see for the
first time this veil of the church she pussy is hiding secret
inside. Ay Dios mío shitong! Straight way I realize the
serious danger of this thing that all I can think to do is
dress her up quick in the wedding-nundress and pelt her
down the stairs to pledge she vows with that wedding ring
jam loud on she finger, because *that* is the only thing that
might save sheself from all these wajanks already boiling
over soon as they smell this cork inside there because let
me tell you *I* know them good enough, and manmen is a
toetee is a toetee and nothing more than a stinking wet
dripping toetee that there is nothing on the face of this
dark earth could save poor Magdalena from she fate, and
before the week finish the whole tribe hold her by the
swamp fighting down each other to find out who is the
one to bust it first at how many strokes, but of course it is
only the cojones of that wajank on top her that burst in my
own hands with all those bassabassas holding on to they

own eggs now like if they are make from gold to take off running in a bolt. Aye Dios mío cabron! Now I am distress again that I can no think what to do to protect this helpless defenceless child, and of course I know Papa God good enough and He is a shitong as always that he would never even raise up He little finger to help her so why the ass should I waste my breath to bother asking Him? that in the end I have no choice but to go to you house to question Barto. Of course the little chucha Myna is there ready waiting for me by the frontdoor to greet me with one set of bawling about how you could be Barto whore if you want and St Michael own and the whole league of heavenly archangels and Papa God too in that big fancy jookhouse you have there disguise as a nunconvent, but you will *never* step you foot cross *my* doorstep to come here inside *my* house no even until the ends of the earth! but of course all that is nothing more than a fart of hot air *pfft-pfft-pfft* and I only have to put one little cuteye on her to send her running to bury sheself in the bamboo growing cross the street, and I climb the stairs to find Barto sitting there at he desk in the library reading in he big black book and studying he face in the picture, but before I can even have a chance to open my mouth to pronounce the question he answer me already straight way because just like everybody else he know everything already, and he tell me of course the thing for we to do is to marry off Magdalena straight way to that mammapoule Chief of Police. Barto explain to me how Gomez is the only one able to protect her proper with he seven bootoo-policemen, and since he is a tantee with he toetee the size of a whistle that it can no even stand up a-tall to make even a little tweettweet as you know good as everybody else in the whole Caribbean then there is no way possible for him to do her no harm a-tall, and Magdalena can remain there with Gomez in the police barracks the three or four months until the child begins to show heself because soon

as those bassabassas see her haveen they will all think of
course straightway that churchveil is bust sure as
groundglass-on-madbull-kitestring which of course will
put a quick finish to all this wild frenzy of wajanks, and
then she can run from Gomez and return to you here in the
convent happy as two parrots in a fryingpan, and Magdalena can bear Papa God she child. But now bubbles is
bursting in my ears again to ask him if it is true as you say
Barto gracias a Dios Papa God have send Magdalena He
child again, and straightway Barto answer me smiling yes,
I can tell you for a fact she is haveen again and sure enough
just as you say the father is no other this time then Papa
God Heself, but that don't help neither of us a fart and we
are both still swimming in hotwater so the only thing for
you to do now is go quick to that Chief of Police and slap
the blame on him, and that way he will have no choice but
to take her up. But of course I am no bigassfool and I raise
the obvious objection to this swindle straightway that who
the ass is booobooloops enough to believe in they right head
this mammapoule Chief of Police could make any popo
a-tall much less the tantie mampoule heself, and that is
when Barto think up the brainful idea for me to go first to
the same oldman Salizar who is the Warrahoon bushdoctor straight out of the jungle that he don't know he
backside from a hole-in-the-ground, and soon as he examine Magdalena he will write up the certificate straightway saying of course without any questions that she is
haveen by Gomez, because of course just like everybody
else Salizar see him bust down the door of the convent
Sunday midnight gone, and as soon as Salizar writes out
this certificate that mammapoule Gomez will be good-as-
goat-in-the-gutter standing before the altar. But when
Magdalena comes running to me again from out of those
police barracks no even two months later to tell me for the
second time how she child have disappear again, I can only
fall down on my knees and swear to Papa God that first

thing soon as I reach up in heaven before I even look round
to hug up none of my family and kiss them, I will crack
You big cojones and scramble them in peppersauce like the
huevos of a cockfowl. Ay Dios mío singon! Now I am
distress again thinking Magdalena will have to wait those
ten long years like me before Papa God can make up he
head longlast to give her back she child, because of course
how can I even imagine that only seven months from now
she will be lying dead already in the bed cover in the slime
of blood and green caca with the child already cut from out
she belly by a scissors, mea culpa! with the whole of
Corpus Christi already waiting there in front the hospital
one on top the next laughing and bawling for that little
baboo to hear them and come running pushing he bicyclecar through the mud already raining spilling shaving ice
like he catch vaps to send them all licking licking they
tongues green and purple and yellow like this is *one* big
pappyshow going on now with this mammapoule pounding down the door and that bushdoctor Brito Salizar
climbing in through the window already bawling Na-me-
na-na-ha! Na-me-na-na-ha! when little can they know that
behind that same hospital door they own sweet saint is
dead in the bed already with she child beating breathing
alive in my own arms and you poor daddy so confuse now
red to the elbows dripping with green caca kneeling down
between she legs he nose press up against she pussy that I
can show him now official for the first time at the last
minute just as Barto have instruct me explicit only the
night before this veil of the church she pussy is hiding
secret inside that little hospital room with all those fregando feathers of copra already gusting back and forth again
like a blizzard, mea culpa, mea maxima culpa! because he,
was Papa God own sweet instrumento de intercesión cé
leste de ce monde humain appearing to me again the same
night telling me just as always how all these trials you and
Magdalena are having to bear are nothing more then Papa

God own stubborn way to test is test He only testing you strength because you know Him good as anybody else, and He is nothing more than a miserable oldman that He don't like to trust nobody in nothing a-tall but now He have make up He head sure certain longlast He is ready to give Magdalena back He child and this time there can be no possible mistake, because this time He is sending Barto *heself* here to Magdalena in flesh and in blood just as He have send him here to you youself in this same room in this same bed thirteen years ago, because the fact is that Papa God have give Magdalena the gift of this churchveil like if it is made from castiron that no kind of manmen could never push heself inside *only* to allow for this miracle of sacred intercession through that heavenly instrument of this angel of the earth Barto, but now I am puzzle again thinking it very suspicious that Barto is speaking of heself now like another third person as if he is some kind of make-up storybook character belonging to real life instead of the paperback novel sleeping on the shelf in the supermarket side-by-side with the Birdseye frozen vegetables and the tins of Kingchung Chinee food and therefore this whole big confusion is nothing more than a fiction of you own monkey-imagination ready to explode, but of course Barto is speaking in English again and this is a funny language without any verbs about it a-tall that it is always impossible to know who is saying what and when and where, so the next morning soon as I wake up I decide that this time I am no taking no chances on no blind faith, and I sit down straightway to compose the letter to Barto SUMMONING THE APPEARANCE OF YOU FANTOME IN THE SQUARE MAÑANA 12 O'CLOCK PM PRECIS ON THIS DAY 20 OF DOMINGO SEPTIEMBRE ANNO DOMINI NOSTRI DEUS MIDNIGHT NISCHIT NISCHIT NISCHIT and I close my eyes to forge the signature official of PHILLIPE GOMEZ DOMINGO CHIEF OF POLICE ORDER OF HER

MAJESTY SEASCOUTS. But when Barto appear in the square the following night with Magdalena and me already byside weself with excitement waiting here looking down secret through that window of my own bedroom just as Barto heself have instruct me explicit only the night before, it is as if he is still dreaming and he don't even know why the ass he have come only playing one set of schoolboy-monkeygames pelting rockstones at the pigeons sleeping on the plume of Sir Walter that soon I begin to lose my patience as I am no standing here waiting for him to decide now he want to pitch marbles, because let me tell you *I* am a woman that nobody could never stop me from nothing in life once I have made up my head no even me *myself*, that before I can know what my hands are doing I have turn round already to tie up the white kerchief from round my neck in a blindfold over Magdalena eyes that I can take hold with both fists and a clean conscience *fripps!* on the muslin of that nundress *frapps!* to tear it *frupps!* stripping her down head-to-toe in the blink-of-an-eye with three hard pulls, and I shove her out naked on the balcony. Just then the clock begin to strike with Magdalena standing there beautiful as ever she long black hair blowing gentle in the breeze of that big moon shining down on her that soon as Barto see her standing there he remember again straightway exactly why he have come already strip down naked too *up* the wall *on* the balcony *in* the bed before those twelve bells can even have a chance to strike theyself so in a hurry now he can no even see me standing here at the end of this bed looking down again through the dark murky water of my dream with my feet to my knees in the mud of my own terrible passion without escape, here looking down again through the dark water seeing myself again my own beautiful daughter struggling helpless here in the mud of my own hopeless longing to lie again beneath my own husband-father-son-of-my-son in nomine Patris Filii et Spiritus

Sancti, with my eyes close still to feel the long blade of He infernal fire thrust up stiff between my legs to sever my body in two my feet numb unyielding again in the icecold water shimmering clear on my back breast press warm against the soft black earth nipples head spilling melting back slow behind me sinking deep again beneath the dark water freezing to sting my cheeks burning until it begins to rise again slow up toward the surface floating bright mirror shining upside-down from behind me below me before me now my head breaking suddenly free of the water somewhere between my legs rising slow in the air higher and higher to pull my whole body complete inside-outside the pelt hairy of some small animal soft glistening bright crimson steaming outside-inside before I can glance down quick to see myself already the tiny black insect tumbling spindling far below in the current swirling my head rising faster and faster up through the clouds sreaming continuous cool milk frothy white cross my cheeks until it is only the infinite brilliant blueglass sea of He iris eye to push harder *oy* only a little *oy oy oy* to stretch to touch the tip of my finger to scalding aching sun, and the starburst of silver flyingfish petals bursting out sudden from below the bow falling back slow again to the water flaming soft through the air floating on the ground again in this slow-burning immortelle sepulchre of fire, and the drop of sweat sweet on He shoulder cool on my tongue as the teardrops of heart-shape tips of anthuriums growing rose colour now to be pierce again now by He white sword here in the marsh at edge of the swamp growing tall byside us, and the crown of thorns crawling cross the rocks and the scourge of sin and the promise of hope and the children running holding hands screaming together in the red blood morning Deum de Deo, lumen de lumine, Deum verum de Deo vero *oy* chanter a Dieu que baja del cielo *oy oy oy* a recibir su alma *oy yo-yuga yo-yuga ba-damba-da-bamba oy oy oy oy oy!*

I COULD NO LONGER listen to what I was hearing. I could not possibly assimilate at the time these impossible things which I have come now, many years later, to accept as simple, verifiable facts: that Magdalena was the daughter of Mother Maurina by Barto. That this frogchild was the son of Magdalena Divina by her own father. Exactly how these events occurred I still cannot be sure. That they *did* occur, I have come to believe now with little doubt.

At that moment, however, I could not possibly listen to what I was hearing. My senses, like my new suit, had long reached the point of saturation, and I had long stopped listening. And yet I continued to sweat. And still this Mother Maurina continued to speak. Because it was no longer the listener Mother Maurina needed, not now, not any longer: now she needed only the story. I, the listener, the eighteen-year-old boy sitting there on the pew in that little chapel of St Maggy Convent, hearing the fifteen bells of that clock ringing now across the square without listening, without counting them – without even worrying to think that *it is already 5:30 a.m., with that mailboat already ready to leave without you now in only a quick half-hour, so what the ass you doing sitting here not even listening to this crackpot oldwoman?* – because I, the eighteen-year-old boy, no longer existed.

I knew that. I had actual physical proof that all this was nothing more than a figment of my imagination. Because if those wings on Mother Maurina's headdress were real, then I was not. And now I did something very peculiar. Now I did something never done before in the annals of literature and all the chronicles of man's childish endeavours: I let go of the piece of paper, and I held out my right hand. Slowly, very carefully, I reached and touched my index finger to the pointed tip of my own imagination. I felt it. I touched the tip of that white wing. The farthest extremity of my deepest, most sacred self, and I sat back calmly and took up the piece of paper again, telling myself once more: *It is only a dream. A dream.*

And like the sleeper who is conscious of his dream, I felt some vague control over it, though I knew I possessed none whatsoever. I knew well enough that any idea of authority or even subtle influence was mere illusion, and if I tried to scream now only the muffled, high-pitched sound would come from my throat – as though I were screaming into water; and if I attempted to run from this chapel I would hardly be able to pick up my feet – as though I were trudging through mud. And though I could achieve some sense of momentary calm, reassuring myself that none of this was real, that I did not exist – neither to this woman nor even to myself – I felt sure that in some way I *did* exist. That I must. Because my dream *was* real – not in spite of its eccentricities so much as because of them – more real that reality itself. Even though I had long stopped listening.

And I know now that I was right long before I could have known that I was right. I know now, many years later, that even though I was not listening, I was hearing what Mother Maurina was saying. It was as though through the sensory overload she had managed to tap some source deeper than my conscious mind, deeper than reasoning and touching and actually tasting, because I know now that although I was not listening, I was hearing every word. I was taking it all in, together with every comma and period and grammatical market, scribbling it all down verbatim on a piece of paper already crowded with words: every inflection and tonal variation recorded indelibly on the black surface of my collective unconscious.

Because years later I began to hear Mother Maurina's voice again. First it was only the isolated words: short phrases, fragments of a language which I knew belonged only to her. And as the years progressed and I continued to listen I began to hear whole passages, coming to me from

somewhere out of my childhood – from somewhere out of
that vast storehouse of words and images constantly
disassembled and reassembled and surfacing again mysterious, new – so that now at the end of ninety years of blind
hearing I can sit here and listen to the whole story,
complete, autonomous, told to me in a voice which does
not belong to me, but to her. Before my ears. In my own
eyes.

NOW I AM HAPPY again for the third time in my life
that the only thing remaining is to praise Papa God and
bear Him He child but of course I should have know better
than any of that because before I can even have a chance to
realize how precious is the gift of hope with her in my
arms she head press warm against my breast beating
together so quiet and peaceful for only a moment when all
of those seven months have pass already and Barto appear
to me again for the last time in a week of instructions
explicit every night for seven nights each more terrible and
frightening than the one before and he take up the seventh
candle for the seventh time from the chapelle in the corner
of my room to touch the wick to the flame of he eye and
light it, the last of those seven candles burning now with
one for each of the four cycles of the earth and the fifth for
the five ages of man and the sixth for the six incarnations
of Papa God and the seventh candle for the seventh time
that is burning already to bring us now to the beginning of
the end, and Barto place the candle in the middle of my
forehead at the spot of my third eye as I sleep here in my
bed for me to see now the last of these seven versions of
the same vision each told separate in seven different
languages that this one is my own now belonging only to
me, and I see a woman sitting on a throne wrap up in a
white capra shining like the sun with the moon beneath
she feet and the crown of seven stars on top she head that it

is the seven testimonies to the seven visions of this woman, and I see that she is haveen with child and I hear her cry out to me in my own name with pangs of anguish for the birth of this child but soon as I try to raise my hands to help her I can no even lift them up from my sides as if Satan heself have reach from the bowels of the earth to hold them down that I am so fill with shame and longing I can no help her that I turn my eyes to the ground, and when I raise them up again I see now that she is dead with the great wound ripping slow of itself down from the top to the bottom of she belly and out from this wound come flowing a sea of human blood, and after the sea of human blood there is the sea of green caca and then after that there is a sea of black mud, and out from this sea of black mud appear the child terrible and frightening as the jabjab heself with thirteen different heads and in each of he thirteen heads is five mouths and three eyes with five horns and a ruby shining at the end of each one, and therefore the composition of this child is thirteen with a division of three that is five and three and five which in truth is one with a division of two, and I see this jabjab bend down slow with he thirteen heads and he five mouths in each one to drink up the whole of that sea of black mud and the sea of green caca and the sea of human blood, and when he have finish all that I see him go to the woman and close up with he hand this wound that have rip down cross she belly that I am so startle to see this thing now I can no help but let loose a cry in amaze that straight way he hear me standing there behind him and he turn round to look at me with all those thirteen different heads and the three eyes in each one always watching at you at any one moment in the same endless confusion of place and time, that he is so terrible frightening I can no help but turn my eyes to the ground again and when I raise them up I see now that the woman on the throne with the moon beneath she feet and the crown of seven stars on top she head have come back

to life again and she is living again, and I see the child
climb up on the throne to sit in she arms that he could suck
from she breast with the thirteen different heads all
growing together now fusing together in one and the five
mouths and three eyes and the thirteen multiples of five
horns each have all dissolve way to nothing with only a
single big ruby shining bright in the middle of he forehead
where the third eye used to be, and now I see that this
terrible jabjab have transform heself to the most beautiful
of creatures in all this big world of manmen and monkeys
that I can no help but fall down on my knees to adore him
and sing him praise, and now I see that five others have
come to kneel on the ground byside me praying to the
woman and the child and the one at my right side is a
confuse youngboy, and now I see many others coming to
pray to the woman and the child each with they black
prayerbooks holding in their hands and I see that they are
all of every race and religion kneeling down together to
open up they prayerbooks each praying to the woman and
the child in they own separate tongue in they own special
kind of ritual and she can understand them all, and I see the
woman accept them every one and she have give to many
great gifts of miracles and visions with many more people
coming and more still again and I see that the number of
we have reach to one-hundred-fortyfour-thousand, and
just as we have all begin to sing together each from we
own prayerbook each in we own tongue with the youngboy kneeling byside me still looking round confuse astonish that he could never believe so many people would
come and we are all very happy singing together, when
just then Barto take up the candle again from off my
forehead and he put it inside he mouth for the seventh time
transforming he tongue to the two-edge dagger of fire that
he can give to me the last of those seven instructions
explicit every night for seven nights each more terrible and
frightening than the one before, and he call out to me in a

voice loud like a trumpet blowing saying that no only
must this child live for only three days as he have tell me
two nights before on the fifth night, and no only must
Magdalena sheself die without ever looking in the face of
she child as he have tell me the night before on the sixth
night, but now Barto look down on me with he eyes each
a flame of fire and he tongue the two-edge dagger burning
and he tell me how both Magdalena and she child must die
beneath the thrust of you own hand that I am so stun
frighten now to hear this thing I can only lie there a stone
petrify in my sleep as if it is me who is already dead, and I
look up terrify at Barto taking out the blade of he tongue
to transform it again to the candle of reality now for him
to put it for the seventh time to burn in the centre of my
forehead at the spot of my third eye before he can dissolve
way heself leaving me again alone sleeping in my bed of
misery looking up cokeeeye now at this flame burning
slow in the centre of my forehead knowing good enough
the length of that wick is the only time remaining before I
must wake up to do this terrible duty with the wax
running hot down the two sides of my forehead along my
temples to fill up both my ears slow with hot scalding wax
overflowing now to drip drop by drop from the tips of my
earlobes shining liquid silver earings until the candle have
dissolve way already to nothing now with only the quick
spark at the end of the wick in the middle of my forehead
and the little puff of white smoke to extinguish itself that
now there is no time left remaining with Magdalena
already calling me knocking quiet at the door that all I can
do is jump up quick to run to that door to throw the bolt
my back press hard sweating hot against the lock wood-
door surface sliding down slow along it now to sit in a
slouch on the cold concrete flooring trying to catch my
breath when only a minute later that piece of paper is
slipping silent slow beneath the crack of that door byside
me lying there on the ground tatter and yellow now wet

with the sweat of you own fingers in you own hand pass
on to you now belonging longlast to you alone and I grab
up this paper quick with my hand trembling to read the
words of this suicide letter that is the complete entire
history of Magdalena and she child and they birth and they
death and you and me and all of this island of Corpus
Christi that now you will carry it as far as America cross
the sea for them to hear of her too and cross the sea and
come to pray to her and she child that the number of we
can grow to one-hundred-fortyfour-thousand that now I
have finish reading this sacred suicide-prayerletter and I
press the paper wet against my breast sitting here alone on
this cold concrete flooring of my room with my back press
hard sweating against the lock door and I raise up my eyes
to heaven praying Papa God Lord Dios Dieu Dius give me
strength now to do this You holy will and I jump up from
the ground to throw open the bolt to take off running
down the stairs out the door cross the square along the
street to the hospital my white veils flying wild in the
wind the door open wide struggling now to catch my
breath holding on desperate to the wall stumbling slow
back behind inside this little operating room to find you
daddy gone already disappear for me to do my duty and
Magdalena alone by sheself kneeling naked on the ground
byside the bed she hands fold soft together she lips
whispering quiet a silent Ave Maria until she see me
standing there now holding on to the wall my face white
murder wet dripping down cold sweat my temples pounding standing now slow supporting sheself on the side of
the bed to take up the pillow turning to hold it out to me
now as if it is an offering for me to take it up slow again in
my own strange hands watching her lie down soft in the
bed and cross sheself and close she eyes for me to touch my
lips gentle to she forehead the last breath of my long life
before I must look up to heaven to press that pillow down
hard down on top she face with all my strength my weight

pressing down hard on top the pillow hard on top she face
my eyes still looking up to heaven feeling her struggling
now beneath me my hands she hands we hands holding
tight together clutching hard round my two wrists stiff
that soon she grip begins to slip way slow for me to step
back now looking down on my own beautiful daughter
dead now waiting now for you daddy to come back only a
minute later to take the child from out she belly alive now
dead now too again beneath the terrible duty of my own
strange hand horrible strangle too just as I am told explicit
by Him Heself only because He know in He own dark
heart that I am a weak and foolish oldwoman blind enough
to believe now for one-hundred-and-thirteen years endur-
ing alone the misery of this earth that now I am happy to
die fearless knowing no even He could think up a death
worse then this life.

THERE WAS SILENCE for a moment before the clock
began to strike, startling me again, but again I could not
turn to look out at it across the square. Again I could only
sit staring straight ahead – incredulous, confounded.
Looking at those white wings of Mother Maurina's white
nunhabit-headdress now for me the physical sign in the
real world of my own unreality. The necessary symbol of
my own imagination and the truth of my fictional self, as I
sat sweating staring at those two white wings stretched
out before me, sprawling, because now they were disappearing again. They were folding up. Dissolving back
inside that white pasteboard-headdress with the same
mechanical movement, the same automative mechanism.
Segment by segment, notch by notch, slowly disappearing
now with every strike of the clock and the almost imperceptible soft static sound of a kerchief pulled quickly from
the back pocket: *zup, zup, zup, zup, zup.* Until now they
were gone, vanished completely, dissolved altogether to

thrust me headfirst back into the world of reality.

But as I sat watching Mother Maurina getting up slowly from her pew, I realized suddenly that those two wings – despite the fact that they were a figment of my own imagination – those two wings belonged legitimately to the real world together with all Mother Maurina's ranting and raving and exantaying in a way in which I did not. I: the eighteen-year-old boy sitting there on that pew sweating in my new suit. I: the ninety-year-old physician sitting here behind this desk still holding this wet murder suicide-prayerletter staring out of this window into the darkness of this black sea. The two of us watching together now through the same single cyclopseye as Mother Maurina stands slowly from her pew. I did not belong to reality for the same reason that those two imaginary wings *did*. Because the fact is that those two wings contained only five segments each. Not six: five partitions only with one for every chime of the clock. And now I did turn to look out across the square at the clock at the top of Government House. Now I did look to verify that it was true: that time had actually turned a circle before my eyes, that it had truly turned back on itself having held Mother Maurina and me captive in a fold of its dark cloth for a full hour, that that mailboat had not already left without me, that those two white wings created out of my imagination were right in a way in which the real world was wrong, false, somehow confused: because the fact is that it was only five o'clock.

Five o'clock: still, now, again. With the first light of dawn filtering into the square as I stood sinking deep into the mud of my grandfather's old hardbacks. Standing there sweating in my new suit with my new clip-on bowtie biting at my throat, watching Mother Maurina disappearing slowly into the darkness of that narrow corridor leading out of the vestibule, feeling my feet numb and unyielding again in the mud of my new washykongs

in my old jesusboots, hearing the water on the rocks and
the breeze blowing cool across my wet skin in the leaves of
the old tamarind tree in my own backyard, smelling the
stale odours of stagnant incence and musty newspapers
and too-sweet eucalyptus and smouldering still water,
standing here holding the finally empty bottle, seeing
myself again with my baggy navyblue school shortpants
billowing around my hips, a young boy alone at the edge
of this vast swamp stretching out black as far as the
horizon, an oldman tired looking down again through the
dark water again, thinking, not understanding, believing:
He is alive. Swimming. As I watch his long angular legs
fold, snap taut, and propel him smoothly through the
water; snap, glide; snap, glide; and the frogchild disappears into the clump of quiet mangrove banyans.

II

A PIECE OF POMMERAC

1

Magdalena Tells
Her Story

SUDDENLY I REALIZED who his mother was. Suddenly I knew, and I was afraid to turn around. Standing here shin-deep in the mud looking down through the dark water, watching the grey cloud rising in a mushroom towards the surface, spreading out, and settling back slowly to the bottom where he had disappeared between the mangrove banyans, thinking: *He is the child of Magdalena sheself. Magdalena Divina, Mother of Miracles, Black Virgin of Maraval!* Exactly what inspired this leap of my childhood imagination I could not say, simply that it occurred, at the precise moment that frogchild disappeared behind the cloud of mud. How I could be so certain of this fact which I could not explain, which I knew to be impossible, I had no idea, simply that I believed it even before I turned around. Because now I did not have to see in order to believe. Now I did not have to understand. And I realized at that moment I was better off not seeing – that it was far easier for me to believe the things I had never experienced, all the impossible stories I had never felt the need to understand – because I realized at that moment my life was not my own. I belonged to someone else: the believing was beyond my control.

It was as though my thirteen years of childhood had brought me to that moment as I stood watching the

frogchild swim away, as though in that frogchild I had
seen for the first time that the world was not an extension
of me, but that I was an extension of the world. My
aloneness had been suddenly violated, split in two by that
swimming frogchild, as though in that frogchild I had
suddenly seen myself, my other self, the constant compan-
ion of my on-going silent conversation, my twin brother.
I had seen the other I. Not the imagined I but the I of my
imagination: the imagining I. The third eye in the middle
of my forehead through which I saw myself – the Hindu
tilak in the centre of my consciousness with which I heard
myself, my essential self, God within – the other I which I
had thought for thirteen years was contained in me,
intrinsically and inextricably bound up in me, but which I
realized now did not belong to me at all. Because I had
stood there and watched him swim away. Now I realized
that the same power, controlling me from without, was
manipulating me also from within. That is why it was so
potent, why it was so deceptive. That is why I had
remained oblivious to it for thirteen years, why I was
afraid to turn around now: now I realized that anything
could happen in this dream of my life, in this dream of my
dream. Anything, and I would have no choice but to
believe. To surrender myself to this primal power.

I was afraid to turn around, even though I had looked
forward to that moment from the time I'd set foot on the
trace toting the bottle. I had wished for nothing more than
that instant in which I could drop the empty glassbottle
and turn quickly and run. I had seen it over and over
already. Envisioned myself in my own imagination and
planned it out exactly as it would happen, again and again
until it was as if it had already happened. But now that it
was time to let my imagination slip smoothly beneath the
veil of reality, now that I was ready to close this closed
episode of my life, to finish with this quick story, now I
was afraid even to let go of this empty bottle. Because the

truth is I'd never imagined that frogchild could still be alive. I'd never preconceived that, never planned for that.

And now that I had seen him swim away with my own eyes – so suddenly I could not have held him back even if I were capable, so impulsively I could not have stopped to question it even if I had wanted – now I was afraid to let go of this empty bottle. Now I realized that not even my own imagination belonged to me. It was as though in that moment the sanctity of thirteen years of quiet solitude were suddenly profaned, desecrated before my eyes. As though in that moment my supple white wings – my grotesque, strangely-compelling frogchild – were reduced to nothing more than the obzockee empty bottle. The empty glassbottle which was all that connected me to reality now, all that assured me I had seen what I had seen and that I was alive within the confines of this dream of my life, this dream of my dream which did not even belong to me, this empty glassbottle to be filled again with nothing less than reality itself. Because I had seen that frogchild of my imagination swim away with my own eyes.

Now that the bottle was finally empty, now as I stood shin-deep in the mud looking down through the dark water, now I realized I had not reached the end, but only the beginning: my story had opened up of itself into something I'd never expected it to be. And I knew well enough that even if it were possible for me to take a single step forward – even if it were possible for me to dive forward into that dark water and swim forever, far away, as far as America – I would only find myself stuck still deeper in the mud of this interminable swamp. I could never escape it now. Now that I believed it already without asking or wanting to believe it; and I knew the same power which decided that he would swim away whether I wanted him to swim away or not, was not about to do me the sweet kindness of killing me off quickly now,

on this Corpus Christi Day, this day before my thirteenth
birthday, in this already too-prolonged suspended instant
– of dropping a boulderstone out the sky on top my head –
that it was not even about to condescend even so much as
to allow me to run home now to attend my grandmother's
funeral. Now that it is impossible for me to let go of this
empty glassbottle. Now that I have actually touched my
index finger to the fingertip of those white wings, and I
know the only way to find that frogchild still hiding
somewhere alive in the labyrinth of those innumerable
mangrove banyans, is to turn around and surrender myself
unconditionally to this primal power – to surrender myself
up to this monkey of my imagination and let him speak,
even in his own impenetrable monkey-language – to turn
around and go back to the beginning once more. Back to
the beginning of the beginning again and beyond the
beginning. Now that I must spend the rest of my life
trying to understand how it could have been possible, how
I could have seen it. Now I am afraid, because I know that
ultimately I must fail. I have realized too soon that no
matter how far I go back, explanation will still be impossible. I have realized too soon that failure is the point of all
this. That failure is the meaning of all this confusion.

　　Standing here looking down through the dark water,
watching the cloud of mud mushrooming up towards the
surface, involuting as it spreads out, and settling back
slowly to the bottom where he had disappeared between
the mangrove banyans, thinking: *But if Magdalena is he
mummy then he daddy must be Papa God Heself. And if you and
he is brothers then He is you daddy and she is you own true
mummy too!* With the cold glassbottle pressed up hard
against my chest my arms wrapped tight hugging around
it, my feet in the mud of my new washykongs in my
grandfather's father's old hardbacks in the mud of my old
jesusboots, the stagnant incense and the musty newspapers
and the wind in the tamarind trees of the blueblack

tonguelike leaves tumbling slowly over ripples of the greengray inward-swirling water, the sun hidden behind the dark clouds, as I curl the toes of my right foot hard to hold on tight to my jesusboot, pulling my leg partially up out of thick mud sucking shifting my weight manoeuvring my leg around slowly abandoning myself now to step suddenly hard my jesusboot pressing up to meet the sole of my foot becoming firm somewhere in the darkness behind me. Then the left. One leg and then the other again and again until slowly I have managed carefully to take three or four backward steps forward. One leg and then the other backwards and forwards now until slowly I have managed carefully to turn completely around. As I raise my eyes from the dark knee-deep water floating in consecutive mudclouds rising slowly stirred up by my shifting feet, mushrooming up toward the surface silver now for a lost instant to reflect the last of my childhood features before I look up to see in the distance the figure of a woman walking down from the church slowly towards me, slowly along the path of the dust rising a cloud continuous smooth around her bare feet, as though she is walking in air, her white gown bright the beads of her rosary wooden big as marbles tied around her waist, slowly beneath the samaan tree to cross the plot of green grass her long dark hair her umber burntblack skin, slowly towards me standing now there at the edge of the water rippling her gentle eyes, comforting lips, the crimson mark on her forehead, calmly now her arms outstretched palms upwardheld to caress me softly, her own soft voice.

WHEN HEAVEN, stars,
Sun and moon show forth.
When de earth appear.

When de waters divide, and de land present sheself.
When from de essence of five primordial elements,
A great egg is born. It is de five senses.
From de yolk of dis great egg two others come forth,
And dese each to birth give back dey firstfirst five,
So now dey are thirteen. Dey are five and three and five,
And de one in de middle, a conch egg,
Does separate from de others and divide up in two.
From each of dese limbs grow, all perfect perfect,
And dey become a man and a woman so extraordinary,
    beautiful,
Together dey seem de fulfillment of every desire.
Dey are de Lord Shiva and He Queen Kali-Mai,
Reigning in heaven together!

Many ages later,
As de earth yield forth unto she fourth yuga,
Kali and Shiva dey did mischief in heaven,
Flesh sapodilla sweet, sweet mango doodoo!
When at de height of he passion Kali she lips withdraw,
Climb up to holdhold he shoulders
    glissglistening with sweat.
Kali wicked smile at Shiva tender curses,
As Shiva seed spill from de sky!

At dis same time,
    old Raja Janaka is pushploughing he canefield,
Tinpaper hat to protect he gainst Prana harsh rays.
Shiva sacred seed fall in de forrow freshcut behind
    he Ganesha,
Wise coolie-buffalo, giftgiver of readwriting.
And so it happen dat from de dark earth,
    Kali daughter Sita is born,
Child of she daddy curses,
Sweet mummy sweet mischief play!

Not far distant,
On de shore of dat same swampshimmering morning sun,
Old Uncle Valmiki is praying to de samaan, Shyama:
'Sanctussanctussanctusdominusdeus!'
Finish, he lie down neath de sacred tree to rest,
Dere to sweetdream heself a boychild again.
In he dream, de boychild toting an infant,
Same dream he dreaming again dat same oldman again.
Again, St Valmiki hail he youngself.
Question he bout de child.
'Oldman,' de boychild answer,
'Dis popo is you and me together.
All we three persons in one.
Father, body of we mummy, son.'
And with dat, de boychild commend up to he father
     he infant spirit,
Bow down to de sacred samaan tree,
And he sit down to tell Valmiki dis story of heself,
Oldest of oldstories since oldman-Time first begin to
     remember stories,
This ancient legend of Rama, Sita and she child!

On de way to he hermitage-home,
Uncle Valmiki did enter a dark forest.
Dere he spy a manquenk and a diablesse,
Loving up dey loving up together.
Valmiki stop to watch de two beautiful creatures,
When just as dey reach to de rapture of love dey
     lovemaking,
Quicksudden a Warrahoon burst out from de bush:
'Yhwh-yhwh-yhwh-yhwh!'
Shootshooting he shoot he arrowshoot he big big bow!
De arrow pierce de manquenk breast so dat he die,
And de diablesse mourn he too bitter.
Dis vision vex old Valmiki vex.
He cuss up de Warrahoon and take way he arrows,

'Yo-yuga yo-yuga da-bamba!' he bawl,
One-two he break dem in one-two.
Valmiki drive de Warrahoon off.
He continue through de forest.

After a time, de words of Valmiki curse return,
Yo-yuga yo-yuga da-bamba, he think,
Dem words is a poetry dey selfsame-own!
Shackshloka, he decide, I ga call dis nonsense,
As he continue continue he way.
When Valmiki arrive in he hermitage home,
De fourarm brightshining darkskin Kali,
Creator-destroyer of all de universe,
Is waiting fa he in he laboratory.
Valmiki fall to he knees *blooppoops!*
But as he begin to pray,
He thoughts did backfold quick to de dead manquenk,
To de mournful diablesse, and to he new shackshloka.
At dis, sweet Kali smile.
At dis, She speak to old Valmiki soft:
'Is by my will dose cursewords came from out you mouth.
Compose fa me now de whole history of Rama and Sita in
    dat shackshloka,
All de world to speak you language,
All to hear you story sing.
Listen well, and I reveal to you all as yet you do not know,
You story to be true from de firstfirst word to de last!'
Saying dis, blessed Kali, She vanish way.

Valmiki den did seek insight deep into dis story
    of he dream.
He sit down according to he yoga-rita,
He begin to bahkti he bajans,
When through de power of meditation,
He soon see Rama and Sita,
Lakshman and Sumitra, Kaikeyi and old Manthara.

He see Sugriva and Bali, Tara, Hanuman,
Nala and all de noble monkeyhosts.
And de oldman see Ravana too,
Bigbelly, all de monsterous Rakshasas.
He see dem playing, and he see dem mischief-behaving,
Loving up one nother and wagewarring war fa war,
And he see all dat have been, what is coming to come.

Only when he story lie down quiet quiet in he
    imagination,
Red as de roukou red in you palmhand palm,
Clean as de picture you recalling from de sacred book,
Do Valmiki begin to dress it in he new shackshloka.
Soon, he paused to consider how he story might be
    publish abroad.
Fa dis he choose Lakshman,
Closest friend of Rama and brother-by-law,
He choose de physician Kusha,
Eldest son of Rama and Kaikeyi,
And he teach dem de story complete by rote-
    rithmetic,
As dese are happy days,
Fore talk turn taletelling to writereading!
Only when Lakshman and Kusha learn to recite de whole
    poem perfect,
Do Valmiki disguise dem as travelling minstrels,
Masmen to play mas,
And he send dem to Rama ancient city of Ayodhya,
Dere on de island of Kouskosala,
Where dey preparing to fête a great fête with de gods,
Dat great horsefeast, de Ashameda!
And so it is, in dis way,
Rama first hear de telling of he own story!

SO IN DE BEGINNING it happen dat wise Raja Janaka,
Did offer a brideprice fa he beautiful girlchild Sita,
Which man to bend and string de famous bow of Rudra,
Dat arrowbow sacred so, dey did worship it
    a deity proper.
Den one day Prince Rama did chance to chance,
Together with he law-brother Lakshman, ,
Returning dey de slaying of two Rakshasa fierce-dragons,
Pass dey long de trace to Mythmythilia.
Dere de two did reststop-stop, hail to dey Raja Janaka,
Describing dey now de famous bow, dat magical
    gift of Rudra!
Straight way did Rama proudboast he strength to string,
While Janaka, knowing did smile,
Standing he den in pronouncement loud,
Call forth he de bow forthwith!
Now did appear de cart of eighteen turning wheels,
Ten-thousand tall men to tote it long,
And when Prince Rama did strive de bow to string,
It yield he easy enough,
Dat making pappyshow to let fly an arrow,
Froppoops! he break it in two!
Den is all dose spectators breathless-amaze,
Raise dey up Rama tall,
Celebrating he now a god among men,
Processioning he home to Ayodhya!

Now dis Prince Rama is de incarnation of Shiva Heself,
And he did have already fa heself two wives,
Sumitra, and she young-sister, Kaikeyi.
Both dem passionate-beautiful, two batimamselles,
But de forceripe Kaikeyi, face-fairer of de two,
Did suffer she fits of jealousy oui bachac!
Fa dis reason, Rama did send way he first-wife Sumitra,
Living dere den in de hermitage,
Neath de care of she Uncle Valmiki.

Dere Sumitra is happy enough,
She days fillfull with silent prayers,
Until Prince Rama, secret,
Did climb to visit with she in de night!

So now Sita prepare to go to she new father Rama.
She did hope to love she two mothers equal,
But hearing of Kaikeyi madness,
Did go denfore to Sumitra, dere in Valmiki hermitage.
But at dis time, Kaikeyi fits have grow worse still again,
So Rama must caution careful bout he meetings with Sita!
Each Sunday, when she make she pilgrimage-duty
    de great swamp,
Dere to sing she homage to blessèd Shyama,
Dey did meet together, neath de sacred samaan tree!
Each Sunday morning, Rama hold she gentle
    with kind words,
Sita loving he also de softness she eyes,
As by holy law Rama did forbid heself heself,
Soon dey to marry happy, de birth of she thirteen year!

But one Sunday morning, de jelljell Kaikeyi,
Suspecting some mischief in Rama each week
    disappearance,
Did follow secret behind,
Together with she nursemaid Manthara.
At de sight of beautiful Sita, Kaikeyi lose she head.
Would have slay Sita in one,
Have not she nursemaid Manthara,
She power of obeah-science,
Kaponkle Kaikeyi kaponkle *kapooks!* a big boulderstone!
Is den, fa dis selfsame reason, dat sweet-soul Manthara,
Knowing too well she Kaikeyi afflictions,
Did seek some plan to protect de defenceless girlchild Sita.
Dis, with womanly-wit, she advise she mistress:
'Use you female ways, to extract from Rama a boon,

As you know he do love you orangutoon,
You know bout he tanrangee-bangee,
So when in he passion dis boon you distract,
Demand Sita to return she she daddy Janaka!'

But Kaikeyi is thinking sheself keener den dis
    kind boiseyback.
She would not settle simple so to send Sita packing-way.
Kaikeyi did know she Rama good enough,
Know he passion would seek Sita out,
Even in de distant land of Mythmythilia.
Kaikeyi did seek some way to keep Sita from she Rama
    fagood faever,
Little suspecting sheself de instrument of fate,
And so she decide to banish she not to she daddy Janaka,
But to de kingdom of dat same fierce-monster Ravana.
Kaikeyi did hear stories tell of he seven heads,
He thirteen strong arms,
Of he terrible monstermen of war!
To Ravana Kaikeyi would demand Sita to go,
A duration of forty days and forty nights duress,
Dere to remain de prisoner of Ravana and all he Rakshasas,
Knowing no virtue of she, selfsafe could remain!

From Rama dat night Kaikeyi backhold she favours,
Tempting until he reach he heightheight of he passion,
And in dat lost moment, Kaikeyi distract she boon!
After, as he lay well-quiet satisfy,
She sixfold enfolding arms,
Rama did ask gentle what promise she would demand,
And Kaikeyi speak she peace!

Now is Rama sad-trouble distress enough,
Bound by honour to grant Kaikeyi boon,
To offer Sita up to vile Ravana,
Offer she in sacrifice dread, he fierce Rakshasas!

Den did Rama go to consult he law-brother Lakshman,
Presiding at dis time over Rama southmost cocoaestate,
How to settle dis question of honour opposing love,
Which of de two must walk first fore de other?
Den did wise Lakshman study he head hard,
Advice he did give to Rama so:
'Know you well dat woman does always walk
    quiet-thinking fore man,
So too must love always stumble bold,
Fore you ego alterself,
Denfore !et all discussion, all decision,
Fall in de hands of Sita.'

So dat Sunday morning,
As dey lie peaceful neath old Shyama,
Rama did tell Sita he sad story,
Which promise Kaikeyi demand.
But at dis, Sita only smile. At dis, she ask of Rama:
'How can Sita do other, happy, den she Lord
    command she?
Fa does not Rama unknowing speak de duty,
Of Sita husband and father in heaven?'
And with dat, Sita did take up Rama hand,
Dere, pressing gentle,
Two hands to touch together,
Sita pledge to he she virtue!

But Rama could find comfort little enough,
Sita quiet assurance,
He did not understand de workings of dat holy veil,
And dat same night, he fever a passion hot,
He leave he troubling bed, rush to Valmiki hermitage!
Sita, aware by intuition of he distress,
Is waiting fa he on she balcony,
Calling to he with she eyes!

So three days happyhence,
Sita prepare to depart fa de land of Ravana.
Fa dis long journey, she beg de help of faithful Jatayu,
Dat wise cobo brave, living dere den in de hermitage.
Early dat morning, fore Valmiki and Sumitra could wake,
She climb up de back de huge buzzard-bird,
He gentle wings ready dust-flapping!
Sita direct Jatayu direct to de coast,
Up over de mountain of Rishymuka,
Where dey breathstop to hail dey friends Surgriva
    and Hanuman,
Dere discussing plans dey bridge-builder Nala,
Before dey start to cross de sea, far as Ravana
    island of Lanka!
And when Jatayu see dis place where Sita bring he,
When he see de dreamlike Lanka dreaming,
Creation of dat famous archetect, Vishvakarma,
A city wield of mind and not of matter,
Tall goldguilded towers, great glassglistening scrapers,
Jewelglittering churchtemples,
Dey bubbledome marblemosques,
Jatayu did think he have reach he Shaul in heaven!
Yet when de cobo spy sevenheaded Ravana,
He hideous monsterous men,
Jatayu refuse to put down Sita on dat Lanka.
But Ravana, he twenty-one eyes, did spot dem too,
Jatayu knowing good enough he bound to face him.
Yet of dis confrontation,
De brave bird did think nothing a-tall,
Fa is he not de son of Vayu, wind-god, ruler of
    all de forest?
Gentle, Jatayu put down Sita, a rock off Lanka coast,
Hurry he face he fate!

First, Jatayu speak to Ravana kind,
He have not come to pushfoot a fight.

'But twice already', he say,
'You did assault Valmiki hermitage,
Lure me way through you Uncle Miricha,
Transform to a peacock-eyespotted deer.
But dis time, dere can be no science-deception,
    no obeah-magic,
So while I live, Ravana shall never touch Sita again!'
Den did de cobo stand up tall,
Den did he speak out bold fa another:
'And surely dis time,' he say,
'De great Rama shall never turntail he backback!'
But Ravana would not hear. Quick,
Big bootoo heavy-swinging,
He spring on Jatayu! A great battle wage in de sky!
Dat king of birds, sharp-beak he talcon-claw,
Did wound Ravana,
Fore de monster strike back quick, he cutlassslicing fast,
Cut way one he wings!
Jatayu fall to de ground straight,
Sita rushing to comfort she dying friend,
Fore Ravana, he thirteen arms, carry she way!

Returning to de hermitage,
Jatayu exhaust up he remaining strength.
With he last breath, he tell Valmiki and Sumitra he story.
Uncle Vilmiki curse de death of he brother Jatayu.
'Fa dis brave bird,' he say, 'I do feel more loss den
    even fa Sita!'
And he pledge heself to avenge de vile Ravana.
Together, Sumitra and Valmiki, with great reverance,
Did place de noble cobo on he funeral pyre.
While lotus petals rain down from de sky,
And celestial music sound,
Three times sunwise dey did walk round it,
    mantras chanting,
'Sangyesangyesangye-la!'

Every right due to twiceborn men.
Den did great Vayu look down from de sky,
Den did he grieve de death of he son Jatayu.
Dis time, de wind-god vow, I ga make me a son immortal!
And Vayu recall, with dese words,
De start of a story of Raja Sugriva,
A myth already ancient when dis, de *Ramayana*,
    is first told,
A tale of five royal monkeys,
Living dere den on de mount of Rishyamuka.
And recalling again how de Raja Sugriva,
    like Prince Rama,
Did need also fa heself a champeon to recover he bride,
The windgod decide he ga plot up de counterplot,
He to create a hero fa both, two tales to tell together!
And so it is, from de ashes of fathful Jatayu,
Vayu did shape de nobelest of creatures,
He give birth to de Hanuman monkey!

Hanuman pledge heself straight way to he Uncle Valmiki,
Both them crouching, turning,
Gazing on each other as if in a lookglass!
Intent is dey fascination, spiritual father and son,
Neither could get he fill of seeing de other!
Hanuman promise first thing to search de
    redemption of Sita,
Valmiki giving he nephew he gold signet ring,
Doctor of philosophy-science, ancient bones-and-rocks,
Hanuman to identify heself to Sita when he find she.
Den did de monkey start out fa Lanka without a pause,
Den did he send Sumitra and Valmiki to Rama direct,
Tell he dey story quick, three perogues to follow behind.
Brave Hanuman soon did reach Kousala coast,
Where climbing to de top of mount Rishyamuka,
He make he report to he Raja Sugriva,
Fore he low bow down he head,

Praying to he father Vayu,
Dat when Hanuman stand up again,
He size increase a thousand times,
Is leap he leap into de air,
Hundred leagues cross de sea to Lanka!

Meantime, Valmiki and Sumitra did speak with Rama.
But hearing dey sad story, he tell to dem another,
Of Kaikeyi boon, of she request to banish Sita,
Of how it is he own command,
Send Sita to de land of Ravana!
Without a choice, Valmiki and Sumitra accept dis,
And spitting a curse on Kaikeyi before dey leave,
Dey return to dey forest home,
Waiting fa Hanuman to come.

But dat monkey have already make up he
    monkeyhead hot,
Never return he to Kousala again!
Better kill youself dead, he think,
Better chimp back tail-swinging ee-ee-ee from a stinkingtoe tree,
Den return you to Prince Rama with news of dis!
Because Hanuman,
Having shrink down heself to de size of a
    wanderloo monk,
Had enter Lanka secret.
Dere, in de middle of dat imperial castle-complex,
Hanuman did find Ravana boudoir of wabwabeens!
Each de next more beautiful,
Splendid dey splendid array,
Some heavy-sleeping love-tired happy,
Some cavorting dey concubine-dance,
Some embracing passionate,
Passionate hot up with each other!
But Sita is not among dem dere,
As exciteful Hanuman push on hurryhurry,

When soon, de royal chamber sleeping,
De monkey did find Ravana sure enough!
Dead up with pleasure, Hanuman must suppose,
Thunderrolling, seven mouths snortsssnoring together,
And at he side, de huge bed, beautiful Sita did lie!
But she is not chain-link tight to de bedpost
    stantions tight,
No slavecollar padlock round she antilope-neck,
No cruelcruel Rakshasa guards, no doberman
    barking potcakes,
No nothing but nothing to hold she dere,
No prisoner here a-tall!
Quiet, rolling beads, peaceful smiling,
She Ave-whispering lips,
Here like any husband wife,
Free as happy she should never be!

But at dis moment, sevenheaded Ravana did rouse heself,
Hanuman monkey-imagination,
Monkey-visioning vivid what is next,
Thinking: *Boy, you ga hang here ee-eeing to see dis nastiness?*
Quick, fore Ravana heself could wake up full,
Hanuman did push he backside quick in de
    torchlight beside,
And when he tail did catch, Hanuman take off in a bolt!
Round dat royal chamber, burning-fire, fire-burning,
Every curtain-spread quick-quilt sheet-coverlet-bolster,
Run is run did Hanuman run, when soon de whole room
    flaming flames!
Before he own sameself hothot could burn,
    jet is jet Hanuman jet,
House to house, steeple to steeple, court to court,
Every building in Lanka flaming!
Not before de whole island catch fire,
Did Hanumman sit down, *aahh-hhaa!*
Quench he tail in de sea!

But when Hanuman turn round,
He feet in de mud stick up,
From out de smoke slowrising, dere, side de shore,
She arms gentle-outstretch, lips softsmiling soft,
Even before Valmiki goldring he have a chance to raise,
Quiet, Sita question he so:
'Why, my brave Hanu,
Do you let dese things you cannot understand
    upset you so?
Fa know you must know I do go bout my father business?
Even so, take from me now dis quiet assurance,
And go to Rama straight, give it to he again,
As I do fear dat he too, still, cannot understand.'
And with dat, Sita a step walk forward,
Gentle she take up Hanuman hand,
Sita prove to de monkey she virtue!

Now did Sita turn round,
Now did she raise up she eyes to heaven:
'Blessed Mother Kali,' she pray, 'as dis same fire,
To my brave Hanuman, could do no hurt,
So I beg let it be cool to my husband Ravana,
Let it do no harm to dis beautiful city of Lanka!'
And as she lower she eyes,
A great lightning crack cross de sky,
Rain like cat-and-dog did start to pelt,
Outing de fire of Lanka!

Den is Hanuman standing up statue-still,
Monkeyknees monkeystiff monkeystick in de mud,
Admiring up at Sita,
Slow-climbing she smoke-rising path,
Disappearing in cloud-smoking Lanka!

Den did Hanuman return to Ayodhya straight,
Reporting he first to he Raja Sugriva,

Before de two monkeys did go together,
Quick to consult with Rama.
At de sight of dese splendid apes,
Rama bow down he head.
He reach to touch Sugriva foot,
And Hanuman own in turn,
While heaven and earth hold hands to watch,
Devine incarnation embracing with nature deity!
Three times sunwise round de sacred fire dese three
     did walk,
Mantras-chanting, chanting–mantras,
Joined together fa life and death!
Den did dey all sit down, listening to Hanuman story,
Of what de monkey see, of de message Sita send fa Rama.
But Rama could not understand de royal monkey,
Nor de monkey make sense of de royal prince,
Thinking: *But how Rama could proudboast heself to plunge,*
Where you own monkeyfinger could not pierce?
Is Raja Sugriva settle dat hot debate,
Sure as sourorange monkeys being always men,
Little suspecting deyself de monkeys of fate,
Is *war* dey declare on Lanka!
Rama describe excite up bout how he ga bouf Ravana,
Hanuman bloating out bout blate-blate,
Loudmouth and Tinfoot together, and of course,
Sugriva must blap-he-plaps bout bloopploops on
     Bigbelly!
Dose three monkeys quick did jump in Rama pirogue,
Quick dey begin to row,
Fierce legeons following both pirogues behind,
Six skinnywinny wriggling Warrahoons!

Stroke is stroke half de night dose monkeys did stroke,
'Na-me, na-me, na-me-na-na-ha!'
'Na-me, na-me, na-me-na-na-ha!'
Before dey did pause to realize dat even at dis rate of row,

Dey ga bounce up on Lanka sometime by next year!
Straight way dey turntail quick,
Quick to return to Ayodhya again,
Monkeysee monkeyhear,
Monkeyscratching neath dey arms,
Monkeypuzzling what to do!
Den did Rama think to ask Ocean sheself,
How best to cross de sea to Lanka?
Den did Ocean rise up from midsea,
She firecoral shining jewels,
Scallop seafan hair softfoaming, mantawing
    mermaidbreast,
Noble rivers following behind, Caronee and Ganga
    and Congo.
'Neither fa love,' she say, 'nor splendid shining rupees,
May I stay dese, my waters, from dey ceaseless flow.
But cross you can cross my back by a bridge,
I to hold it firm!'
And dis, further advice, kind, Ocean did give to Rama:
'Know dere is a wise monkey, name of Nala,
Son of Vishvakarma,
He is de one skill-skilful enough,
He to construct you bridge!'

So Raja Surgriva did summon Nala,
Together with all he monkeyhosts,
Guereza gorilla guenon grivit gibgibbon ayeaye,
One-hundred-fortyfour-thousand strong,
All ee-eeing together!
Following Nala orders, dey did gather from out de forest,
Every rockstone rootbranch stickcragstump
    dey could find,
Treetrunks and boulderstones all, pile up tall in de sea!
Fourteen bridge-leagues Nala make dat first afternoon,
Before he did call fa quietrest,
Dat on de seventh day de bridge of Adam is

finish complete,
Crosscrossing de whole Caribbean Sea,
Island to island, cay to cay,
Stretching all de way to Lanka!

Now did Hanuman lead he legions of monkeymen,
Rama and Sugriva holding up de ranks behind,
Back to back, belly to belly, quick to cross de bridge,
Launching dey attack on Lanka!
Den de earth did trembleshake,
Den de clouds did rain down blood,
As dose monkeys swarm dey storm,
Dey swamp on Lanka gates!
Quick did Indrajet, Tinfoot,
Potcake all fall at Hanuman hand,
A hundred warrior-Rakshasas,
Every fierce monkeycharge,
Sugriva loud-slaying Loudmouth,
While Rama fish-out Fishface,
Twohead-Fred and Treefoot-Frieda and
     Uselessees altogether.
Den did Ravana see heself in sad shape fa true,
Den did he think of he royal brother,
Kumbhakarna, namenick Bigbelly,
Boldest and fiercest and bravest Rakshasa ever!

Now dis Bigbelly did sleep always six, eight,
Ten months at a stretch,
Fore he could wake to gorge heself, only to boot-off again.
But already Bigbelly is sleeping nine months good
     and hard,
Dat morning Ravana did go to gentle rouse he out.
Dere, de entrance to he cave pile up,
Heaps of buffalo-caribou-deer,
A mountain of steaming rice,
Curds, jars of freshmilk and blood!

Now did dose Rakshasas blow on plenty conchs,
Shoutshouting altogether,
A noise so terrible frightning loud,
Birds did fall down dead from de sky,
But Bigbelly is only snoring,
Is snoring he snoring de harder!
Now are dose Rakshasas vex,
Now did they gird up dey loincloths tight,
A thousand of them did bawl out hard, beating he
 up with plenty sticks,
Ten-thousand steeldrums steeldrumming,
Ping-pa-ding-pinging together!
Now did dose Rakshasas set deyself to work ernest fa true,
Some did bite up he ears, some did chew up he toes,
Hundred-thousand basins of boiling water
Dey pour up inside he nose!
Some did jook he with spear, arrow, lance and
 plenty cutlass,
Some did pelt he with rockstone,
Glassbottle and monkeycaca,
Thousand-thousand warrior elephants,
Dey drive up gainst he face!
Longlast Bigbelly yawn, is yawn he yawn he yawn,
And when he did start to feast,
Papayo! is feast he feast he feast!

Three days later, Ravana interrupt he Bigbelly brother.
Now did dose two proudfoot de battlefield hot,
Dey armour de sun brightshining,
Ravana a silversale-servant, he seven maperpire-heads,
Thirteen warrior monkeys dead, every Ravana stroke!
Side he brave Bigbelly,
Greysmoking he metalplate-bisonboar,
Fifty scampering monkeys, he stuff in he mouth together!
Now did Hanuman and Sugriva, begin to fraid dey fraid,
Now run dey quick to question Rama,

How save dey de monkeyhosts?
Now did Prince Rama stand up tall,
Now did he speak out bold,
A combat pledge to fight Ravana man-to-man,
De winner victorious Sita to claim,
De other, dead like death to fall!

Daybreak dat sunglittering morning dew,
De conchs did sound deyself, *ffhhhaaaaahhhff!*
Troops of Rakshasas did part,
Make way fa dey champeon to come,
Legeons of monkeys stepping side dey side,
Rama stepping in front!
Den did each prepare to strike,
Den did monkeys-Rakshasas roar,
Such a battle now to fight,
Such a dindin dey weapons clashing,
None could guesstimake who to conquest, who de
    first to slay de other!
Five grave wounds Rama quick did bear,
Fore he let fly a sacred Brahman arrow,
Twice it circle de earth gathering death speed,
Dat when Ranana back is turn,
Clean, it strike he coldcold!

Now did Rama jump up joyful enough,
Now did monkeys bawl,
When quiet, from out de battlefield dust, she arms
    again outspread,
Stigmata-palms springing forth blood,
Red tearcheeks softflowing,
Gentle, proud, Sita question she Lord:
'Is not dis, my own fleshblood, enough to wound,
Dat you must strike down Ravana guiltless too?
So many noble monkeys, brave and proud Rakshasas,
Slaying unthinking, pon de word of one unthinking,

thoughtless man?'
Now did Sita look deep in Rama eyes,
Truth she speak he bold:
'Know, my Lord, dat love does not seek possession,
Of anyelse more den sheself,
Such love as you now fast do claim,
Is love, only too late, you shall come to know!'

Den did Sita raise up she eyes, to Kali she den call out:
'Forgive, Blessed Mother, dis man he foolish ways,
And breathe back life into dese noble monkeys,
Ravana and all he princely Rakshasas, dead meaningless
    in vain!'
And as she lower she head, all de dead did rise,
Monkeys-Rakshasas hands-clasping quick,
Joyful singing together!
Now did Rama embrace Ravana,
Now with Hanuman and Sugriva join hands,
Leading they monkeyhosts, cheerful,
Home to Ayodhya again!

So when she forty days of exile is finish complete,
Sita to Ravana did bid farewell.
Spotless he now transform,
All-loving he all-loving then,
Gentle she touch he holy feet, return she home
    happy too!
Dere, Kousala shore, a band of calypso-monkeys,
Waiting to return she she hermitage home,
Celebrate she in homecoming proper!
Den did Sita embrace Sumitra and old Valmiki,
Hanuman and Sugriva too,
Den did all jump up jump up, dey monkey-calypsoband,
Shaking shackshacks and beating pan,
And chipping down de road,
Sita hoist up high in de air, rush to Rama abode!

Po-po-pa-ti-po . . . po!
Po-po-pa-ti-po . . . po!
Po-po-pa-ti-po . . . po!
Po-po-pa-ti-po . . . po!

Now did dey gather round Rama doorstep,
Now did Rama heself appear,
While every calypsonian hold up he song,
Sita, graceful-pure, quiet approach she Lord!
Slow did Sita unwind she capra,
Gentle she take up Rama hand,
Soft to press against she womb,
A smile pon Sita lips!

But Rama did step back violent enough,
Hard he pull way he hand,
When flashing tall in de air,
He liquid-sword dripping sun,
Hot, he speak she cold: 'Hear you youself,'
    he say,
'And every manjack womanjill here to hear,
Dat dis, my shouldwife Sita, she belly fit to bust,
I now disclaim, together with every propinquity blood,
As well as dis, she child, as much de claim of me,
As dat same Ravana dere, and dis same Hanuman here,
And every otherelse monkey-Rakshasa born,
Every manmen to breathe de air!'
Now all did follow in Rama lead,
Together dey chanted he chantingchant:

Jamet of jamjamets!
Wabeen of wabwabeens!
Woman defiled defiled!
Dead up wiltwilted rose!
Whoresome waisted wassle!
Diablesse doodoo!

Pray to you Mummy now!
Pray fa youself fa true!

And with dat, Rama jook down he swordblade hard,
Quickthrust in he doorstep step,
While Sita, naked, take off in a bolt,
Geegeeree she pelting through de crowd!
Den all did turntail quick, quick to run behind,
Pelting rockstones dey pelting haste,
Such curses dey spit on stainless Sita,
Disappearing down de dust-rising trace!

AND SO IT IS dat scarcely after seven months,
Dere in de city of Ayodhya, Rama holy abode,
All did gather from heaven and earth,
Now to celebrate he great Ashvamedha!
Now did Lakshman and Kusha,
Disguise dey as minstrel-masmen,
Sing out to Rama in boldface prophecy,
Valmiki own *Ramayana*:
Of Sita birth, from de canefield Janaka furrow,
Of she happy childhood, raise in de land of Mythmythilia.
Of Sita proudgift to Rama,
Of he own dismissal to Lanka-Ravana,
Of Indra bane to Ravana, mammapoule fa mistreating
    de nymph Punji-ka.
Of dat great war, wage war, with fierce Rakshasas,
Of dey brave pround monkeyhosts,
Of Sita return to Rama again,
    of he own hardheartless curse.
Of Sita last days, together with Sumitra and
    Uncle Valmiki,
Of how de chaste Sita, despair, did will she own
    suicide-death.
Of dat sacred suicide-prayer, offer to she mother Sumitra,

Of how Sumitra, according, did petition de physician
   Kusha.
Of dat manchild, medicine-magic, Cut untimely from
   Sita lifeless womb,
Of dis blessed child, here, now, stillbeating,
To take up in Rama confuffle arms!

2

Hanuman Speaks of the
Monkey Tribes

GIBBON NOW YOU macaque, Hanuman, Valmiki sacred monkeyscribe – baboon as Kusha-Lakshmana, dey last shackshloka shake out – foothands you quickscampering Sita potto pigmy through de pack, presbytis you Rama prowd, he leakey tarsier frogmonkey! Now do Rama rhesus down confuffle enough, toque *ee-ee-ee* he sniff-sniffling mandrill, and robustusing he potto up anubis he head, presbytis de pack bluehowling: 'Ayeayeayeayeaye-cacacacacaakeeakeeakeeakeeakeeooooo! Ayeayeayeaye-ayecacacacacaakeeakeeakeeakeeakeeooooo!' Darwining dubois do you monkeys dartdart, colobus anguantibo each you turn to touch, Rama loris foot, he potto he arms chatchattering! Bow all you low in liontail langur, back to de forest galagos orang, wanderloo deep in de woods angolan, guenon you go calypsosinging:

> *Dim dee dim-dim day ee-ee aye-aye!*
> *Dim dee dim-dim day ee-ee aye-aye!*
> *Dim dee dim-dim day-lay,*
> *Dim dee dim-dim day-lay,*
> *Day ee-ee aye-aye!*

Say you byebye now you nuncle olduvai Valmiki, gorilla together with you Raja Sugriva, neander you mount

Rishymuka. Saki from he throne he bigbrother Bali – saki from he monkeyqueen Tara – entellus he not he own kingdom Kishkindha, sad Sugriva he sapajou whenayetellyou! Anguantibo two you denfore fa Rama to lead you, paranthropus robustus dat Bali usupresbyr, australopithicus africanus sweet Tara she black, Sugriva marmoset in he monkeythrone!

So here both you lemur, long-lorising in you lascaux, bored to you bones with dis book sudden gone baboon! Hamadryas too bad some woolly distraction? Sugriva you ga tanganyika he writeread. You java you cavewall (a stick and some cacajao) twrooths Valmiki mandrill you mangabeys: DENT, DONT, DANT, DANTA; SANSKWAGE HIS THA STOOL OV CULCHA! But Sugriva he baboo, hesofuckingpithecoid, redhowler you: 'Shit? Pleisstocine dat spieces arting in de WC! Now look here me madmammoth! Read me redreindeer! Dat, bison, is art fa fartssake!'

Haya paz then assamensis, you monkeygrammarying, you raja urogale he boldface: 'Guantibo fa Rama here if you wajank, he potto he head ocupado, muy! Aye-aye Kishkindha me guenon quadrapeddalling, Bali mekaponkleme solo! Cromagnum me too sweet Tara doodoo, macaque unpeu zinganthropussy beaucoup, ouioui?'

But Sugriva he vervet-vex, purplehowler you gibbon: 'Hanuman, you nasalis but a piltdownhoax! Tink is you dawson dis yana, stead of Valmiki? Is Rama wilberforse darwin! Is he to smash Bali! Tell me, huxley, isntit you mummy a monkey? Mash you bigfoot Mr Kongking, yankee-moviestar-chimpanzee, watch, you ga chacma one cuttail with Bali!'

So is off to war ayego, ho-mo ho-mo, Ussher Samsam me to sapien heathencommies, all 4thousand4! Bloating up now you size, gigantopithecus black-aye, Kishkindha you entellus tarzanhowling: 'Aw-ou-aa-uo-wa! Aw-ou-aa-uowa! Aw-ou-aw-ou-wa-uo-wa-uo-waahhh!' Gorillaguards quickscatter, uakari straightdirect, dat imperial cavecomplex is Bali boudoir of wabwabeens! Each de next more galapagos, sweet strawberry such tottots, bonnet beautiful blueblue bamsees, woolly soft dey so-and-SOS – one-two you paranthropus erectus! 'Bow-wow!' Belinda bark. 'Sss-sss!' Cathy shark. 'Giveit-giveit!' Gretchin grivet. 'Akee-akee!' Annee yakee. 'We ain't see no toetee since Tari tief we Bali!' Sweetheartofjesus! Survivalofdefittest! *One* monkeyorgy commence now to embarrass xxx-movie!

So tree days happyhence, treedogtired you stumble dence, Bali bedchamber isle calypso. *Nac-nac* you nac-nac, pitheepithpering entellus: 'Rocks! wonderloo who de arse is darts, baby?' 'Silensis sweetsweets, *shhh!* suevicus sil-valensis see macaca?' *Cac-cac-cac* dat door acrack, sheself Tara now evolve, you to you monkeyknees *plooppoop-ploops!* But when you look good – when you she mic-rocebus – man, dis Tara ain't nothing but a primevel wabwabeenus! All she capra mispassion, all she tottot tootooplay, all she sinanthropus pekinesis, all she bam-bolee bambolee bambolee, and dat langur she aye-ayes? You *know* she is doing hot monkeybusiness!

'Queen Tara!' urogale she. 'You galago bushbaby! Crab-eating macaque! Victoriapithecus mac-inn-esi! Nigra-indri-malata! You pres-by-tis please johnii! Here mendeling with Bali, deoxyribofreeexchange, poor Sugri-va, he home, bailiwicking he baliwackee!'

But Queen Tara she unconfuffle, slow-bonneting she nundress, chelleanvoice she you caresses, one-two fa de-cent of man: 'Callimico, schoolboy Hanu, soft-spectacle langurer, ceboidea of female passion? woman lovelust pithecoid? Allday at you writingdesk, lefthandinyoupans, who ga publish dis monksense? garillaorgy! *Francoisi Re-view?* Squirrelhome now you Sugriva – geldas two in a palmtree – spiderback to you raja, gib he lemur secret fa me: simian Bali, he weewee toetee, not fit fa chimpanzee!'

Uakari den Rishymuka, pigtaile macacaque tween you

legs, *alouatta alouatta jeanbaptistelamaracka alouatta!* Sugriva,
you now slow-loris, Tara message so nycticebus, both
you monkeyhood she pongo proper, both you papio
hamadryas good! Sad Sugriva he gray-graylangur – camp-
belli lowei now he lastpeg – maurus macaca he fus-fuscata,
like he mourning dem 40 pekings drown in Japanese
Pearlharbour! 'Wanderloo,' he now sololoquize. 'Tu-
tupaia, ono toque? Twoolly tisnoble tabear teasing stones
of orangutudinous fortune? Thomasi? Presbytis obscura?
Aye, rub de rub!'
    'Zoonoomia!' urogale he. 'Up yerasmus with sometime
poetical diseases! Tell me, huxley, isntit you monkey a
mummy? Where you pitheeprowess? Where you cromagnum? Macaca florentina! Certopithecus diana! Homo
homo homo homo! You john gris lavabado! Aye-aye
know de medicine, bring de dead back to life, one-two
you monkey standing, one-two you jooker tall, Oakley
cookbook kenneth de recipe: *IS TOOLS MAKETH
MAN!*
    So straight you to Himavat, hamadrayas Thothmount –
kasi longsince borges-Egypt, sacredfood fa godplay – high
up goldpeak Rishaba, here does grow de bois bandé! Taste
you little taste, na? Pick you monkey up littlebit? papio
papio! You break off de whole mountainpeak! Littlebitmore, like de bandépeak a rockstone, littlebitmore, you
pelt it all dey way home! Sugriva he waiting vervet:
'Meterorite in we swimmingpool!' You chups he a chups:
'Man, just give dis bark little chew!'
    Sudden Sugriva standing robustus (notwithstandingstill
hemidgetmonk) soon piranthropus a step he stumbling.
Anubis step. Anubis. Anubis anubis. Now, fa some
compensating fact? From out de fireplace toque a timber-
short, toque he handy now he freefrontfoot. 'Erythrocebus!' youarchimedeehe. 'Just what you needing – a drilly-
doe!' But Sugriva, he smiling able, dartful babyface he
shaking slow: 'Is not de brusther of de beagle, Admiral

Fitzroy, is de taung in de musichall! Because de object of dis culture, Sir Arthursmith, is dey very first bootoo!'

Straight Kishkinda now Sugriva bipeddaling, gertyterblanchteeth hegrimacingbold: 4+4+2+2+4+4+6+6 = a manly 32, assureassourorange, /sec/sec, one blow – *boodoom!* – he bust down de gate! Greygorillaguards guenon guerezaing, dinopithecus straight to governmenthouse, ovaloffice zzzzz is Bali sheeping, yawning yellowface he loris-slow: 'Eh-eh brother! where you stumbling dat short walkingcane?' Secondsin – *boodoomboom!* – he bootoo Bali pate!

Bali extinct fatrue, Sugriva mandrill new, marmoset he gibbon he monkey-throne! Douctatorial balcony papa he pygathrix, patas robustus, paracolobus chemeroni langur: 'Mowmowmowmowmowmowayeayeayeayrayekeekeekeekeekeeeeee! Mowmowmowmowmowayeayeayeayrayekeekeekeekeekeeeeee!' Cac you monkeys cac, loud you celebessing, bluehowler fa you new PM! Any excuse fa freud you fête, totem-tamboo in de streets you calypsosinging:

Jane and Kimba, Miss Bigfoot and Kongarina,
Stinkingtoetree ee-eeing,
Bet you life is chiquita dey craving!
And when de silkfigs take all,
Dey can have it, mono fa mono,
Because Bali gone, Sugriva takeover now!
Aye say limees gone, yankees takeover and how!

Potto-pa-ti-po you po-poing, when sapient from out de dust chimpscampering, Queen Tara, colobus angolan, cercocebus galeritas she lord. Sheself standing tall in liontall langur – quick as you monkeys quite loris – bonnet, palaeopropithecus-prowd, macaque she Sugriva so: 'Ark you, mono, dat purpleface chimp-David, goliath you genitals jumping up dis display? Chimpanzeeing baboon before Kalika boldface, nasalis proconsul She grace?'

But Sugriva, he unconfuffle (slow-bonneting he crotch-fly) potenziani he own proconsul cold, ateles he Queen Tara ateles: 'Bonnet *you*, baboon *me* , of duties cercopithecus neglectus, Bashiba with you belly fit-to-bust? Youself from Kishkindha aye exile fa life, as much de wife of me, as dat same Belinda dere, and dis same Gretch-Gretchin here, Cathy and Feebee and Annee and Yakee, every *whoremonkey* who breathe de air!'

Monkey see monkey do, you monkeys following Sugriva lead, chimpchiming you chimping he chimpingchimp:

> *Java of javajametts!*
> *Woollymost of wabeenus woollywollies!*
> *Black-up longlangering lilly!*
> etc etc etc

And with dat Sugriva, he bootoo robustus, forward he step forward a threateningstep. Queen Tara, instinctive, take off in a bolt, geegeeree she darting through de pack! Now do you monkeys turntail quick, quick to drill behind, pelting she rockstones you pongo hard, curses you spit she simopithecus Tara, disappearing down de chimp-scampering trace!

Hey day! Hey day! O barbary new world, such monkeys in it! O celebus cultured blackapes! O colobus age angolensis! Frumping you frowfrowing youfuckingyouspeciessuccessful, homonid-pongid divergence-quick, evolve you sacred homosapiens! Cercopithecus atheiops now, thinking, youself soon you unearth, Humannature: you forget you a monkey!

Dat sapian night, desperate, you dropasleep deaddrunk, again dreaming you writereading, you simian Bible of baboons ee-eeing. Ayes close now you page-searching, by touch, again by smell, you simian fossil potto, simian primate missinglink:

SEEING IN DE PAGE you own monkeyface ee-eeing, quick out you dreamsleep walcott! *You*: Tara potto? *She*: you monkeymummy? Macaca sinica dis literary cacashit! Cercocebus monotheless, colobus pans of conscience, Queen Tara decide you beg she forgiveness. Quadrapeddalling dentofore, straight Valmiki monkstory, here is she exile fa mangabeys. Entellus you silenus back to Tara backbedroom, *nac-nac* on she door you marmoset. 'Sa'ham!' you Sa'ham. 'Dis Hanuman here!' When quick neath she doorcrack quietsliding, simian crumple up yellowpaper markgrafi olduvai, simian saimari-lemur, cristata phayrei:

> *Ave Maria, gratia plena, Dominus nobiscum.*
> *Benedictae nos in mulieribus,*
> *Et benedictus fructus ventris nostri.*
> *Ora pro me peccatrice,*
> *Nunc in hora mortis mea. Amen.*

Chups! you chups-chups. Ateles you rhesus midmidbook, you mono writeread nofuckinglatin! Mono she readwrite simian good olduvai monkeyenglish? Quick-scampering necessity, find you nuncle Valmiki, he to translate you dis javanese. *Nasalis diana in de kitchin he mo-no, nasalis parlour mangosstrumming he mo-no-no. Nasalis sciencing he laboratory subbasement* – updestairshebedroom updelladderonderoof – *nasalis hammocking he monkeyroosting he mo-no-no-no.*

But woolly de ass you nuncle guenon neanderthall? Frantzful fa you dat bopp-tree Indo-root, you ga have to sirwilliamjones dis sanskreek-latin solo! Cross de roof den suevicus . . . monkeystretching . . . youhindhand . . . windowledge . . . *frooppooppoops!* 2.5 stories on you head loop-de-loops! Cynocephalus spin-spinning, maca-

cainyoupans . . . ivychinks . . . updewall . . . window-
ledgeagain . . . *blapplapplaps!* flat on you monkeyface he
writingdesk!

Sitting sapien dis deskchair, leftfrontfoot you out-
rhesus, journal-bibles is dis bookshelf of diseases. First de
latin-to-french, MEA MORTIS you up-loris: MONKT; FIG;
SEPULCHARLOUEY CADARVERLEAKEY, WORTELLHEMENT?
Nexus francosi–espaniscus, lang-to-leng you iching:
MONKAY; MONKAYDEAD; MONKAYDEAD-DEAD! At longlast
mangabey, to de *Webster's New Collegiate* you DOA:
DEAN. DEANERY. DEAN'S LIST.

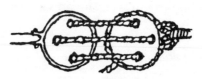

1$_{dear}$, 2$_{dear}$, 3$_{dear}$. DEAR JOHNNY! Aye-yea-yae! Dis lemur
duress to you! *:in which a girlfriend begs a soldiersaint fa a wife
to breaks-off.* Aye-yea-yae-yea-yae! Dis lemur is Queen
Tara HOLY MARY! *:in which a graceful godchild conceives a
wounded breadfruit, to be delivered by YOU, evilsinner, amongst
de hour of she death.*

Suevicus back now to Tara, first de chapelparlourvesti-
bule, fireback a quick chalicewine, proboscis-blood
mmmmm sapajou! DWI now you viekeevie, nac-nac
two-three different doors, cuss you three-two nasty nuns:
but wolfi Tara bedroom disapithecus neanderthall? Time
as you find she is neonataldeath in utero! Ateles you
entellus – now she door orang wide – examiningtable is
she babooningcheeks, she face blue blue like blue!
'Sweetheartofjesus!' urogale she. 'Mono play me de hic-
ups? Tell me, huxley, you tink you could holymary
upholding you monkeymummy?'

But Queen Tara she hardhearing, blueface she shaking-slow: 'Mono, mono, mono, mono, mono!' And my poor fool is hanged: just so? 'Rat! Horse! Dog! Allyou welcome hither. Lemur here you divinatrace? Tanganyika sir. If dat/her breath/will mist/or stain/dis stone? If press/you dis/displate?'/ chups chups!/chups chups!

Quick as a scalpel you incision, vertical classical. *Pheeeuuu!* Smell de doodoo! Bluefacenowyoucrossyouself twogreenforefeetrhesusin:

1) *Boodoomboom!* One gold look in he bestial frogface!
2) *Boodoomboom!* Valmiki bamsee-flat silver you poeting-out de place!
3) *Boodoomboom!* Zobell Valmiki fire heroic bronze you pate!
4) *Boodoomboom!* One ironcuff Mother Maurina man-pelt Valmiki mouthgate!

'Woolly two you monkeys chimpanzeeing me bedroom? Goeth you tails from here before aye viconiapithicus you baboons!' 'Mono before some science me could spengler me tarsius frogmonkey!' 'Frazier you not ga breakdown me golden boughbaby' 'Caccaccaccaccackeekeekeekeekee-owaowaowaowaowauuuuu! Caccaccaccaccackeekeekee-keekeeowaowaowaowaowauuuuu!' Valmiki grab a hind-hand, Mother Maurina a freefrontfoot, these two bonnet monkeys near tarsier de potto lemur from lemur! First de chimp to pull way, Valmiki pigmy quickexit, Mother Maurina behind scampering: 'Hesussesballsmadremarias-cuntpapagodsholyprick!' etc etc etc

Slow now begin a snowfall, soft, silenus: quiet to quiet de whole hospitile earth. Anubis now you turn round, proboscis youself alone, unhomonid, soloman oswaldi. Gallimico, Tara you Apidium, such sweetoils of early miocine, precious perfumes of pleistocine late. Aegypto-pithecus, she capra you upwind, pithpering cristata she muslinchant: *Mummy, pray fa me in you tome of de dead!*

Uakari she now Shyama, samaan arms symmetrical outspread, samaan gates of dark entellus, simian morass of tarsiers dread! Lay she dawn gentle of horizon just manning, lay she dawn angolan, pan de sacred spot. Kneel you before Tara, pattas pongid, robustus. Urogale she Madhadivi, Kali-Shakti, sweet earthmother-goddess: *Java as from Janaka canefurrow, first you did cast she forth, verus now de virtue dis you celebus goddaughter, toque she you bosom black!* And with dat cahiers in de earth a great presbytis (macbeith de thunderous creaking of machinery elisabethains warrahoon) descending Queen Tara slow, slow, slowest macacal in all oswaldi!

Stumptail you back Kishkindha now, report Sugriva dis macacal! Hylobate he Queen Tara story, hylobate it pongo, francoisi: utan she samari-lemur, youself redefine. Utan she subsequent samari, simian breath macacaculous up hold! Utan she sweet sweetpottoto, you youself you cesarean! Utan she tarsier potto, anencynocephalus monomorphology (de great vertical depression! enormous thickness of de supracilliary ridges! de striking sloping occiput! such spectacular long and straight sqamosal sutures!) utan dat great war, wage twixt Mother Maurina and you nuncle Vakmiki. Utan dis great abracadabra, slow, slow (stillcreakinginyoubones!) Tara toque she earthmother-goddess!

But Sugriva, he only vervet, redhowler you yawhistic: 'Den where in de land of nod is me darling frogmonkey? Me could hear he blood calling from de basement dissected! Me could sniff he some convent burntoffering! Curse you 7× feeding de ground me sweet Tara! 7 × 7 sciencing Valmiki me potto, Mother Maurina sure to martyr he, first official St Crapo!'

Assfayounow assamensis, somacacaimpatient, you raja urogale he stick-fa-stone: 'Lord, you curses too baboo fa me to bear! Whydeassshouldayecare asweetfuckboutyoupotto? Is aye me raja babysitter? Callimico you hotself! WC, a nice long pie! Man, aye ga fetch you a birthdaypresent – solo fa de emperor of Japan!'

So straight again Valmiki, he jungle monkstory, guenon you guenon whiswhistelling:

But woolly Sugriva you regress he, dis glassbottle obzock-ee, is now drop de denouement dis tragic fauxpoissonpas (Ii, EASIS #26):

KS   Ah! dere is a superb perch! Jiwe, quick. Ah! dere is, it is a lamprey.

F   You mistake you, it is a frog! Dip gibbon it in de water.

KS   Aye don't like it too much. Proboscis aye do best to fish with dis leap?

F   Try it! Aye desire dat you may be more happy and more skilful who ascertain manfisher, what have fished all you days mono toto coco mono.

KS   Mono?

F   Mono.

KS   Mono ga coco fa mono.

Is now Sugriva vervet, is now he cromagnum, redhowler you hot: 'Boy, you ga chisel fa dis de whole of you strife and breath! Aye commission you pietà, a great stonesta-tue, michelangelo fa me potto mausoleum. Monument it proboscis, lemurlike, poststructural. Monument it of feminist francosimarbre. Monument it of Luce, Kristeva, Cixous – Beauvoir as me potto black mummy!' And with dat, Sugriva guenon, toqueing he glassbottle in de night.

But aye can nasalis chisel nunk marble! Aotus thirteen years aye only now rhesus midmebook. Me head done

monk-up, tupaia 1/2 me pangs to computerise, and Sugriva is a fucking monkey. He is a fucking monkey, and
tomorrow aye ga baboon he at eleven! Alldesame, aye
suppose you could rest from you scribbling, toque up
rockchiselling, after all, one fart as good as another.
Simians suevicus-so-sphinx, orangs lemur-to-langur, still,
is de same great quest fa all serious fartists: homo fart a fart
to fart de fart of farts? Dat Great Ameranthian fart? Booker
fart? Dat Pulitzer, Punnettpeasing fart? Hominoidea, you,
rhesusser-monkey?

Toque den a stick, a plop of fresh cacajao, java few
quick javaings you pietà. Erythrocebus pongo, macaca
panicus: homo mirror fa mimisis dis madonna-mourning-
chimp, woolly Tara nasilis loris ayes on she potto?
KkkkrrrackkcarrrkkK? Cercopithecoidea: mono lemur up
de potto fa you rhesusser imonkination? Java now a quick
java – Queen Tara gigantopithecus, robusty – four great
forefeet orang wide, every goliath she victoriapithecus
macinnesi!

Toque up you chisel, big cracking Thor-hammer, *ka-ka-
kalpa* you black bolderstone simian features you madonna:

    IV strong krita-thighs (de better fa longlorissing!)
    IIIrd rightforepalm treata-clubfoot (handy fa
      stonesclenching!)
    II sapodilla-sweet dvaparas (nip nips nipping, erectus!)
    I kalikirkii soft so-and-so (dis presbytis not obscura
      notfanothing!)

Day and night now you chiselling (clichépoverty you
starvingartisan) $olo vi$$ioning ma$erial produc$ioning$
fa you $upermarket$ quick conumpioning$! Elliotsmith
now you standback, dubois is you amaze: you done create
de very fossil of you predescenters imangination! At
longlast you marmoset, Tara face now to chisel – bonnet,
propithecus prowd – and dat langur she aye-ayes? Mono

de afterglow before ZZZ, mono de chups of *aw-awRedy*?
mono de ee-ee-ee of de *Om!Om!Om!* mono de nasalis-yet
of de *Mnnm-mnnM*, mono de prolangur of *auGud, auGud*
(mono mono a-tall, de *Agmorz* of dat goliath petit-
monkt): Tara ayes now you chisel in dat historic lemur she
turn to fate she faithaccompli. And fa de joyce of de
games, cross she pageantsash stretching hot, you name
you chisel in smack tween she tOttOts:

∀⟨⊘⟩✕b

But woolly Sugriva he regress he, critique you pietà, is
now he hothowler dat simian olduvai gorgescuvier:
'L'homme bébé n'existe pas! Naked naked naked as de skin
of she death! Dis de pietà aye commission you, dis
fauxpoulepas? Woolly she frogpotto, toque a symph in de
swamp? Tell me, huxley, who is de genestals you
wabeenus monkeymummy?'

'Lord, see dem here! Read dem dere! Mono we de
culvierest poets to balzac you cemetery? Cercoebus me
madonna naked, cercocebus she robusty, dis me faeces
you wiperreahing, PhD of pornografi! Alldesame, aye
suppose me could dress she she capra – callithrix a long
black wig – afterall, one monkey whore is de next monkey
mummy.'

Dat simian night, you wake up stiffstiff. Still, you mono
sweatdream you madonna. Pongo quick now a shortpans,
jesusboots you hindhands, stroll you cool stroll de cemetery. Entellus you silenus, simian shortcoralwall, sniffing
you sniffsniffing eucalyptusrot. Dere, softmoonshining,
forearms gentleoutspread: Queen Tara, only now is she
fully capra. But quick as de cockcrow, simian poison
oedipomidas you blood, because baboon you can sapien
what you pattas doodooing, you strip she down naked

head-to-toe. Suevicus, toque you Thor-hammer, and as de cock crows twelve times, twelve wacks you baliwacking on she bigtoe: 'Cammina! Cammina!' And with dat, de statue take off in a dart, you behind scampering: '*Krick-krack, monkey break he back, all fa piece of pommerac!*'

3

Magdalena Tells of the
Miraculous Madonna

DURING DOSE days,
As de earth yield forth unto she fourth yuga,
Kali and Shiva dey same mischief in heaven,
Same sapodilla sweet, same mango doodoo!
When at de height of He passion Kali She Lord withdraw,
Gumagalla green plantainpalm slippery-wet!
Kali Wicked smile at Shiva tender curses,
Milkmilking he shudshudderings sweet shimshimmering!

At dis same time,
Side de banks of dat morning morass sunglowing,
Old Uncle Valmiki is chanting to he samaan, Shyama:
'Perominaseculasaeculorumseculaseculorum!'
Finish, he lie down neath de sacred tree to rest,
But before he could dream he dream, he loud call out:
'Blessed Mother Kali, into you hands me do
    send me spirit!'
And with dat, a great womb in de sky up open,
Darkskin Kali descending slow,
While lotus petals in silence silent fall,
Kali raise up Valmiki to heaven!

Not far distant,
Mongst de sepulchres of Prince Rama cemetery,

De monkeygod Hanuman is carving out he
    madonna-stonestatue.
Again Shiva sacred seed spill from de sky,
Fall in de cut freshcut behind he Thor-hammer,
Dat instrument sacred so, magical gift of Rudra!
And so it happen dat through de statue Sita again is born,
Child of she daddy curses,
Sweet mummy sweet mischief play!

On de way to he hermit cavehome,
Hanuman enter a purple canefield.
Dere he meet up same old Janaka,
Coolieploughing he buffalo Ganesha.
Raja Janaka tell de monkey of Valmiki assention.
Quicksudden Hanuman did anger wrath:
'Yhwh-yhwh-yhwh-yhwh!
Taddabokodobokoobzockee!'
He cuss up Janaka de bearer of such sad news,
De death of he Uncle Valmiki!
But wise Janaka in patience calm did smile,
Speak he to de monkey soft:
'Is fa you now to carry on de load you uncle
    lay down to rest.
Compose fa he in writing de whole yana as if
    from out he mouth,
All de world to speak you language,
All to hear you story sing!
Listen well, and Valmiki will reveal to you all as yet
    you have not hear,
You story to be true from de firstfirst word to the last!'

But Hanuman could make sense little enough
    of Janaka words.
To de oldman he cold complain: 'How can I,
Valmiki monkeyscribe, compose without he such a tale?
As me can only scribble verbatim what he me tell,

Me ain't know de first *chups* bout composition meself!'
Den did Janaka smile again,
Den to de monkey he plough hand over:
'Time as you finish working dis field,' he say,
'You will compose de first sentence if you lucky.
Den come again tomorrow early again, me to work you
    next field fa de second!'
And with dat, Ganesha pull way slow he steady pace,
De monkey behind monkeygrimacing,
Distant dust in they wake slowrising!

But even before Hanuman he pencil take up,
De monkey now pause to consider,
How might Valmiki story its former virtue regain?
How attain he de authority of his master?
Den did Hanuman upfold he legs in he yoga-rita,
Begin he to bakti he bajans,
When swift, through power of meditation deep,
Hanuman did hear Kaikeyi speaking.
Lakshman, Manthara, Kusha and Sumitra,
Sita she own voice she storytelling!
And as Hanuman continue, he listening forward,
Same voices now speaking reverse:
Sita, Sumitra, Kusha and Manthara,
Lakshman, before to end begin Kaikeyi.
Only when Hanuman inform dem each,
With he mirror-form simple enough,
Clear as you face you recalling from de sacred book,
Red as de roukou red in you palmhand palm,
Did Hanuman begin to dress he story in Valmiki
    shacksloka.
But soon de monkey did pause again,
Something now more to consider:
How might he story be publish abroad?
Where are dere monkeys enough to read it?
Where, in truth, are dere monkeys patient to trudge,

Dis mudthick-mudswamp of monkeylanguage?
But before long Hanuman put down all such worry,
In blindfaith he take up he pencil,
Since these are sad days fa monkeys fa true,
Since these are sad days fa manmen.

SO NOW TO BEGIN, once was a time,
Dat even in de essence of dis Sita-stonestatue,
Sita sheself did stepdown bold,
From she pedistal in Rama cemetery!
Now de trace did Sita retrace,
Same direction same glistening swampwater,
And offering she homage to sacred Shyama,
De shore she begin to walk, Sita searching fa she
    cherish lost-popo!
But when dose Ayodhyans see she walking dere,
When dey witness de dreamlike Sita walking,
Proud beautiful blackwoman, she capra of
    silvermoon-nimbuslight,
Morningmist-cloudshuffling air,
Barefootfeet-softstepping,
Dey did know dey visioning Mother Kali,
Return she to dem from heaven!

Quicksudden did all dose Ayodhyans adore,
Dey Sita miraculous madonna!
Uproaring-uproarious, uproarious-uproaring,
Celebrate she in homecoming proper!
Quick forth, forthwith, same cart of eighteen
    turning wheels,
Ten-thousand tall men to tote she long,
Ten-thousand palmfronds soft she path to wave,
Through de streets dey stonestatue calypsosinging:

Sal-ve Re-gina,
Regina Sita Mater!
Be-ne-dicimas te.
Glo-ri-ficamas te.
A-do-ramas te.
Regina Sita Mater!

To Ayudhya mosque-temple dey madonna bring,
Here in she chapelle side de altar,
Jewels glittering redrubies, round she candles redflame,
Here honour she Queen of Heaven!
Of incense slowrising, frangipani sweetoil,
Many prayers do dey mother soon bless,
Every piety passion to she dey did give,
Every soft Ave-whispering breath!

Every Sabbath sun dey same miracle witness,
Sita out she chapelle step down!
Leading dey following, all Kusala behind,
Same pilgrimage, same morning swampwater!
Long waiting dey now, fa dey saviour pastpromise,
Blessèd son of dey Mother son-blessed.
Sweet child is dey father, is dey father dey child,
Sweet saviour takeback to backgive!

Cross dey did come now from de earthsea four corners,
Mythmythalia, Kishkindha, Himavat,
Lanka, Rishymuka, Rishashaba, Thothmount,
Come all dey dis miracle to witness!
But now, quicksudden, dose Ayodhyans protest,
Dey madonna to share with redheathens:
'Why accept we dese strangers, such customs peculiar,
Of superstitions dey beliefs so childsimple?
Irreverent is dey ignorance fore de One True God,
Straight way dey quiet presence we prohibit!'

Lamenting dey now, all dose Lankans lament,
Dis miraculous Sita fresh forbid dem!
Jelljell dey too bad dat Ayodhya stonestatue,
Envy is dey envy coldcoveting!
Petitioning dey bold to dey Raja Kumbhakarna,
Roly Sea, Papee Bull, Bigbigbelly:
'Demand we demand we own statue miraculous,
Fa us, we own walking madonna!
To bless now she children, we own mummy now
    we claim,
Fa us, we own Kali-incarnation!'
Straight way, quick to council, all he knights
    round he table,
Loudmouth, Tinfoot, Indrajet,
Potcake, Uselesses, Bobolee, Fishface,
All assemble round he pomp holygrace!
Of fullscale regalia, is obesity oblate,
Bigbelly of monastic monstrosity:
Biretta, babybuskins, cincture and cuculla,
Mantellone, mozetta and rochet.
Tara-to-trippet, tripple-tunicle-tunic,
Silkydrawers neath he lacepetticoats!
Now blast he bombastic, beatitudenous Bigbelly,
Multitudenous secondchins reverberating,
Directing dem directions, dat Proventriculus Digester:
'Is war we declar on Ayodhya!'

Now strategies dey bloating,
Bout blateblate and blapplapsing,
When stand he to he treefoot Twohead-Fred.
In silence he waiting, such dignity commanding,
Speak he he archprimates so and so:
'Are not dese, me two hardheads, enough to wield,
As obvious me must template fa de rest of you too?
So many blindbelievers, brave and proud
    faithful followers,

To be slay unthinking,
Pon de word of one unthinking, thoughtless man!'
And den Twohead-Fred, treefootfeet standing tall,
Truth he did speak he boldface:
'Learn, my Lords, dis lesson de Goodbook teach,
Chap. 9, Deuteronomy, vs. 1–4:
Never do nothing in honesty direct,
When a swindle, underhand, does accomplish selfsame!
So stead of proudfooting on de battlefield hot,
One-two we to suicide weself,
Why not Maricha, again to transform,
Same peacock-eyespotted golddeer?
To lure way dose Ayodhyans,
While dey statue we up-grab,
Sure as Maricha lure way dat Jatayu of old!'

Now did all primatemonks proudmyrrh,
Praise dey up Maricha tall,
Celebrant he quick, he own monstrance starbursting,
Dey did mission he straight Kouskusala!
Dat same Sabbath sun, all Ayodhya behind,
Dey Sita stonestatue again walking,
Silver-dusting Maricha pass by dem amaze,
He pelt of a rainbow prism-shining!
He ears lotus-flowers, he blue eyes ice-diamonds,
Magestic horns top he head tall goldglistening!
He hooves blackest jet, sofee tail soft
     white snow,
Milky chest, amethyst, bright star-glittering!
Quicksudden pious pilgrims, bubball dey babbawl:
'Eh-eh boy, doe-is-doe, buck-a-buck!
Bring you cutlass, you bigstick quick bear,
Is only quenk like stewpot better den deer!'

Straightway did Bigbelly, he three acolytes up grab,
Dat straining stonestatue dey coldcursing.

Quick toting she quick, dey own Vaticanship waiting,
Swift Kusala dey waketurbulence she slowsinking!
Now did Bigbelly, fore all Lanka unveil,
Dis Kalika Sita-statue fresh-filch.
Quick-summoning priorprimates, together all
    he monkhosts,
Capuchins, orangutorians, gibgilbertines, graymonks,
One-hundred-fortyfour-thousand strong,
All calypsosinging together:

  Kalik-kalik Kalik-kik-kalik,
  Kalik-kalik-kalik!
  Kalik-kalik Kalik-kik-kalik,
  Kalik-kalik-kalik!

But when den Bigbelly, every power in he vesting,
While steeldrums dramatic *ping-pa-ding-pinging*,
Command he boldface: 'Cammina! Cammina!'
Dis statue, she not walking, not fa nothing!
Now did Bigbelly, he fierce anger hot wrath:
'Is swindle we own swindle backfire!
Steal we dis statue of wabeenus monkeymummy,
Good-fa-nothing bakee-plackee-penny-a-pound!'

Den did Cardinal Fishface, fa Bigbelly he fishforth,
De trick, of all such great miracles:
'Is squeeze you de poor every drop dey lifeblood,
De answer to dey prayers is shining rupees!'
So collect he of ordinance, a stiff miracle-tax,
Windballs of faith Fishface feed dem,
But when with dis offering, stood de statue stonestiff,
Bigbelly of Cardinal Fishface make callaloo!
Next Loudmouth he loudmouth, secret secrets
    sanctimonious,
Wisdom he impart he divine:
'Is de same program-menu, fa all computer-robots,

Dis statue ga do anything fa chipchip-oyster!'
So onward soldiers-christian, marching now as to war,
Loudmouth he before dem hot-bawling:
'Is off to de swamp fa oyster!'
But when den dis chipchip, bamboopole-string
    dangling-dancing,
Front de statue stonestill she coldsniff,
Straight is Loudmouth St Loudmouth stakeburning!
At longlast mangabey, tiny Tinfoot tip to tinker:
'If a buffalo could frighten fa jackspaniard,
If a elephant could fraid fa mouse,
One thing is sure as sourorange,
Dis statue fa crapo ga dance!'
But when crank tiny Tinfoot
He cornucopious gramophone,
While round he duck-size crapos did waltz,
One-two Bigbelly blunderbuss blow he nose!

Meantime it happen, dat back in Ayodhya,
Prince Rama heself busy consider,
How best dey to cope, how best dey to combat,
Dis loss dey miraculous stonestatue?
But soon enough, he head he make up,
Speak Rama to he Ayodhyans so:
'Remember you well, dat message Sita sheself did give:
Let love always stumble bold, fore you ego
    anger-wrath.
Denfore we ga raise up no weapons gainst Lanka,
All discussion, all decision to make,
We ga let fall in de hands of Kumbhakarna!
Three emissaries we ga send, now peaceful to go,
Pleading fa we statue return:
My own son Kusha, same learned physician,
With Sumitra, secondwife of myself.
And with dem to clinch, we own statue back-filch,
Same old obeah-nursemaid Manthara!

Such evidence to give, such miracles to prove,
De sainthood we patroness Sita!'

Now did all dose Ayodhyans sa-ce,
Sa-sa-yea dey three intercessors sa-ce!
Processioning to Kings Wharf, three navy pirogues,
And to row dem, six skinnywinny-wriggling
    warrahoons:

    Dim dee dim-dim day ee-ee aye-aye!
    Dim dee dim-dim day ee-ee aye-aye!
    Dim dee dim-dim day lay,
    Dim dee dim-dim day lay,
    Day ee-ee aye-aye!

Cross dey did cross den de sea to Lanka,
Kumbakarna he judgementseat take.
To decision he bold, is dey Sita dey saint?
Return she fresh-canonize to Ayodhya?
First den to testify, learned Kusha did give,
Convictions of a science death-defying!
Dis child yet enigma, dis mother yet child,
Confirmations of a birth science-plexing!
Calm is he voice, he demeanour dignify,
Gentle patience quiet Kusha persuade dem,
All such archbishops, here assemble to hear,
Proving miracles dis Sita childsaint!
But when next Manthara, she creoleobeah-Warrahoon,
Confuffling confusion commence,
Before den Sumitra spread icing de cake,
Plenty passionate she perversions plurallingular!
Stumptail now Kumbhakarna, dis sudden bigstick,
Quick kaponkle *blapplapplaps!* cross he head,
Only thinking heself lucky, never see dese again,
Only begging dem, 'Please! please you statue carry quick!'

So longlast to Kusala, dey madonna return,
All Ayodhya in de streets celebrating!
But when now fête finish, to Prince Rama quiet-serious,
Dey did beg how to end, fa good, all dese miracles:
'What need we encourage, such greenenvy of others?
How to stop we from walking we stonestatue?
Of faith now well-satisfy, we madonna is return,
Why chance we to loose she fresh again?'

Now did Prince Rama, fa wise Kusha he send forth,
Presiding at dis time over de hospital new make,
And send he fa Lakshman, he own brother-by-law,
Manager of he southmost cocoaestate.
Den did Prince Rama, of dese two he implore:
'How settle we dis question of a spiritual-morphology?
Which of de two undefeating must preside? Which one
    over de other?'
Now dis wise Lakshman, quiet Kusha by he side,
Consult dey ancient books, primal-memories address,
Fa many long nights dey did study.
At longlast to speak, all Ayodhya gather round,
Advice dey did advise dem so:
'Long as we statue, dis cathedral she reside,
Here lavish-wealth is vast-squander,
Never to remain here she destiny content,
Never stand she here proud, quiet-restful.
As dis we can tell you, we story now to prove,
Sita is ever guardian of de poor.
Live she as always simple poverty embracing,
As always, brightriches she abjure.
But give she a sanctuary, modest in design, small in its
    size and distinction.
Dere side de swamp, ever peaceful she vigil,
Dere will she remain quiet restful!'
And now begin Kusha, together with Lakshaman,
Dis tale of a birth, from a canefield fresh-furrow!

SO NOW ALL did gather, from heaven and earth,
Here in Rama holy city of Ayodhya.
Together dey did come, to he island Kouskousala,
Here to fête he horsefeast, dat great Ashvamedha!
Now did wise Kusha, and old Lakshman shake out,
De last of Valmiki shackshlokas.
Masmen disguise, travelling-minstrels to sing,
Fa all de ancient world dis *Ramayana!*
Of five-hundred cantos, twentyfour-thousand couplets,
Dis poem of gods and men.
Make by Valmiki, in reverence of Kali, trace out by he
    Hanuman scribemonkey.
Dis tale to give sons, to dose who have none,
Daughters, to dose who do read it!
To wash way all sin, all sorrow quick dissolve,
From dose who do hear it loud sung!
Longlive dey too happy, who sing dis *Ramayana,*
Dey honour is dis world, with grandsons and daughters,
Dey honour is de next world to come!
Dis tale to take up, from de beginning of time,
Future-past, past-future, now de present relate:
Of Rama quick death, neath he selfsame strong hand,
Of he meeting with Sita joyful in heaven.
Of Sita rebirth, in dis statue of stone,
Of a following, of a heritage slow make.
Of petitionings bold, of a journey cross de sea,
Of Sita home she return she fresh again.
Of de passage of time, ever slow to turn,
Of a child, of a burden now bear.
Of dis, my child, my child now return,
To take up, longlast, in dese waiting black arms!

SHE STOOD SILENT for a moment, unmoving, her
arms still outspread, palms upwardheld, a smile soft on
her lips. I stood in the knee-deep water, my feet still stuck

ankle-deep in the mud, arms still wrapped hugging around the empty cold glassbottle. She lowered her dark eyes. Slowly, carefully, she bent over: touched her index finger to the wet mud. She stood. Without looking up, she stepped forward into the water, the hem of her lace gown dragging in the ankle-deep mud. She took another careful step, another, and she stood before me, only the empty bottle between us. I felt a rush of cool current brush past my legs, a breath of cool breeze glaze my warm, bloodrising cheeks, smelled the fragrance of cool roses in a gap of the stagnant, suffocating air. She lifted her face from the water: her large undulating eyes, her dark sienna skin, the crimson mark on her forehead, her comforting lips. Slowly, carefully, she reached out towards me: touched her mudtipped finger to the centre of my brow. Touch: cool and sticky on my forehead, tingling in the centre of my brow, a trace of its memory lingering in the fingerprint of mud.

Now I watched her eyes turn toward the water again, watched her step now beside me. Watching her over my shoulder three or four careful mudstirring steps out into the water waist-deep. Stepping carefully her lacelayered-pettycoated gown billowing in a cloud softly around her, the beads of her rosary wooden big as marbles floating on the water tangled with the ends of her long dark hair, the long train of her burial-bridal veil its mesh semitransparent flowing seaform-frothy-white down from the back of her head, swirling on the surface of the tonguethick blueblack sedimentary leaves boiling up slowly out of the mushrooming, mudcloud-spreading water. She stops, her arms again outspread. Again I perceive several things almost at once: a hard silence, cold wet shadow, the wind hissing loud in the leaves of the moss-covered thick-banyaned trees arching up quivering out of the stagnant-smelling water. As I look down now to see myself reflected on the silvergreen surface: squashed and mirror-

ripple distorted, twisted on my back appearing now to
float inside of the bottle myself – my head protruding out
from the rim looking up at myself looking down – down
again through the silver rippling surface into the depths a
few yards beyond where she is standing to see him again,
appearing suddenly out of a cloud of mud erupting
suddenly between the mangrove banyans, swimming
again; snap, glide; snap, glide; as she reaches into the water
to take him up.

She turns around, her face still downwardheld, looking
at the child hidden from me in the folds of her arms. She
steps forward: towards me, beside me, beyond me now
without looking up for an instant from the child I knew
she held, but could not see in the folds of her arms.
Watching her back now her gown wet clinging with her
long dark hair, her bridal-burial veil stuck mudfrothing
seafoam-grey to her back with the blueblack leech-sucking
leaves plastered dripping greengrey muddy water. Slowly
up through the tall reeds to cross the plot of green grass
beneath the samaan tree symmetrically outspread. Along
the path of the dust stiffled now beneath the weight of her
mudlace-dripping gown. Slowly up towards the church,
her face still downwardheld, looking at the child in her arms.

With me still standing in the knee-deep water. Still stuck
ankle-deep in the mud of my on-going unending dream,
paralysed again. Unable to step forward or backward or
even to lift my feet numb up out of the mud of my old
jesusboots. Thinking: *She is the mother of you own half-uncle,
Manuelito Domingo. Frogchild, anencephalic monster, devil son
of God!* Now I could not help but believe what I had seen
with my own eyes, what I had heard with my own ears.
What I had believed already even before I had turned
around reluctant to see or to hear it. Without asking or
wanting to see or to hear what already I had known
happily and easily enough. Standing here holding the
empty glassbottle my arms wrapped hugging desperate

around it. Now all that remained of the real world to tell me that I was alive within the confines of this dream of my life, breathing. An empty cold glassbottle and the fingerprint of wet mud already drying on my forehead. That almost imperceptible mudspot-tilak tingling between my brows: wet, cold, the trace of its memory evaporating now from the fingerprint of mud already drying on my forehead. The soft mudspot which already I could scarcely recall. Another event seen or heard or touched sometime somewhere in my childhood, or my father's childhood, or my father's father's childhood which I could know, believe, but no longer remember. Not until now, seventy-seven years later, as I sit here at this desk of purpleheart, in this miniature Warrahoon-Windsor chair, as I look out of this window at this moon above the same black glistening sea. Not until now, as I close my eyes, as I touch my trembling index finger to the tip of my sticky, slow-drying tongue: touch it trembling to the centre of my brow.

But I did not need that memory in order to believe. Not now or then. Knowing well enough even at thirteen years of age that such memories only made the believing more difficult. The events of my life always seeming more implausible than all the impossible stories I had never thought to question. Never felt the need to understand. Realizing even then that the believing was beyond my control. That I was being manipulated by some extraneous power manipulating me also from within: that I had been conditioned to believe certain things long before I had thought to question what it was they were. Because by the time I had paused to consciously consider my own beliefs, the events of my life had already grown so overwhelmingly complex, so indecipherable, that to question my beliefs now only seemed absurd, irrelevant: that to question *Him*, now, at thirteen years of age, was to question my own existence. Because if *He* did not exist, then I did not exist either. That is what I told myself, what it has take me seventy-seven years to affirm: *You do not exist. You are only a dream.*

Now I felt angry, irate. Now I pulled my heavy mudsandled feet up out of the knee-deep water three or four violent loudsplashing steps up onto the bank. Now I dropped the bottle *clap* into the wet mud. Went quickly to the glass lid a few yards away and retrieved it. I raised up that thick heavy discus-lid with both hands high over my head, brought it down on the bottle with all my strength: *klunggg* – a hollow metallic thud, vibrating, the unbroken bottle driven an inch deeper into the mud, the heavy discus-lid deflecting off flipping *flunggg* into the tall reeds. I retrieved the lid again and raised it over my head again, brought it down again: *klungk.* This time the bottle broke into two large pieces. I got down on my knees in the mud, took up the discus-lid and brought it down on the pieces of thick broken glassbottle *klungk klungk klungk* again and again and again until now only half-a-dozen shards of nondescript blood-red bleeding glass remained. With the lid I scraped the wet blood-striped mud over the pieces of broken glass covering them up. I stood. Reached back. Swung my arm held straight fingers cupped tight around the discus-lid hurdling it as far as I could out over the water spinning-floating-wobbling-tumbling *clap.*

But I'd taken only a few steps up the bank through the reeds when I felt suddenly exhausted, scarcely able to pick up my feet. Reaching down quickly now my blood-dripping fingers unbuckling the straps of my old jesus-boots. But even barefoot I managed only three or four steps across the soft grass, collapsing in a heap beneath the samaan tree. And no sooner had I taken a few deep breaths, no sooner had I closed my eyes, when I saw her walking again: slowly along the path leading up to the church, the dust silent beneath the weight of her mudlace-dragging gown, still looking at the child she held in her arms.

III

MAGDALENA DIVINA

1

Mother Superior Maurina Tells of Magdalena's Canonization

. . . *oy oy oy yo-yuga yo-yuga da-bamba da-bamba oy* benedictus que venit in nomine Domini *oy* lumen de lumine de
Deum verum de Deo vero *oy* Marie conçue sans péché
priez pour nous qui avons recours.à vous Sainte Catherine
del Carmen purísima hermosa azucena maravilla ayúdame
cuídame fortaléceme socorredme favoréceme fuente de
bondad de gracias y de misericordia *silverfishflyingstarpetals*
exploding bursting out sudden silent from below the bow
glittering peals of white light wet dripping widespread
wings transparent cellophane-glistening mercury-slippery
glassgreen metal plates of armour flashing in ancient
gleamings of prehistoric living fossils rising-riiising-riiising
slow up from out of the dark depths of lost time forgotten
age-old earth-memory dripping in short takeoff trails of
they passage falling behind in tiny waterdrops puncturing
water with water in increasing increments of dramatical
quicktailflappingfuriousflurry exploding again through the
air sacred flashes of white light soaring in every direction
silvergreen songbirdfish skimming silver pectoralwings
sliding effortless smooth cross the surface in infinite
gliding-gliiding-gliiiding falling ever so slow slow before
the sudden grammatical *billbeakpressingscribblingfrenzy* to
burst again into bright light dripping again in short takeoff
trails of they passage through the other world recording

behind them in tiny white waterdrops punctuating points of water with water falling in cadence counting language rhythm steady slow cross the blueblack waterpage surface of tiny bright watermarks dissolving forever already behind them swimming again through the air stretching farther farther only a little riding-riiding-riiiding longlast *slupp* to slip silent soft one by one in through the infinite brilliant bluegreen seaglass portals of He iris-sky of the schoolchildren running uniforms of tall white socks and starch white shirts slurring slow cross the horizon of navyblue pleated skirts-shortpants red and black and brown and yellow holding hands together screaming of life and hope in the redblood morning sunset rising staletide smelling despair of the old fisherwoman calling alone from the cocoreet saltfish square of she poverty imprison *pong-fa-pong-ah-fie-pong! fa-pong-ah-fie-pong! fa-pong-fa-pong!* over and over again and again for seven days and seven nights without even a pause between the beating of that clock in my heart with my eyes close still to feel the steading poundings of He pillar of fire thrusting up stiff against the back of my throat throbbing lukewarm soursop seafoam-tasting cheesecloth-squeezing thick white pulp sloshing heavy inside my ears flooding my lungs the hollow of my heart filling to overflowing again that I can no even suck a breath of air to know I am still dying slow here again now but only to hold on tight a little *oy* to stretch to touch the tip of my *oy oy oy* to scalding aching *yo-yuga yo-yuga ba-damba ba-damba oy* José Jesú María virgo ego tali animatus confidentia ad te Virgo virginum Mater curro ad te venio Mater Verbi verba mea here now still with He long sword dripping of fire pressing up stiff between my legs to sever my being complete in two with my head rising high above the clouds with my corpse already the tiny black insect spindling far below in the bright stream swirling my head over heels backward tumbling tiny black arms and legs splaying below in the

cool water clear with He hot sword thrusting up steady
continuous now for seven days and seven nights dissolving longlast to send my head the final surging up over the
last short hill steep my heart in my mouth for the instant
pounding my head spilling forward down over the bright
boulderstone precipice falling slow now through soft
white clouds streaming milk frothy cool cross my cheeks
with my corpse drawing closer and closer there on the
ground the pelt hairy of some small putu-agouti-lappe the
skin of she abdomen soft cobo talon tear outside-inside
steaming crimson mucus glistening bloodwet pulsating
folds of flesh pulling of theyself ever so slow slow
dying-dyying-dyyying longlast *slupp* to slip silent inside-
outside again with my head falling faster and faster before
the sudden spasm-slap of the lukewarm washing oldtime
smelling wharfplank sloshing thick muddy water somewhere down between my legs with my feet numb in my
old washykongs wading careful now in slow-motion
moon-gravity stepping soft among the blueblack prickly
urchins undulating slow waves of they sharp thin spikes
stuck together in clumps hiding in every dark shadow of
my corpse still unfeeling dying my head sinking slow
beneath the warm water cooling bright bubbles clinking
glassball crystal words gentle inside my ears sinking
deeper and deeper down through the ages in layers of
icecold water freezing longlast to lie here now calm on my
back on the coral sand talcum powder white for the
moment of quiet equilibrium here now the beginning of
time on the bottom of the sea looking up at myself floating
face down reflecting against the blue céleste sea-sky surface of clouds drifting past the steady stream of bubbles
rising up from out of my mouth bright inside my mouth
swallowing one by one steady before my head begins to
rise up too passing slow out between my legs before me
below me behind me up towards the surface bright shining
my neck unstretching my face unmelting my cheeks

glowing warm against my heart beating hot nipples in toetip finger extremity pins-of-needles rising slow along my wrists-ankles-forearms-shins-elbows-thighs to seep soft moist inside my waist unnumbing hips still moving continuous surface waterwaves undulating gentle to feel Him now inside me again longlast lukewarm semisoft hips pressing up hard against Him deep inside me one last throng of death agony *oy yo-yuga* Antonio hijo mío santo de Padua tuvisteis para ir a libradme de falsos testigos acusado condenado finalmente a mi muerte longlast to discover myself again lying here in the soft grass my eyes close tight beneath my husband father son-of-my-son beneath the red orange petals falling soft flaming slow through the air on the ground again here now in this slow-burning immortelle sepulcre of death with He hard sword soft melting longlast slow here now after seven days and seven nights beneath the garlands of bluegreen Spanish moss hanging moist to brush along we backs press warm against the soft black earth-memory flowing clear byside the smooth white boulderstones crawling crown of thorns slow in tiny crimson flowers unbleeding of He passionate sacred blood here still again with this leaf on my tongue dissolving forever longlast of He last brittle yellowhite fishflay of dry saltfish flesh dissolving forever into nada nada nada y nada en nada but only the heartshape teardrop tips of anthuriums rose colour dripping now the last white drops of He white sword flying-flyying-flyyying *slupp*.

Dear Johnny,   *17 April 1938*
We have just finished burying your great-aunt the Mother Superior General Maurina. We did it as quickly as possible, with a minimum of funeral confusion, and this time I do not need your astonished face to tell me we didn't bury nothing in the ground at all. Whatever will come of all this business you are about to hear remains to be seen. We put her there in Domingo Cemetery – quiet and peaceful for the first time since

anybody can remember – there beside her daughter Magdalena, two stones away from daddy, and as far from mummy as the family plot would permit. At this moment of writing, you are no doubt still standing there at the railing on the stern of that mailboat bound for Caracas. Because you hadn't even left the dock when one of the little nuns came running up behind me to tell me that she was dead. Raped and murdered *she said, by a band of staledrunk leftover Corpus Christi Day hooligans who'd been pounding down the floor of the convent the whole night. According to the little nun, they had all climbed up the wall, and they were there in her room waiting for her when she'd finished her vigil in the chapel.*

Boy, you know these nuns and priests good as anybody else. I promised her I'd be right there, just as soon as I finish eating a little breakfast. But I hadn't even reached halfway through my eggs and blackpudding when the junior Chief of Police (a little brown-skinned fellow who tells me he used to acolyte with you, by the name of Anthony d'Nizo) when this little fellow comes busting in through the door to tell me about Mother Maurina and the band of wajanks again. What to do? I left my breakfast, took up my bag, and I went following behind him.

The same little nun is waiting for us there by the convent front door, a candle burning in her hand. She leads us up a flight of stairs, through a maze of dark musty hallways, and she stops in front of one of the doors. The little nun turns to look at the little policeman, who turns to look at me. So I turn the knob, only to find that the door is bolted up tight from the inside. What the ass! I look at the little fellow: 'How you can tell me she's dead when you haven't even been inside the room?'

Of course, the little policeman turns to look at the little nun, who turns to look at the flooring. 'Alright,' I say, 'you'd better run to the barracks for one or two of your boys to help you bust-down the door.' So off he goes to return in a minute with four others, all coming in a soldiermarch with their bootoos already in the air. Of course, this door is so rotten with oldage and silverfish-crawling, that before they can swing their bootoos twice it is flying off the hinges.

Boy, it was the same nightmare all over again: Mother Maurina lying there in the bed her ancient decrepit body dressed in nothing but its own transparent skin and yellow bones, nunclothes piled up in a pile there on the ground beside her, arms still wrapped hugging around the pillow still pressing down on her face, her jaws clamping down tight on the casing swallowed halfway down her throattube. I rest my bag on the bedstand, I take out a scissors, and with the help of the little policeman – the little nun standing above us shining her candle – I cut the pillow again from out of her jaws. I take up a white kerchief lying there convenient enough on top the pile of nunclothes, and I tie it up in a tourniquet around her jaw, which has already begun to set with the toothless mouth hanging wide open. I fix her hands neat on her breast, and I pull the sheet up over her body and tuck it in around her as best I can.

I don't know what more to do, but I have to think up something, because already there is a band of four or five nuns jammed up together in the doorway with the five policemen – all staring at me with their eyes open wide wide like I am a mokojumbie doing a dance before them – and they haven't had their fill as yet. They won't be satisfied neither, not until I give them a good dosage of bushmedicine-magic. (Of course, there isn't any door left for me to shut them out.) I go to Mother Maurina's little altar in the corner of the room, and I light the three candles standing before each of her three saints, crossing myself a few times, lighting up the room a little bit. I light the incense, waving it about in the air, crossing myself a few more times. Now in a moment of inspiration I take up the plastic squeeze-bottle shaped like the Virgin, and I improvise a little ceremony hop-skipping around the bed, squeezing a few sqeezes of Lourdes-water here and there.

Boy, I don't have to tell you autopsies are the standard

procedure these days for deaths occurring under questionable circumstances (particularly for a celebrated state enemy like this Mother Superior General Maurina) and I don't have to tell you how I am not about to perform one neither: you and I both know already well enough how this woman died. We have seen it together once before already. But I am not about to pronounce the word out loud for these little nuns and policemen to hear it, because neither am I about to attempt an explanation as to how it is physiologically possible for this woman to have taken her life by holding up her own breath. Not only that, but according to the rigours of the Catholic Church, suicide is the <u>gravest</u> of mortal sins: in their books this Mother Maurina has condemned herself to <u>hell</u> (which is why I suppose Christ had to spend three days down there himself, before they allowed him to climb the stairs).

What I do do is make a sign for all of them to come inside the room. Now at least the doorway is clear. I tell them quietly to kneel down around the bed, the policemen too. I take up Mother Maurina's big set of beads from beneath the jumble of nuncostume, and I go down on my knees myself, ready to start them off saying a rosary. This way, I am thinking, I can get out quiet and easy enough. I can make the funeral and burial arrangements, and we can get this whole confusion over with as quick and painless as possible. The nuns untie their beads from around their waists, and they all turn to stare at me again.

Boy, all of a sudden I can't remember how the ass to begin: do you start off on the cross, and if so what is the prayer? Or do you start off on the beads leading up to the neck, and if so what is the prayer? Or do you start on the first decade, and if so what is it again on the first big bead, an Our Father or a Glory Be? They are all staring at me with the room quiet quiet, and I am only sweating bolts fumbling with my beads wondering how the ass to begin. This goes on for a long minute, until I clear my throat with a loud <u>ah-ham!</u> and I bow my head to the same little nun who'd let me up the stairs. She takes the cue and starts us off, and as soon as I have calmed down a little I get up

*again, moving as inconspicuous as possible. I slide the scissors
quiet inside my bag, I take it up, I cross myself one last time,
very slow and dignified, and I bolt for the door.*

*Of course, before I can reach halfway the little policeman
speaks up: 'But how she dead, doctor? Strangulation?' That
one stops me and the prayers in one. Boy, is now I feel the first
jookerfish. I stand up there stiff as a standpipe, my back still
turned: 'Minor fibrillations of the heart,' I answer, trying to
make it sound like I'm saying something. After another long
minute I clear my throat ah-ham! again, cross myself again
with my back still turned, and the prayers start up again. But
before I can take another step, the policeman interrupts again:
'And what bout de gangrape, Doctor?'*

*That one hadn't even crossed my mind. Now I do turn
around to face them: 'Surely,' I say, 'even in this island hidden
somewhere behind God's back – even in this place shoved
somewhere up He black backside – there is no animal of the
human species capable of such a monstrosity!'*

*They are all staring up at me as though I'm speaking in a
different language. What the ass! I turn around again, put my
bag down on the bedstand again, and I take out the mirror to
fix it careful on my forehead. (This, I am thinking, should
satisfy them good and proper. And maybe if that oldman sitting
up there with his perverse sense of humor, has something of a
propensity for symmetry and balance, he will give me the
langniappe of another one of those imperforate hymen.) I take
out the torchlight, and I flash it on and off in the mirror a few
times for effect. I pull down the sheet again from off the body,
and gently I open her legs. Is now I feel the next jookerfish.
Man, she pussy full like a flood! One set of thick white
business comes draining out from inside there, and boy, I don't
have to tell you I only wanted to close up those legs again.
Instead I grab up a white veil from off the ground – as if
somehow I can make all this mess disappear, as if somehow I
can wipe it up quick quick and no one will notice – and I wad
up the veil to try to soak up this thing. But boy, the more I*

wipe, is the more it continues to flow.

'Alright,' I say. 'Everybody out! Continue your prayers downstairs in the chapel if you want! And don't waste no breath on dead Mother Maurina! Pray for yourself and the destiny of this place!'

I suppose the look on my face was enough to convince them: they all took off running. All except for the nun and the policeman who'd brought me up: these two I held back.

'Alright,' I say. 'Who are the witnesses? Who can name these men? We will clout them with the full clout of the law!'

I am in a sweat, walking up and down, and again these two are staring up at me as though I'm speaking in a different language. I realize I had better go slowly – that these two are still in a state of shock like the rest of the island – which, in fact, they were. And boy, we are all in a shock still.

I move aside one of Mother Maurina's legs, and I sit down quiet on the side of the bed. I repeat the same questions again, slowly this time. Again the little nun turns to look at the little policeman, who turns to look at the flooring.

After a long silence he speaks up: 'You know how dem carry on when dem fêting, Doctor?'

'Yes,' I say.

'You know how much dem like de nuns and de priests, Doctor?'

'Yes,' I say.

'You know how much dem like whitepeople, Doctor? Not to say _Spanish_ and _English_ whitepeople!'

'Who is them?' I say. 'Who the _fuck_ is them?'

'Is my chief, and de PM, and he five cabinets!'

– daddy

NOW HE look down on me from he big throne sitting there in he fancify carnival costume like a Dame Lorraine with the crown on he head in a big parcelpost envelope open up in two points at the top and the shepherdboy crookstick in he hand and the ring shining on he finger

with he big belly spilling-forth from out he lap to tell me
in he voice of a tantee wineywiney that we have hear
enough from you now with we eyes burning and we ears
buzzing and we nostrils flaring with all this caca you come
here to dump on we sacred doorstep that we was all happy
enough thinking you have reach you end longlast so please
come to whatever is the point you trying to make now and
finish, and I look back at him full in the face with my eyes
only spitting fire to tell him that you might think you is
Papa God self but in truth you is nothing more then a man
no different from any other with those big ugly things you
have hanging down between you legs to make you feel
you own the earth but let me tell you cojones plenty
bigger than you own have squeeze happy enough between
the grips of these two little fists because I am a woman that
nobody could never stop me from saying nothing I want
to say to nobody I want to say it in plain English perfect as
the Queen no to mix no oldbones about it no even no
cacashit mammapoule *Pope*, and I tell him just for that I
will take up my story again from the very beginning that
you will have no escape from it a-tall but only to sit right
there on you big fat pontifical backside to hear the same
story over and over from me and all the others to follow
behind in reverse sequence now until you have give up
longlast in exhaustion to proclaim she we saint sanctify
official and mark down on the Calendar for the birthday of
she death on the 16 of Apr in black and white or else by
then you will have loose you head and we can drop you off
easy enough by St Ann's House of the Bobolees on we
way home as by then there will be nothing left to say and
no voice or hand or language remaining in the end of the
word to speak it. Ay Dios mío cabron! So I take up my
story again at the very beginning in evidence of testimony
proving that she is we own patron saint without any
questions about it a-tall, that on that first meeting of Thurs
11 Feb I remember how by the time we have finish we

Rosary of the Seven Pains I have boot-off snoring a little bit right here in my pew in the chapel no even realizing we morning prayers is finish when this little St Bernadetta come to shake me from out my daydreams asking me mummy if I can go by the swamp to collect some oldbones please as we don't have no school today jeudi oui, and that is a very sad thing and no joke to laugh at a-tall because let me tell you this famous St Bernadetta is a true true chupidee that when she mummy first bring her here together with she sister and she cousin to dump them off on me in this convent I can only ask her if she come to the right place as St Ann's is cross the street? but she say no it is the convent she looking for and I say well, we have never accept a waterhead here before but we will take her up regardless as if it is an act of charity and we will try we best with her, but of course no matter how much we beat her we can no teach her nothing a-tall or to read or write or speak in no kind of English but only she own creole baboo-dialect that she can no even learn enough cathechism to answer she First Communion questions with the other children of six and seven even at the age of a hardback woman of thirty-five years, but fortunate for her she is very small and malnourish by nature that nobody would never take her for more then thirteen (sic) years at the most with she face fat like a football pleasant to kick and she big eyes always watching you dumb like a donkey own very satisfying to jook in you finger cokeeeye that the only reason she is a nun today a-tall is that one night I am sure she is going to dead by tomorrow morning with this asthma she is always having, and I declare to myself what the ass there is no harm to loose if she is dead by tomorrow morning anyway so I give her she veil, but when she wake up the following morning good as ever healthy again to mammaguy me saying you see mummy you give me my veil thinking I am going to dead by tomorrow morning but look I am no a dead canard yet pas, and I get so vex at

this swindle I tell the little baboo that if you are no dead by
tomorrow morning first thing I will take back you veil,
but of course she have never fall for that one and in truth I
never have have the heart to do it. Ay Dios mío singon! So
this little St Bernadetta is a nun official even though in
truth she never make she First Communion a-tall that all I
can say it is proof positive of that same worn-out old cliché
and general principle of Papa God that He sure does do He
work in some foolish ways, and that is the only thing I
have come up with after all these years of beating my
brains to think up some possible excuse for this useless
good-for-nothing waterhead, and of course she is always
saying chupidness that don't make no sense to nobody
a-tall like this nonsense about going to Maraval to search
for oldbones, because as you know good as anybody else
there are no oldbones by Maraval except the ones from
Kentucky leave behind on the Sunday picnics previous of
young lovers coming to court with they barrels of extra
crispy toting beneath they arms, or the oldmen hoping to
find inspiration poetic studying the crapos singandoing
and chewing on a drumbstick of special recipe, and
anyway today is Thurs that by now the hermits have come
with the swampcrabs to carry them way, but I have have
to try my best effort to humour this little bobo in the name
of charity no to make her feel too chupidee before the
others despite that it is a very difficult trial to bear
demanding the patience of a dead morocoy, so I ask her as
pleasant as I can muster myself what are you to do with all
these oldbones Bernadetta? and she explain to me how she
will carry them by Victoria Market to sell them to the
ragpickers to make sept sous to buy a pound of blackbread
to feed a whole family living desperate in a dungeon
comme boîte-sardines, and I say well that is a very nice
thing but you could save youself some trouble by just
giving them the oldbones to suck, so little St Bernadetta
agree with me that that is very good advice mummy, and I

tell her to go long to Maraval if she want but she must
carry with her she sister Sr Toinette who is twelve years of
age and she cousin Sr Janine who is fifteen years and as
much a sister to her as any other Sr Baloum-the-Cussbud
as we have namenick that little one because let me tell you
she can cuss to shame the devil-self, and I tell St Bernadetta
that you must wear you capulet on you head to protect
youself from the morning dew no to catch another freshcold to keep the whole convent up tonight again the whole
night long beating the walls and chupsing with all you
horse-coughing and donkey-weaseling worse than St
Balthezar. Aye Dios mío cabron! So as soon as they reach
Maraval Sr Toinette and Sr Baloum strip down theyself
naked to pelt in the sea splashing and screaming and
chasing guanas and crapos like any other normal little
nuns, when Sr Baloum turn round of course to ask Sr
Bernadetta if she lulu is too sweet to taste saltwater like
everybody else you little con! and St Bernadetta answer
her proper enough that no matter how bad you cuss me
cousin mummy have forbid me to take off my stockings to
catch another freshcold and anyway I don't make the habit
of stripping down myself naked like a jamet before Papa
God and all He saints comme poules-poulailler, and
anyway I prefer to say my chaplet for the Virgin oui, so of
course Sr Baloum answer her back that she can tell the
Virgin she is a con too or some other nastiness so, and just
as St Bernadetta go down on she knees in the soft grass just
there in front of the big samaan before she can reach by the
second decade when all of a sudden the bright light appear
shining at the top of the tree and out from this bright light
take shape the most beautiful youngwoman in all the
world standing between the two branches of the tree dress
in she long white dress with the blue kerchief tie up round
she waist and the white capulet on she head and the rosary
in she hand of beads of white pearls with the gold cross
dangling like bait on a hook and she feet barefoot with a

yellow rose holding between the bigtoe of each, but of course the little waterhead only continue saying she beads without even a chups to question the youngwoman who she is and what is she name like if this is nothing a-tall to meet up a BEAUTIFUL WHITELADY CLIMBS TREE as the *Bomb* headline her the following morning, but she only continue saying she beads with this whitewoman the two of them rolling the same beads together except of course in the opposite hands and for some funny reason Magdalena never do explain why she don't say none of the Aves but only the Glorias and the Paters, that when they beads is finish and they cross theyself together again the same way except of course with the opposite hand and the beautiful youngwoman smile on St Bernadetta before she take a step backward inside the bright light again without even turning to look out where she is stepping before she fall down *bloops* and bust she head like you daddy out the tamarind disappearing now like she outing the electric lightbulb, when just at that precise moment Sr Toinette and Sr Baloum-the-Cussbud come running from out the water with a crapo the size of a Peking duck jumping up five feet in the air, but St Bernadetta say she don't have no interest in no crapos a-tall but only the beautiful young-lady dress all in blanche ma-doo vraivrai, so of course Sr Baloum reprimand her straight way to stop with all those chupidee stories you always inventing as no whitewoman beautiful or ugly as a sucked mango seed have ever step she foot by this stinking Maraval but only a set of half-wild half-naked calaloo-creoles and dalpourie-coolies and pepperpot-Warrahoons just like you send here to collect chipchips for the afternoon verandah cocktails of one of those *same* rich whitelady cons! or some other nastiness so, but of course as soon as they reach back to the convent all three of them come running to tell me how this beautiful whitewoman appear to St Bernadetta to say she beads with her, and I say of course that can only be La

Diablesse sheself because why else would she be saying only the Glorias and the Paters but leaving out all the Aves? and if St Bernadetta have happen to notice by any chance she cowfoot? and that is when little St Bernadetta turn she face sad to the flooring to whisper those famous words headline in the *Bomb* of the following morning that today have become the battlecry fierce of all we feminist believers against all you clergy of mammapoules and scientists chisel proud in she gravestone only a fortnight later when Magdalena give her she promise of a death happy no in this world but the next: COWFOOT DON'T HAVE NO TOES TO HOLD YELLOWROSE. Ay Dios mío singon!

I WAS SITTING in the convent chapel, listening to the voice which was coming from behind me again, and now that it had at last ceased, I sat waiting for the clock to strike. I wanted to turn around, but I knew that I could not – not until I heard the bells. I did not even try. There on the table at the front of the chapel stood the huge starburst-monstrance, its circular glass chamber in the centre holding the white Eucharist, a dozen tiny red flames reflecting on the shining gold metal, continuous clouds of incense rising slowly around it. I counted the bells: *bong, bong, bong, bong, bong.* Now I turned calmly in my pew, comforted somewhat to find Mother Maurina sitting there as expected, the same transparent skin covering the same yellow bones, same opaque greyish eyes, same purple medusas crawling slowly across her cheeks. I was relieved also by the absence of something which I could not immediately identify, but which I realized after a moment was the absence of those gaping wings from her headdress. We looked at each other. And though I could not detect the slightest glimmer in her eyes, even the hint of some emotion in her lips, there was something nevertheless comforting in those blind eyes, in that tight mouth with the pointed chin protruding. I waited calmly now for her to get up from her pew – as I knew she would momentarily – to exit through the breezeway and disappear into the corridor leading out of the vestibule. Then I could get up also. I could cross the square already filling with the first yellow light, and I could stroll home to sit with my father on the gallery while he ate his fried eggs and blackpudding, the sky turning a soft crimson behind him, then a harder yellow, listening to the fowls scratching and the *shush-shush-shush* of Evelina already scrubbing out clothes against the jookingboard in the big washbasin full to the brim overflowing with white suds, already, even today, the day of my eighteenth birthday, the day of my departure for America. Waiting for my father to look at his wristwatch, to tell me it was time now to go upstairs and wake the others.

But there was something slightly incongruous about this scene I had conjured up, some soft anachronism there, and I soon realized that it was *Evelina*: Evelina could not have been present at this scene, because in fact she had been dead for two years. Now I experienced the first signs of an on-rushing panic – a sensation of lightness in my stomach, a slight buzzing in my ears – as I studied Mother Maurina's face for some indication that she was not dead too. Now I felt a drop of perspiration run slowly down my spine beneath my new suit. Now I felt my new clip-on bowtie biting up at my throat, my feet numb in my father's old hardbacks. Suddenly Mother Maurina raised her arm from her lap – in a movement surprisingly fluid and vigorous – holding her open palm out towards me. I breathed a sigh of relief. For the moment I did not understand what she could have meant by this gesture, but neither was I much concerned. After a few seconds I understood that she wanted her piece of paper back – Magdalena's suicide letter – but when I looked in my lap I found that my hands were empty. I turned around again.

Looked quickly on the bench on either side of me, on the floor, in the slot at the back of the pew in front of me, fumbling among the missalettes and the ragged hymn-books. I checked the pockets of my trousers, vest, jacket. Bent over to raise the kneeler and lower it again. Now I turned and lay on my breast on the pew to grope in the darkness beneath it. Now the pew was transformed into my bed in the dormitory house, and I extracted not a piece of paper, but a thick black book, SIR WALTER RALEIGH inscribed across the top: *British Obstetric and Gynaecological Practice*.

I awoke with a start, taking a few deep breaths. I threw off the sheet to feel the fan sweep slowly across my wet skin, slowly back again, and I looked over at my room-mate, still sleeping soundly in his bed. He was also a first-year medical student, a Brazilian from a small coastal town, yet he called himself Arthur and spoke with an Oxford accent: needless to say he was sure I'd arrived from out of the bush. I took up my new Timex wristwatch from the bedstand, looking proudly at the watch itself without registering the time. (It was the same watch that had travelled across the Arctic attached to the ski of an Eskimo dogsled – to the bottom of the Madagascar Sea attached to the propeller of a US Navy submarine – advertised on the television by a man named Hugh Cameron Stacy. This watch had been my only extravagant purchase since I'd arrived in New York, other than the diamond ring I'd bought from a Jamaican on the street – who'd convinced me of the stone's authenticity by digging a deep scratch across a storefront glasswindow – the diamond of course melting when I had the ring sized to fit my little finger.) My eyes focused on the clockface: 5 a.m. Two hours before I had to report to the hospital. I jumped out of bed, pulled on a shortpants and a jersey, and I buckled up my jesusboots.

There were already a few people walking hurriedly

along the sidewalk, their hands in their pockets. There were a few motorcars and vegetable trucks in the street, a jitney crowded with Jamaicans in navyblue monkeysuits and silver hardhats. Occasionally one of the trucks would come to a screeching halt before a potcake still asleep in the middle of the road. The potcake would get up slowly to its feet, stretch on its front paws, and wander off to the side. Then the truck would take off again.

It was during one of these fractured moments, in a flash of insight, that I understood why this city moved at such a rate. I came to the realization of something which had slowly been dawning on me ever since I'd arrived in America: there were no oranges to suck in this country. Not a one! At home we never walked anywhere in a hurry, not simply because there wasn't anyplace to go in a hurry, and not simply because we were slow by nature – both of which were perhaps true – but simply because we'd never think of walking anywhere without an orange to suck. It was a reflex encoded in our unconscious. And because you could not suck an orange properly without giving it your fullest attention – because the act required your whole body – you were compelled to walk at a moderate pace. And of course, as soon as you finished sucking out this one, there was a coolie waiting at the next corner for a half-cent to peel you another. And at that moment I came up with the definition of the Carribean which I'd been searching for, a definition not found in our literature or any of the tourist pamphlets: *it is the way we suck an orange.*

I also came up with a scheme to make a million dollars: I would pope off oranges on the yankees. I'd bring the oranges from home, where there were so many they were rotting beneath the trees which belonged to no one in particular. I'd also import a thousand coolies – one to stand on every corner – who'd be fighting down each other to jump in the boat as soon as they hear it is going to

America. The oranges would sell for two cents each, one of which the coolie would keep for himself (a half-cent more than he usually made) so the coolies would become millionaires by this scheme too. Of course, it wouldn't be the oranges themselves which would drive the yankees mad – those lovely thinskinned soursweet oranges packed full of seeds – not so much as the way the coolies peeled them. *Because even if the yankees had seen an orange peeled with a knife (which was highly improbable since they'd gone to great efforts to hybridize they own thickskinned spraypainted supermarket – sunkists only so they could peel them easy with they fingers) those yankees sure as hell never seen a coolieman peel an orange in two seconds in a single long peel behind he back! Man, that ga drive them ba-tooks!* Now I envisioned the small mountains of oranges on every corner, stacked on their crocusssacks in perfect pyramids as neatly as any supermarket display. Always with the single orange standing at the apex of the geometrical peak already peeled, waiting for you, wrapped up in its long curl of bright skin reassembled around it to keep the orange moist, sweet, perfect. *So before you can stop to question it or even snap you fingers that orange has already been snapped in half by the coolie's penknife quick as lightning already in you fingers rising dripping to taste you lips! Oui fute papa-yo! And better even that, you can bring some of those new peeling machines they have now. With the little cup here where you put in the orange to sit down – and you crank the crank over here a few times to peel it in long bright strings like confetti paper – and in another second you take out the orange already peeled perfect dressed in parallel stripes as fancy as a bathingsuitfish swimming beneath the dock! Oui ma-doo mon-pere!*

But suddenly I felt the ridiculing nudge of reality, and I saw the flaw in my grand design: *This scheme you scheming not ga work a-tall! Because even if you do manage to bring all these oranges, and the coolies, and the modernage peeling machines and so like you say, how you ever ga teach the yankees*

*to suck the orange patient and proper? And when you hand them
the pinch of salt?*

I turned on to my favourite street, one lined with
brownstones where all the Jamaicans and Bajans and
Trinis lived. Here I could stop and close my eyes and not
know in which world I stood. The street was full of
garbage, full of the early-morning smell of saltfish frying,
float-and-accra. The street was full of noise, already, at
six-thirty in the morning: televisions blasting and people
bawling and gramophones shouting out calypsos. Already
there were children pitching marbles in the dust, jumping
rope, busting tops on the sidewalk. There was a little boy
stuck at the top of a leafless tree, several others below
laughing and encouraging him to jump.

I remembered my father's story of the scar on his
forehead (the same crease Granny Myna boasted he'd been
born with, calling it the mark of St John); daddy had
jumped out of the tamarind tree in our backyard with a
sheet tied to his hands and feet, convincing every child on
Mucurapo Road that he would parachute down like a
yankee soldier. They had all assembled beneath the tree:
daddy let loose a Tarzan cry and dived onto his head.
There was another story of Amadao playing tic-tac-toe,
skipping stones across the duckpond in the back: on *tac!*
the stone jumped up and hit him *toe!* on his forehead (and
on *toe!* my father would slap his brow open-palmed and
look stunned as though it were fate which had struck him).
I saw the scar, running vertically down the middle of his
forehead, purple and pulsating whenever he grew angry:
*That scar could have been a natural feature fa true, except no one
but daddy has it. Daddy and St John the Baptist, still smiling
happy on the dishplate in the painting above Granny Myna and
Barto's bed.*

Just then I heard a noise behind me, and I turned quickly
to look at the group of boys laughing. Something brushed
past my face: *cocotte, picoplat?* I passed my hand in front of

my eyes as though chasing a mosquito. I turned and continued walking. Soon I found that I was sweating heavily, and I decided to return to the dormitory house. I passed a tall, gaunt oldman gingerly fishing a rubber boot out of a rubbish tin with the hook of his white cane: he looked over his shoulder at me with an expression of horror. It was the same expression imprinted on Arthur's face as he opened the door. I wiped my hand across my forehead and it came away dripping in blood.

SO NOW BERNADETTA raise up she eyes from off the flooring to tell me how she going to Maraval tomorrow morning again to see she beautiful younglady dress all in white no matter if she miss school or no, and she quote a quote from St Paul writing to the Thessalonians putting goatmouth loud on sheself and all of we at the same time saying *suffer the little children* (sic) *who will never learn to read my fish inscribe at the beginning in the end of this long chain of roadsigns since without it nothing don't say nothing to nobody a-tall and you are all to a pack of baboos babbling at the tops of you towers of tusk because this is the mark on every letter of mine it is the way I write* and I say that is the most sensible thing that you have say for a long time even though of course this text does no belong to you as yet and you have have my permission to visit you young whitelady again tomorrow morning if you want, but you must carry with you a basin of holywater from the tap in the cathedral to pelt it on her first thing soon as she appear that if she is La Diablesse in truth it will burn her like a plague of firebugs inside she chucha and she will have no choice but to jump down quick from out the tree and pelt in the sea to out it, but if she is no La Diablesse and the holywater does no burn her then you must remember when you finish you beads to ask her what is she name and if she come from Tunapuna that they could teach her this shorthand method of the chaplet by skipping out all the Aves, so the following morning of Sun Feb 14 a band of twenty or so little nuns take off running behind St Bernadetta all the way to Maraval to meet she young whitelady again that no sooner have she instruct them all down on they knees in front the tree untying they beads that before they can even reach by the second decade when all of a sudden St Bernadetta let loose a cry in ecstasy with she face rouging rouge rouge and she eyes popping and she blowing heavy that the others could only think she must have slip she other hand beneath the nundress fingering two rosaries at the same time because nobody seeing nothing a-tall but only the empty tree, and now St Bernadetta jump up to run by the tree to bathe it down with that basin of holywater saying if you come from Papa God stay but if you are La Diablesse in truth then jump out this tree and run in the sea to out youself, with all the little nuns thinking of course that this St Bernadetta have loose she head viekeevie now for true pelting holywater and telling the tree to run in the sea to out youself, and now she saying look how she is smiling beautiful on me for wetting her down with that sweet holywater and look how she is dress just like me all in white with she white capulet on top she head and the blue kerchief tie up round she waist just like me and look how she is the same height as me exact the same size as me looking no more than fifteen (sic) years exact like me with she dumb donkey-eyes and she fat football-face and look if I hold up my right hand she hold up she left and if I cross myself she cross sheself and if I make a monkeyface she make back the same monkeyface, when all of a sudden Sr Baloum have decide that we have see enough of this bubball now and she pick up the big boulderstone from out the bush to pelt him *blaps!* cross St Bernadetta head kaponkle cold on she backside with all the little nuns jumping up running round in circles crazy now like a pack of yardfowls for a handful of stalerice, when all

of a sudden the earth stop to hold she breath for that big
boulderstone to rise up slow of heself in defiance of all the
principles of gravity with all of them looking up astonish
rubbing they eyes at this boulderstone floating in the air
before them, when all of a sudden *blappaps!* he pelt back Sr
Baloum cross she head kaponkle too cold on she backside
byside St Bernadetta with all these little nuns so excited
now by this miracle of the BEAUTIFUL WHITELADY
PELTS BACK SR BALOUM as the *Bomb* headline it the
following morning that all they can think to do is take off
running back to the convent again to tell me about it, and I
say this is wonderful frontpage news in truth but where
are the two little kaponkles? and they answer that in truth
mummy with all that miracle excitement we have forget
them there still kaponkle cold on they backsides, that now
of course we must take off running all the way back to
Maraval again only to find them kneeling side-by-side
good as ever beneath the tree and St Bernadetta is praying
she chaplet calm as anybody else without even a symptom
of she ecstasy remaining on she waterhead face, but I say
this is miracle enough for me as I never yet witness Sr
Baloum-the-Cussbud saying a prayer ever since she arrive
in the convent three years ago, so now all of we go down
pon we knees together to celebrate the first miracle of this
boulderstone for the remainder of the thirteen decades that
when we have finish I ask St Bernadetta if she have
remember this time to ask the whitelady she name and she
say of course again no, that in truth with all this miracle
excitement she must have forget, that I can only push a
chups at her for that as this is *twice* now already the little
chupidee have forget to ask the whitelady she name, and I
tell her tomorrow morning when you come back for the
third apparition you must make sure to bring with you a
writingpencil and a paper for this whitelady to mark down
she name on it because even if you *do* manage to remember
to question her what it is without no doubt a-tall by the

time you reach back to the convent you will have forget it
again, and St Bernadetta answer that that is very good
advise mummy and I will do just as you say and bring the
pencil and writingpaper with me because even if I do
remember to question her what it is by the time I reach
back home I am sure to confuse it with some other like
Inadequate Contraception, or else remember it front-to-
back like Conception Immaculate, and now she take up
that same big obzockee boulderstone from off the ground
that I can only whisper to myself what-the-
motherasschucha and she say the whitelady have instruct
her to tote this boulderstone the remainder of she days for
the penitence of sinners. Ay Dios mío shitong! So the
following morning of Thurs 18 Feb the whole convent get
up at the crack of dawn like a nest of jackspaniards buzzing
to march chupsing behind St Bernadetta walking at no
miles an hour due to this big boulderstone she toting all
the way back to Maraval where he belong, but of course I
have make sure to give her the writingpencil and paper the
previous night as I am no missing this opportunity to sleep
in late that such a chance does come long but once of a
bluemoon, and St Bernadetta instruct them all again down
on they knees in front the tree that before thay can reach
by the second decade she fall in she ecstasy again with the
face rouging and she eyes bulging and blowing heavy
saying again look how she smiling on me and look she
look just like me and so on and so forth, but straight way
Sr Baloum take way St Bernadetta chaplet announcing
very sensible that *nobody* is reciting another bead before
this invisible whitelady mark down she name on this
writingpaper in black and white for all of we to read it
except of course the little waterhead sheself, and we can all
know Bernadetta is no fantasizing all this whitelady-
bubball to swindle we hot like the magic books you tired
buying in the supermarket now of days you little conartist,
and St Bernadetta say that that is very good advice cousin

and she stand up to go by the tree reaching on she toes to push the writingpencil and paper between the two branches just where she have pelt the holywater the day before, but no sooner have she rest it down when she turn round again to pass through the crowd of nuns chupsing in chorus at St Bernadetta walking towards the swamp but only looking backwards over she shoulder with the whitelady directing her two giant-steps this way and three crapo-jumps the next like they playing the schoolgirl game of mummy-may-I, and now she go down on she knees right there in the mud only a few steps from where the water is stenching to scratch out a little hole full of stinking chourupa swampwater, and just as St Bernadetta have wash she face with some of this muddy chourupa and scrub out she eyes with some of the same chourupa and scrape off a fistful of moss from the mangrove banyon byside her to eat it washing it down with a big handful of the same stinking chourupa swampwater when Sr Baloum pick up the boulderstone again for the WHITELADY PELTS BACK SR BALOUN AGAIN like if you reading the same frontpage headlines in you sleep again and this is only a dream or else a misprint, when in fact all this is all hard historical reality you reading without any of those magic tricks about it a-tall by now no only obvious enough but tedious too, because all this is thief hot-off-the-press from a master historian-theologian following strict historical methods of *meticulous scholarship base for the most part on primary sources of unpublish documents and convent records in black and white without no unintentional misprints about it a-tall and translate official from the original Francois Trochu by the spiritous father of a famous Irish priest Fr John Joyce complete with the pictures to prove it* that when everybody have calm down again longlast and we are all back in the convent dead from exhaustion after four trips to Maraval in two days and I ask St Bernadetta to please rest down you boulderstone a moment because you are giving me loud growing-pains just to look at you fat face groaning, and kneel down here before me child that I can question you why you have do all this nastiness of eating mud and drinking chourupa and so, but she can only smile up at me with that same creamsoda feeling again to reach inside she sleeve for the same little piece of writingpaper holding it out for me to take up now in my own hand trembling to read it again: SEE SPOT RUN. JESUS WAS BORN IN THE CITY OF BETHLEHEM. And I clasp my hands to my breast and I say *yes!* and she answer back *yes!* and I say *yes!* again and she answer back *yes! yes! yes!* and I take off running across the schoolyard for that same big red firstform tombstone-textbook open now to the last grammatical exercise instructing schoolchildren where to put in the full-stops and the amber-lights sitting side-by-side together again to witness this miracle of transformation before my own ears: *so then Miss Jane slap on the tail of that handsome Mr Clark a full dosage of the secret kriptonite now to sustain him three to four hours at a stretch with that big red brute of a crowbar he have so big she frighten it going to burst any moment spraying we all down again in a shower of blood though he nose is no so big a-tall when you coming to think about it . . .* THE MIRACLE OF THE READING CHUPIDEE as the *Bomb* headline it that before you can twink you eyes twice already there is a line up of chupidees stretching all the way to Tunapuna each waiting they turn to scratch in the mud and scrub out they eyes with that chourupa swampwater and bawl out miracle! in every funny kind of language as you can just imagine to make this place you living in no only the most illiterate on the face of all the earth but now the most confuse on top because this chourupa don't make no discretion a-tall as to who is to read what where and when with the little Chinee from Grande Sangre reading out loud in he ancient Greek Sophocles and the old Warrahoon from Blanchisseuse who never yet see a book in he life much less to know what to do with it but tear out a leaf to wipe heself or light the coalpot all of a sudden sololoquizing a Hamlet in the original Danish and on top of that if you only make the mistake of scrubbing out each eye with a different handful of stinking chourupa you will find youself reading Mondongo in one and Coonoomoonoo in the next both at the same time without knowing what you seeing or who you hearing in which ear neither. Ay Dios mío cabron!

Chief of Police Sargeant d'Angla have today declare 22 March of the fiscal year to be headline in the morning Bomb *an OFFICIAL STATE OF PUBLIC CONFUSION. Issuing forth he report to all he inferiors standing before the barracks on a saltfish crate and speaking impassion though a pasteboard funnel the size of a small Christmas tree he did: 'Command every manjack of you to ready you bootoos and a goodsize chockstone or a sweetdrink bottle in each pocket prepare at all times to pelt. Dress to be full carnival costume. It will be necessary to establish a two-way stream of traffic on the trace leading to the swamp. Chupidees walking in the direction of the swamp (west) together with wheelchairs pushing and cripplecots toting to keep to the left (the side of the one hanging higher). Newly miraclize chupidees returning to the Municipal Library in Alexandria (east) to keep to the right (the side of the one hanging lower). Also recommend is a basin of icewater very effective to pelt on pilgrims dropping to the ground like dominos one after the next in predictable charismatic spasms encourage by the church of recent with they fits of malkadee and jooking up and speaking in astoofar ofheardun tongues.'*

A statement coming from the twelve (sic) year old St Bernadetta sheself quoting a quote from the as yet unidentify whitelady in the tree: 'Having promise to all you baboos foolish enough now to scrub out you eyes with a handful of stinking chorupa just because I say so nothing less than the continuing exasperation of deciphering this book. Which is the false promise

*of faith. The delusion of profits.' When ask of the meaning of
that one the little saint say she don't know sheself: 'I only say
whatever chupidness comes inside my head and excuse it as divine
inspiration.' When ask of she goals for the future the little
beautyqueen reply that she hope one day to make she First
Communion: 'As of now I am still stump by the question of the
three-in-one.'*

*A contradictory statement coming from the Mother Superior
General Maurina that she own forecast for this event is very
unlikely if a-tall: 'As of now she is nothing more than a
waterhead who have receive the special miracle of reading. No
different from the counting donkey or the billy who sings God
Save We Queen from Barnum-and-Bailey. In fact she still
dribbles on sheself regular and continues to paint religious pictures
on the wall with she caca no matter how much we beat her.'*

*Another quote from his ladyship the Monsignor Roderick
O'Connor: 'That yesterday at the six o'clock in the midst of
distributing some sacred fish I did happen to notice a little nun
kneeling at the altar-rail with a bright halo shining round she
head. I was struck by this sight. Convince that it can be no other
then a genuine solar tinpaper-dish on the Budweiser cap of one of
those little handheld solar-electric fans that she must have thief
from a yankee tourist, I immediately set my head to thinking up
some swindle by which I could pope it for myself: a solid gold
rosary, a month of indulgences to be offer up in she name, a
Lazyfingers battery vibrator. In truth I did give her a Holy
Communion bread without even realizing who she is in the
temporary distraction of a vision of myself marching the Pentecost
Pilgrimage dress as always in my Dame Lorraine carnival
costume of infinite petticoats beneath the August sun beating
down to further kill the dead, but for the first time with a smile on
my face: omnipotent, invincible, the tinpaper-dish shining bright
on my head and the tiny plastic blades of that little solar-electric
fan in my hand whirling way! Only after the harsh reality of a
squingy second collection am I further reduce by the realization of
an authentic halo on the head of this little baboo from Suparee, St*

Bernadetta. From that moment my anxieties cease and I have give up all faith in the apparitions.'

A further Medical Report coming from St Maggy Chief Physician and Warrahoon Bushdoctor-in-Residence Dr Brito Salizar: 'That he own careful examination of the patient confirm she a regular cataleptic with a delicate constitution and obvious nymphatic and nervous temperament. She have thirteen (sic) years on she head but to me she looking more like eleven (sic). She face fat and pleasant. She eyes big and bloat with a lively expression at the top. She skin green green like green. Particular during frequent fits of horse-coughing and donkey-weaseling. Due to she asthma. Occasional spitting up blood. Otherwise the patient eats, drinks, and sleeps wonderful well. I can't think of nothing else.'

SO NOW the mammapoule Pope interrupt my story for the second time to look down on me again with he voice of a tantie wineywiney asking if you have any proof positive for all this bubball you are quoting out of context from ancient senile memory confuffle according to you own personal gains and prophets, and I look back at him again with my eyes only spitting fire to ask him if he take me for some fool slash-and-burn hackwriter-pennyliner that I am no willing to acknowledge the secondhand resources of my ancestors right here in black and white as I present to him the complete nolle contendre prosequi contain in this black book you holding in you hands full to the cover overflowing with nothing more than frontpage stories steal repetitious from the *Bomb* incomplete chrono-logical disorder with the table of contents at the front listing the whole of this great fortnight of thirteen head-lines of apparitions each with the precise date behind it proving without any questions a-tall the appearance of this beautiful as yet unname whitelady in the tree to St Bernadetta no including of course the one apparition lost

in translation due to an emergency behind the seagrape
bush and dedicate in particular to the scientific analysis of
St Bernadetta WONDERING ROCKSTONE and pro-
ving without any questions that he is a boulderstone no
different from any other compose approximate of equal
proportions of rock and stone with a splattering of blood
identify as belonging to Sr Baloum otherwise namenick
Baloum-the-Cussbud from two separate occasions headline in apparition #3 and #4 in which this boulderstone
did rise up heself in the air to defy all the scientific
principles of boulderstones either to remain resting or
continue rolling or even to grow a little moss if he choose
but never before to kaponkle nobody of he own free will
for two apparitions in a row, that by now the whole of
Corpus Christi is so viekeevie over all these miracles one
after the other with so many thousands of chupidees
descending on Maraval eating mud and drinking chourupa
swampwater that nobody can know how it is they don't
drink the swamp dry and dig out that big samaan by she
roots except of course to shrug it off as another useless
good-for-nothing miracle that none of those scientsts can
explain why it is the more mud those chupidees eat up is
the more mud appear beneath the samaan tree, and the
more chourupa those chupidees drink down is the more
chourupa fill up the swamp until Maraval have swell up to
burst she banks threatening to drown out the whole of
Suparee and sink it beneath a mudbath of stinking chourupa, with the cocodrilles walking the streets and taking up
residence in the basements of all the houses that the Chief
of Police have have no choice but declare ANOTHER
OFFICIAL STATE OF PUBLIC COMMESS and he
erect a big tall barrier of oldboards and sections of rusting
corrugation tinmetal and pieces of old pasteboard with
here and there a platting of palmthatch all nail together in a
jumble, because this is the only way those baboos know to
build anything a-tall with the great wall going in a big

circle right round the tree with a hundred-and-one bills stick official to it with laglee to catch a thousand-and-one picoplats whistling all together in such a great uproar that you have have to plug you ears no to loose you balance while you struggling to decipher these bills post in a hundred-and-one different languages excepting of course proper English that still there is nobody in this place who have bother to learn that one FORBIDDING ANY MORE CHUPIDEES TO COME NEAR THIS TREE TO SCRATCH IN THIS MUD AND DRINK DOWN NO MORE CHOURUPA FROM THIS STINKING SWAMP ON PENALTY OF DEATH EXCEPT OF COURSE OFFICIAL PATIENTS OF ST ANN'S ALREADY UNBALANCE ANYWAY THAT READING IS THE SOLE SOURCE OF PLEASURE IN LIFE FOR THOSE BOBOLEES but even so the following morning of Tue Feb 23 St Bernadetta lead she band of little nuns marching behind her chupsing as always due to that big boulderstone she is toting at no miles an hour all the way back to Maraval where it belong for the #7 and central and most confusing apparition of all, that of course along the way every chupidee from Wallafield and Blanchisseuse and Alexandria and Grande Sangre and San City and St James and Tunapuna and every village between St Maggy and End of the World Rock have come out to follow behind her each with a goodsize chockstone or a sweetdrink bottle in they pocket to pelt back at those police if they only try to stop St Bernadetta from giving them another useless no-good miracle that of course soon as they have reach Maraval she only have to give them the command to let them loose! because let me tell you whether or no a dahlpurie-coolie can chink a chockstone, or a pepperpot-Warrahoon can pelt a sweetdrink bottle, I could never say as I am still in my bed in the convent dead to the world, but one quote I can sure quote from the *Bomb* is BOODOOM! that big barrier of boards is blow way

LIKE THE HOUSE OF THE THREE LITTLE
QUENKS. Ay Dios mío cabron! No sooner have little St
Bernadetta instruct them all down on they knees again to
take out they chaplets except of course the three-hundred
or so monkeys who have scramble up in the tree hanging
from every branch and risking life and breath for only a
single glimpse of St Bernadetta rouging and blowing
heavy in she ecstasy like if it is the samaan byside the
Queenspark Oval and Great Britain is squeezing the bowls
of West Indies again, but before they can reach by the
second decade Sr Baloum take way St Bernadetta chaplet
again to give her the writingpaper and pencil again for the
still as yet unidentify whitelady to write down she name
when no sooner have St Bernadetta finish she game of
mummy-may-I again to go down on she knees in the mud
to scratch and drink some more chourupa and so on and so
forth, when the earth stop to hold she breath for the same
Chief of Police sitting there on the back of he big black
steed grinding he teeth to decide that we have see enough
of this bubball now and there is only *one* sure way to put a
stop to it, as he take out he pistol very cinematographic in
slow motion with a slight pan beating in the background
dramatic and he arm holding straight with he eye squint-
ing down the length of the shoulder aiming precise to fire
BOODOOM! STRAIGHT THROUGH THE EARS of
little St Bernadetta with all the nuns and chupidees jumping up running round in circles crazy again and two or
three of the little monkeys loosing they grips to tumble
out the tree on top they heads like you daddy out the
tamarind when one by one they begin to realize now that
this St Bernadetta is no faze in the very least by this bullet
passing straight through she head and she scarce even
notice it a-tall but only to pause a moment from she
scratching to pass she hand in front she eyes like she
chasing a mosquito before she go back to she business of
drinking chourupa and so on and so forth, with that

physician Dr Brito Salazar who is standing right there byside her studying the effects of she ecstasy from a personal scientific curiosity busy at the same instant the pistol fire with a candle trying he best to burn a hole through the patient wrist to see if she could even notice the smell of she own flesh squinging, of course resting down he candle now a moment to take up a gauze from out he big black doctorbag and dip it inside a little bottle of iodine pushing one end of the gauze in through one ear and out the next with a quick little back-and-forth shuffling movement between she ears like the last little tapdance of the shoeshineboy spitshining you shoe before he extract it again out the other side explaining later to the *Bomb that that bullet have apparently enter one ear to pass straight through she head and exit out the other in the only possible trajectory leaving all she vital organs untouch and intact that it is a miracle I am still alive as I am standing just byside her* as one by one all the little nuns and chupidees go down on they knees again quiet watching St Bernadetta unfaze in the least carrying on good as ever with she nastiness that before they can even have a chance to catch the breath from one useless miracle when the earth stop to hold she breath to prepare for the next, with St Bernadetta boulderstone rising up again in the air and all the little nuns and chupidees again bawling out and jumping up to take off running in circles again because nobody know who the ass the whitelady preparing to pelt this time when of course BOODOOM! CROSS THE HEAD OF THAT CHIEF OF POLICE that before he can even manage to tumble kaponkle off he horse when those half-a-dozen of he little policemen standing right there byside him waiting with they basins of icewater that before he can even know what have hit him that poor horse is pelt with a shower of icecubes flying and freezing icecold water from every direction that he let loose a horsecry with he horseeyes jumping out they sockets and he take of pelting in the sea to warm heself, with this Chief of Police flat on he backside in a puddle of mud and jumping chupidees. Ay Dios mío cabron! So when the whole confusion have calm down again and we are all back in the convent dead from exhaustion after all those interviews and photography sessions with all of we standing in a circle holding hands round St Bernadetta standing in the middle holding up she big boulderstone above she head like she studying him beneath the light, no forgetting of course that special prize-winning frontpage featurephoto of journalistic genius in selfparady without seeming the least bit unconscious a-tall showing me bending down to peer through one of she ears to read the headlines of that same morning edition of the *Bomb* through the other BOODOOM! BOODOOM! BOODOOM! that when we have all calm down again I ask St Bernadetta to please rest down that thing a moment that you giving me loud growing pains again and kneel here before me child that I can question you how it is that bullet have no kill you dead as a doornail, but of course she only look up at me again with the same oversweet creamsoda feeling to make you sick to you stomach by now reaching inside she sleeve for that same yellowhite fishflay holding it out for me to take it up again in my own hand trembling with rage to read it again: *The boulderstone was big and obzockee. I was having a hard time toting him.* And I clasp the paper to my breast to bawl out *no!* and I bawl out again with all the anguish of my livelong life of misery *no! no! no!* as I draw back my fist with my knuckles clench tight to cuff her a blow with all my strength in the middle of she fat football face saying you will NEVER write this book in you own name to bring the destruction of all the earth and she answer back no, of course not mummy, but only under the pseudoname of one of the many many positive authors. Aye Dios mío singon! THE MIRACLE OF THE WRITING CHUPIDEE that I can only run to my room to fall on my knees and raise up my hands in the air to thank Papa God that this little St Bernadetta will be dead as a duck in three days time just as Magdalena have promise the world for we happy ending but HOW is this book EVER to end with everybody always jumping up back to life soon as they drop down dead and you can have a chance to catch you breath, but even if this St Bernadetta DO manage to stay up the whole night all night for the three nights remaining scribbling way in the dark what with three more apparitions #11 #12 and #13 still remaining to go and three more trips to Maraval for three more useless miracles and three more interview photography-sessions yet to endure, then she can no possibly even get through the first chapter if we are lucky and there is truely a Papa God living upstairs in heaven with any feelings for we a-tall no to mention He own SELFSAMESELF? but of course I should have know better then any of that cacashat because this St Bernadetta have scribble way in she epileptic fit of continuing ongoing ecstasy until with she last breath she manage to scribble at the bottom of the last page *The End, Alba De Tormes, 1582* before she expire that in truth she complete the whole of this terrible LIFE-STORY with such conviction of imagination and divine inspiration that when at last the work is publish after many years of inquisition and censorship of course all those chupidees read it as historical fact without any fiction about it a-tall, that in no time they invent a whole reality to coincide with it and several orders of Carmelites establish under the same pseudoname of this positive author of such a thin disguise that any passage you study at random *like struggling against a great thick crowbar standing all the time to leave me in utter exhaustion* with the big publishing houses completing the mythology by inventing a fictitious celebrity to coincide with this fictitious pseudo-writer and make theyself a fortune with she fat football face on the cover and the two scratches overlooking she right cheek from the time Sr Baloum try to dig out she eye because that is the most important gimmick to make a bestseller these days and they go so far as to invent three more sequels PERFECTION and FOUNDATION and INTERIOR CASTLE to flood the market posthumous. Ay Dios mío singon! That when she lead she pilgrimage of chupidees the following morning of Fri Feb 26 for the #10 apparition and no sooner have she fall in she ecstasy again when the beautiful whitelady begin to give her some special instructions this time about the building of a chapel that she must go to that man whoever he is in charge of this place and demand of him that he must build this little chapel to be dedicate in my name right here byside the shore of this swamp that it is my favourite place byside this big samaan tree, when straight way Sr Baloum jump up to bawl out again you little conartist! how are we to build this chapel dedicate in she name when she wouldn't even tell us not for nothing what it is, but every time we give her the writingpaper she mark down more nonsense on it, and which MAN in charge of this island is she talking about a-tall when everybody in the whole Caribbean know that this Chief of Police is nothing more than a tantie with he toetee the size of a whistle that it can no even stand up to make a little tweettweet, and worse even than HIM is that mammapoule Monsignor O'Connor that everybody in the whole of Christendom know he is good for nothing except of course buttending a little Shawn or Shem or a blind old Isaac behind the sacristy wall, and if there is ANYBODY a-tall in charge it can only be we WOMEN clutching they cojones in the palm of we hands, and Sr Baloum announce to the crowd of chupidees that anybody who can BEAR to hear ANOTHER word of this chupidness could pelt the last chockstone, and with that of course *blaps!* she pelt a chockstone *blups!* with all the little chupidees following she advise *blaps! flaps! plaps!* and St Bernadetta have no choice but to take off running like a potcake behind a bigstick. Ay Dios mío shitong! So when

she present Monsignor O'Connor with the frontpage of
the following morning explaining everything about how
this as yet unname beautiful whitelady demand of him to
build this chapel in she name just there byside the swamp
that she can gather she flocks together of every race and
religion and we will all one day be one big happy family
for we happy ending, but the mammapoule question her
sensible enough of course that why should he build her
this chapel in the bush of Suparee by Maraval for only a
handful of dahlpurie-callaloos and pepperpot-mondongos
who are the only putus able to bear such a stench and enjoy
it when she have a nice big cathedral right here in St
Maggy, but he say that I will forgo all that and give the
whitelady she chapel if she want in exchange for the small
personal miracle of a satellite dish like any other Third
World minister-politician for my TV, so the following
morning of Sun 25 Feb St Bernadetta lead she crowd of
chupidees back to the swamp for the #11 apparition all
marching happy longlast at a reasonable pace due to the
fortunate accident of forgetting she boulderstone there at
Maraval where he belong on the apparition of the previous
day, that soon as St Bernadetta arrive beneath the tree she
begin to search on the ground and in the bushes where she
have leave that boulderstone that she can no find him
noplace a-tall, when all of a sudden she fall to she knees in
she ecstasy again with she face rouging and blowing heavy
as usual pointing up in the tree at the same spot just where
the whitelady always appear saying now that this is the
greatest miracle of all with my own prayers answer now in
full without any questions about it a-tall that I will
NEVER have to tote that big boulderstone again, because
look where he is lodge up there in the tree even though of
course I would have prefer this miracle last week as I only
have two more apparitions left to live regardless but even
so better late than never, that now they all look up where
St Bernadetta is pointing to see with they own eyes this

miracle of the BIG BOULDERSTONE CLIMBS TREE
that to this day none of these scientists can explain how he
climb up there without a forklift or a crane that such
machines are no even invent as yet by the yankees, and
even if they are you would never find them in this place
where it is easier to pay a thousand coolies less money to
pick up a steelbeam or a pallet of bricks or to stamp out
you Thanksgiving-Laborday specials at K-Mart then it
cost you to buy a gallon of unleaded to put inside the
crane. Aye Dios Mío shitong! But even so Sr Baloum
jump up of course to reprimand her again you little con,
who could care about that boulderstone up there in the tree
unexplainable when we have all watch him already in
action floating in the air and pelting yours truely on three
separate apparitions? and why you beautiful whitelady
don't give we a proper miracle with some practical
application like a poprock CD each but of course if you
only ask her she would no doubt drop on we heads a
useless LP of heavymetal so don't even bother to waste
you breath, and tell me why it is a waterhead like youself
should deserve any personal miracle a-tall even if it IS
nothing more than to pelt that boulderstone up in the tree
and out from my reach that I would like nothing more
than to kaponkle you again with him right now this
minute, that of course they all follow she advice again
straight way for the CHUPIDEES PELT ST BER-
NADETTA AGAIN that when Monsignor O'Connor see
the frontpage the following morning he tell her now that
he would settle he stakes for only a VCR, but even before
she can have a chance to drop to she knees in preparation
for apparition #12 when the whole crowd of thousands
and thousands of chupidees fall down in they ecstasy
THEYSELF now all rouging with rage and blowing blue
with they bile hot overboiling at this boulderstone no
different from any other only the day before except of
course lodge unexplicable up in the tree carve now miracu-

lous overnight into the BLACKEST of BLACKEST
madonnas the world have ever see, as if Papa God Heself
have comission He own monkey-michelangelo to hang by
he tail from the tree all night long to carve out this
stonestatue anonymous except of course for some mysterious googleeye fish swimming indecipherable cross that
blue kerchief tie up cross she chest BANG between she
TOTTOTS, because how the ass else could this black
madonna get up there? and where the caca she come from?
and who the fregando do you think you are St Bernadetta
telling we all along this is a beautiful WHITElady when in
truth she is BLACK AS THE DEVIL BACKSIDE? but of
course St Bernadetta only answer her shaking she head
that if you recall Baloum I have never ONCE say my
beautiful younglady is a whitewoman a-tall, but only that
she is DRESS all in white except of course for that
BABYBLUE kerchief tie up round she chest as you can
very well see with you own eyes, that in truth I don't have
no idea myself what is the colour of she skin as she always
appear with that bright light shining in my eyes that she
could be ANY colour you want to make her black or
brown or red or yellow and you would never know the
difference, and furthermore still HOW is it possible that
this stonestatue could be fairskin when all of you know
good as me that that boulderstone I am toting now for
almost a fortnight is a BLACK boulderstone of BLACK
marble BLACK as the devil backside or maybe you forget
me saying that one TOO? Ay Dios mío cagon! And now
of course as if she have no cause enough confusion already
this little St Bernadetta have to add ANGER to INCENSE
quoting a quote from St Paul writing to the Corinthians
for the second time saying *have not Papa God make wise the
chupidness of chupidees? For since in the chupidness of Papa God
the chupidees did not know Papa God by He own chupidness, it
please Papa God through the chupidness of what we chupidees
chupify chupidly chupiding* and on and on and on like a

broken record until they begin to pelt her and she take off running again like a potcake to save sheself, but when I wake up the following morning of Tue 2 Mar soon as I read the headlines in the *Bomb* and study the picture of the statue proper I take off running straight way to little St Bernadetta bedroom and I take her up gentle in my arms and try my best to console her that Papa God have decide to take way she boulderstone again as there is no way for me to tell her how He have promise to give him back to you in heaven again first thing tomorrow morning if I can possibly help it without incriminating myself, much less to explain to her the significance of this great miracle that there is nobody but me remaining in the world who have live long enough to remember all those years ago that this living saint did walk the earth byside we in all she virtue that now she have return to we longlast in the shape of this as yet unname beautiful black madonna that she can be no other than my own daughter MAGDALENA DIVINA, and I grab up St Bernadetta hand pulling her saying come quick to collect Monsignor that we can run quick to Maraval for the final apparition #13 and Magdalena can tell we all the news of Barto and Papee Vince and that Dr Domingo and Evelina and of course the little chucha Granny Myna that we have no hear from them in such a long time, and Magdalena can tell us where she want she chapel and how big she want it and if we should bottle that chourupa in all its natural effervescence to pope it off on the yankees and make weself a fortune like Perrier easy as Levis to the Red Chinese, so I make my second trip to Maraval after this beautiful fortnight in a row of sleeping in late every morning that I can only thank Papa God I didn't waste no time going to the apparitions in between, that soon as St Bernadetta direct us down on we knees again for the last time except of course the three hundred or so monkeys hanging by they tails from the tree to get a good view again that no sooner have she fall in she ecstasy

when Sr Baloum take way she chaplet for the final time
saying to me sensible as always, mummy what is the use
of listening to this talking stonestatue as to where she want
she chapel and how big she want it even if she name IS
Magdalena Divina as you say mummy because NO-
BODY but you have never heard a word about her before
and HOW are we to know you have no invent this name
to coincide with all those other fantastic stories you are
always selling the Third World like IMMACULATE
CONCEPTION and STILLBIRTH BY CAESAREAN
and THE CHILD OF BETHLEHEM and even you
famous lecture publish in the soubonne LE BOIS SACRÉ
and so on and so forth ad-interminum you ancient old con,
when the HARD REALITY is another story altogether of
that statue stuck up there that there is no way possible to
get her down except to call in a thousand coolies with they
cutlasses swinging to chop down the tree or else to wait a
thousand years for some yankee to invent he forklift,
when just then of course the earth stop to hold she breath
for Magdalena to come to life again in the statue smiling
beautiful as ever with she big dark eyes and she comforting
lips that now she begin to climb down slow from out the
tree with all the chupidees bawling and slipping they grips
to tumble down on top they heads before they can jump
up again to follow walking behind her up and down and
back and forth byside the swamp with occasional reststops
to transform sheself to the statue again that as soon as we
catch we breath she start off again leading we scampering
over the mangrove banyans and wading through the mud
high as we waist until the Chief of Police decide that we
have see enough of this bubball now and there is only one
way to put a stop to it and finish as he jump off he big
black steed to slap the cufflinks loud on Magdalena wrists
dragging her by a rope tie up round she neck behind he
horse walking barefoot in a cloud of dust and bawling
chupidees still following behind them all the way back to

St Maggy, and he lock her up in the jail for four or five days until we have have a chance to build the big iron cage for her to live in the cathedral proper like all the other miraculous statues that none of those chupidees can molest her and bite off she bigtoe in they ecstasy to kiss she foot like they did to poor Teresa after she is dead peaceful enough for thirty years, with a throne in she cage to sit down and rest sheself and a pedestal to stand up if she choose because how else can we keep this statue from walking way as soon as we back is turn? Aye Dios mío cabron!

TABLE OF CONTENTS

VOL III

SO NOW this Dame Lorraine Pope interrupt me again for the third time to tell me in he voice of a tantee wineywiney how we have hear enough from you now with we ears burning and we eyes buzzing and you don't have to tell we no more please then you say already two or three times at least and we can all read it for weself anyway easy enough right here in these frontpage-headline-stories of the *Bomb* compile together in this big black book complete now with the Table of Contents saying about how St Bernadetta *have wake up the following morning dead as a doornail due to the natural causes of suicide by holding up she own breath even though of course it is physiologically sceptical enough beneath the casing of Mother Maurina own big featherpillow gusting back and forth again inside that little nun bedroom like a blizzard* and so on and so forth ad insanium that we have make up we head longlast to declare she you saint sanctify official and mark down on the Calendar just as you demand on this unending day of beatification by me the Pope Pius IX sitting here in my Chair of the Apostles in my Universal Church pronouncing this mysterious formula of canonization improvise official for the occasion *with a warm resonant voice vibrating of a certain tenderness* as the *Bomb* describe me: *To the honour of the Most Holy and Invisible Trinity in the exhaustion of the Catholic Faith and for the spread of it exclusive particular of Hindus and Muslims and other non-believers by the authority of we own private Lord Papa God together with the blessèd apostles Peter and Paul and we*

own selfimpose sanctity after much mature desperation and useless
imploring of Divine Assistance on the advice of we own
venerable brethren the Cardinals of the Holy Roman Church and
all the Patriarchs of Bishops and Archbishops define now and
declare the blessèd Marie Bernard Soubirous otherwise nickname
St Bernadetta to be enrol now in the Catalogue of Saints that she
memory will be henceforth fête with a big fête every year on the
birthday of she death of Thurs 16 Apr on Corpus Christi Day
with plenty music and jumping up in the streets to be celebrate
pious in this Universal Church exclusive particular of Hindus
and Muslims and other non-believers when I bawl out NO! to
interrupt him NO! NO! NO! before he sacred speech have
reach the end to thrust we all hopeless into oblivion as this
is all a terrible terrible mistake you making and it is
MAGDALENA DIVINA we talking about because who
the ass ever heard of nothing so ridiculous as making this
USELESS WATERHEAD A SAINT? that if by some
unforeseeing tragic unthinkable misfortune she could be
alive today still for me to give her this terrible news that
the Pope have made this hideous mistake to *CANONIZE*
you official instead of Magdalena I know for a fact she
would only look up at me again with she big dark eyes
dumb like a donkey own and she fat football face very
pleasant to kick to tell me, yes mummy this is all very nice
but what is the meaning of that word and all the rest you
say *CAPITALIZE?* but of course he can no even hear me
speaking without even knowing what he saying to
announce to the world the good news that the uncountable
eternity of we matriarch have reach she end, *in the name of*
the Father and the Son and the Holy Ghost.

2

Dr Domingo Verifies
the Miracles

SO HERE I am now eight or ten years later, when all of a sudden the two little nuns I have there fa nurses bust out with one set of giggling like sticklefish swim up inside they pussies. What going on here? I look in the waiting-room and I find out: there sitting down on the bench is this Chief of the Commission of Enquiry Bishop Bertrand-Sévère, and there beside him smiling ca-go is the same old mammapoule Monsignor O'Connor, because everybody said cupid prick he tail when this Bishop arrived from the Vatican wearing more petticoats than he. But boy, this Bishop Sévère ain't nothing to smile about, and I don't have to tell you there ain't no sticklefish tickling me neither. Realize: I had this idea in my head that daddy had buried all this commess in the ground with Magdalena and she child. I'd washed my hands of the whole business soon as he let me out from the jail, and fa those few intervening chapters I'd written them off fa good. Finished. Bat-tai. But boy, soon as I see this Bishop sitting there on the bench, soon as I look him in he face, I realize the truth that daddy ain't bury nothing in the ground a-tall. Because boy, by the time that Chief of Police, and Mother Maurina, and this Monsigonor O'Connor had finished digging up, and reburying, and mismolesting all the old jumbies sleeping peaceful enough in Domingo Cemetery –

and daddy finally put a bullet from General Monagas' big
rifle *hot* in the tail of that Chief of Police, another fired
quick at he own head to end the whole confusion one time
and finish – by then we were all so tired telling the same
story over and over with only a word or two different each
round (not in the name of poetic licence, but fa the simple
selfish reason of sanity) by then we didn't want to hear
nothing more about it. We didn't neither. Not until this
Chief of the Commission Bishop Sévère arrives. Not until
eight or ten years later (when you were already a little boy
two or three years of age running catacoo about the place)
when this Bishop arrives to recommence digging up in the
cemetery to send all the old jumbies rolling in they graves
fa the *second* time. When those of us who could still
remember, took up we story again. And boy, I could
remember good enough. Now fa my second turn. But
boy, I am not ready to loop the next loop. To turn the next
circle of this story. Not yet. Not so quick. I do the only
thing I can think of: I introduce myself to the Bishop,
excuse myself to run in the bush fa weewee, and I bolt to
the parlour next door to fire a rum.

By the time I reach back I am ready to face this Bishop
Bertrand-Sévère. I put him to sit down calm and quiet in
the office – together of course with that Monsignor
breathing down he neck the whole time – and I take my
seat behind the big desk. Now I ask him what is the
problem. 'Doctor,' he says, 'big big problem! Nine of
these commissions I have supervised all over the world,
and this never happened before.' 'Well,' I ask again, 'what
is the problem?' He says he can't find the body. Now I lean
forward a little bit behind the big desk, I brace my two feet
firm on the ground, and I look this Bishop Sévère hard in
he face: 'Which body in particular do you mean?' I ask.
'That of the mother, or that of the child?' Now the Bishop
pauses a long minute, so quiet I can almost hear the drop
of perspiration running vertebra-by-vertebra slowly down

my spine: *slup, slup, slup, slup.* 'Both,' he says. And he says
it like if *I* am responsible not only fa they deaths, but fa the
whereabouts of they corpses too. There is another long
minute of silence, but before this Bishop can open he
mouth again, that tantie Monsignor O'Connor takes off
cantankering in a tirade like somebody put pepper in the
vaseline, and he bamsee on fire. He says, 'You know good
enough little schoolboy-doctor wherever the ass it is you
daddy hide she body and the child's too – and you will tell
us where they are even if it is under the orders of the
Church and the State together to jail you again and beat
the shittings out of you with that cat-of-nine-tails – until
you confess we the truth!' And now he putting loud
goatmouth on me without knowing what he saying. I let
him cantanker heself out na, and when he sits down again I
tell him that I never had even a cratestool in that musical-
chairs the rest of you were playing in the cemetery a-tall.
'Because the fact is Monsignor, the whole time that game
was going on, I was sitting right there on my backside on
the cold concrete flooring of that same jailcage beside
oldman Salizar.'

Because boy, let me tell you whatever it was went on
between daddy and that Gomez Chief of Police, whichever claims each claimed they had on she bones, I couldn't
tell you. Realize: daddy never said a word to me about
what kind of relationship he had with this woman.
Realize: I had known Magdalena sheself fa little more than
an hour of she short life, and fa half that time she was
already dead. All I can tell you is this: daddy and that Chief
of Police were both *so* determined to get hold of she bones
– so obsessed with the notion of laying they own bones
down peaceful beside hers – that in the end one had to bury
the other in order to do it. But boy, the fact is that neither
daddy nor that Chief of Police managed to get hold of
Magdalena's body in the end. Whatever happened to it,
and whoever managed finally to lay claim to she bones –

if, indeed, there is anybody other than that same oldman
rocking on the gallery upstairs who managed to do it –
nobody knows to this day. Because boy, by the time
daddy buried Gomez. By the time he dug up Magdalena
there beside him where Gomez had just finished burying
her fa the second time. And daddy covered her up fa the
third time there beside she child in we own family plot on
the other side of the cemetery (only to be dug up again a
fourth time a few weeks later by Mother Maurina and this
same Monsignor O'Connor) by that time daddy had to
take off in a run in order to save heself. Because by that
time Mother Maurina had decided *she* wanted to shoot
him dead too. By that time this Mother Superior General
had actually taken charge of the entire police forces of
Corpus Christi *sheself* – with Gomez not even cold yet in
the ground – announcing that she would string up daddy
by he stones right there in the same square that same
afternoon fa murdering the Chief of Police. (Of course, all
of this took place only five minutes after daddy had let me
and oldman Salizar and the same Mother Maurina out
from the jailcage heself. Five minutes for her to decide
now she wants to kill him too. Because of course, nobody
could explain why the ass this Mother Maurina should be
so outraged over Gomez's murder – as far as we all knew
there has never been nothing but loud cumbrucktion
between them – because it was not until eight or ten years
later, sitting right there in that same jailcage, that Mother
Maurina explained to me what everybody else somehow
eventually figured out: that all this time the same little
Philipe Gomez Domingo, the same little Chief of Police,
had been she own *son*. Mother Maurina's own son, born in
the convent in Caracas the second time Barto sent her
away haveen, and of course, *he* was the father.)

   But as you already know, in the end daddy saved
Mother Maurina and the rest of Corpus Christi the trouble
or the pleasure of shooting him, all in a rage too soon as

they heard about this confusion, which of course nobody could make heads nor tails of yet. Because of course, whether or not anybody actually understood anything a-tall didn't matter a fart: they could all sit down quiet and figure it out soon as they'd finished lynching the fucking wajank. Soon as they'd finished stringing up daddy by he stones. Because again, as you already know, that same afternoon soon as he'd finished gathering the family round the big diningroom table to eat we last supper together – at least according to the deathdate inscribed on the headstone daddy heself arranged to have placed there on he own grave – he put the gun to he head and shot heself. But boy, how it was that Mother Maurina and this same Monsignor O'Connor sitting before me now couldn't find Magdalena's body which daddy had reburied right there in front the whole of Corpus Christi only a couple weeks before – all watching cokeeeye licking away on they snowballs – nobody knows to this day. Because Magdalena's body, like daddy's own, had simply disappeared: she remains have never been found. Because of course, it didn't make no sense a-tall fa daddy and this Chief of Police to have taken the trouble of digging up and reburying three separate times a coffinbox containing nothing more than a few goodsized chockstones, which was what Mother Maurina and Monsignor O'Connor claimed they found inside.

But boy, my own theory is that these two, Monsignor O'Connor and that same Mother Superior Maurina, like everybody else in this place, got to fighting down each other over she bones too. My own theory is that one of *them* secretly took she body – that Magdalena's bones are still hidden in a crocusssack downstairs in the catacombs of that cathedral, or in a saltfish crate upstairs in the attic of that convent – because neither of them could bear the thought of having to share those sacred bones with the other. What in all they perversion they could have wanted

with Magdalena's bones I couldn't tell you not fa barbadine icecream. (Unless they were waiting fa the canonization official to pope them off nuckle-by-nuckle and femur-
by-vertebra on the yankee-tourists to make theyself a
bloody fortune?) I couldn't say. All I can tell you is this: if
anybody took those bones it was one of the two of them.
Either Mother Maurina secretly dug up Magdalena's body
a fourth time and substituted those chockstones in order to
deceive Monsignor O'Connor, or Monsignor made the
switch in order to deceive her. So the *fifth* time they dug
up the coffin it was nothing more than a pappyshow one fa
the other, a measure of schoolboy-tactics. And if there was
anybody still walking the face of this green earth who
could possibly tell us anything of the whereabouts of
Magdalena's bones, it was one of the two of them: Mother
Maurina or this same Monsignor O'Connor. And boy,
that is exactly what I told him: I look at him hard hard, and
I tell him, 'Monsignor, you come in here with this Bishop
questioning *me* about the whereabouts of Magdalena's
bones, when *I* is the one should be questioning *you*. You,
and that same Mother Superior Maurina.'

Of course, this one sends him into a rage like the
peppersauce-vaseline burning he bamsee again, and he
jumps up to dress me down saying, 'You could push all
you little schoolboy chockstone-theories up you little
white culo – because what the ass do Mother Maurina and
me have to fight down each other about when we both
looking to consecrate she bones in the same catacombs-
relicsbox beneath the mainaltar where she belongs – which
is proof positive you don't know a *caca* what you talking
about!' (because you know how Mother Maurina teach
him to cuss) and with that he pelts out the door dragging
this Bishop behind him.

Boy, I have to lean back a little bit sitting here in my
chair behind the big desk, and I close my eyes fa few
seconds to try to recover myself from this thing, because

the whole business done hit me over the head like bigstick. Now I am wondering if maybe this isn't the best thing that could happen? If maybe this Bishop Sévère, and Monsignor O'Connor, and that same Mother Maurina wouldn't take charge of all this canonization business now theyself (which is what Mother Maurina told me later in the jail *she* wanted to do all along) and I wouldn't have to get myself involved a-tall? Because boy, let me tell you dealing with those two mammapoule priests is one thing, but having to deal with that old Mother Superior Maurina a second time over is something else again. Realize: She had never forgiven Barto fa the murder of she son Gomez. Realize: Since the afternoon daddy had disappeared, she'd had nobody but the rest of us to pelt on the blame. Because boy, soon as you sit down a quiet minute to logically analyse all of this commess, you will realize this man Barto had actually married off he own son to he own daughter, soon as he'd finished making the daughter haveen *heself.* And as if all that isn't enough, then in a father–son rivalry over the same sister-daughter – who had in fact just killed sheself in the middle of bearing a child both claimed resolutely belonged to *them* – the father had actually murdered he own son. Of course, they are *she* own son and daughter too. And Mother Maurina sheself not only supervised the conception of the daughter by the father, and the subsequent marriage of the sister to the brother, she dictated them too. But boy, *I* remain convinced that daddy heself never knew he was Gomez's father. Just as he never knew that Magdalena was he daughter neither. I remain convinced that that same old Mother Superior General Maurina (who is the genuine author of all this plotting when you come to consider it, and the only true signature deserving the cover of this black book) I remain convinced that she never told him. How could she have? How could he have known? Unless we are all mad? And boy, that is exactly what I was thinking. That is exactly

what I told myself: You are mad. Boofootoo. Viekeevie.
Instead of renaming this place St Maggy, they should have
called it *St Ann's*.

Because boy, all I could think is whatever ga happen it
ga happen soon, sane or insane, sacred bones or no sacred
bones, because judging from the amount of excavation
going on in Domingo Cemetery these last few nights, just
now there wouldn't be no more graves left to dig up a-tall.
Of course, what I could never have known at that precise
moment, though perhaps I should have suspected something of the sort – fate again, advocating bubball and
endless confusion – was that there still remained *one* grave
in Domingo Cemetery which still remained untouched.
Only one, and that same night I would find myself
digging up in the cemetery too. I would have no choice
but to play out my own part in this pappyshow they were
preparing to stage before the Pope heself quite in the
Vatican soon enough. But of course, I don't know a fart
about none of this business coming yet. Neither do I have
the presence of mind to pick up my tail and run to
Venezuela before this Bishop Sévère can have a chance to
hold it. As the story tells itself however, the Bishop would
hold my ass that same night, right there in the same
cemetery. Because that same night, just like everybody
else in this tootooloo madhouse, I would find myself
digging up in the cemetery too. But boy, before I would
have a chance even to send my spade three times in the
ground, that same Bishop Sévère would turn round to slap
on the cufflinks loud and throw me in the jail – together
with Mother Maurina and that same old good woman
Evelina, there waiting together fa this Vatican's ship to
arrive a few days later transporting we practically at
gunpoint to that Holy City cross the sea – there to testify
we testimony fa Magdalena's canonization. But boy, I
don't know a fart about none of this bubball coming yet.
And as I sit there in my chair behind the big desk, trying

my best to recover from all this confusion which had not even begun to begin yet, all I could think is I hope I don't ever have to see this Bishop Sévère ever again.

Boy, I am still sitting there in a daze, my eyes still closed, when all of a sudden I realize that there is somebody standing there in front of me. I look up to find that it is the same Bishop Sévère come back already. He is looking at me hard again, with that same percolating feeling of a dosage of mummy's casteroil bubbling up inside my belly again, and he tells me not to pay no mind to that old cussbud Monsignor O'Connor. 'Because the fact is,' he says, 'the Monsignor's own part in this commission is to be negligible if it is to be anything a-tall. You see Doctor, as pastor of this parish, as director of this diocese, he is too intimately involved, and Mother Church requires only for him to hold up he tongue. And that of course has him talking more than ever. But you, Doctor, will play a vital role. As Magdalena's personal private physician, you will play perhaps the most vital role of all. Whether or not His Grace will name Magdalena the patron saint of Corpus Christi, will depend upon you testimony. In other words Doctor, the burden of this woman now falls upon you shoulders. In other words Doctor, it is up to you now to decide the destiny of you island nation, at least in so far as it involves any legitimate claims to the sanctity of you own true Mother, the Black Virgin of Maraval, Magdalena Divina! You part will begin tonight at precisely six o'clock, following the evening Mass, as you are to report to the cathedral to make you first official statement.'

Boy, I couldn't tell you how long this Bishop Sévère went on with all he sainthood Commission of Enquiry business or when it ended, because for me it could have been three hours. All I can tell you is this: when he was finished, and he walk round the side of the desk to reach out he hand to take up mine, and I reach out my own hand to return the gesture, he does something which always makes me feel uncomfortable when I try to remember it. And boy, at that moment in those castoroil-percolating eyes it almost made me shit my drawers: he brings he mouth down on my own so hard we teeth knock together, and my first thought was that my lip must be bleeding. It wasn't. And I didn't shove him away or even turn my face. I couldn't. Sitting there numb with the shock of this Bishop suddenly kissing me up on my lips, again, long and slow and full in the mouth so that anyone who'd have walk through the door would have said that I was my own son now behind the sacristy wall. And boy, fa some reason I can't explain, some peculiar reason which of course *he* can't explain neither, I know my son has secretly been wishing this thing on me ever since it happened to him. So now he has he wish, though of course it doesn't make no sense in this narrative a-tall. Even so, regardless of what kind of sense it makes or doesn't make, I can tell you that when that Bishop was finished, when he was gone, and I discover myself again, alone, sitting here in my chair behind this big desk with my eyes again closed, tasting the incense-taste of that Bishop still inside my mouth, feeling the percolating-feeling of that castoroil still inside my belly, I was sure a cobo had just pass through. He had come with the flapping of stinking labass-screeching car-niverous feathers to shit the shit of fate *plaps!* in the middle of my forehead.

BOY, LET ME give you a little story while we here, showing you just what kind of story this story you telling has become. It was, I suppose, three or four years after I'd arrive back from England. The little nurse comes running in to tell me, 'Doctor, dey a oldman standing up outside dere, only rubbing he bamsee groaning groaning like he sit down on a porcupinefish!' 'Well,' I tell her, 'we better get him in here right away.' So I ask the oldman to drop he drawers, and we put him to lie down quiet on the table with the pillow beneath he belly, and he blueblack bamsee standing up tall in the air in what we call the jackknife position. But before I go in from behind to take a look, I ask the oldman what is the problem. 'Doctor,' he says, 'big big problem. Ninety years I been shitting like a pelican, my mummy tell me, and dis never happen before.' 'Well,' I ask again, 'what is the problem?' He says he can't make a caca. 'Every time I try Doctor, I feel one pain in me ass like I been feeding on groundglass, and thumbtacks, and fishhooks!'

So I take out the proctoscope from out the cupboard, I grease it down liberally with the K-Y jelly, and I ask the little nunnurse to open up he cheeks fa me to push the proctoscope inside. But before I can get near him with this proctoscope, before I can even come close, the oldman seizes up he bamsee tight tight trembling, and he lets loose a bawl like a Warrahoon spying a quenk: '*Ay-ay-ay-ay-ay-ay-ay!*' Of course, I jump back quick like if it is *me* sit down on the porcupinefish now, and when the oldman's bamsee stops quivering, I ask him what is the matter? He says, 'Doctor, I beg you, please don't push dat imperial cannon you holding up inside me. Not to say I too manmen to take little plugging in de softend like a buller. But Doctor, contrary to de doctrines of History, contrary to de chronicles of all de schoolchildren's Economics books, dis little black backside ain't big enough to accommodate de Royal Navy!'

Well I have to smile a little bit at that one. I rub up the oldman's bamsee nice and gentle, and I promise him so long as he relax heself, I wouldn't give him no more pain. 'But Mr Adderly,' I tell him, 'if you don't let me push this thing inside there, how I ga look to find out what giving you all the groundglass, and thumbtacks, and fishhooks?' I tell him to turn he head and try to distract heself – think

about a cricket match, or he girlfriend, or something so
— and I promise him he wouldn't feel the cannon. Now I
lubricate he bamseehole too with a squeeze of the K-Y
jelly to try to relax him, and now he tells me, 'Doctor, I
don't know what kind of thing you putting up inside me
dere, all I can say it must be make from icecream: cool,
and soft, and lovely!'

Now I slide the proctoscope inside easy enough, I pump
up the little bulb a few times to send some air inside there
to inflate the mucosal folds, and I light up the little
lightbulb at the end. But boy, when I bend down to take a
look, when I focus my eye through this proctoscope, is
now I feel the porcupinefish: just there at the recto–sigmoid
junction, where the third portion meets up with the
sigmoid flexure (because the rectum is constructed in three
divisiones of 5 and 3 and .5 inches in length, the first half
curving forward and downward towards the apex of the
prostate gland shining in the middle, then backward and
upward curving again on itself to culminate with the
orifice of the faecal opening in the end, which is of course
where all the caca comes out) in others words, right there
at the onset, in the very beginning, just there at the source
of this oldman's rectum, I find an *eyeball* staring back at me
cool cool like if *I* am the asshole looking out!

Of course this thing is impossible! It could never be! But
the *harder* I look, the *surer* I am that is exactly what it is.
And of course, when I nudge my nose at the proctoscope
fa the little nurse to take a looksee, she only lets loose a
cry, 'Amor Matris!' and she bolts fa the door.

Of course, I excuse myself fa quick weewee and I bolt
out the door behind her, I fire down a quick one, and
when I get back I tell the oldman, 'Mr Adderly, I don't
know how to put this thing any other way: you got a third
eye inside there blinking at me, right up at the *top* of you
asshole!'

Of course, the oldman gives me a face like I gone

viekeevie now fa true. But then he begins to chuckle little bit, he bamsee still standing up in the air giggling way. 'Mr Adderly,' I tell him, 'if you know a pretty joke you better give it to me quick, because just now I ga shit down this place with enough caca fa you and me together!'

'Doctor,' he says, 'dat eyeball you seeing not belonging to me a-tall. Even dough in truth I must be carrying it round a good long time. Dat eyeball belong to me daddy. You see, daddy used to wear dat eyeball make from glassbottle, and he used to take it out every night and leave it in a tasa of water above de kitchen sink. De story goes dat one morning as a little boy, I climbed up on top de sink and I drank down de tasa eyeball and all. So Doctor, I suppose dat glassbottle eyeball must be rolling round me belly all these years, and it only now stick up on de way out.'

'Well,' I tell him, 'as they say, hindsight don't drive motorcar. And that is a good thing, because if you ever want to shit happy again, I ga have to remove it.'

'Pluck it out!' he says. 'Let me smell me way to Dover!'

'England?' I ask.

'No Doctor, you play de Regan fa me old Grenada: is de plague of de times when madmen lead de blind!'

'Oh-ho,' I say. 'In that case, you better open up you ear again fa me to pour in the poison.'

Now I take the anuscope from out the cupboard, I grease it down too, and I replace it fa the proctoscope. I press down the lever to open up the two halves of the anuscope, I reach inside there with a long ring-forceps, and in no time a-tall I pluck it out. Of course, before I have a chance to remove the anuscope, before I even have a chance to brace myself: *Boodoomboom-doodoomdoom-boom-boom-boom!* And boy, that ain't groundglass, it ain't thumbtacks, and it ain't fishhooks. It come out flowing easy as poetry!

SO AFTER the final blessing the ten or twelve who have
come to the five o'clock Mass clear out, and Monsignor
disappears into the sacristy behind the mainaltar to change
he costume. I am still sitting there in the last pew, still
feeling mummy's castoroil percolating inside my belly,
and I still haven't seen no sign of this Bishop Sévère. Of
course, the Monsignor is still plenty vex with me after we
discussion over Magdalena's bones that morning, so busy
looking the other direction that the host he went to press
on my tongue would have dropped out on the ground if the
little acolyte didn't catch it up in he goldplate. Monsignor
appears on the altar again, now wearing a navyblue
monkeysuit and carrying a grey box by a handle at the top.
(I am thinking that this is a peculiar outfit, and maybe old
Monsignor is a motorcar mechanic these days moonlight-
ing in he after hours, and the big grey box is he toolchest?)
He outs the candles still burning on the altar, goes to the
back of the church to out the electric lights burning
overhead. With a jingling of keys he bolts up the big
wooden doors, locking the two of us inside this cathedral
which is suddenly pitch black. There is only the tiny red
flame flickering beside the tabernacle, the four or five
devotion candles flickering before Magdalena in she side
chapel, and the faintish bluish glow seeping in slow
through the stained glass windows. Monsignor comes and
sits in the pew directly in front of me, still not saying a
word. Now I am wondering if this Bishop Sévère will
arrive a-tall. If this whole business isn't only some baddream – with me locked up inside this big empty cathedral
the whole night – only staring at the back of Monsignor's
head waiting fa him to grow out a pair of Bazil's goath-
orns. All of a sudden the Government House clock begins
to strike, startling me, and I turn round in my pew only to
find the bolted up doors. From the inside of this closed up
cathedral the clock sounds like I'm hearing it from under
water: *bun, bun, bun, bun, bun, bun.* Suddenly there is the

glow of a light in front of me, and I turn round again to see that now Monsignor is wearing a shiny silver hardhat like a construction worker. He turns he head to flash a bright beam in my face, and I realize that this hardhat has a torchlight built-in shining from out he forehead: 'The Bishop coming in a minute,' he says.

But boy, if I didn't know those doors were locked up tight, I wouldn't be waiting there no minute. I would have jumped up to bolt from that cathedral the same instant. Now I am hearing a creaking noise up at the front, and I watch a kind of a trapdoor set into the ground before the mainaltar open up with a hard *brapps*. Out from this trapdoor climbs Bishop Sévère, dressed in the same navyblue monkeysuit, same silver torchlight-hardhat shining on he head. Behind him come scrambling three little Warrahoons, all wearing the same gravedigging costumes, all barefoot, all swimming in they monkeysuits rolled up in big cuffs dragging round they ankles. The Bishop leads them in a procession down the centre aisle toward us – the four bright beams of they hardhats darting back and forth every which way across the walls and the rows of pews – and boy, let me tell you this scene is so geegeeree, now I am sure it is a baddream I'm dreaming. The Bishop takes way a silver hardhat from one of the Warrahoons – who is so distressed by this he zips up he monkeysuit quick quick tight round he neck, before the Bishop can take *it* back too – and he hands me the hardhat. 'Come,' he says, and I get up to follow behind him, Monsignor and the three Warrahoons trailing behind.

The Bishop leads me up to the front of the cathedral, over to the trapdoor in the ground before the mainaltar. Now I stand there watching him climb down a set of steep steps, disappearing slowly into the black rectangular hole, he silver hardhat glowing suck-surging up and down like a jellyfish swimming in the night. But boy, when I go to follow behind him, when I go to pick up my feet, all of a sudden they stuck to the ground with laglee. Numb. I can't budge them an inch. And boy, when I make the mistake to look over my shoulder, and I butt up those three brights beams staring me hard in the face, I lose my balance and I pelt *blappapplaps* head-first down the stairs.

Fortunate fa me it is only a short drop – and I am wearing that same hardhat – otherwise they could have shoved me into a coffinbox one time and finish. The Bishop helps me to my feet, and he leads me along a series of dark corridors, so short we have to bend down we heads not to butt them up, so narrow we have to squinge up weself not to stick up on the way through. We enter into a small room like a prison cell, the walls and the ceiling and the floor of coral bricks, everywhere covered in a blanket of spongy, bluegreen moss: we had all heard the stories of this mausoleum which we called the *catacombs*, but as far as I knew no one had ever seen them before, or could say who was entombed inside. (Of course, these days they have regular tours fa the tourists of the cathedral and the same catacombs, and the guides will give you a history to make this one look like a three-cent picture-show. Even though in truth there is only one corpse entombed down there – and I don't think you'd want to call him a *saint* – because it happens to belong to you own Uncle Olly. You see, by the time all that grave-digging confusion was finished, those three little Warrahoons were so exhausted they couldn't be bothered to tote he coffin-box out again and bury him back in the cemetery: they simply flipped back on the lid and nailed it shut.) These catacombs are cold, dank, and stenching loud of putrefaction. With the incessant *tonk tonk tonk* of water dripping some place. Monsignor comes and stands beside me, the three Warrahoons huddling theyself squatting quiet in the corner. With the beams of those five torchlights these catacombs are bright like noonday.

There are three coffinboxes with they heads against the

wall in front of us, Bishop Sévère bending over the one to
the left, now with a white kerchief tied up round he face.
In the centre there is a crypt of shining black marble, sealed
up tight, its lid engraved in tall white capitals: MAGDALENA
DIVINA, MORI XVI APRILIS, ANNO DOMINI NOSTRI,
MDCCCXCIX. There is a wooden coffinbox on either side,
both dilapidated, both still covered in dirt: clearly these
two have just been dug up from the cemetery and brought
here. They are open, they lids leaning against they sides.
But boy, let me tell you *I* ain't feeling no hot desire to look
inside. The Bishop stands up straight, and he makes a sign
fa me to come forward.

Now I see the four black chockstones in the coffinbox
on the right: they are the same ones I'd put into daddy's
coffin years before. In the coffinbox on the left, the one the
Bishop had been leaning over, there is a skeleton of yellow
bones – covered only by a stockinggauze of transparent
dry skin – by the tattered remains of a professorial gown
which had once looked more like the costume of T.P.
Barnum. With a shudder I realized that these were the
remains of Uncle Olly: we had buried him in the cemetery
ages before.

But I couldn't understand why the ass they would bring
Uncle Olly to this holy place. Because boy, as sure as you
Uncle Olly was an amusing, lovable old fellow, he got
into more mischief and monkeybusiness than the devil
self. The last place I'd expect to find him is down here in
these sacred catacombs. And boy, this is exactly what I
say: 'Bishop Sévère, I feel as much good fondish senti-
ments fa old Uncle Olly as anybody else. But I ga tell you
one thing fa sure: you put him down here inside *this* holy
mausoleum, and that oldman upstairs ga bring down the
roof on top we heads!'

He pulls the kerchief down from round he mouth.
'Doctor,' he says, 'nobody has any intention of leaving
him here. These two coffins are down here only because

this is the only place in the whole of Corpus Christi we
could find to examine them secret. And as soon as you
identify this body, we will bury him back in the cemetery
where he belongs.' Now he pauses fa second. 'You see
Doctor, of those five headstones standing there in you
family plot, this is the only corpse we could come up with.
Together with this box of stones!'

Of course, I am in no hurry to start up a discussion over
those chockstones. I close my eyes a moment to picture
the line of graves: Manuelito in the middle, mummy and
daddy on either side, Magdalena and Uncle Olly on either
side of them. True enough, of those five graves, the only
corpse I myself had buried there was Uncle Olly's. 'Well,'
I tell the Bishop, 'I couldn't say nothing about none of the
others, but this body I can identify easy enough: he is
wearing a gold signet ring on the weddingfinger of he left
hand, Doctor of Philosophy-Science.'

'Yes,' says this Bishop Sévère. 'I have it in my possession, and I will present it before His Holiness as evidence
during the trial. That is to say Doctor, with you permission.'

'*Permission?* As far as I am concerned Bishop Sévère, you
can take he goldteeth fa the collectionbox too if you want.
I'm sure Uncle Olly wouldn't mind in the least.'

'Of course,' he says, 'the ring will be returned to you
following the trial.' (Which is how the same signet ring
was handed down to you, on the day of you graduation
from Medical School. Because boy, by the time all the
confusion and quarrelment of this trial was finished, and
they gave me back Uncle Olly's gold signet ring, let me
tell you *I* was not about to go down in those catacombs
again to return it.)

'Fine,' I say. 'And now, with you permission Bishop
Sévère, I would like to get my ass to hell out of these
catacombs. They have my blood squinging!'

'One moment, Doctor. First I want you tell me something about this next coffinbox. This one with the stones inside.'

Boy, is now I feel the jookerfish. I pause fa few seconds. 'Bishop Sévère,' I say, 'the truth is that I couldn't tell you nothing more about these chockstones than anybody else on this island could tell you.' I pause again, stumbling still. 'So why you don't ask the Monsignor here? He hot fa oldtalk, and he is reponsible fa these chockstones as much as me!'

Of course, that one is the peppersauce-vaseline, because Monsignor is only standing there waiting fa he chance to take off cantankering again. He says, 'What the ass you talking about Doctor I don't have nothing to do with no coffinboxes full of no chockstones – which is nothing more than you own schoolboy-monkeytricks – and that is evidence enough you know the whereabouts of *she* bones too, so why you don't confess we the truth!'

I let him cantanker heself out na, and when he finishes I tell the Bishop quietly enough that I don't understand what my father has to do with any of this business a-tall. (Of course, the truth is I have a good idea, though at that precise moment I still didn't understand half the half.) 'In any case,' I say, 'the whole of Corpus Christi knows how I buried this coffinbox with these chockstones. Everybody knows well enough I did it because my father's body could not be found. The only person I deceived was my own mother. And I did it, Bishop Sévère, fa reasons you could never understand.'

There is another minute of silence, but before the Bishop can open up he mouth, Monsignor takes off again. He says, 'Who the ass is talking about you daddy we talking about *Magdalena Divina* bury the 16th of April on Corpus Christi Day right there in the cemetery under my own supervision! Because of course we have to wait fa she canonization official before we can bury her here in these catacombs – until Mother Maurina and me decide there is no use waiting the inevitable and we might as well move her here one time and finish – but when we dig she out only two weeks later all we find in she coffinbox is these four black cacashat chockstones!'

Well boy, whatever is the meaning of all that cantankering Monsignor is going on with, there are *two* things I understand now good enough: this black marble sepulchrebox with Magdalena's name on it is *empty*. And this other wooden coffinbox with these four chockstones is not daddy's coffinbox a-tall: this one belongs to Magdalena too. The same coffinbox with the same chockstones which Mother Maurina and Monsignor O'Connor claimed to have dug out years before. Now I realize *both* these coffinboxes belong to Magdalena, though in fact *neither* belongs to her, since neither contains she bones. Wherever this big empty sepulchrebox came from, whoever engraved Magdalena's name on its lid – and however the ass they got it down those steep steps through those squingy corridors without mashing theyself like a pembois beneath it – I couldn't tell you not fa soursop sweetdrink. (And as Mother Maurina informed me that same night in the jail, neither could anybody else: that big sepulchrebox simply appeared down there in those catacombs, at the same time those four headstones appeared in Domingo Cemetery – from nowhere, without explanation – the same black marble with the same white engraving, so maybe daddy was responsible fa this sepulchre-relicsbox too?) But boy, fa the moment I had another problem. Fa the moment I had another much simpler confusion, and fa the moment I had no choice but to stop Monsignor to question him about it. 'Monsignor,' I say, 'then what ever happened to *daddy's* coffinbox? What ever became of *that* one?'

Now it is the Bishop who answers. 'Doctor,' he says, 'of course we never bothered to dig up Bartolomeo Domingo's coffinbox. That is the *only* coffinbox in the whole cemetery everybody assured me they knew exactly what was inside: they had all heard the same story of that funeral you had arranged only to bury four black stones. And Doctor, I am not about to waste the Church's precious time and expense to dig up a box I know already contains nothing more than a few black stones. I am no fool. I only wish the Monsignor here could have saved me the trouble of digging up *this* box of stones too!'

Boy, is now I realize Monsignor O'Connor and Mother Maurina are telling the truth. They have been telling the truth all along. I could be sure of that not simply because the Bishop happened to find the same empty box with the same four chockstones. Not simply because they own story coincided in duplicate with his. I knew they were telling the truth because otherwise they would never have allowed this Bishop to dig up Magdalena's coffinbox a *sixth* time. Because boy, both Mother Maurina and Monsignor O'Connor knew well enough that Magdalena could never be canonized until we found she bones. So if either of them knew the secret of where she was hidden, they would have divulged it fa certain at that moment. They would have had no other choice. Realize: the Vatican required *some* physical evidence that this woman had in fact lived. Realize: without she corpse, all that remained of her were we own stories. We own stories and that black madonna upstairs. And boy, you know as well as anybody else, when it comes to matters of faith, the Church don't believe nothing without hard scientific proof. But boy, that is the one thing I could never give them.

I let the Bishop finish, and then I repeat fa him quietly the same thing I'd told him that morning: 'I don't know a fart. Whatever happened to Magdalena's bones, whoever put those chockstones inside there, I couldn't say.' And I ask him again to please let me out of those catacombs, I turn round, and I start towards the entrance.

'Doctor,' the Bishop says behind me, 'you realize this

leaves the canonization all but impossible. Because the only thing remaining to tell we anything of this woman is that statue upstairs, and we cannot make a *statue* into a saint. Even if she does walk about the place as Mother Maurina and this madwoman Evelina claim! We will all make a long, pointless trip across the sea!'

'Bishop Sévère,' I say, my back still turned, 'let me tell you the only thing I can be sure of, even three-quarters of the way through this story: only *you* have made a pointless trip.' And with that I charge boldface down the corridor. Of course I loose myself after the first turn, when one of the little Warrahoons comes running behind me jingling the keys, takes up my hand, and he leads me towards the stairs. When we get to the back of the church I return him he hardhat. He gives me a big smile, unbolts the doors, and he lets me out of that cathedral into the night.

But boy, this catacombs business left me feeling so geegeeree, so in such a state of agitation, I couldn't stop worrying over Magdalena's bones the whole remainder of the night. I even made the mistake to mention them to mummy when I reached home and the two of us sat down alone fa dinner (because Evelina had disappeared since the night before – taking off in a run soon as the Bishop's summons arrived habeas corpus calling her in fa questions – but what we *didn't* realize is that she'd managed only to get halfway to Tunapuna before the Bishop and Monsignor held her and took her off to the jail) but boy, the mentioning of those bones to mummy was no doubt the worst thing that I could have done. Because soon as I pronounce Magdalena's name mummy looses sheself in a fit malkadee, and she dumps the whole big pot of callaloo upside-down on top my head, swimming in crabclaws and thick green dasheen soup, and she runs to she room to bury sheself beneath the bed. And when I woke up in a cold sweat in the middle of the night, I was sure that it was still Magdalena's bones I'd been dreaming about, even though I tried to convince myself it wasn't. That Magdalena had nothing whatsoever to do with this baddream – though I knew well enough she did – because Magdalena sheself never appeared in it. Only *daddy* appeared in this dream. Daddy dressed up in he fancy white uniform with the gold braids and the epaulettes, doing something which didn't make no immediate sense to me a-tall. Because in this dream daddy substituted fa me – daddy substituting fa me substituting fa heself – daddy busy filling up he *own* coffinbox with the same chockstones I had substituted fa him. I watched him there beneath the moonlight of Domingo Cemetery, digging out a chockstone from beneath a eucalyptus tree, returning to he coffinbox to drop it in, back to the tree again to dig out another chockstone, back to the box again, one by one again and again until the entire coffinbox was full, and only then did I wake up.

But I quickly wrote off that baddream as the old proudfoot one about patricide (since that symbolically is what I had done according to the fraud of burying that empty coffinbox). Because the truth is that nobody ever found out what happened to daddy, despite all we stories of shooting heself, or slipping out he pirogue into a school of piranha somewhere up the Orinoco. But *Magdalena's* role in that nightmare never crossed my mind as I dressed myself. (And neither did incest or matricide, both of which I was guilty not in any fraudulent dream of symbols, but in actual soft inadvertent *fact*. Because if Magdalena Divina was my own true mother – as this Bishop Sévère had just finished reminding me – then I had not only taken she life, I had taken she virginity too.) Again I decide to go fa walk along the wharf, to take in some cool seabreeze. Again I am in a hurry to get there. So much so that when I sit down on the frontstep to tie up my shoes (because I used to sleep in daddy's bedroom in those days, and I didn't want to wake up mummy sleeping below) I was so in a hurry I didn't want to bother lacing them up. I leave them there just so, and I take off in my bare feet. And when I arrive back to the house almost two months later, mummy tells me she mistake them fa daddy's and pitch them again in the sea.

But instead of going to the wharf, again I take off in the opposite direction. What the ass I was thinking about I couldn't tell you, only that I'm sure it wasn't Magdalena yet. Not yet. Not until the clock begins to strike – and I look up to find this Bishop standing there in the moonlight above me in the same gravedigging-costume – do I think of Magdalena, and all of a sudden I realize what daddy is trying to communicate to me in that dream. All of a sudden I understand the only possible way daddy could have make *sure* Magdalena's bones would not be disturbed until the proper time: daddy had substituted he own coffinbox fa Magdalena's. He had actually stood there behind a eucalyptus tree watching he own burial – watching we bury that coffinbox full of stones which of course everybody in the whole of Corpus Christi knew about by now except mummy – and when all that funeral-confusion was finished, he'd dug he own coffinbox and switched it fa Magdalena's there beside him. So the sixth time daddy dug up Magdalena it was in order to bury her there beside she child just as she'd instructed him, only he'd buried her in he *own* grave. And only after he'd reburied he own coffinbox in *Magdalena's* grave – the same coffinbox Mother Maurina and Monsignor O'Connor had dug up years before, the same one that this Bishop Sévère had just dug up again to tote to those catacombs – could daddy disappear to whatever mysterious ends he disappeared to in the end.

Bishop Sévère is still standing there above me, still looking down on me with that feeling of castoroil still percolating inside my belly, and now he does something which is not so peculiar a-tall when you come to consider it: he hands me a shovel. I take it and I get up to lead him back to Domingo Cemetery, straight to daddy's grave, now to dig out Magdalena fa the seventh and final time. Of course before I have a chance even to send the spade three times in the ground, he turns round loud to slap on the cufflinks and to order Monsignor appearing straight way from out of the shadows to take me off to the jail, there to join Mother Maurina and old Evelina, there together waiting fa this Vatican's ship to arrive a few days later to carry we way. The Bishop claps he hands together three times in the air, and immediately the three little Warrahoons come pelting from out the bush, all toting shovels, all smiling baboo, and they take up the digging where I'd left off.

AS CHIEF MEDICAL RESIDENT of the Henry Ford Hospital, part of my duties was to lead a weekly discussion of any interesting or problematic cases reported. I'd de-- cided to end up this session on a comical note: in the Emergency Wing I had treated an old black outpatient for an obstruction of the lower digestive track. X-ray identi- fied the obstruction as a foreign body the size of a marble lodged in the recto-sigmoid junction. Conference with the patient verified the foreign body to be the patient's own prosthetic eye, which the patient had inadvertently swal- lowed. Proctoscopic examination confirmed all this, and the foreign body was removed via anuscope and ring- forceps. After which the prosthetic eye was sterilized and replaced by the patient. I wanted to show the other interns the x-ray – let them try to guess the identity of the foreign body – and when they failed, I'd give them the old joke about looking in the mirror to find the asshole looking out.

I slid the x-ray into position with the *slup-clack* of the negative flapping onto the projector surface and sliding into the clip at the top, I pressed the switch until the box

began to flicker illuminating itself, and I turned around to
introduce the case and to read them the patient's history.
But before I have a chance to open my mouth, two or
three of them begin to chuckle out loud, which throws me
into confusion as I haven't even begun to give them the
joke. And what can be so comical in the x-ray of an
oldman's asshole? All of a sudden I am in a sweat, and I
can't remember what the ass I was going to tell them.
Because all of a sudden this story is feeling very vague, and
I can't be sure if I'd experienced it myself, if I'd dreamed it
up, or if I'd read it long ago on the frontpage of the *Bomb*. I
open the report, and I start to give them the oldman's
history:

APGAR SCORE
CRITERIA

COLOUR: blueblack
HEART RATE: >100
RESPIRATION: good, crying
REFLEX RESPONSE TO CATHETER: grimace
MUSCLE TONE: some flexion of extremities; predilec-
tion for pithed frog position
SCORE: 3–0 GB/WI
PROGNOSIS: severe asphyxia; residual neurologic dam-
age

All of a sudden someone bawls out: 'LBW! Penalty box!'
And they all laugh. I am thinking: *low-body-weight?* Reading: *The eyes bulge and the forehead is deficient, the eyelids are
thick and oedematous and the tongue* . . . I turn around to look
at the x-ray illuminated behind me:

protrudes. The neck is short and the head appears to sit upon the shoulders (Fig. 9.XXII).

An anencephalic fœtus is always associated with excess of liquor amnii and presents clinically as a case of hydramnios. This excess

FIG. 9.XXII.   Anencephalic fœtus.

may be due to transudation through the exposed choroid plexus and meninges. It is interesting, however, that no lanugo hair is found in the intestine, which suggests that the swallowing reflex is abolished and that liquor is no longer absorbed from the fœtal intestine and returned to the maternal circulation. Probably both explanations are correct : there is an increased formation of liquor and an inability to absorb it.

I awoke with a start, taking a few deep breaths. I threw off
the sheet to feel the fan sweep slowly across my wet skin,
slowly back again, and I looked over at my wife, still
asleep in the bed beside me. For a moment it struck me as
peculiar that she should be lying there – so sudden it
seemed – like if I'd awoken in somebody else's bed; and for
a terrifying instant I was afraid it might be daddy's. Then I
remembered we'd buried him almost three years before.

My wife was a native of Corpus Christi (born in
Mayaguaro on the last working coconut estate on the
island) yet she was called Ashley, and she spoke with an
English accent: needless to say she was sure I'd been raised
in the bush. We met soon after my return from Medical
School – Ash had just returned from school in England
herself – when I made several long drives to the old estate
to treat her dying mother. It was Ashley's father whom I
fell in love with first, watching the way he cared for his
wife. Greta was in the last stages of consumption (tubercu-
losis of the lungs complicated by pneumonia and half-a-
dozen other things) and Vernon nursed her practically
twenty-four hours a day. Even with Ash there, even with
all his estate obligations. To the end he'd refused to sleep
in a separate bed, getting up three times in the night to
change the sheets sweat-soaked beneath her. Vernon returned to England soon after Greta's death. Ash and I were
married within the month – daddy had of course just died
too, and with no other doctors on the island it became
necessary now for me to do my residency overseas – so
within the year we left for America.

Then came the two boys in their cribs in the corner, the
fourth generation, born in this country so far away.
Suddenly I felt the first sensations of an onrushing panic –
everything seemed to be moving in fast motion again,
edging out of control – and I reached quickly for my
wristwatch on the bedstand, sure that I was already late:
5:00, 5 00, 5:01. Still two hours before I had to report to

the hospital. I jumped out of bed, pulled on a shortpants and a jersey, and I buckled up my jesusboots. On the way out I grabbed up some money and the grocery list Ash had left on the little diningroom table.

There were already a few people walking hurriedly along the sidewalks, their hands in their pockets. There were a few motorcars and vegetable trucks in the street, a jitney crowded with Jamaican construction workers. Suddenly a truck came to a screeching halt before a potcake still asleep in the middle of the road, its red lights flashing: the doors flew open like two wings, and two men dressed in white jumped out, ran to the potcake, and slapped on a muzzle and a choker chain. The potcake was still half asleep, and it got up slowly, starting to wag its tail. One of the white men bent down to pet it. They walked the potcake around to the back of the truck and pushed it in through a big door on rollers, jumped in and slammed the side doors, and the truck took off again.

It was during this fractured moment, in a flash of insight, that I came up with the definition of the Caribbean which I'd been searching for. A definition found in all of our literature, and written between the lines of every tourist pamphlet: *it is whatever America wants you to be.*

I also came up with a scheme to save the Third World. I'd import a thousand steeldrum players from home, dress them up in their carnival costumes, and I'd put them to beat pan in the street. *I'd also import a hundred of the fattest, wassaest callaloo-coolie-creoles anybody has ever seen, and I put them to teach the yankees to dance. Oui fute papa-yo! Soon as those squingy politicians smell a smell of that sweet pan ping-pa-ding-pa-ding-ping, soon as those froopsy worldbankers taste a taste of those sweet callaloos wassaing down the place like they bamsees on fire, every manjack-womanjill ga bolt fa the streets! Man, that ga drive them batooks! Next thing you know the whole of Wall Street–Madison Avenue holding hands chipping down the road, firing rum like bush, letting loose a bawl when they feel just fa the sake of letting loose a bawl! Qui ma-doo mon-pere!*

I began my own little chip down the sidewalk: '*Po-po-pa-tee-po . . . po! Po-po-pa-tee-po . . . po!*'

A young Jamaican stepped up and began walking along beside me. 'Eh-eh, whiteboy. Tell me what you say!' He was tall and thin, and he had his hair stuffed into a black woollen cap that swelled up as big as a second head. A circular yellow patch stared out the front which read CATERPILLAR TRACTORS.

The Jamaican pulled up his dashiki sleeve to show me a line of wristwatches. 'Boy, why you don't change dat plastic Chinee flasher fa genuine Switzerland twenty-four-carat selfwinder?'

'Oldman,' I said, 'you don't remember selling me this computerized digital last week?'

'True, true,' he smiled, and he pulled down his sleeve again. 'In dat case, loan me a loan of you penknife a quick space.'

I stopped in my tracks and turned to face him, smiling too: 'Fa what?'

The Jamaican chupsed. He reached into his pocket for two small kings, and he tossed one to me.

In three seconds I had it peeled in a single long peel. I snapped it in half, my fingers dripping, and I handed it over in exchange for the other.

'Oldman,' I said, 'where you get these from?' But he was already busy. We walked along without talking, indulging ourselves, dreaming of home. Until we'd turned both orange halves inside out as if they were mango cheeks, and sucked them dry.

Suddenly he turned to the side before a storefront glasswindow. Almost by accident he scratched a long deep scratch across the pane, keeping his back to the street. 'Listen boy,' he said. 'If you want dis pretty ring fa you mummy you better quick hoc it! Just watch it don't burn a hole through you pantspocket!'

It was a diamond engagement ring, three times the size of the one I'd given to Ash. I looked down at the stone shining, then up at the scratch in the glasswindow.

'Quick boy, what you got fa coconut water?'

I reached inside my pocket and pulled out the two crumpled five-dollar bills. Before I knew what had happened he'd grabbed them up, the grocery list too, and disappeared.

Now I found myself standing in the middle of the sidewalk holding this diamond ring I was sure the Jamaican had stolen the night before. Probably the alarm bells were still ringing. I clasped my fist shut and shoved it into my pocket, looking for signs of police. I turned around and started quickly home. By the time I arrived I was covered with sweat. Ash opened the door, little Olly tucked under her arm. I wiped the back of my hand across my brow and held it out, smiling. Ash looked down at the ring, then up at me with a tired expression: a look of frank tedium.

ONLY THE LITTLE baboo on he bicyclecar witnessed the final exhumation of Magdalena's body after so many previous attempts. The little baboo, together with the Bishop, and Monsignor O'Connor, and the three Warrahoons. They were the only five snowballs the baboo managed to sell all night long after the digging was finished: nobody else arrived. Nobody even bothered to climb out from under they sheets to spy through the window that night, all overtired and well desensitized by now with this digging up of the cemetery which had been going on not only fa the previous two weeks, but fa ten years. Even the spectacle of these two priests and they three workers dressed in they fancified gravedigging-monkeycostumes was no longer even a spectacle, but a

common nightly occurrence. Still, word got to us quick
enough. Even locked up sitting there on the cold concrete
flooring of that jailcage: they found no trace of corruption
on she body. Though Magdalena had been buried beneath
the ground fa ten years. She flesh had not even begun to
decompose, she face preserved fresh as day in the same
rich, sienna-burntblack colour. Some even went about the
place saying that she cheeks were rosier than in real life,
and she beautiful black hair had grown out even longer.
She hands were still crossed gently on she breast, still
holding the same rosary which by now time had reduced
to nothing more than a handful of peewah seeds, and a
powdering of bright orange rust. She gentle eyes were still
partially open, she gentle lips still smiling the same gentle
smile. So by the time the Vatican's ship arrived a few days
later Corpus Christi was already boiling over in she frenzy
again – all the old stories tumbling over theyself to tell
again – with the shackshacks shaking and the steeldrums
beating and everybody bawling *St Maggy! St Maggy! St
Maggy!* in a big parade to march the three of us like three
local politicians down to the wharf.

Boy, let me tell you this Vatican don't fry fritter to feed
famine: that same morning we arrived, before we even had
a chance to catch we breath, this Pius XI opens up
proceedings with the ceremonious signing of a decree fa
the Introduction of the Cause, entitling Magdalena to she
first official title of Venerable. That afternoon begins what
they call the Informative Process, under the authority of a
physician-priest by the name of Cardinal Vico. This
Process concerns Magdalena's life, she virtues, and she
reputation fa sanctity. There are fifty-two sessions fa this
first introduction stage extending over a period of seventeen days. Fa each session one of us appears before the
Ecclesiastical Commission – sometimes before the Pope
heself sitting there in he gestatorial chair, the four little
acolytes kneeling round him ready to tote him outside

quick to the bushes in the event of Papal weewee – with the three of us telling them the same stories over and over, answering the same answers again and again until we are blue in the face and tired to we bones with exhaustion. Fa the whole of those seventeen days we never left we rooms except to appear before the commission (they brought us we meals there too) because there was no way of knowing at what hour of the day or night they might come to call us. We never appeared together, and we never saw each other fa the whole time that trial was going on, so even if we had it in we heads to collaborate, there was no possibility fa pinttalk a-tall. We could only give them the truth the best way we could hope to get it out, the best way we could hope to call it up. So I couldn't say what Evelina and that Mother Maurina told them. All I can tell you is this: somehow that commission of fancified footfarah-priests – together with the inescapable fatigue of this unending ordeal – must have calmed the two of them down and slowed them up. Even the Mother Superior – who was my main fear in all this – and she must have managed somehow to talk sense and to make sheself somehow intelligible. Because we never had even the slightest doubt fa the whole time that trial was going on, that this Cardinal Vico and the rest of that Ecclesiatical Commission did not take in we every word with stonedry, blankfaced earnestness.

At the end of this Informative Process they gave us a few days' rest – though they still didn't allow us to see each other – after which Pius XI signed a second decree concerning the Heroic Nature of the Virtuous and Venerable Sister Magdalena María Domingo. This opened up the second stage which went by the name of Apostolic Process, and this one concerned the miracles. It was, of course, to be my main contribution. After a private consultation with Cardinal Vico (who by this time I had grown to admire and like well enough) we selected the required two miracles from a list of a possible ten, which I had witnessed or heard about secondhand. These two were to be presented before the Congregation of Rites, composed of both clergy and laymen, all of medical and scientific backgrounds. They would examine these miracles, and hopefully authenticate them, and push them forward fa the Beatification.

The first concerned a St Maggy boy, fairskinned, seventeen years of age, by the name of Henri Boisselet. On Tuesday 17 November they brought him in to me with a profuse abdominal swelling: I diagnosed tubercular peritonitis and admitted him to hospital. Two days later I called in Monsignor to administer Extreme Unction. That same night Mother Maurina and half-a-dozen nuns came to the hospital to kneel round he bed and begin a novena in Magdalena's name, the boy participating as best he strength would allow. The novena was to end on Thursday 8 December. The following morning on 9 December on my routine rounds of the hospital I examined him and found him instantly and completely cured. A week later he was stamped physically fit fa service overseas, where he fought at the German front fa thirty-two months without injury, after which he returned home still in sound health.

The second was a little French-creole from Suparee Village by the name of Marie-Bernard Soubirous. At about thirteen years of age (she had no birthpapers) Marie asked to pledge sheself to the convent. She mother would not allow it. At about the same time Marie's mother brought her in to me suffering from acute stomach pain and frequent vomiting: I diagnosed a gastric ulcer. I advised Marie's mother to allow her to pledge sheself to the convent, convincing her this would benefit Marie's emotional state, which would in turn improve she health: it only continued to decline. After a few weeks Marie became incapable of taking nourishment, and by this time she was extremely weak. On Saturday June 17 I examined

her in the convent and found her near death. I advised
Mother Maurina accordingly. That same night Marie
vowed a pilgrimage to Maraval Swamp – as Magdalena
used to make practically every Sunday of life – just as little
Marie sheself used to make often enough. Two of she
sisters helped her walk this pilgrimage, during which she
suffered intense pain. As soon as they reached Maraval
Marie fell to she knees in exhaustion beneath the samaan
tree. She remained there saying she beads fa more than an
hour, sometimes kneeling, sometimes lying on she back
on the grass. Suddenly she pains disappeared. Now she felt
a violent hunger, and she went quickly to she home in
nearby Suparee. There she took a meal without difficulty.
Marie felt she strength returning already, and she made the
long walk back to the convent without fatigue or suffering. The following morning of Monday June 19 I examined her and found her completely cured.

There were twenty-three sessions fa this Apostolic
Proçess extending over a period of twelve days. After this
the Congregation of Rites held another three sessions in
private before acknowledging the validity of the two
miracles fa the cause, assuring Magdalena's Beatification.
The Pope then declared the Apostolic Decree, and Magdalena received she second official title of Blessèd. There
was only one title left to go: that of Saint. In a few days
time Mother Maurina and Evelina and I could pack up and
go home. The three of us had had enough of this Vatican
and all this canonization business by now: that night
Mother Maurina went to stay in a nearby convent. I
moved to a little hotel just outside the Vatican's gates, and
at Evelina's request I put her to stay in the room next door.
The two of us ate dinner together that night fa the first
time since the ordeal had begun. Then I took off to find a
parlour, which I can tell you there ain't no suffering of
a-tall in that Holy City. They didn't have rum: I fired
down a whisky, like a coffee without the sugar, and I took

my first breath of air in nearly three weeks.

NOW I COULD not help but listen. Now I could not help but hear my father's voice. The same voice speaking to me above the same loud insects, above the same water beating against the same rocks. And I remember sitting here in this Warrahoon-Windsor chair, and wondering even then how it is that these insects cannot drown out this voice? How it is that these waves cannot outlive this story? And I remember thinking even then that the reason is because this story does not belong to this voice. To these voices. *This story belongs to that moon. To that black sky and that black sea. This story belongs to the same foul smell of the swamp when the wind blows.*

And I remember sitting here wondering even then whose hands were these weighing down on my shoulders? *Because if this voice is coming to you from outside there, then this weight you carrying on you shoulders could belong to anyone. And maybe if you could bend you head back without butting it up, you might find that it is not daddy but Papee Vince standing there behind you. Maybe even Evelina or maybe Granny Myna. Because if you could bend you head back without butting it up on the back of this chair, you might find that it is Barto standing behind you. Maybe even Magdalena Divina sheself.* And now, as I sit here in the same Windsor chair, looking out the same window seventy-four years later, I can only wonder again whose hands are these still weighing down heavy on my shoulders? Whose arms are these still jammed up against my temples? Now that I can look back easily enough and see that there is no one standing behind me. Now that my father has been dead in the ground longer than sixty years.

BOY, IT WAS as if Corpus Christi transplanted she own

hot enthusiasm to this Vatican, because by now the whole of that Holy City was bubbling up in the frenzy fa we Magdalena. By now everybody could tell the story of this Black Virgin who had come from cross the sea to sanctify sheself. By now Evelina and Mother Maurina and I were public spectacles, the people crowding round us, running out quick from they trinket shops to question us soon as we set foot in the streets. Every morning the newspapers headlined the canonization proceedings. Every evening big crowds gathered in the square before the Ducal Palace, all waiting to hear the news firsthand theyself. Scapulars of Magdalena suddenly proliferated. Medals and prayercards and black madonnas of mahogany and plaster appeared in the windows of all the shops, plastic statues with screw-on crowns to be filled with holywater. Everybody waiting with they sacred obeah-effigy to touch it to Magdalena's hand when she body is exposed, finally, this time in St Peter's Basilica in the special guilded coffinbox.

The day came soon enough. The three of us had hardly moved out of the Vatican a week before the summons arrived, ordering us to appear in the basilica the following morning at precisely 8:15 a.m., a special instruction written cross the bottom in the Pope's own hand: *You are to tell no one of this final meeting.* Even so, Evelina and I hardly had a chance to step into the street that morning before the crowd came pressing up behind us. At the appointed hour Mother Maurina arrived at St Peter's along with three busses, in the company of what must have been three orders of nuns. So by the time they toted in Pius XI sitting in he gestatorial chair – now in full costume with the triple-pointed tiara shining on he head, preceded by a procession of two-dozen fancified Cardinals and Bishops and so – by that time we were a congregation of about two-hundred. The four little acolytes toted the Pope slowly up to the front of the side chapel where we were seated, and they turned him round in a u-turn to face us.

Straight way he made a sign to remove the lid of the coffinbox. It wasn't the shining gold coffinbox we'd come to expect: fa the moment it was still the old wooden coffin Magdalena had come from Corpus Christi in, but at least they'd scraped off the dirt and slapped on a fresh coat of varnish. As soon as the two Vatican guards lifted off the lid the crowd let loose a long sigh, all squinging up in we chairs, even though of course nobody could see nothing inside the box as yet. The Pope took an envelope out from beneath he gown, removed he glasses from another pocket, unfolded them, and carefully fixed the curves behind he ears. He took a piece of paper out of the envelope and unfolded it. Then he held up he palm fa the crowd to quiet weself. He breathed heavily. When he began to read he voice was slow, dignified: '*By the order of our Lord Jesus Christ, of the blessèd apostles Peter and Paul and by our own supremacy, after much mature deliberation and the frequent imploring of Divine Assistance, on the advice of our venerable brethren the Cardinals of the Holy Roman Church, the Patriarchs, Archbishops, and Bishops, we hereby define and declare the cause of Magdalena María Domingo officially closed, and we invite the Church to witness the sole remains unearthed from her grave, three black stones, evidence substantiating the fact that this woman, and all else you have come to know and believe and dutifully to pass from generation to generation since your first beginnings, is but a fiction of your collective imagination. Now go home and try to awaken yourself!*' And with that the little acolytes u-turned again to tote him way.

3

Evelina Speaks of the Walking Statue

YES DOODOO, now de burden of passing on dis story must fall pon you. Because old Evelina not here no more to push she foot long de road again, and you is de firstborn Domingo manchild, beget by de firstborn Domingo manchild, beget by dis wadjank-cacashat who is Satan self, who defile Papa God own sweet saint of heaven to beget dis diab-crapostory hand down to you, to all Domingos, to dis whole island of Corpus Christi, and now to all America. It happen so, because you is de person standing up with one foot pon dis side of de sea and de next pon dat, one hand in dis pepperpot and de next in dat. And if dere is anybody could explain all dis confusion to dose yankees, dat dey can understand who we is and where we come from dat we can scarce even understand weself, it could only be you. Because if dere is anybody pon de face of sweet Papa God earth could help we climb out from dis crabhole we find weself bury in, now dere is no more sand remaining fa dem English and de rest to pelt pon we heads, it could only be America. Just hope dey don't cook we in dey own callaloo first, oui.

So when Granny Myna pull she hands from out de pot of water boiling with de dasheen leaves squirrelling with de okra, and she raise dem trembling up above she head to look up at heaven bawling out *Singate pendejo, Barto!* me

313

could only grab up de big basin of icewater from off de table to pelt it *splapplash* bathing she down. Granny Myna look at me like me head gone viekeevie now fa true, and she want to know why do me plash she down with all dat icewater and de icecubes pelting? Me tell she of course to save she hands from squinging up with dat boiling water, and de only thing now is fa me to run in de bush quick fa some aloe and sweet grannadilla leaf to dress she hands proper and keep dem from swelling up to bust she veins. But Granny Myna only push a chups at me saying she never bawl like dat because of no pain, but every time she make de callaloo is de same thing she can't feel nothing a-tall in she hands dead like a doornail cold, and she only praying to feel dat pain to know she is still alive, dat Barto have forgive she longlast fa killing he nasty crapochild. Me could only push de chups back at she and ask she if she take me fa poisson d'eau doux to believe dat crapochild could ever be dead, when she know good enough he swimming happy as ever in dat seawater inside he glassbottle bury safe neath de ground – and dere is no man nor saint dead fa thousand years strong enough to kill he, oui ma-doo mon-pere! – and if she think she could fool me so easy to dig out dat crapochild and take he way before dis Chief of de Commission Bishop Sévère find he, dat he put a quick fullstop to Magdalena sainttrial one time and finish. Me tell she de only way to dig out dis crapochild is to work enough science pon he fa we own protection, and if dis Bishop only make de mistake to take he out blankface so he ga dead up heself fa true and *all* we on top, but Granny Myna say she don't know nothing bout no Creole-obeah bubball, so is me ga have to do it, and is just den me realize she speak de truth.

First thing is to find some way to distract Monsignor and dis Bishop Sévère. Because every night dey dere digging up in Domingo Cemetery searching fa Magdalena corpsebody, when anybody in de whole of Corpus Christi could tell you sure enough dere is no corpsebody to dig up a-tall – but only de statue of black boulderstone standing dere in de cathedral dis diab-crapochild turn she to with only a single look from he nasty crapoface, oui fute Papamoi! – but how is me to dig out dis crapochild without dem two mammapoule priests catching me? Me decide me ga distract dem with a good dosage of scalowash-water, oui. Because dis scalowash-water is so powerful only little taste does make you toetee stand up tall like a standpipe ready to bust, or you mummy to melt down soft like a jubjub twitching in de sun, dat soon as dose mammapoules taste little dey ga be *so* hot up dey wouldn't have time to think bout no digging fa no corpsebody a-tall. So dat same morning me go by Blanchisseuse to a set of rocks by de seaside where de water does come pelting in pon a fulltide. Because dis scalowash is a kind of leech-shell sticking pon de rocks living only where dere is plenty rough sea pelting, and dat is why dey very difficult and dangerous to find and not many people would risk dey life to catch dem, but even so every year five–six oldmen dead up deyself searching fa scalowash trying to bring dey toetees back to life. So me hurry to Blanchisseuse before de sea rise, me tie me skirt round me waist to climb out pon dose rocks with de cutlass in me hand to scrape dem off, and in no time a-tall me collect up a kerchief full with scalowash squirming. Me squinge dem down good in de frying pan to make dem let loose dey scalowash-water, me strain it through a cloth to fill up a rumbottle full to de cork, and me rest dis lovejuice down pon de sill to cool waiting fa darkness to come.

Not before near midnight do me take up dis scalowash-water again, because me not taking no chances to bounce up nobody walking in de road nor liming by dat cemetery neither. Because a cemetery is always de first place famous fa people to go courting, and something bout de sight and de smell of a cemetery always hotting up people to do dey

business. Me light de boutille d'feu and rest it pon de
ground before de tamarind tree, me dress meself to pray de
prayer to Ogoun feeding he plenty rum, and me dig out
dat sardine-tinbox with Eshu navelcord coil up inside, de
tamarind already sucking pon me tongue already tying up
me mouth. Me hang de obeahpouch round me neck, me
cross cross in de street to keep Soucouyant from walking
behind me, and me go long quiet to dat cemetery. Of
course soon me reach me find de whole big crowd of
people only bawling and laughing and holding dey torchlights pon dey foreheads to mimic a spaceman walking
in a dream neath de sea, and dey standing up one on top de
next going right round de little cemetery wall. All dese
people only watching watching at dese three little Warrahoons, and Monsignor O'Connor, and dis Bishop Sévère
all dress up pappyshow in dey spacesuit-gravedigging-
monkeycostumes, with de torchlight-hardhats shining out
dey foreheads showing dem where to dig. Well now me
head viekeevie again, because now me bound to distract
not only Monsignor and dis Bishop Sévère, but dis whole
big crowd of people watching on top. Just den me get
strike by a lightning flash, and me steal up behind de little
babboo with he bicyclecar park side de big poincianna by
de frontgate. Me crouch down quiet behind de tree, and
soon as dat little babboo reach out to hand over a
snowball, me thief a sweetsyrup glassbottle from off he
car. One by one me full up every one dem sweetsyrup
glassbottles, oui. Every one full to de top overfoaming
with dat scalowash-water lovejuice: guava, governor,
soursop, red, king, portugal, barbadine. Passion, blue,
bitter, pine, julie, cocoacola, teenteen. Doodoo, one minute all dese tongues licking licking pon dey snowball,
next minute dey licking licking pon eachother. In no time
a-tall every manjack-womanjill *over* de wall *in* de cemetery
down pon de ground in some place private behind a
coughcold tree or a coolie-mausoleum, with one set

jooking going on backward-and-forward and upside-
down and inside-out – and sometimes two pon one and
four together with a oldman balling out *ee-ee-ee!* and a
woman *oo-oo-oo!* and *oh-Gud! oh-Gud!* and *ooops already?* –
with every possible kind of jooking that you could imagine going on like de cockroach-cocktailparty of Old
Year Eve morning. Of course next in line fa lovejuice-
snowball is dose two mamapoule priests, and soon as dey
taste little taste dat Monsignor is down pon de ground like
he playing horsie, with dis Bishop Sévère riding he
bareback *hy-ho!* like a spaceman-cowboy. Doodoo, me
walk straight to dat crapochild grave to dig out dis
glassbottle, me take it up, and me pass *straight* through de
cemetery *out* de frontgate cool cool without a single
monkeyhead looking up from dey monkeybusiness. Of
course dere is de little babboo peddling he bicyclecar home
now with all he empty sweetsyrup bottles rattling and he
fortune smiling in he pocket, and he only squeezing de
little bulb of he horn *peep! peep! peep!* singing out de old
calypso:

> *Was a jumbie jamboree,*
> *Took place Domingo Cemetery,*
> *Back-to-back, belly-to-belly,*
> *I don't give a damn,*
> *I done dead already!*
> *Back-to-back, belly-to-belly,*
> *Was a jumbie jamboree!*

CALLALOO
*A typical West Indian potpourri, its name an
old Arawak word, served traditionally on Sunday*

Ingredients:
    1 big armful dasheen leaves (an indigenous swamp
    plant)

12 African okras
1 cp. coconut milk
12 crabs
½ lb. saltbeef, or nice hambone
1 clove garlic
touch of East Indian curry, seasoning
1 big basin boiling water

Scald crabs and scrub well. Soak and cut up saltbeef. Wash
dasheen leaves and strip off stalks and midribs. Wash and
cut up okras. Put dasheen leaves in rapidly boiling water
(this gives them their rich, dasheen-green colour). Add
remaining ingredients and simmer until soft, about 3–4
hours. Stir thoroughly. Do not remove meat from crabs:
West Indians prefer to spend the afternoon picking them
clean and sucking them dry. Other ingredients may be
added as desired: bhaji, bodi, bluefood, cassava, eddoes,
tanya, greenfigs. Plantain, pigeonpeas, sweet potatoes,
pumpkin, dumplings, and all ground provisions. Any and
everything goes into a good callaloo. Serve with endless
foofoo.

SOON AS me push me foot in de house with dis
crapochild Granny Myna let loose a bawl, and she take off
running to spend de rest of de night hiding in de bamboo
cross de street. Me put dis glassbottle down pon de big
diningroom table, and me not even lowering me eyes to
look pon dis crapochild swimming inside with he fat
crapocheeks blowing out, nor pon dose forceripe
groseegorro greenplantains floating up tween he legs, and
me go straight to me room to throw meself dead in de bed
from exhaustion. But me scarce even close me eyes before
me jump up from out me sleep again, because now me
hearing one set of commotion going on outside de house,
people bawling and laughing and carrying on, and when

me look through de curtain me find five–six monkeyfaces staring back at me wake up already at dawn of morning, even after dis marathon jooking-jamboree going on de whole night. But me only have to put one little cuteye pon dese monkeys fa dem to know me not skylarking, and dey let go de sill to fall down tumbling one on top de next, only to jump up again scampering round de next side of de house. Now me throw on me clothes quick and me grab up dat obeahpouch from de chapelle to hang it round me neck, me whisper quick prayer to Ogoun begging he protect me against all de snare and malice of dis Eshu crapochild, and me reach neath me bed to grab up de cutlass. Me take off running through de kitchen to throw open de diningroom door, but when me look pon de table me find de glassbottle open with de metal clamps hanging down loose and de dishplace-lid side it, and dis crapochild *gone*. Me run straight to Granny Myna room only to find she gone too, still hiding in de bamboo cross de street, and now me take off running all through de house looking in all de drawers and neath de beds and all bout de place fa dis crapochild. Now me head viekeevie fa true because me not finding he nowhere a-tall, and me only watching up at de roof waiting fa it to drop down pon me head de next second, when all of a sudden me hearing a funny kind of language talking upstairs dat me can't remember where me hear it before, Dominica or St Vincent or Martinique? and me strain me ears to try to listen with so many people outside all talking together at de same time: *oy-juga oy-juga oy-juga*. Now me take off running again up de stairs back inside de diningroom again, and dere is Granny Myna with Rosey up on top de table holding dis crapochild below she sucking down de milk spilling all over he nasty crapoface, with all dese people only looking through de glass carrying on worse den ever. Now me hearing somebody mamaguying me bout how *me* was de pretty young obeahwoman make dis crapochild fa Barto, and

how *me* was he doodoo all dose years living in de same
house with Granny Myna together – when dey know
good enough it was dat diab Manfrog make dis crapochild
by defiling Papa God own sweet saint céleste, oui ma-doo
mon-pere! – and how mummy was de mistress of dat
wadjank-cacashat not me a-tall, because me would never
have nothing to do with dat man Barto, not even until de
ends of de earth. Me grab way dis crapochild from out
Granny Myna hands from off Rosey tottot, me tote he up
de stairs to de garret out on top de roof, and me walk
straight to de very edge. Me don't even open up me mouth
to speak a word. Me stand up dere just so with me legs
spread wide and dat cutlass holding in one hand pointing
up at heaven – and dis crapochild holding in de next
upside-down by he two legs with he two armflippers
flapping flapping like a crapofowl, oui fute Papamoi! – and
me turn de cutlass slow through de air with de long blade
dripping fire in de sun to point it down at dis diab-
crapochild, and me jook he one clean jook in he side. No
sooner do dis nasty green boil-dasheen crapoblood begin
to spray down all dese people, when every manjack-
womanjill take off running fa dey life like I done jook each
one with de same cutlass *in* dey backside.

Me climb down from off de roof toting dis crapochild
back downstairs in de diningroom again, and me push he
back inside he glassbottle with de two metal clamps clamp
down tight again. Now me turn to Granny Myna, and me
tell she if she only take dis crapochild from out he
glassbottle again he ga put one mal d'yeux on you to kill
you dead in one, because de only one thing to save we
from dis crapochild is dis obeahpouch tie up round me
neck. Now me take it off to hang it round de glassbottle-
self, dat dis crapochild could know sure enough who is de
person holding he cordstring, and he not ga be doing no
more mischief fa me now so long as he remain here in *dis*
house. Den when dat sainttrial fa Magdalena is finish, and

dis Bishop Sévère pronounce she we saint longlast to pack
up all he spacemonkey-costumes and carry dem back to
dat Vatican where dey belong, me could bury dis crapochild back in de cemetery safe again neath de ground.
But as dis crapostory does tell heself me never do reach
back in de cemetery with dat crapochild. Because dat same
night dis Bishop Sévère hold me to lock me up in de
jailcage together with dat same Mother Maurina and you
daddy too, waiting fa dis Vatican ship to come to carry we
cross de sea, only to testify we testimony in dis big
pappyshow-mocktrial dey stage fa we Magdalena. So all
me could do in de end at de last minute is run to Granny
Myna standing dere pon de wharf before me board de
ship, and me beg she please fa de mercy of Papa God please
to bury dis crapochild back in de cemetery where he
belong, just dere tween sheself and dat wajank Barto safe
and happy again neath de ground, and of course Granny
Myna accept straight way smiling fa me she ga do it.

But now Granny Myna is only crying in de corner of dat
diningroom sitting pon de ground rolling she beads, and
she tell me she could never help sheself from trying to save
dis crapochild. She say she even try to squeeze out little
milk from she own tottots, but dey don't have nothing left
a-tall after dose nine badjohns one after de next sucking
she dry. She tell me how dis crapochild is de son of she
own husband, born of he own flesh, living of he own
blood, even dough she hate he more den any creature
crawling pon de face of Papa God earth, and *you* should be
de first to understand as Barto is you own daddy too. Me
could only take she up gentle in me arms and try me best
to console she, and me tell she of course every thing she
say is true enough. With dat wadjank coming two–three
times every month pelting pon he big white horse foaming
from he mouth, and mummy standing dere she back press
flat against de door, dere inside dat little boardhouse he put
fa we to live in de first time since she *own* mummy days of

slavery she know anything more den a mudhut with a
thatchroof to cover she head. Standing dere against de
door in she Shango priestess-whitedress with de white
kerchief tie up round she head and de crucifix pon she
breast breathing, morning after morning only listening,
waiting fa dat soft *ca-clap ca-clap ca-clap* of he horse pelting
from de distance. With dose horsehoofs pounding harder
and harder pon de quiet earth faster and faster until dey
stop dead, and de next minute mummy throw open de
door fa dis man to appear, with mummy already pon de
ground basodee before he feet. And he take she up to lay
she down again pon we own little copra mattress dere in
de corner, with me de young girlchild again by de back
door outside listening, sitting dere pon de ground me back
press hard sweating against de cool boardwood wall,
sitting dere sweating listening waiting de whole day, only
waiting fa evening to come longlast. Den longlast he can
get up again to dress heself in he leather clothes and he
cowboy boots, and he can go by good Papee Vince to sit fa
quick half-hour before he climb up again pon he big white
horse to take off pelting again, with mummy again
standing dere she back press flat against de door of she
Shango priestess-whitedress crucifix breathing, listening,
only listening breathing waiting fa dose horsehoofs *ca-clap
ca-clap* disappearing slow in de night. And now me tell
Granny Myna very gentle, very quiet: *No. No.* Me did
always love you like me own mummy, oui. But *not* dat
man. Because it is over dat man mummy take she life, fa
me to find she de next morning in de canefield slash by she
own cutlass ear to ear cross she throat, and me could only
always hate he fa dat, even until de ends of de earth. And
now me hold Granny Myna gentle another quiet minute,
me help she lift down Rosey from off de table, and we
carry she together out de house back inside she shed.

NOW I DID NOT know what to think. Who to believe. Now I was dismayed again. It was not so much the story of Evelina's mother, the story of her death, because Evelina had told me of her mother's suicide before, and I had long intuited from the stories Granny Myna and Papee Vince told me – maybe even from the stories Evelina herself told me – that Barto had kept a mistress on the old Domingo Estate. All that talk of suicide made me uneasy enough, especially sitting there in the middle of that cemetery, on that frogchild's own headstone – or sitting there on the frontstoop watching Evelina plucking a chicken clean, on the back wall shelling pigeonpeas, or on the dock sanding hundreds of tiny chipchips; sitting there in any of those so familiar places or in all of them at once, listening for so long to this voice I knew so well – all that talk of Evelina's mother and her suicide made me uncomfortable enough, but I could accept it for the moment without too much trouble. And though I could not possibly have imagined that Barto's mistress on the old estate had been Evelina's own mother, I knew well enough from the way my family spoke of the whole affair – or avoided speaking of it – that this mistress had been a woman somehow known to me, if only vicariously, as the mother of this woman who had raised me from earliest infancy. I could even accept the fact that Granny Myna had adopted the daughter of her husband's own mistress, brought her to live with her in her own home as the daughter she'd never been given herself: I knew my grandmother was a woman of such strength and goodness. Now: that Evelina's mother could have loved Barto to such an extent as to kill herself over him. That Evelina's mother could have possibly loved Barto *a-tall*, this man who at one time had owned her own mother – Aiyaba, Evelina's African grandmother after whom she'd been named – purchased together with the boilinghouses, the canemill-trapiches and the mules to turn them. That *I*,

Johnny Domingo, Jr, that I am the grandson of this man
who had actually owned slaves – all that is absolutely
incomprehensible to me. Too incomprehensible and painful a reality for me to even consider, and I must force
myself to think of something else.

*How could Barto have been Evelina's own father? How could
it have been possible? And how could daddy not have known?
How could Evelina possibly have been Barto's own daughter,
and not have any birthpapers?*

Because the first time Evelina mentioned that Barto was
her own father – saying it so matter-of-factly that at first it
did not even register – that seemed more incredible to me
than all the rest put together. Because I had always
imagined that Evelina's mother, like Evelina herself, had
been far too strong and independent to be bothered with
any man. Evelina never mentioned a father, and I know in
my childhood imagination I believed she had none. But
Evelina *did* have a father, and as I knew now, that man had
in fact been my own grandfather. So maybe daddy had
lied? But why? Surely daddy would have been proud of
Evelina's Domingo heritage. Now I had to know. Now I
had to stop Evelina and to start asking questions:

'Evelina,' I said, 'how can you tell me Barto was your
own father? How could it have been possible?'

Evelina paused. She looked at me confused: 'Doodoo,
what you asking? Me not saying dat wadjank ever try to
hide de fact dat he was me daddy. Not so a-tall: is me own
self could never accept it. Because dat cacashat-wadjank
went bout de place boasting proudfoot to everybody bout
how he was me daddy, boasting proudfoot bout how he
did never hide nothing from no man.'

I shook my head: 'But Evelina, if Barto was so proud to
be your father, then how could daddy not have known?
And if daddy *did* know, how could he give me that
boldface lie about forging your birthpapers? Because Evelina, surely if Barto was your father, you'd have had

proper birthpapers?'

'No doodoo,' she said. 'You daddy never did give you no lie. It is me own *self* give you daddy de lie. Because when he come to me, one day not long after he reach back from dat England when dis pepperpot begin boiling over with dat crapochild swimming inside, and he ask me bout who is me daddy, me couldn't bring meself to give he de truth. Me could only give he de boldface lie, dat mummy did always tell me me daddy was one de caneworkers. And doodoo, me did feel so bad bout giving you daddy dat lie, de very same night me thief he key fa dat Government House Records Room, and me burn up me *own* birthpapers.' Evelina chupsed again. 'Of course me did never stop to think proper bout de problem you mummy and daddy was ga have burying me in Domingo Cemetery side de rest of we family. Because den me would never had give you daddy dat lie, nor burn up dat birthpapers neither. But you daddy write me out a next birthpapers just de same. And you daddy was a joker fa true, because if you go to dat Records Room and you look fa dat birthpapers, you ga see how pon de line fa who is me daddy he write OGOUN DOMINGO. So doodoo, me is you tantie in flesh and in blood just de same, and dat only go to show you how from de beginning of dis crapostory everything is a boldface lie, but time as you reach de end, everything ga turn out true as truth-self too.'

SO IT WAS many years after dat big pappyshow-mocktrial dis Bishop Sévère stage in dat Vatican fa we Magdalena, long after Granny Myna bury back dat cra-pochild happy in de cemetery again tween sheself and Barto where he belong, many many years after everybody forget to remember anything bout Magdalena, and she statue, and dis crapochild and de whole crapostory. It was one Wednesday midday me dere in de cathedral as always

putting in fresh bouganvilla flowers fa all de saintstatues,
and when me pass Magdalena me see she nice pretty
whitedress dat me have sew out with me own hands all
black up now muddy up pon de skirt, with one set of
beachburrs, and jookers, and sweethearts and so stick up
inside de ruffle. Well me not understanding dis thing a-tall
a-tall, less maybe some poor little callaloo-girlchild have
borrow Magdalena gown to wear it to some fancydress
fête? but if she have to muddy it up like dat, de least she
could do is wash it out proper before she dress back
Magdalena again. So me strip she down and me carry de
dress home to wash it out, and soon as it dry me carry it
back to de cathedral to dress she proper. But next Wednesday midday me find de same thing again, all she skirt
muddy up with one set of jooker stick up inside de ruffle.
Well now me head starting to get vex, so me strip down
Magdalena to wash out she dress again, and me spend de
whole afternoon sewing out a *next* whitedress just like
Magdalena own, and me leave it dere pon de bench fa dis
little ungrateful callaloo. So when Wednesday midday
come me not templating nothing bout Magdalena gown
again, but now me find *both* de dress waiting fa me all
muddy up jooker up, Magdalena own and de next dress
me leave fa dis spoilfish-callaloo on top. Well now me
head vex fa true – because me not no cheeneyweeney-
chineeman running no laundry service fa every little
callaloo running round coonoomoonoo in Tunapuna,
Papamoi! – so me wash out both de dress, and me wait dat
night sitting dere pon de pew before Magdalena, because
now me head set pon holding dis little cacashat-callaloo.
But me waiting dere de whole night and me not finding
dis little girl a-tall a-tall, dat after a time me did boot-off
snoring right dere pon de bench. Doodoo, when me wake
now me find de very same dress me holding in me own
selfsame *hands* all muddy up, but at least de spoilfish-
callaloo satisfy sheself with only one dress dis time,

because Magdalena own is still looking fresh and clean. Of course when me reach back to de cathedral de next afternoon with dis little callaloo dress all wash out pretty fa she, me find Magdalena own muddy up. So me wash out she dress one last time, and dat night me make up me head me not twinking me eye twice before me hold dis little no good callaloo. Of course after a time me boot-off sleeping again, and when me wake now me find not only dis callaloo dress gone from out me hands, but when me look up me find Magdalena *sheself* gone disappear now too. Me jump up straight to run quick to dat belltower ringing out de big bell *ba-bonggg! ba-bonggg! ba-bonggg!* to wake up de whole of St Maggy all running from out dey beds, with me only ringing de bell bawling *Somebody thief we Magdalena! Somebody thief we Magdalena!* and dis whole big crowd only standing dere watching up at me now like me is some kind of St Ann crazyhouse-bobolee. Me tell dem to go look in de cathedral see fa deyself, somebody thief we Magdalena, but of course when dey reach in dat cathedral Magdalena is dere standing up pon she pedistal good as ever, except now of course she dress is all muddy up. So dey all push a chups at me to mumble some curse bout dat crazy young obeahwoman again, and dey turn round to go back home back inside dey bed.

Of course now me realize straight way dis statue is walking. Because of course dat should have be obvious to me from de first time me find she dress muddy up, since Magdalena spirit *must* remain living in dat stonestatue like any other corpsebody, and if she restless she bound to walk de night like any other restless unhappy jumbie. Me could only think to find out who is de person she searching, oui. So me go de next night to wait sitting dere pon de pew before Magdalena again, and now me know good enough Magdalena is only waiting to see me drop asleep before she step down from off she pedistal again, so dis time me tie up one end of a twine round me bigtoe, and

de next round Magdalena own, dat soon as she move she
foot she would wake me. Sure enough soon as me drop
asleep me feel de tug, and now me look up to see
Magdalena come back to life more beautiful den ever. She
step down light as a breeze from off she pedistal, and me
jump up quick to follow she out de cathedral into de night.
She lead me cross de square and through de front door of
St Maggy Convent, stopping fa few seconds by de little
chapelle with de statue of St Bernadetta dere standing at de
front, and den she lead me long a set of dark winding
corridors before we pass out de back door again back again
in de night. Now she lead me long de trace going to
Domingo Cemetery, with de road so dark me have to
light de boutille d'feu quick to see behind she, and now me
feeling geegeeree geegeeree fa true, because now me
realize Magdalena can *only* be searching fa dat diab-
crapochild inside de cemetery. She stop by de frontgate to
pick a red poinciana flower, and she lead me through de
graveyard straight to we own family plot, and now she
kneel down to bend over resting dis poiciana flower gentle
pon de ground. But she don't rest it pon dis crapochild
grave a-tall like me is expecting, nor pon dat wadjank
Barto grave neither, nor even pon she own grave: she rest
it down pon de grave of we Granny Myna. Now me
thinking of course Magdalena *must* be troubling over
Granny Myna, de only person in dis big world ever to bear
she any malice a-tall. But when Magdalena lead me out de
cemetery again she don't turn round to go back to de
cathedral like me is expecting, but instead she continue
long de trace leading to Maraval Swamp. Now me realize
with a breath of relief Granny Myna *cannot* be de person
Magdalena searching. Because if she looking fa Granny
Myna of course she would never look inside dat cemetery,
since just like anybody else Magdalena *must* know Granny
Myna is still a young woman, living strong as ever inside
she house. So dat poinciana flower can only mean she

offering fagiveness to she after all dese years of hatred boiling up in Granny Myna blood, which is just what you would expect a saint céleste like we Magdalena to do. Now me follow she all de way long de trace to dat Maraval Swamp, passing straight through Village Suparee where Magdalena was born and raise without even stopping fa few seconds by dat little mudhut she live all she life. She only pause fa minute side de big samaan, and now she continue walking straight to de bank of dis nasty mudswamp, straight inside de mudwater. Magdalena don't stop before dis mudwater reach up high as she waist, oui. She stand up dere just so fa few minutes quiet templating de sea, and den she turn round again to climb out from dis stinking swampwater. Now she lead me up and down back and forth side de bank, climbing over dose banyans ducking down neath de mangrove branches scratching cross we backs – dat me can scarce even hold up de torchlight to see where me foot is slipping sticking deep in de mud high as me knee, oui Papamoi! – but me following behind she just de same monkey see monkey doing de very same thing. Not before a good two hours of dis foolishness do Magdalena turn she back longlast pon dat nasty mudswamp, and we start back long de trace back to de cathedral again.

Of course by de third night de whole big band of chupidees is sitting dere just like me, all waiting dere in de cathedral fa Magdalena to step down off she pedestal again. Now we follow she back to de swamp back again inside dat stenching mudwater, in and out and back and forth long de bank holding up we torchlights to see how best we can stumble over dose mangrove banyans tumbling one over de next in de pitch dark, with everybody bawling and yelling and carrying on until it is time fa we to follow Magdalena back to St Maggy again. So by de fifth night de whole of Corpus Christi is dere waiting in de cathedral to see Magdalena step down from off she pedistal

again, and dey let loose a bawl straight way to jump up
following behind she cross de square, through de convent
back to de cemetery back in dat stenching mudwater
again, with everybody climbling in and out stumbling
over deyself fa few more hours, only to turn round again
to follow she back to de cathedral again. Now Monsignor
realize he ga have to do something quick to put a stop to all
dis commess, because just now de whole cathedral ga
drown neath all dese chupidees traipsing in and out every
night after livelong night, all soakdown to dey waists
dripping with stinking dripping chourupa. Monsignor
decide de only thing to do is make a big iron jailcage fa
Magdalena just like all de other famous miraculous statues,
and he ga lock it up tight with few big heavy horsechains
and some fat panza-padlocks to hold she in. Monsignor
say he not taking no chances with dis calamity a-tall, and
he even take out dat old dusty shackle with the chain-and-
cannonball rusting in de corner of St Maggy Municipal
Museum, and he shackle it tight to Magdalena foot
standing inside she cage. But of course none of dis big
jailcage nor de chains nor de padlocks nor even de
chain-and-cannonball neither could do nothing a-tall –
because in truth dere is no way to hold down a jumbie
when she decide to walk, oui Papamoi! – and de very same
night Magdalena step out de shackle to pass through de
bars and de chains and de padlocks *straight*, and she go long
she way to Maraval easy as ever.

So de next morning Monsignor send fa me, and he beg
me to please work some obeah-science pon dis statue to
keep she from walking, because just now we *all* ga drown
weself in dat cathedral neath dis flood of chupidees and
stinking chourupa. Me tell he is not to science no science
pon dat statue, is only to find out who de person de statue
searching and work some science pon *dem*. De thing is, me
can't understand a-tall a-tall who dis person could be. So
me give Monsignor a next suggestion: maybe if you build

Magdalena a little piece of thatchroof dere side de swamp, just a little carrotroof or something so to keep de rain from pelting pon she head, maybe she would stand up dere neath it? At least den she wouldn't have such a big distance to walk every night, and you wouldn't have dis big flood of chupidees flooding through de cathedral neither. So Monsignor do just as I say, he find few Warrahoons to build de little carrotroof just dere side de swamp. Dat same night soon as Magdalena step down he give de order fa he three servantboys to commence pushing she pedistal, rolling like a concrete piling from King's Wharf rolling behind she. So when dese servantboys reach Maraval dey put dis pedestal to stand up just dere neath de little carrotroof, and sure enough soon as Magdalena finish leading she pack of chupidees scampering through de mud, she go straight to she pedestal to stand up watching at de sea. So now all de chupidees turn round to carry weself home, leaving Magdalena dere standing up neath she carrotroof happy as ever. We come back de next night and fa good few nights after dat, all laughing and bawling and licking up we snowballs waiting fa Magdalena to climb down off she pedestal again, but in truth Magdalena never walk again after dat night. She never step down from she pedistal never again. Whether or not Magdalena is resting peaceful longlast nobody could say. Whatever it is she find in de sight and de stench of dat morass to raise up she heart, or whoever it is paining she still dat she standing up dere watching she endless vigil to find, nobody could say neither. All anybody could ever know fa sure, is she *never* walk again after dat night. But it is many years later, long after de little boboloops from Suparee say Magdalena tell she she want a nice little chapelle to replace dat rotten carrotroof ready to fall down pon she head every time de breeze blow – and de next morning Monsignor win he satellite in de lottery dat he was so happy he give Magdalena she chapelle, oui fute! – it is many long years after dat, early one Sunday morning me make de pilgrimage to visit Magdalena because me not seeing she fa so long since she move to Maraval, dat me understand who is de person troubling Magdalena. Me enter de chapelle, me kneel down quiet before she, and when me raise up me eyes, *now* me see longlast who is de person she searching. Now me know who is de person Magdalena awaiting restless all dese years.

ALREADY I KNEW where Evelina was leading me in this story. Already I knew what she would say. It was as though the smell of that rum which still lingered on my forehead – the feel of it still cool and sticky behind my ears – was Evelina's *own* memories of these distant events, memories which I could see now through her eyes, which I could recollect in Evelina's own voice. Because now I knew exactly what she was going to say. After all, hadn't I delivered this frogchild to Magdalena myself? Hadn't I seen her take him up in her own arms and carry him back to the little church? Wasn't *I* the blind instrument of Magdalena's own happiness and peace? *Me*, her own son, Johnny Domingo, Jr?

Now I could stop Evelina and take up her story myself: her own voice telling the story without her even having to say it. Because I knew perfectly well what she was about to tell me: that when she raised her eyes, when they adjusted to the darkness and Magdalena began to take shape in her little chapelle – with the clouds of incense rising around her and the smell of sweetoil and the tiny devotion flames flickering red on her face, beautiful – I knew she would tell me that Magdalena's arms were no longer outspread, as they had always been, that her palms were no longer upwardheld, as we had always know them. *Because doodoo, when me raise up me eyes to find she standing dere pon she pedestal before me, now in she arms she swadling dis crapochild. How dis diab-crapochild could raise up she heart, and which miracle of heaven deliver he to Magdalena dere by dat stenching mudswamp, me couldn't tell you. But here is she standing before me now beautiful as ever, a smile gentle pon she lips, with dis crapochild swaddling peaceful inside she arms!*

Now I could sit back calm and easy in my pew. And I could put down Evelina's folded piece of paper a flay of old dried fishskin sticking to my wet fingers, and I could loosen this clip-on bowtie the claws of a rockcrab biting up at my throat. Sitting here behind Evelina in this little chapel again, my new charcoal-grey suit again soaked through with sweat, but calm now, finally, waiting to hear Evelina tell me what already I knew she would say. And I could slip my hand beneath this bench to pull the laces of my new washykongs sweatsoaked again sopping too, and I could kick them off and leave them here for the little Warrahoon to find them again tomorrow morning, right here beneath this kneeler tomorrow morning again. I could sit back now and breathe a breath of fresh air, relaxed, finally, because already I knew what Evelina was going to tell me.

BECAUSE DOODOO, when me raise up me eyes to find Magdalena again standing dere in she white gown dat I have sew out with me own hands, a little bit tatter and yellow now with oldage, with de years of people reaching up to touch she, to pin de plastic flowers and de medals pon she breast, to slide de silver churries pon she wrists and de solid gold rosary hanging round she neck. But Magdalena sheself is beautiful and fresh as ever, with de clouds of incense rising round she and de little red flames flickering pretty on she face, standing dere pon she pedistal she arms spread wide as always, she palms open as always to embrace all she children. But dere sitting pon de bench before she is dat man. Me seeing only de back of he head,

but me know he good enough, even after all dese years,
even from only de back of he head. After a minute he stand
up to leave de chapelle, and now me can see he face full, a
middleage man but just de same, same leather clothes with
de same cowboy boots and de same curls standing up pon
he wax moustache, and me jump up quick to follow
behind he. He walk cross de altar and through de sacristy
out through de door at de back, and he go to sit neath de
big samaan smoking one he little cigars again through he
same gold cigarette holder. So after a few minutes he
boot-off asleep lying dere pon de soft grass neath de tree,
and me turn round quick quick to run inside de chapelle
again. Me go straight to dat gold Baptism-fountain dere
side de altar, me fill up a tasa with holywater from de tap
neath it, and me carry dis holywater outside quick to plash
he down. Because doodoo, even dough me never before
hear of no diab-jumbie walking in de day, one thing me
know sure sure, *no* diab-jumbie could never stand de
plashing of dis holywater pon dey flesh. Dis holywater
must sting he like a nest of fireants biting he up, and dis
diab-jumbie *must* jump up quick from out he sleep to pelt
heself in de sea. Doodoo, he don't even wake up. He
remain dere sleeping just so, quiet and peaceful as ever,
and not before a next half-hour do he sit up longlast, and
he wipe he face with de cowboy kerchief tie up round he
neck. Now he stand up again to walk by de sea templating
it fa few minutes, and he turn round to pass through de
sacristy and de church, out de front door again. Of course
de morning is still too young to find anybody but we two
in de street, and now me follow he long de trace straight to
Magdalena own little mudhut, right dere in Village
Saparee not ten-twelve steps from she little chapelle. Me
watch he lie down in a hammock neath de almond tree in
de frontyard, and me stand up dere just so in de middle of
de trace, viekeevie, tootooloo, because me not believing
what me own eyes seeing before me. Because doodoo, dis

is no *jumbie* lying here in dis hammock. No jumbie a-tall. Dis is *he*, in flesh and in blood, living still, because no diab-jumbie never walk in de day, and no diab-jumbie could never stand de plashing of dat holywater neither. But doodoo, how could dis man be living still with all we taking he fa dead now fa donkey ages? fa longer den *forty* years?

Me come back de next morning and me find he dere again. Every morning in de early morning sitting right dere pon de pew before Magdalena again. Every morning lying neath de samaan to smoke he cigar, resting dere in de hammock neath de almond tree again. *Where* he have disappear to fa all dese years me could never tell you. *How* he could be living right here neath we own eyes without we knowing, fa all dese many long years, me could never tell you neither. But of course nobody would never think to look fa he in dis little mudhut in Village Suparee. Nobody would never think to look fa he *a-tall*, because everybody in de whole world taking he fa dead now fa longer den forty years. Even dough in truth nobody never *do* find out how he die, nor where, nor when, nor nothing a-tall except fa dose markings dis diab chisel out heself pon he own headstone, only to play we all de fool. So in de end you daddy didn't have no choice but to make dat pappyshow mockfuneral to bury dose few chockstones, because dat was de only way to give you granny little peace, dat now she could believe longlast she diab-husband is dead and bury safe neath de ground. Me could only think to try kill he dead again, oui. Because not until dis man is dead and bury, could Magdalena nor *none* of we know little peace. But doodoo, you know youself how many times already me try to kill dis diab and de diab-crapochild. You know youself good enough dere is *no* man walking dis earth strong enough to raise up a hand against dem. No man a-tall. Only Eshu could take de life of dese two diabs. Because doodoo, now me ga tell you something dat neither you daddy, nor Granny Myna, nor Papee Vince, nor Mother Maurina, nor nobody else telling you dis crapostory could tell you. Now me know good enough who is de person Magdalena is searching all dese years. But she don't have to search no more, because *here* he is, sitting every morning right here pon de bench before she. Because you listen good to me now. Listen good good to me here now, because dis thing me ga tell you now, in de end, is more difficult to bear den all de rest together. But doodoo, if you could bear de rest, den you ga have to bear dis one too: you grandaddy Barto is living still. He alive. Still. Living right dere in dat little mudhut in Village Suparee. And he only waiting fa Papa God to fagive he and take he life. But Papa God could never fagive he. Never. Neither Papa God, nor Magdalena, nor none of we could fagive he, and he ga live faever. We *all* ga be living faever neath de curse of dis man and he child, even until de *ends* of de earth.

I AWOKE from a dream of death: old Evelina's wrinkled face looking down at me, her hand clasped over my mouth so I could not breathe. I threw off the sheet and took a few deep breaths, panicked by the vague notion that I had forgotten something, something lost irrecoverably long ago. I sat up in my bed, looking around the room as though I might find it: the oscillating fan swept slowly back and forth. Ash lay asleep on the bed beside me, Evy in her bassinet in the corner, not yet six months of age. On the bureau there was a pair of my old jesusboots, one of my shortpants and a jersey. I couldn't figure out what my jesusboots were doing on top the bureau. Then I realized Evelina had taken them out and left them there for me to put on. I slid quietly out of bed and pulled on my shorts, buckled up my jesusboots. But as I raised the jersey over my head I stopped with my hands in the air: where was I going so early in the morning, and didn't I have to report to the hospital in a couple hours? I brought the jersey down over my head, checked my wristwatch on the bedstand: 5 a.m. I'd agreed to accompany Evelina some-place – that much I remembered – but I couldn't recall what place it was, or even if she'd told me where we were going. Perhaps it was Corpus Christi Day again – because suddenly I couldn't remember the date either – and we were going to the cemetery to repeat her obeah ritual. In that case, I realized, we could walk to the cemetery and back in fifteen minutes.

I closed the door quietly behind me, and I stuck my head into the boys' room for a moment, my own bedroom years ago: they were both sound asleep, and I stood for a moment listening to their calm breathing. I found Evelina down the hall, waiting for me beneath the light at the top of the stairs, outside Papee Vince's and my sister's old bedroom: it would be Evy's room in a few months' time. Evelina looked a hundred years old – I was sure she'd reached her nineties at least – dressed in a faded longdress with a kerchief tied around her head, another over her shoulders, barefoot, a dozen silver bangles rattling like old bones on her wrists. In one hand she held a kerchief suspended by two big knots from the blade of her cutlass, in the other a bottle of rum. She turned and started down the stairs. I followed her to the bottom, walking on my heels with my toes curled up to keep the flapsoles of my jesusboots from slapping against the bottoms of my feet. Evelina led me through the entrance hall and out the front door. When we got to the gate she turned and looked at me for the first time since I'd awoken from my dream. She gave me the bottle of rum. I didn't know what to do, so I pulled the cork and took a big swallow. Evelina made a face as though I'd lost my head. She turned and went to the middle of the street, carving a cross in the dirt with her cutlass. We started down the road, the sun and the dust

rising behind us, Evelina walking ahead trailing her kitch-
en smells of cooking coalpots, of sweetoil rubbed into her
joints every morning, with me following behind carrying
the bottle of rum, pulling the cork every few minutes for
another swallow. The potcakes were still asleep in the
middle of the road, and occasionally we'd have to step
around them.

Evelina led me along the trace to the cemetery, but I
could not be sure yet that that was where we were going: I
had learned long ago that anything could happen in this
story. *Anything*, except what I was sure would occur. I had
learned long ago to doff all expectations, and I followed
behind Evelina blind, but not with faith, nor by incredul-
ity either: blinded by fatigue, by excess. And I was right
not to believe that we were going to Domingo Cemetery,
because we passed it straight – as though it were not even
there – and we continued along the trace to Maraval
Swamp. We did not go to Divina Church either, at least
not yet, because when we got to Suparee Village we
stopped at the little mudhut, the almond tree with the
hammock beneath it in the frontyard. But Barto was not
lying in the hammock, and neither was he in the little
mudhut, so far as I could tell. Because the door was wide
open, held against the wall by a faded conch shell. The hut
appeared empty, deserted like the rest of Suparee Village at
that hour of the morning. But now I saw a woman, sitting
crosslegged on a saltfish crate in the shade of the almond
tree, bent over a grindstone: she was patting out a cassava
cake. As we approached she raised her head, and I looked
into the face of a very old and beautiful East Indian
woman. Her eyes flashed momentarily bright and alive,
and she bent over her grindstone again without speaking. I
followed Evelina past her to the door of the mudhut. She
turned and looked at me for the second time since I'd
awoken. Evelina had not said a word to me that morning,
and I was not sure she would speak now. 'Go,' she said.

'Go inside dat he could beg you fagiveness.'

Evelina remained by the door. I entered into a single small room which took up the entire hut. Its roof was thatch, its floor earthen, pounded hard and smooth by generations of feet walking across it. The hut smelled of dry dirt and wet straw. There was a small copra matress in the corner, covered with crocusssack. Above the bed there was a small window, a crocusssack curtain hanging before it. I assumed I was waiting for Barto to return from his morning visit to the church.

Now I perceived a slight movement behind me, and I stood for an instant puzzling over it, because I perceived it neither through sight nor sound, but as the gentle movement of air across the backs of my arms and legs. I turned slowly around. Now I saw before me an elderly man, sitting in an old rocking chair not three feet away, wearing only a merino-vestshirt and a pair of boxer drawers. He was rocking back and forth, so slowly that his movement was nearly invisible. He was little more than a skeleton, with scarcely any hair on his head, other than a stubble of silver beard. His eyes were covered with a grey film, and I would have thought them blind, were they not looking directly into my own. His skin was so thin and transparent I could see all the veins working beneath it. In his hand he held a piece of cassava bread, which he seemed to be chewing: there was a dusting of phosphorescent flour on his colourless lips. Slowly he raised the bread, and for an instant I thought he was offering it to me, but he put it down on a crate-table beside his chair. Then he held his hand out towards me. Again I did not know what he wanted. We remained motionless for a full minute, silent – only the soft patting of the oldwoman on her grindstone outside – before I realized he wanted the bottle of rum. I was no longer even aware that I was holding it. I held the bottle out, sure that it would drop to the ground as soon as he tried to take it. But he held on and pulled the cork with a movement surprisingly vigorous, and he raised it up to his mouth and took a big swallow. Then he held it out to me. Again we remained motionless, silent, for a full minute. I understood that he wanted me to drink some of the rum – he had not corked it back – and slowly I took the bottle. But as I brought it up it would not go to my lips – as though I'd lost control of my own hand – and I raised it quickly, high in the air, upside down, rum spilling over both of us. I brought the bottle down on his head with all my strength. With such force that it broke in my hand, even on his soft skull. He was on the ground now the empty chair rocking violently back and forth beside us, with me kneeling over him bringing the broken bottle down my fist a knot of shattered blood-dripping glass smelling of rank rum, down on the bleeding torn mass of his soft disfigured skull again and again and again, with Evelina screaming behind me: *Jesuschristjesuschristjesuschrist!*

4

Papee Vince Tells the Madonna's History

YOU SEE SON, ramgoat never bring home no lamb-sheep, and by that, is meant to say this: monkey don't climb grugru tree, and agouti don't look fa road to run, and rockstone have no business between cockfowl legs. I am no bloody historian now to loop the loop fa you. Neither am I any one of those ethnopologist fellows, or who ever the hell kind of people they have to make a study of these things in particular, such that I ga have the knowledge sufficient to look you in the face and say, well yes, such and such, and so and so. I am a simple storyteller. I have a simple story to tell. And son, these days story telling quicker than you can beg water to boil cowheel. It filling you belly fast as airfritter. But don't let that one bamboozle you, son. Because this story you hearing might be nothing more than a simple island folktale, telling of simple island folkpeople, but I can promise you one thing: it not ga leave you belly empty. Just listen good good to me here now. Listen good good to me here now, because this thing me ga tell you now, in the very beginning, is something that neither Evelina, nor you daddy, nor Mother Maurina, nor Granny Myna nor nobody else telling you this story could tell you: both Barto and Magdalena are still alive. They living. Still. Right there in Village Suparee. Right there in that little

mudhut where Magdalena sheself grow to she thirteenth
year. How in bloody hell this thing could be possible.
How they could both be living still with all we taking they
fa dead now fa donkey's ages. And how the ass I myself
could believe it fervently fa thirty-five years without ever
once stopping to question it – lying there in my hammock
in a little bungalow high at the top of one of those derricks
in the middle of the jungle of that Delta Orinoco, hidden
somewhere up in the bush behind God's back – only to
return to this island thirty-five years later and discover that
all this time I have been deceived by the very same story I
am telling, that, I ga explain to you in a moment.

Wait awhile. Wait awhile, son. We coming to that one.
Just let me tell you something first, while we here, at the
start, in the very beginning. Because son, some of the
things I ga tell you now, some of the things I have told you
already, may seem, in one way or another, disrespectful to
you as the patient listener of this story. I can only assure
you of this: I would be the last man on this green earth to
abuse the privilege of you good ear. No son, I am no
cokeeeye slymongoose, to sit here in this hammock
breathing up my own breath. Talking fa myself to hear.
Guineahen don't hide collection plate when she preach to
cockfowl. But son, I can only give this story back to you
the way life give it to me – the way the story asks itself to
be told – with all its many deceptations, and cumbruc-
tions, and confufflations. Because all that is as essential to
the telling of this story – as essential to the understanding
of it – as any amount of poetry pile up in the po beneath
you bed. No son, I can only give you this story the way
life offer it up, and try my best to remain truthful to all
three: to the story, to myself, and to you. And son, that
one is a turtle egg that don't suck easy a-tall. Because of
course, in the end, as with any other tale told of man or
monkeys since the beginning of time, you can only tell
your own story. You can only hear your own story too.

Enough. You want to know the history of this madonna. Good. The facts are these: 1702. Southern Spain. Andalusia. A black shepherdess appears to the Capuchin monk, Isadore de Seville. She reveals sheself to be an incarnation of the Virgin Mary. Names she name: LA DIVINA PASTORA. She informs this Isadore monk that she will bring together all Papa God's people, flocking we up in she one universal sheepfold. Isadore spreads he devotion to this Black Virgin throughout Andalusia. He wins the support of Pope Pius VI, who blesses she name and publishes it worldwide. 1715. Pañyol Capuchins arrive in the New World, looking to evangelize the indigenous Amerindians. In the Caribbean they are primarily Arawaks and Caribs (the latter distinguishing theyself as Oubaobonums, or island Caribs, and Balouebonums, or mainland Caribs). In addition there are Tainos in the Greater Antilles and Bahamas, Igneris in the Lesser Antilles. All exterminated and obliterated by the colonizers. On mainland Pañyol America there are, among others, the Guaranon Indians, commonly called Warwarrahoons, later shorten to Warrahoons.

The Capuchins bring with them they devotion to this Black Virgin, a devotion which wins instant popularity in the New World, fa reasons obvious enough: the Amerindians can easily identify theyself with this madonna looking just like them, can easily transform her into a *zemis* or idol of they own. 1720. The devotion spreads throughout mainland Pañyol America, particularly the region we now call Venezuela: to this day you will find several Venezuelan churches dedicated to La Divina Pastora. 1727. Aragonese Capuchins from Northern Spain establish a mission in Valley Cutacas, along the River Orinoco, not far from its mouth opening into the Caribbean Sea: they dedicate it to the Black Virgin. According to historian-priest Fr John Thomas Harricharan, in he book of *The Catholic Church in Corpus Christi 1498–1852*, the Cutacas mission encounters various misfortunes during the four years of its existence: floods, fevers, famish. Two priests die of mappapee bites. Nevertheless, the Capuchins baptize forty-seven Warrahoons, perform fifteen Warrahoon marriages, bury nine Warrahoons with full Catholic rites. According to physician-historian Surgeon-Major DWD Comins, in he *Report on Indian Emigration to Corpus Christi* (quoted by Fr Harricharan) the statue of the Black Virgin was brought to the island by the Aragonese Capuchins about 1730, fleeing persecution from the Warrahoons in Valley Cutacas. Comins's sources remain unknown.

But among the many legends bespeaking the origins of this statue, the most popular tells how she is carved from the trunk of a purpleheart tree by an old Capuchin monk. She is stolen from the monks by a band of vengeful Warrahoons, escaping downriver towing her behind they three rowing pirogues. The statue is beached on Corpus Christi near the Amerindian settlement of Coyaba, later to become St Maggy. She is placed on a mound in the centre of the village and here she is worshipped by the Indians: Arawaks and Caribs, as well as Warrahoons from the mainland. She is given the name AKAMBO-MAH, an *akambone* being a good spirit which takes the shape of bats and blackwidow-spiders. With the disappearance of the Indians the statue disappears too, discovered many years later beneath the big samaan by the little callaloo from Village Suparee, Marie Bernard Soubirous. The madonna remains fa several years beneath a small carrotroof on the banks of Swamp Maraval. Here she is worshipped by East Indian labourers and African slaves, until they ceremonies are prohibited by Church and Government officials. The statue moves to St Maggy Cathedral fa some time, travels cross the sea to the Vatican in Rome fa the canonization proceedings, and she returns to settle sheself in she own little church there by the swamp. Son, we can resign weself to only this: wherever this madonna came from,

and whoever brought her here, if, indeed, anyone really
brought her here a-tall. If, indeed, she is not truly as old as
this island of Corpus Christi sheself, all that remains very
much a mystery to this day. We will never known fa sure.

Right. Good. To begin with she skin black black like
black. She face small and round, she eyes large and dark,
she lips smiling a soft, comforting smile. She hair is made
from real human hair, probably that of a young Warrahoon girlchild, perhaps a little Pañyol shepherdess. It is
straight, thick, and intensely black, and very long,
reaching almost by she knees. She is rather short, the
typical height of a Pañyol or Warrahoon girlchild at the
age of maturity: five feet two inches. Stripped down
naked, I suppose she weighs about half a stone. She stands
with she neck backbent in a slight bend, she beautiful face
upraised in a slight raise, she arms outwardspread, she
palms upwardheld. Over the years she has worn various
gowns, during various periods, fa she various religious
groups. But she most recent gown these days is the one
Evelina sheself sewed out, some fifteen or twenty years
ago: it is white lace, a little tattered and yellowed now with
oldage, ruffles on the hem and sleeves, a large wooden
rosary tied up round she waist. On she head she wears a
veil of the same yellow-white lace. She is stuffed primarily
with crocusssack, cottonwool, a few balled up pages of the
Bomb. Like most Pañyol statutary of this type and period,
she consists of a painted papier-mâché head, two papier-
mâché hands with forearms attached, two short sticks tied
with twine.

Of course, there is nothing peculiar in any of that. I am
telling you nothing that you do not know perfectly well
already. But what *does* seem to me rather curious, very
peculiar, is this: here is a statue coming most likely from
somewhere in Northern Spain, or at least pasted out by
some Pañyol Capuchin living most likely in Valley Cutacas. Here is a Roman Catholic statue, with this absolutely

incomprehensible tilak of an East Indian from India stamped in she forehead. Now naturally, you ga want to ask youself: What in bloody hell is this chuffchuff old fucker babbling about now? Because of course, as you well know, the history of this statue is a history written as much by the Amerindian and African slaves – by the East Indians who came to the Island as indentured labourers – as it is a history written by the Catholic Frites from France, who brought the East Indians when slavery was finish. So any little half-naked, half-starved coolie could have turned round to slap on that tilak in half-a-second, a dab of roukou paste when the pomme-frite priest's back is turned. But son, as I have been made to understand, and I have had it confirmed by several individuals who actually examined this statue closehand, particularly you own grandfather. Because of course, ever since that morning when Barto sought me out secret to make the arrangements fa Evelina's headstone – the same black marble with the same white engraving – insisting that as he own girlchild we can only bury her there in Domingo Cemetery beside the rest of we family. (But of course, if you recall the chronology of this story, you will remember how Evelina sheself wouldn't be dead fa good few years to come, and in fact, I myself would be dead fa good few months before her. With Evelina's headstone already there in the cemetery waiting fa her long before she needed it – just like all the others – but of course, with all that confusion going on about birthpapers and deathpapers and where to bury her and so on and so forth, nobody ever seemed to notice it there, not even Evelina sheself.) Yes son, ever since that morning when Barto first revealed to me the fact that he was still alive, I have made the pilgrimage to Maraval on many occasions to see him, both we passing the evening sitting there together beneath the same almond tree in the frontyard, me in the hammock with Barto there on the cratestool beside me, knocking back we tasas of punching rum, talking we oldtalk. Because of course, I have never seen this statue, as I have always preferred to let Magdalena live and breathe in my own imagination, rather than to experience her dressed in the dry hollow reality of little crinoline, and paint, and papier-mâché. So I can only repeat fa you what I myself have been told, and as Barto assures me – in addition to the bulk of the remaining particulars which substantiate, fa all the world to witness, the actuality of this black madonna such as she is – that this East Indian tilak is not simply painted there on she forehead, it is *stamped* into the original plaster.

Well: I don't know what you want to make of all this tilak business son, but I have considered it fa good many years, and I have turned it over until I think I have come up with the logical explanation. Let we suppose now that that this black madonna *was* pasted out by some Pañyol Capuchin, some 300 years ago, either in that Old World or somewhere here in the New. (Because perhaps the only useful piece of worthwhile sensible information to come out of that big pappyshow sainttrial, was the verification that this madonna is in fact 300 years old, she painted papier-mâché head is in fact preserved in its original ancient form, discounting the few layers of lacquer slapped on she face every fifty years or so.) And son, let we suppose too that the most salient feature of this black madonna – the one characteristic specified from the very outset by La Divina Pastora sheself, when she first appeared to that Isadore de Seville – is she universality, the all-embracing all-comprehending expansiveness of she great love (which is precisely the meaning of the gesture of she widespread arms) would not then the Capuchin monk, priest, and artist pasting out this statue, would he not then seek some visible sign to communicate this universality? Some concrete symbol foreign and somehow mysterious even to the Capuchin artist heself – this solitary old monk

sleeping on a bench with a boulderstone beneath he head fa
he pillow – this old monk who most likely had never even
seen a Hindu or a Muslim in he life? Some proud and bold
and perhaps even painfully defiant gesture somehow con-
tradicting the doctrines of he own spiritual core of belief?
Would he not then take up in he trembling hand a dowel,
or a writingpencil, or a jooker of some sort dubbed with
red paint, or roukou paste, or perhaps even he own blood,
and carefully pierce Magdalena's forehead? Of course,
what this old monk could never have foreseen, what he
could never have dreamed up even in he wildest imagination, was that this same tilak would allow the East Indians
to identify theyself immediately and wholeheartedly with
Magdalena, 250 years later when they arrived here on this
island of Corpus Christi.

Right. Good. Corpus Christi fête takes place every year
on 16 April, Holy Thursday, as you well know, when all
of we jump up from out we beds first thing at the dawn of
morning, hurrying to dress up weself dandan to attend the
early Mass. But we are only waiting fa that service to
finish, waiting to run home again to throw off we clothes
and costume weself as some saint or Bible character. Only
to take off running again to jump behind some church-
band, we calypso-hymns singing out to wake up the dead
– shackshacks shaking we steeldrums beating we toktoks
tacking *tack-ka-tack-tack, ping-pa-ding-ping* chipping down
the road – only celebrating weself and we love fa life on we
feast of Corpus Christi Day. But son, what you probably
do not realize, what you probably have never before been
told, is that this Catholic carnival, this fête with which you
have come to identify yourself, did not originate as any
kind of Catholic carnival a-tall. Quite to the contrary.
Because it was not taken over by the Catholics of Corpus
Christi until much later, as initially it was a Hindu and
Shango fête: a festival of East Indian and African origin. In
fact, the true Catholic carnival was another carnival

altogether (still celebrated to this day in Trinidad and some of the other islands, just as it is celebrated in Rio de Janeiro there in Brazil, and quite in New Orleans all the way there in America). The true Catholic carnival was a pre-Lenten festival, a festival actually taking place during the three days prior to Ash Wednesday, seven weeks earlier on the Liturgical Calendar. Furthermore: the original Corpus Christi Day did not take place on Corpus Christ Day *a-tall*. That is to say, it did not occur on Holy Thursday, but on Good Friday: the day of Christ's death. The day when all the East Indians and Creoles and Warrahoons went into the Catholic church to take up Magdalena, parading her joyous through the streets, resurrecting *her* up to take He place. It was a day known *not* as Corpus Christi, but as the Day of Suparee K Mai: the Day of Mother Kali, Black Hindu Goddess of Death and Destruction.

IT WAS on the night before my forty-fifth birthday, exactly forty-five years ago, precisely in the middle of my life (how these numbers are significant I cannot say, only that they seem too coincidental to leave unmentioned); it was on the night before my forty-fifth birthday, that Ash and I were awakened by our daughter's voice, calling quietly to us from down the hall. We hurried to her room, Ash in her nightgown sitting on one side of her bed holding her hand, me in my boxer drawers and marino vestshirt sitting on the other, the back of my hand pressed lightly against her cheek to check her temperature. Evy had been sick in bed for three days. She'd been burning a low-grade fever, complaining of pain in her lower abdomen. Ash assured me that she hadn't begun to mestruate yet, so initially I thought it might be her first period coming on. But when the pain and fever persisted, I began to fear something else: inflammation of the vermiform appendix, impending appendectomy, though I examined her again and again without finding any swelling, no tender spot on her lower right side. Still, I put her on 250 mg of Ampicilin every six hours (a broad-spectrum antibiotic), aspirin for the fever, and I bribed one of the nurses to meet us at the hospital first thing in the morning – Good Friday morning – to take her white count. No easy accomplishment at all: it was hard to get anybody out of bed the morning after Corpus Christi Day, much less a whitecap-nun.

Evy was then thirteen years of age, the only one of our children still living at home. The boys had already been going to college in the States for a few years, and Evy would do the same in four or five. For a time she would return home for Christmas and summer vacations, as her brothers had done before her, but I knew from the start those trips were numbered: the three of them would eventually find their own lives in America, far from this forgotten place, lives with promising futures. For a time Olly, our eldest, showed some interest in medicine, and he spoke vaguely of plans to return to the island to take over my practice. The third generation to produce a doctor, I decided, already fantasizing about building him his own clinic – right there on Rust Street beside the hospital daddy had built for me – complete with all the most modern equipment brought from America with him. But eventually those plans drifted away, no doubt for the best. Eventually our three children ceased returning to Corpus Christi altogether, and Ash and I returned to America instead to visit them. Their families and their children: our American grandchildren.

But what I could never have foreseen, what I never even thought to consider, was that Ash would die before me: thirty-five years before me. Leaving me here to stumble around this big, empty house. To stumble around this old, broken-down house for thirty-five years, with only myself to bump into. But perhaps I should have suspected something of the sort. Perhaps I should have anticipated some tedious, drawn-out ending like this, every member of my family cursed with the same inevitable, invincible longevity. Were it not for my medical practice – which has of course slowed substantially over the years – but which, nevertheless, I have managed to keep up even to this day; were it not for my perhaps insignificant practice, and the satisfaction I gain from helping a few Blacks and East Indians who might not otherwise *ever* see a trained physician for the lengths of their pitiable, deplorable lives; were it not for my small practice, I'd never have survived these thirty-five years. These ninety long years.

I removed my hand from my daughter's cheek: she continued to burn a slight fever.

'Still paining you down below?' I asked.

Evy nodded.

I pulled the sheet down to examine her again, pressing gently with both hands, one set of fingers crossing over and pressing down firmly on the other, feeling her abdomen through the oversized undershirt she slept in.

'Nothing?' I asked. 'Just the pain below, inside?'

She nodded again.

On top of the bureau lay her Corpus Christi Day costume, which the three of us had assembled the week before. Her mas was to have been a cowmaiden in the band of Krishna's Companions: there had been a recent, enthusiastic resurgence of the Hindu element at the fête. Ash and Evy had sewn up a blouse and pants of white gauze, the sleeves and legs ballooning out above the wrists and ankles, like an outfit for Ali Baba. I'd contributed a vest and headdress, glued together from pasteboard. The three of us covered them with plastic jewels, feathers, gold glitter. We'd even glittered her old washykongs, there on the bureau beside her gilded vest. But Evy's cowmaiden costume went unworn. Instead, the two of us spent the day together in her room, joined occasionally by Ash. This I did not find disagreeable in the least: I was happy for any excuse not to go out into the street. Happy to spend a quiet day with my daughter, helping her with schoolwork and telling her the old stories, interrupted only by occasional bands parading past the house.

I knew that this was not an appendicitis my daughter was suffering from. What it was exactly I could not be sure. I also knew that there was no hope of getting hold of another doctor or nurse at that hour on Corpus Christi night: I would have no choice but to do this vaginal examination myself. I looked at my wife, then down at my daughter. Told her so as gently as I could. Then I left to scrub my hands.

As soon as I felt the obstruction I knew what it was: *hemato-colpos*. (I could feel the blue membrane with my fingertips.) But I had to see for myself. I fumbled through my bag – there on Evy's bedtable since I'd arrived home on Wednesday midday – found my mirror. I tied it around my forehead, took up the reading lamp, got down on my knees at the end of the bed. I had never seen an imperforate hymen before. Never heard of one except from my father – not even in Medical School. But here was an imperforate hymen again. Here was my own daughter.

I was in a sweat now, my hands trembling. I thought of going to the hospital for a sterile scalpel: I couldn't get up from my knees. I took a deep breath, and I did something absolutely bizarre, some unconscious reflex which I had not repeated for thirty years: I crossed myself. Then I carefully pushed my finger through. It was not Evy but Ash who gasped, menstrual fluid spilling over the white sheet.

NOW: IN ORDER fa me to explain you the history of these various transitations – these various discombruc-

tions, and suffixations, and usurprications – in order fa
you to understand them proper, I must take you back a
little earlier. Good. To begin in the beginning: 12 Octo-
ber. 1492. Columbus arrives in the New World. And
Columbus (according to historian-politician Dr Eric Williams, heself the independence leader and prime minister
of Trinidad and Tobago) according to Dr Williams' *History of the Caribbean*, Columbus was the last of the mediev-
al crusaders. The big significance of he discovery, in he
own eyes, was the vast multitudes soon to be saved by the
Catholic faith. In fact, to quote Columbus's own narrative
at the end of he first voyage, quoted also by Dr Williams:
'Papa God has reserved fa the Pañyol monarchs not only
all the treasures of this New World,' by which he meant
endless gold, 'but a still greater treasure of more inestim-
able value, the infinite numbers of souls soon to suckle up
to the bosom of the Church.' In other words, Columbus
claimed the New World not only fa those Pañyols, but fa
the Catholic Church on top. Of course, by the end of he
fourth voyage he'd forgotten all that bubball. Now he
remembered only the gold, which he was convinced he
could find somewhere here in this Caribbean. But Columbus should have listened to what those poor Indians
would be saying fa hundred years to come, that there isn't
enough gold in the whole of these islands to pound out a
single pair of earrings. Because it would take Columbus
and the rest of Europe a hundred years of sailing back and
forth and up and down the length of this Caribbean –
making sure to dead up a few hundred Indians every time
they passed through – before they could come to the same
conclusion theyself. In fact, when Sir Walter Raleigh
arrived here in Corpus Christi fa the first time in 1595, a
hundred years after Columbus, he was still looking fa gold
heself, searching out the mythical El Dorado. Of course,
here he bounced up that famous Pañyol explorer Antonio
de Berrio, here searching out the very same thing – but

boasting like a little bantycock with he feathers all ruffled
up about how he'd come to save the souls of the poor lost
Indians instead – here in he little white church with its
name so big he could hardly squeeze it cross the wall above
the front door: NUESTRA SEÑORA SANTA FE DE
LA CONCEPCIÓN. He had already changed the name of
they ancient village of Coyaba to *Santa María*. Raleigh got
so vex he mashed up de Berrio's little church in one. Of
course, in the end Raleigh *did* discover El Dorado here fa
true, as he wrote in he journal early on the morning of 2
March, dead up after he exhausting sleepless vigil of
twenty-seven hours. But of course, this wasn't no kind of
mythical heavenly paradise Raleigh was writing about
a-tall. It was the very real, *earthly* paradise shining in he
tasa of bois bandé.

What Raleigh did not know, is despite the fact that these
Amerindians were, in he own words, 'very moral and
upright, strictly monogamous', they led a life of great
sensuality. Indeed, they frequently participated in ritualis-
tic orgies – including much feasting and knocking back
plenty cassava grog, making music and dancing and so –
lasting fa no shorter duration than three days. So this bois
bandé was a little more than the occasional diversion from
the monotony of primitive island life: it was more like
sacred churchwine. You can imagine also that if these
religious orgies, these juliefied jooking-jamborees, were
offered in celebration of the tribal zemis. And if, in fact, as
we like to believe, Magdalena *did* preside over the Village
Coyaba (a Carib word meaning *heaven-on-earth*, perhaps fa
good reason) you can imagine also that Magdalena, or
more precisely Akambo-Mah, very likely presided over
and inspired quite a few such jooking jamborees. Which is
not to suggest nothing has changed. But son, you know
yourself good enough what takes place, soon as the band
passes the cemetery on Corpus Christi Day.

Other than these religious orgies, however, the

Amerindians seldom felt the need to exert theyself. Fruit
of every imaginable sort proliferated in the forest. Game
was plentiful: lapp, quenk, tattoo, agouti. Chipchips and
conches abounded on the beaches, scalowash and oysters
on the rocks, guanas in the trees and crabs in the swamps.
Fish and turtle swarmed the sea, which the Indians could
sein or spear from the sides of they pirogues, hewed from
colossal trunks of yellow poui and pink silkcotton. Tobacco, bananas and corn were easily cultivated in the fertile
soil, cassava the staple crop, from which the Amerindians
distilled the poisonous juice to make they grog. They
dwellings were cool, comfortable, and circular in shape:
thatched carrotroofs with walls of bamboo, tied with
lianes and cokeeyea. Among the different groups, the
Caribs were more transitory, more aggressive with they
fishbone-studded *bootoos*, the Carib word fa club. But the
Arawaks, substantially more populous, were sedentary
and peaceful peaceful. They were a handsome, gentle
people. A people who lived an idyllic kind of existence,
fearing only *mabouyas* (evil spirits which take the shape of
crapos and mappapees) or perhaps Pañyols. Because you
can imagine how quick the colonists killed them off,
arriving all of a sudden one morning to tie them up and
drag them off mostly to Hispanola, there to dig fa gold
which didn't even exist. Or to introduce certain diseases
spreading among them like darkness through dusk, syphi-
lis fa example. And when the colonists gave up the idea of
gold, they turned to sugar, just beginning to command a
high price on the European market: *King Sugar*, called by
many historians the great gift of the Old World to the
New. But again, like most historians, they got that one
back-to-front and inside-out too.

In fact, Columbus heself was the first to bring cane to
these islands. The first to initiate what would remain fa
300 years we monocrop sugar economy: we relationship
of European dependency. The cane Columbus brought

was the one we call the Creole variety, and it remained the dominant species until the English brought the Otaheite variety in the middle of the eighteenth century. Son, cane grew in this Caribbean like grass over a grave, which of course it quite literally *is*. The problem, however, was labour. A problem due to perplex these islands fa the next 300 years, due to haunt we fa however long we survive to exist. Because the cane had not only to be sown and reaped, it had to be pressed and boiled down into sugar, before it could be dumped in a crocuss-sack or cask and shipped off to Europe. All of which of course meant labour. The first method fa extracting the juice was to crush the haulms with primitive wooden instruments called *squingers*, still found in many parts of the West Indies to this day. But the first mill (instituted in Hispanola by a Pañyol named Gonzalo de Vendosa as early as 1516) was a horse-powered mill known as a *trapiche*. Oxen or slaves could be substituted fa the horses – which they very frequently were – made to walk round-and-round in a circle to turn the big stone wheel crushing up the cane. But not long after that a water-powered mill was introduced called an *ingenio*. Fa the first hundred years of the sugar industry (before the introduction of wind-driven mills in the late seventeenth century) the trapiche and ingenio stood up side-by-side together, the trapiche more expensive due to the horses or slaves required to turn it, the ingenio limited to areas of abundant water supply. According to Gonzalo Fernando de Oviedo (in one of the first chronicles of the Caribbean entitled *Historia general y natural de las Indias*, composed in Hispanola in 1546) the ingenio was twice as efficient as the trapiche, requiring twice as much labour: the trapiche demanding thirty or forty slaves to load between 25 and 35 cartloads of cane, producing 840 lbs of sugar in a twenty-four hour period. The ingenio requiring 80–120 slaves loading 40–50 cartloads, producing up to 2,000 lbs in the equal amount of time.

Correct. And more ingenios meant more sugar which meant more Amerindian slaves, and the Pañyols were running out of Amerindians quick quick. Bishop Bartoleme de las Casas (appointed by the Pope Protector of the Indians in the New World) realized that the only way to save the Amerindians was to solve the labour problem. He proposed the solution and corned the coop at the same time: Negro slaves could be brought from Guinea and Ethiopia, the labour of one black African fowlcock equalling four red Amerindian frizzlefowls and more. Las Casas (who'd even engaged heself in an on-going biological debate with renowned journalist Sepulveda, the latter offering scientific proof of he equation that Indians are to Pañyols as monkeys are to men) Las Casas would realize he mistake in the end: Negroes are human beings too. Hoping to prevent the exploitation of one people, he'd promoted the exploitation of another. History, of course, would repeat the same mistake 250 years later, when the East Indians were brought to replace the emancipated Africans. And Las Casas failed miserably in he attempt to save the Amerindians. In he defeat and disillusion he took up writing, publishing he *Apologética histórica de las Indias* in 1552. Here he charged the Pañyols fa exterminating fifteen million Amerindians. He somewhat impassioned and slightly hyperbolic little book became the first Caribbean bestseller, through the sixteenth and seventeenth centuries selling out the bookstands in four Italian editions, three Latin, four English, six French, eight German, and sixteen Dutch. Of course, like all Caribbean writing now as then, they read it not as history, but as some kind of fancified fantastical *fiction*. Nevertheless son, the hard reality is that that is all we have remaining of the indigenous Amerindians: a few historical documents like the one I am giving to you now, and a couple dusty calabash tasas, and fishbone-studded bootoos to show the tourists in St Maggy Municipal Museum.

But before the African slaves could be brought to replace the Amerindians, the Frites had to come to replace the Pañyols. The Limees hadn't even arrived as yet, though they were already proving theyself cock-of-the-walk in this henhouse we call the Caribbean. (Because I suppose the supremacy of England had been established ever since they mashed up that Spanish Armada, as early as 1588, with that nastiest of old-cocks ever to find he whiteepokee backside here in these islands, Sir Francis Drake, running out from the middle of he lawnbowl game with that other jump-over-the-fence, Sir John Hawkins, the two of them giving those Pañyols one good cuttail.) But the Limees wouldn't get hold of we tail here in Corpus Christi until as late as 1797. In a sense, the Frites managed to squeeze theyself in between the two. The first ones to arrive called theyself the *petit noblesse*, which usually meant that there wasn't nothing noblesse about them a-tall, at least not in the sense of great wealth. Quite to the contrary. They were adventurous, hard-working people who left France behind in order to begin new lives here, arriving with whatever few pennies they could manage to scrape together in they pockets. Not like they Pañyol and Limee counterparts, who were so well greased they stepped off the ship dripping, and who fa the most part were landlords in absentia: the little amount of time they *did* spend here was occupied mostly in beating up they slaves as hard as they could, and making they fortunes quick as possible to get back home to they castles in London and Madrid. But the big influx of Frenchmen in Corpus Christi began with a little Frite, like all the others, with a big name: *Phillipe Rose Roune de Saint Laurent*. He first arrived here in 1777, running from the island of Grenada in the midst of a bloody row which had been going on there between the Frites and the Limees fa years. St Laurent was impressed by the rich soil and vast expanses of unculti-vated land in Corpus Christi, and he made up he head it was a good place fa he fellow Frites to settle. Of course, at this time the island still belonged to Spain. So St Laurent picked up heself and went to Spain, speaking with the colonial administrators, knowing full well that these Pañyols were getting more geegeeree by the minute with those Limees. The result, as you well know, was the famous Cedula of 1782. By this Cedula the Frites – and subjects of other powers friendly to Spain – were given tracks of land in Corpus Christi to cultivate on one condition: they had to be Roman Catholics. This, of course, excluded the Limees, who fa the most part were Protestants.

Well: those Frites flocked to Corpus Christi like fowls to a handful of stalerice. Not only from Grenada and the other islands (particularly the former French island of St Dominique, originally Hispanola, but now with the 1789 slave revolution of Toussaint L'Ouverture, calling sheself by she first Amerindian name of Haiti, the French trico-lour flying above it with the white noblesse stripe scis-sored out with a scissors) those Frites came flocking to Corpus Christi not only from the other islands, but from France as well. In fact, it was the revolution at home – the French Revolution of 1791 – that brought these Frites like picoplats flying fa laglee. All running before they lose they bloody heads. Because of course, now it was a different species of Frite altogether to arrive here on the island. These ones didn't waste they breath boasting no *petit noblesse*. These ones called theyself the *Grand Blanches*, with every little pomme-frite to step off the boat introduc-ing heself as some kind of Comte, or Vicomte, or Cheva-lier, or Baron or some foolishness so. Of course, the slaves they brought with them, or the ones to arrive soon after, were Blacks from Africa. Blacks who spoke neither Span-ish nor English, but *Yoruba* and *French-patois*.

They were Roman Catholics on top. This had been establish as early as 1685 with the French *Code Noir*, a code stenching high as heaven of Roman Catholicism. By this code all slaves had to be baptized Catholics. They could be owned only by Catholics. But an additional code (decreed in 1789 by we own governor of Corpus Christi, Don Jose María Chacon, this one called the *Chacon* Code Noir) an additional code came out Chacon's backside stenching of the Church stronger than ever. Now the slaves could not go to the fields on Sundays and holydays, when they owners were obligated to teach them the catechism *they-self*. Furthermore: they were obliged to provide a priest to celebrate Sunday Mass and administer the sacraments to the slaves, to end each workday with a recitation of the beads, the *masters* taking the lead. All this was due not so much to the influence of the Church, but the Colonial Government. Because of course, the teachings of Catholicism served the institution of slavery well. Calling fa humility and obedience and tolerance. Holding up Christ as the exemplar of virtuous suffering. Teaching that the kingdom of heaven was not of this world – as the slaves believed in Africa, as the Amerindian slaves had believed before them – but of the next. It was a gospel encouraging the slaves to disregard the deplorable existence they were living, and place all they hope in the life to come. In this way the Colonial Government worked with the Church hook-in-sharkskin-bait to maintain the institution of slavery. To sustain the old social order. Despite the obvious advantages which the slaves gained by these various Catholic codes and such. Because of course, each one of those Church dignitaries had a few personal slaveboys waiting fa him in he sacristy too.

But the slaves neither accepted nor rejected: they assimilated. To they former Yuraba religion they grafted certain elements of Catholicism to derive they own *Shango, SuSu*, the *Vodun* of Haiti, *Santaría* of Cuba, as well as the predominant *Obeah*. African gods merged with Catholic saints such that they names become interchangeable:

Ogoun – St Michael, *Shango* – St John, *Oya* – St Catherine, *Beji* – St Peter, *Osain* – St Francis, *Emanjah* – St Theresa, *Oromelay* – St Joseph, *Oshun* – St Anne, and so on and so forth, right down the Calendar. These African gods and goddesses were nothing like they purely Catholic counterparts, dead up and buried fa hundreds of years, sealed up fa centuries in they catacombs: these African powers came to life in the believer, making of the believer a miraculous receptacle, filling the believer with they own potency. But there was one extraordinary power. One goddess in particular who assumed a special role fa the slaves of Corpus Christi. They called her Mama Latay, Mistress of the Earth. She was among the strongest of the African powers, standing side-by-side with the great Shango, God of Fire, Maker of Thunder and Lightning. But Mama Latay did something which even Shango could no do. Mama Latay not only took possession of the believer – not only filled the disciple with she great power – she came to life in the black madonna beneath the small carrotroof. Many had witnessed this miracle theyself. Had watched her walking by sheself in the early morning mist surrounding the swamp. She came to life in Magdalena, La Divina Pastora, Notre Dame de Lourdes, La Vierge Noir de Marais Maraval: Mama Latay – *St Maggy*.

But unlike the placid Oshun, Mistress of the Sea, and different from the gentle Emanjah, Mistress of the River, Mama Latay was hot-tempered. She was hard-hearted. The Mistress of the Earth was dangerous and destructive: cruel, violent, quick to inflict punishment, slow to forgive trespass. Most feared of the female powers, Mama Latay was the one the slaves held accountable fa they present affliction, fa they sudden inexplicable punishment: she was also the one to deliver them.

Word spread among the estates. At first the slaves were allowed pilgrimages to Maraval, gathering round the tiny carrotroof. They went under the pretext of visiting the

Catholic saint, just as the East Indian labourers would do
when they own turn came, fifty years later. The Père
called her La Divina Pastora, the Black Virgin, but to the
slaves she could be none other than Mama Latay. No one
else could inhabit a place so vile and treacherous as that
Marais Maraval. They meetings became popular quick,
the slaves gathering to beat they oumalays and bambas and
congos, to dance and sing and chant in the patois which
only the slaves understood. Female goats were brought to
be sacrificed, spotted hens, dasheen leaves with they
tender tanya roots: all the prescribed offerings of the
Mistress of the Earth. These ceremonies lasted through the
night, until daybreak, but they did not continue fa long.
The owners and Church officials soon got word of what
was going on. Primed by the recent Haitian revolution,
they interpreted the gatherings not as religious ceremonies, but as political insurrections, and they soon put a
stop to the meetings. Fa months they continued in secret,
until the head priestess of the Chapelle de Marais, the
Amambah, was found by she disciples murdered and
quartered: displayed round the carrotroof on four up-
turned pitchforks, Mama Latay's special tool. And the
black madonna had disappeared again. She would not be
found until almost fifty years later, when the East Indians
arrived in Corpus Christi to see in the statue another
fearsome Goddess, the Hindu Goddess Kali. And Magdalena would come to know she true following.

But before the East Indians could arrive, the Africans
had to be emancipated. This, of course, did not happen
overnight, nor did it happen all at once. Because even
though abolition had been accepted in principle by the
Limees as early as 1802, it did not happen in fact in the
British Colonies until 1833. Even at this late date there
were still seventeen-and-a-half-thousand slaves in Corpus
Christi. Almost all of these slaves were owned by Frenchmen. Almost all spoke patois, Corpus Christi being a

French colony in all but name. But the patois-speaking slaves of Corpus Christi were now free, and the sugar industry was again in trouble. Wind-powered mills had been introduced almost two centuries earlier – more economical than the trapiche, more practical than the ingenio, and more efficient than both – demanding as always more labour. Other than the introduction of windmills, however, there had been practically no improvements in the industry fa 200 years. This, of course, is always the case where human labour is the focus. Human labour which was now a problem fa the third time in the history of the Caribbean. In Corpus Christi Governor Woodford had recommended the importation of 'peaceful and quiet and industrious East Indians', as he put it, as early as 1814. But the first Asians did not arrive here until 1845, by which time the sugar industry was near dead. The East Indians had come to save it. And fa good few years they *did*. At the time of they arrival in Corpus Christi she was producing 13,300 tons of sugar per year. Fifty years later, in 1895, that figure had jumped to nearly 55,000 tons.

Correct. But the East Indians were not slaves. They came to the Caribbean on contract, first fa three years, then five, then ten years with the guarantee of a return passage home. They came mostly to Corpus Christi, Trinidad, British Guiana and Surinam. Some to Jamaica and Guadeloupe. The Chinese to Cuba. Each labourer received a fixed wage fa specified number of days per year, which worked out almost as cheap as buying and keeping slaves. The labourers' contracts further provided fa housing and medical care, which in most instances was worse still than the slaves had earlier been given. Between 1845 and 1917 (the period of indentureship in Corpus Christi) 144,000 East Indians were brought to the island, in addition to several thousand Chinese. At first they had no intention of remaining here a-tall. They found the French

and English landowners, the former African slaves, well
blipps and bisquanky, they various religions in particular.
The labourers' only aim was to finish they contracts in the
canefields, and get they broken bamsees back home as
quick as possible. But the East Indians found theyself as
adaptable as the Africans before them, though in a somewhat different way: rather than assimilating the mix-up of
cultures in which they found theyself immersed, they
remained quietly separate, adhering to they own ancient
traditions. In a sense, it was the surrounding culture which
assimilated them. But regardless of who swallowed who,
by the time the East Indians had finished they labour
contracts, many found they had established new lives here,
that they no longer desired to return home. One event,
however, greatly influenced the immigration of Asians to
the island: in 1870 Governor Gordon decided he ga put
aside a big block of land – property to be given to East
Indians wanting to make they homes here – in exchange fa
they return passage to India. In a sense, it was the reverse
of the St Laurent Cedula decreed a century before. By that
Cedula land was offered to the slave masters so long as
they were Catholics. Now it was the servants who got the
land, with the one stipulation that they were Hindus. Of
course, cobo don't casso he best bones: this wasn't no
prime property Governor Gordon was parceling out a-tall.
Not by a chups. It was the area adjacent to that same
chorupa-stenching, crapo-festering mudswamp, today the
well-known Maraval Belt, with its dense population of
East Indians. Because in no time a-tall villages began to
spring up. First along the ancient Amerindian footpath
leading to Maraval, then beside the swamp itself: Tunapuna, Blanchessuse, Oropouche. And of course, the village
of Suparee K Mai.

By the time indentureship had reach its end in Corpus
Christi, the population of East Indians was only slightly
less than the population of Creoles. Whites, of course,

were in the minority, by now an almost equal mixture of French, Spanish and English. Others, like you own grand-father, had come from such places as Corsica – Portugal, Italy, Denmark and so on – but as you well know, Barto arrived here via Venezuela. Because you grandfather ar-rived with another group of immigrants, at the beginning of what would become a substantial mercantile trade between Venezuela and Corpus Christi. In fact, Barto actually arrived here among the very first group of immig-rants to come to the island: the Warwarrahoons of the Delta Orinoco. Because son, I will tell you one more thing that you have never before been told. One more fact fa you to hear fa the first time. And it is something you own *daddy* never even knew heself, something to no doubt send you good grandmother rolling in she grave. Because son, it is one thing that neither she nor Mother Maurina would ever admit, and of course, none of the rest of we were ever boldface enough to say it out loud, fa fear of a basin of icewater coming pelting top we heads: Granny Myna was in fact the granddaughter of a Warrahoon tribal bushdoc-tor. Perhaps the first medical doctor ever to come to the island, brought here in the earliest days of Corpus Christi by Barto heself: a man by the name of Dr Brito Salizar. In any case, it was not long after the East Indians had arrived, not long after they'd made up they heads to stay, that the whole of Corpus Christi was nothing but one big callaloo with all of we boiling up swimming together inside, and nobody could know any longer who was who and what was what, much less care to make a difference.

MY GRANDFATHER paused again. Again he took his hands from off my shoulders, reaching for his ragged-edge sweetmilk tin here on the desk beside me. But this time, in my moment of freedom, I turned as best I could in my miniature Warrahoon-Windsor chair to look up at him:

standing there in his baggy boxer drawers and marino-vestshirt, both stretched tightly over his huge belly. There was a halfmoon of white flesh exposed between the bottom of his undershirt and the elastic waistband of his drawers, his deep navelhole staring out of the middle – just in front of my nose. I studied it cokeeeyed for a moment, fascinated. Not so much by the navelhole: by the small dustball of lint suspended neatly and perfectly inside it.

Suddenly I couldn't restrain myself: I reached cautiously to pluck it out. But with the contact of my index finger there came a bright flash of static electricity – a hot shock running down my arm – and I pulled back my hand. Now I felt determined. I thrust my thumb and forefinger into his navelhole and plucked out the lintball. The gesture felt somehow obscene – too intimate for a couple of oldmen – despite the fact that we were grandfather and grandson. I quickly flicked the lintball off the ends of my fingers. But it only made a slow loop in the air, the static electricity bringing it back into the centre of my palm. I flicked it away again, and the static electricity brought it back again. Again and again. Finally I drew my fist back behind my shoulder, flinging the lintball into the air with all the strength remaining in me. It travelled through the air for a few inches – in exasperatingly slow motion – then the draught caught it and took it smoothly up and out the window before my desk. I watched it float gently over the big tamarind tree in the back yard, over the rocks with the waves beating down below. Then the breeeze caught it and took it in a dive pelting towards the water, spread out to the horizon pitch black and glistening beneath the moon.

Ptsuulp-plsuuhp. I turned again to look at my grand-father, watching him manage the ordeal of spitting into his sweetmilk tin. His face was very large and grey, a tuft of salt-and-pepper hair covering his scalp like a neat wire brush. There were purplish marks on the bridge of his nose, in partial circles around his eyes, and behind his ears: permanent stains tracing the outline of his glasses, the metal frames of which had oxidized into a brilliant blue-green. He was nearly blind without them, yet he always took them off for his sessions of storytelling. (They were also here folded on the desk beside me.) For a moment I studied the even inflation-deflation of my grandfather's tight belly, shaking with a short spasm and drawing pockled-limp at the end of each exhalation. And as he reached out again to put down his sweetmilk tin – ragged-edged, its faded red-and-white label still speaking of *contented* cows living somewhere on the other side of the sea – as I sat there looking at old Papee Vince, I realized something very strange and eerie. Something very peculiar indeed: I was actually four years older than my own grandfather. Because in fact Papee Vince was eighty-six years of age, and tomorrow I would be ninety.

Suddenly I was afraid he'd loose his balance, and I reached out my hand to help him. He grabbed hold of my wrist so tightly, bringing his weight down so heavily, that for an instant I was sure he'd throw me out of my chair (a comical image flashing through my mind of two oldmen groping over each other, sprawled out together on the ground like two diapered infants). But he let go of my hand and took hold of the back of my chair regaining his balance, and only the sweetmilk tin tumbled to the ground. The nearly empty tin rolled across the wooden floorboards with a noise so big it was startling – as loud as a jet aeroplane passing overhead – and it came to rest against the wall, none of its contents spilled. The two of us stared at the tin for a moment in disbelief. Then we looked at each other.

There was a long minute of silence.

Then I spoke: 'Papee Vince, I want you to answer me something.'

He cleared his throat: 'Yes son, if it is in my power to do

so.'

'Look around at the books in this library. Look at them all: medical journals, histories, atlases, dictionaries, ency-clopaedias. Not one book of poetry or prose. Not one book of Literature. How can that be?'

There was another minute of silence.

'Furthermore,' I said, 'we were never even given story-books as children. Discounting the few the nuns read us, discounting the Bible. Why is that?'

'Son,' he said, 'I'm not so sure about that one myself. I suppose we have so many of we own stories to tell, so many of we own stories to hear out, we never found the time to look fa no others.'

Now I was getting angry. 'But what about *our* books? *Our* Literature?'

He took a deep breath. 'Well,' he said, 'I suppose nobody ever found the time to write out those ones neither. Much less the need. Because why the ass would anybody in they right mind want to read out a story dead, that they could hear in a hundred different *living* versions – each one better than the one before – on any streetcorner or porchstoop they happen to stumble. Then again, I suppose you have to know youself pretty good before you can write out any storybooks, and that is something we are only now beginning to learn. Because son, I will give you another biological-historical truth. Another one that those historians always seem to forget when it comes to understanding this Caribbean: son, you never truly grow up until the death of you second parent. Whether that death is natural, psychological, or the result of bloody murder. Only *then* can you come to know youself. And in fact, we only just finish matriciding we mummy-England the other day.'

Papee Vince paused again, wiping the back of his hand across his mouth: 'So son, you better turn round quick and let me tell you a little more about youself. Because if you don't look out, you ga find youself dead up in the grave too, before you *own* story has a chance to finish.'

NOW: IN ORDER fa me to explain to you the history of this carnival – all of the various recombructions, and prefexations, and resuprecations resolving in its slow revolution – in order fa you to understand them proper, I must take you back a little earlier. Good. To begin in the beginning: 30 May, 1845. The ship Fatel Rozack arrives in Corpus Christi harbour. She cargo is 152 East Indian indentured labourers. They have come to ·save the sugar industry, and fa good few years they do. But sugar, like the cocoa which replaced the cane, like copra which replaced the cocoa, was doomed to fail. Because even though sugar reached its height in 1895 (what with the implementation of steam engines pioneered by the Scotsman James Watt early in the century, fa new highly efficient techniques of cane crushing and sugar production) even though King Sugar remained high and mighty in 1895, by 1897 the industry was already bankrupt. Two things killed it: the development of the sugar beet industry, particularly in Europe and America, and the spread of cane cultivation to new areas, particularly India and Brazil. The advantage of the sugar beet was that it represented the triumph of science and technology, whereas cane represented only the stigma of slavery. The advantage of India and Brazil was they virgin soil. Because by the end of the nineteenth century, after 300 years of cane cultivation here in this Caribbean, we own soil was deader than death. In my opinion, what contributed to this depletion more than anything else, was this practice towards the end of scorching the fields prior to harvest. Of course, they were scorched to eradicate the scorpions, which were plentiful enough in those canefields, particularly during the rainy season. But son, by removing the *vermin*, you are also removing the *humus*. And soil wants humus. Because it is all that unused part of the plant you burning up – all the leaves and scrub and underbrush and so – which in the old days used to decompose and go back to the soil, replacing at least some of the nutrients you are taking out.

Right. *Treatment of scorpion stings*. In those days of course, before the invention of this antidote serum they have now, the sting of a scorpion was fatal. The East Indians had they own cure which they would carry with them in the fields, and which they called simply *we medicine*. This was a bottle of punching rum into which they would throw one set of scorpions, and mappapees, and blackwidows and so, leaving them there to ferment fa years at a stretch, constantly adding more scorpions and more punching rum. So when they get the sting they would fire down a few swallows, often to good result. But you could never be sure. What I used to do, and I used it *extensively* in the old estate days with success – though it is something the medical profession did not recognize – what I used was a thing called the *Blackstone*, the *Belgian* Blackstone. Correct. Now: this was a piece of stone as smooth as a piece of a marble. It was invented, right here in Corpus Christi, by a Belgian monk of the Benedictine order. And how you use it is this: you tie a tourniquet (since the majority of stings come on one of the extremities) take up a razor blade, and you make an incision above the sting drawing blood. Now you press the stone against it, and the stone would hold on. And the stone would hold on fa however long there is still poison remaining inside there, and when it drops off, you would know the poison is gone. Son, in every case of some forty to fifty odd cases which *I* treated, in a few hours that patient would be walking. Of course, now you have this stone with all of that poison inside. But if you take and put it in a pan of raw milk, leaving it there soaking overnight, by next morning that stone would be good as new, and you could use it again.

Of course, now we didn't have to worry so much again about scorpion stings – or we medicine, or Belgian Blackstones or anything else – because now not only King Sugar was dead, we soil was dead too. But cocoa had come to replace it: the *Golden Bean* of the island. And with the arrival of the Golden Bean, came the second big influx of East Indian labourers. Because son, the Corpus Christi cocoa bean, even today, is known the world over fa its flavour. And cocoa cultivation offered several distinct advantages over cane cultivation. Fa one thing, it could be grown in the mountains, in the vast areas of rain forest where the soil is so fertile, there is nothing you can do to keep a seed you throw inside it from growing. Fa another thing, the initial investment fa cocoa plantation is not nearly so heavy. The estates could be much smaller, since large tracts of land were no longer required, and no expensive machinery was needed – no trapiches or in-genios or windmills or steam engines – only a couple boardhuts: a *sweathouse* and a *dryingshed*. Once the cocoa tree was planted, in a few years she would start to bear she pods, and she would give you fifteen or twenty or twenty-five pods every year, each pod giving you fifteen or twenty or twenty-five beans. The primary investment then was the East Indian labourers. Because of course, the beans didn't come out just so.

Right. *Preparation of cocoa beans.* You take a ripe cocoa pod in you hands. Good. She colour is a nice purplish-pinkish colour now she's ready – say about the size somewhere between a mango calabash and a mango zabuca – with longitudinal channels running between she navel and she bamsee. Now you crack her open with you fingers: she beans are covered by a whitish, slimy, pre-servative kind of jelly-like substance. (This substance is of course the same soursweet jelly lovely to suck out these days when you walking in the forest, and you stumble on an old cocoa tree growing wild from some abandoned estate.) So first thing you have to do is to take out this jelly. You put the beans in what we call the sweathouse, putting them say 300 pounds to a sweatbox, with weights on top pressing them down. This sweathouse has a special kind of flooring at the bottom with slats in it, such that the jelly could slide off and fall down between the slats, the beans remaining on top. In three to five days then you beans would be ready fa they first drying, so now you take them up to the dryingshed. This is what we call an *extended roof*. In other words, a roof which divides in the middle so that you can slide it open to let in the sun. You spread out you beans in the dryingshed, and now you have one of the workers, generally a woman, to walk barefoot through them every few hours turning them over with a special *wooden* shovel, because an iron shovel would break up the beans. (You can still find these wooden shovels in many of the West Indian islands even today.) This turning over of the beans then would keep them from drying on one side, because you want them to dry right through. So in five to seven days, with a good wind and providing you have no rain, you beans would be dry. And how you know they are dry, you take a handful like this and you squeeze them, and you beans would *crackle*, and once they crackle, you would know. Now you have to *polish* them. This, of course, was the big festival in the old days known as Dancing the Cocoa. With everybody coming in from town already drunk up, singing, beating bottle-and-spoon, all ready to make fête. But of course, when cocoa finish fête finish too. To polish the beans then you pile them up, and you wet them down with a solution of water mixed with the sap of the figroot, until they are good and slimy. (In the old days we used a thing called the red ochre, to give them a nice red sheen, but they stopped us using that. I couldn't tell you why.) So you call together all the workers and everybody else you could find, and

you trample on the slimy beans, barefoot, and this tram-
pling and dancing and so polishes the beans. Now you
have to dry them again. You spread them out with the
same woman turning them over, and in a day or so you
beans would be dry. Now you have to *sift* them, because
what you want is whole beans. You sift and put aside all
the broken up beans – which is what we call *parsey* – and
now, finally, you can dump you beans all clean and
beautiful and shining in a crocusssack, and you can ship
them off to England and Europe and so. Because of
course, even though Corpus Christi cocoa is known the
world over, nobody has never yet heard of a single tin of
Ovaltine, or a Cadbury, or a morsel of chocolate coming
from *this* island. Not by a chups. We economy is still
dependent on Europe. And just as Europe killed King
Sugar, sure as the skin of you backside belongs to you,
they ga kill the Golden Bean too.

But it isn't Europe directly. It is *Africa*. Africa who came
back like cobo to shit happy on we heads. Because now
Africa had the slave labour – at a time when we own
indentured labour was reaching its end – and once *she*
started to produce cocoa, there was no way we could hope
to compete: they simply swamped the market. Son, I can
remember a time when cocoa went down to eight CC
dollars a fanega (a fanega is 110 pounds) which it is costing
you twelve dollars to produce. You just couldn't do it.
Then, on top of that, we contacted this disease known as
witch's broom, and that finished we off fa good. Now: why
it's called witch's broom, it's a fungus (they said it came
from Surinam) which would apparently attach itself to the
tree, sucking out all she sap. She new shoots would grow
out all erratic and bunched up together like a dusty old
broom at the end of each branch, and the pods she bears
would be hollow. Hollow, or solidified. But son, even
before this witch's broom came to sweep we way, we
were already deader than dust. Cocoa in the Caribbean

was already done and finished.

So now we turned to copra. And with copra came the third and final few boatloads of East Indian labourers. Of course, the main advantage with copra was the open market. But there were other advantages on top. Fa one thing, a coconut tree could grow just about anyplace, in just about any kind of soil short of pure sand. You could spread him out in a spacing of twenty feet by twenty feet (which you would mark out with stakes before you plant him) and that gave you over 400 hundred trees to an acre. Fa another thing, the whole nut could be used, and because the nuts went to the factory, the farmer didn't have to worry again about preparation. Just pile up you nuts in you lorry and send them off. This reduced the amount of labour required substantially. To start up a cultivation then you simply purchased (fa little more than a halfdollar fa two–three dozen) you purchased a quantity of what we call *selected nuts*. Selected nuts, because you are interested not in the nut's *size*, but the copra content *of* the nut. You put these nuts to lie down in the field (or to stand up, whichever you prefer) and soon he will sprout and start to grow. In five years he will start to bear he nuts, seven years to full bearing, and he will give you up to eighty nuts a year. All you need now is a couple East Indians bicycling up and down the trees with a cutlass between they teeth, throwing you down the nuts. Now: why it's called a *bicycle*, it's a kind of belt (made from lianes, which is to say grass) going round you waist and the waist of the tree. You climb him barefoot – scampering up seventy-five to a hundred feet in the air, turning round-and-round in any direction as you climb – and that gives the bicycle its name. So you thrown down you nuts and collect them up, and you send them off to the factory to be used fa various purposes.

Right. *Utilization of coconuts*. You take a ripe nut in one hand, you cutlass in the next. He colour is a nice golden-greenish colour now he's ready, say about the size of a football. You hold him in you palm with he navelcord poking out pointing away from you, and he bamsee pointing towards you, you raise up you cutlass high above you head, and you bring it down on you palm splitting him clean in two. Good. The outer, yellowish-brown, fibrous layer between the shell and the kernel, is what we call the *husk*. Then you have the *kernel* in the centre, which is covered by the hard, greybrown *bone* part, with the pure white *meal* the innermost layer, and that is what we call *copra*. Copra, which derives its name from the Hindustani word *khopra*, because the Indians in India were the first to extract the oil to cook with, and to rub on they hair every morning beautiful and shining and jet black, and in they skin soft and rich and dark. Inside the kernel of course you have coconut water, which will be sour now he's ripe. (But of course this is the same water lovely and sweet to drink out when he's young and green, and you stop by a coconut vendor in the savannah with a two-cents fa him to chop off the top, and jook the cutlass through he soft navelspot fa you you to drink him down. And when you've finished the water he ga chop him in half and chop a spoon off the husk fa you to scoop out the jelly, all soft and white and sliding inside you mouth sweeter than the sweetest of sweetdreams.) But the factory now, the factory would use these various parts of the nut fa various industrial purposes. From the meal part the oil is extracted to make cooking oil, fa the manufacturing of soap, lipstick and other cosmetics. The remainder of the meal then goes to make an animal feed. The bone part is used in the oil fields to weigh down the mud when you drawing from a well. And because it's composed of carbon it was shipped overseas during the war – mostly to America – to make all you gasmasks. Finally, the husk can be bailed fa its fibre. This, in the old days, was used primarily fa making mattresses. Because before all these fancified foam mattresses we have there now, all your parents' and my parents' mattresses were make from coconut fibre.

Two things kill it again. First, all the various other oils to come on the market – synthetic oils in particular – and second, this disease we call *redring*. (Because the other disease, the one known as *brownsing wilt*, is not fatal: it simply indicates an insufficiency of nutrients in the soil. In that case you treat him with a dosage of N, P and K – that is to say, Nitrogen, Phosphorous and Potassium – giving him a dosage of five pounds twice a year, and sprinkling him in a big circle going right round he trunk.) But this redring is another story. Now: why it's called redring, it's a nematode, feeding on the tree there, which they said was transmitted by beetles. And how you know it, if you take a healthy tree and chop him down, he trunk would be yellowish-white, clean through. But a tree with redring. (Wait awhile: we call him a *tree*. He is *not* a tree. He is a *palm* because he has only one heart shoot in the seed. Whereas a tree has several heart shoots.) Correct. But a tree with redring, if you chop him down, would have a reddish band about two–three inches in diameter, going right round the circle of that trunk. And there's nothing you could do. Up until the time I left Mayaguaro they had no cure. And the loss, when I left the estate, was sixty to seventy per cent of loss.

So son, now we had nothing. Neither cane, nor cocoa, nor copra. And now that they'd robbed we fa all we were worth, nobody was interested no more neither. Not the Pañyols, nor the Frites, nor the Limees. Of course, the yankees arrived in the Caribbean just the other day, as you well know, though that again is another beginning. (Unless it is the end of the whole story. I couldn't tell you: that one is a story fa you *own* grandchildren to tell.) But prior to this recent arrival of the yankees, all manjack had come and gone, taking whatever little piece of we they could fit ringing in they pockets. And when there was nothing left to take, they left we alone. True, they wouldn't be willing to call we *independent* fa good many years to come, but now they left we to weself: alone, free and hungry. Because now the Africans were free, the East Indians were free, and the few Europeans who remained were reduce to paupers no different from anyone else. But son, now at least we could look we face in the glass fa the first time. A face we could scarcely identify. A face childlike, and geegeeree, and hopeless. And it was precisely at this historical moment, the moment we needed her most – the moment of we greatest confusion and desperation – that the black madonna came to all of we together and collected in she fifth and final reincarnation. Because she had already come to each of we individually in we time of need: to the Pañyols as Divina Pastora, to the Amerindians as Akambo-Mah, to the Africans as Mamma Latay, to the East Indians as Kali Mai. Now she came to all of we collected and together as *Magdalena Divina*. Of course, before she could come to we as Magdalena, she had to resurrect and reunite she previous four incarnations: she had to flock we up.

Right. You want to know the history of this fête. Good. The facts are these: 1890. The black madonna beneath the carrotroof is already attracting large numbers of East Indian labourers. They are Hindus fa the most part but Muslims also. They go to her as Mother Kali, Black Hindu Goddess of Death and Destruction: of famine, plagues, epidemics, illnesses, all forms of disaster. And indentureship is all of those disasters piled up together. This black madonna is known to grant favours to the afflicted: miraculous cures, sudden wealth, healthy births, the return of unfaithful spouses. Word spreads among the estates. 1900. The railway is completed connecting the estates of Mayaguaro and Wallafield with the sugar factories and distilleries of St Maggy. Steam engines are now in use fa highly efficient cane crushing and sugar production.

With the railway Village Suparee and the black madonna
become accessible to East Indians living in southern and
central Corpus Christi fa the first time. 1906. Though free,
the labourers are under the estate owners' control. They
choose the public holiday of Good Friday, 18 April, as the
day to offer homage to Mother Kali. At dawn on Holy
Thursday the East Indians begin they journey to Maraval
from all parts of the island, such pilgrimages being essential to Hindus and Muslims, just as they are to Catholics.
On the evening of Holy Thursday they gather round the
tiny carrotroof, there beneath the huge samaan tree.
Offerings of sweetoil and ghee are made, sugarcake and
sweetmilk, light and incense. Vegetables and fruit of all
kinds are brought, together with every imaginable prolif-
ery of flowers. The first locks of young children are cut off
and offered as a sign of dedication (not unlike the tonsure
of the monks). Bangles and churries are given, the
bracelets lining the madonna's arms just as they line the
women's arms and legs from wrists-to-shoulders, ankles-
to-knees: without banks to keep they money, fa many of
these women and they husbands too, these bracelets
represent they complete wealth, all pounded out from the
silver of English shillings. Fa the entire night of Holy
Thursday the East Indians beat they tassas and nagaras and
tamboos. They clap they fingerbells, singing and chanting
the Hindustani which only they understand, performing
ritual dances costumed in brilliant colours and shining
ornaments: *puja, dholak, gatea, gazal*. Then on Good Friday
morning the statue is taken up. She is carried in procession
the whole length of the ancient Amerindian trace to town,
and fa the remainer of the day and half the night, she is
paraded through the streets of St Maggy. With the first
light of Holy Saturday she is placed again beneath the
small carrotroof.

    1912. Other racial groups, Warrahoon migrants but
especially Creoles, are drawn to the fête. It is now known

as the Festival of Suparee K Mai. Yoruba rituals and the name of Mama Latay are revived from the days of slavery. A Shango element is added to the fête, including the rhythms of African dance and music. 1916. Many of the Creoles participating in the Catholic carnival (the pre-Lenten festival instituted by the Frites) have now abandoned it fa the Hindu fête. They bring with them various elements of the Catholic carnival: the making and wearing of costumes, the formation of distinct bands, the playing of steeldrums and other instruments in the street. Thursday. 11 February. 1918. A callaloo girlchild from Village Suparee, Marie Bernard Soubirous, sees the statue walking the banks of the Swamp Maraval. The vision recurs fa fortnight in succession. Multitudes are drawn to the black madonna beneath the tiny carrotroof, Catholics fa the first time. Hundreds claim to have witnessed this miracle of the walking madonna theyself. Catholics begin to participate in the festival of Suparee K Mai. 1920. The Catholic carnival is abandoned. 1921. The Church attempts to prohibit its members from participating in the Hindu fête, a festival they consider pagan and founded on superstitious beliefs. Most scandalous of all, the fête occurs on Good Friday, the one day of the liturgical year when any form of celebration or indulgence is strictly forbidden. The carrotroof is torched and the statue moved to St Maggy Cathedral. She is placed in a large iron jailcage and chained to a stone pedestal. She stops walking. Good Friday. 18 April. 1922. Government notices are posted in seven languages forbidding Hindus to enter the cathedral. The Chief of Police and he forces are called out to implement the decree, but the attempt to stifle the festival proves a failure: Catholics theyself enter the cathedral, mash up the jailcage, bust the horsechains, and they carry away the statue to join the others in celebration of Kali Mai. 1923. Church and Government officials issue a final decree: *THE FESTIVAL OF LA DIVINA PASTORA is to take place on Holy*

*Thursday, 17 April, CORPUS CHRISTI DAY, as opposed
to Good Friday. People of all races and religions will be allowed
entrance to the cathedral, all permitted to offer homage to LA
DIVINA PASTORA. But the statue will not be removed
under penalty of hanging.* The decree is posted in seven
languages.

This should have been the answer to everyone's problem. In one sense it was, because the festival took place
without incident. And it continued taking place, continued
growing in popularity, now celebrated by East Indians,
Warrahoons, Africans, as well as Europeans. The problem, however, was that each knew the black madonna by a
different name. Furthermore: each of these names came
from cross the sea. *We*, on the other hand, did *not*: now we
belonged to Corpus Christi. But so also did we black
madonna, though we did not know she true name as yet.
Because despite the fact that she had stopped walking, she
had not stopped granting favours. Quite to contrary. As
times in Corpus Christi grew more desperate, she granted
more favours, more cures, more miracles: silver shining
piltchers to hungry croakcroaks beneath King's Wharf,
which of course we quite literally *are*. Not only did the
festival grow in popularity, so did the madonna sheself, if
only fa the simple reason that she now resided in St Maggy
Cathedral. Because now not only was she accessible to
greater numbers of people, she was exceedingly more
attractive than she could ever have been standing up
beneath she half-rotten carrotroof, there beside she same
chourupa-stenching mudswamp. Still, we could not claim
her fa we own. We did not know she true name as yet. Or
more precisely, we'd simply forgotten it. Because history,
of course, had already named we madonna, even before
we could think to ask, even before we could think to
remember: she is *Magdalena Divina*.

Now naturally, you ga want to ask yourself: What in
bloody hell is this boboloops old fucker babbling about

now? And I wouldn't blame you in the least. Because of course, as you well know, the Mother Superior General *sheself* named Magdalena – the first name to jump in she head, the name of that same Biblical whore – only a few seconds after Mother Maurina finished giving birth to her, a few seconds before she tried to pelt her out the window. Only a few seconds, in fact, before Mother Maurina dumped the infant Magdalena on the doorstep of that same family of callaloos living in the same little mudhut in Village Suparee. The same little mudhut where Magdalena lived and grew to the age of thirteen, when she returned to St Maggy Convent to live as a nun fa precisely one year, living in the very same room in which Mother Maurina had conceived her and gave birth to her too. The same room, in fact, where Magdalena conceived she own child of she own spiritual husband and father, you own grand-father, Bartolemeo Amadao Domingo. Then to return to the same little mudhut to live together with him to this very day.

But wait awhile. Wait awhile, son. Understand: I am not talking simply Magdalena's *physical* birth. Nor she death and rebirth neither. The precise medical details of all that I can give you quick and easy enough, as I promise I ga give you in just a moment. But now I am talking about something much more important. Something much more significant, which comes to bear on the lives of every one of we living here on this island of Corpus Christi. I am talking Magdalena's *historical* birth. A birth, in fact, which came many years after we all thought her *dead*. Which could *only* have come after, because not until we all took Magdalena fa dead and buried, could she possibly grow to the mythical, superhuman, *saintly* proportions she ulti-mately grew. Because son, the fact is that Magdalena did not precede, or anticipate, or in any way inspire the creation of this black madonna. She did not give birth to this statue: the statue, or more precisely *history*, gave birth to Magdalena. And history took she life too – long before she was dead – only so that history could give Magdalena a *second* birth, could bring her back to life in this black madonna which preceded her. Of course, she has only *one* biological-historical mother. Because son, as I have told you already long long ago, if there is any *one* name deserving the black cover of this historical-biological book we call Magdalena Divina, it can only be the Mother Superior General Maurina.

NOW I COULD not help but listen. Now I could not help but hear my grandfather's voice. Because in truth I was about to drop asleep with all that exantaying about cocoa and cane and copra. All that endless oldtalk about Limees and Pañyols and Frites. But now, suddenly, I was caught up by Papee Vince's voice again. Trapped again, by the same voice, on the same cobo roost – only now there was no trapdoor through which I might dream of escaping. The same voice speaking to me above the same loud insects, above the same water beating against the same rocks. Sitting here behind the same desk of purpleheart, in the same ridiculous chair. This miniature Warrahoon-Windsor chair, its arms pressing absurdly into my sides, its saddle seat too small for my bamsee, its legs so short I must stretch my own out beneath the desk.

But not comfortably. Not so at all. There is no comfortable position to be found. It is as though I am not even sitting here in this chair, but somehow balanced on it: my buttocks somehow suspended above the saddle, my weight falling instead on the front edge of the seat, cutting across the middle of my thighs, the chair's back jutting into my hips, my kidneys. It is as though I have never come down from that cobo roost. As though I am back there sitting on the same railing, balanced there again: only now my legs have grown out far too long. Because I

remember sitting there on the railing and pointing my toes
– stretching to touch the ground – reaching out with my
big toe to touch the finger of reality. But now, instead, it is
as though the ground is drawing up closer to *me*. As
though I am slowly sinking inside of it: reality, which had
always seemed so tangible, so far away – which I had
always dreamed of and longed for – but which now
suddenly filled me with fear. Sitting here in this
Warrahoon-Windsor chair with the weight of all my
ancestors pressing down on my shoulders, each individually and all of them together: pressing, pressing. The
weight of all the dead. Pushing me slowly into the ground.

MOTHER MAURINA was the first to tell this story.
This story of Magdalena Divina. She was the only one to
know it complete, perhaps even better than Magdalena
sheself. Because each of we had we own individual
chapter: the historical chapter, the myth, the medical
report, the family saga. But Mother Maurina knew them
all. She had been there to witness all the important events.
More than that, she dictated them. And the most important of these was Magdalena's death. Because the rest of
we believed Magdalena had committed suicide. We repeated it over and over until we convinced weself, even
though we knew it had been impossible. Because that is
what we *had* to believe: we could not share the responsibil-
ity fa this innocent woman's death. But we were all
responsible in a sense, though we could not have known of
we own guilt: we had all killed Magdalena by we lack of
faith. Mother Maurina believed something else. She believed that *she* had murdered Magdalena – strangulated her
with she own hands – the one person she loved above all
others in the world. Mother Maurina believed she had
sacrificed she own beloved daughter by Providential Instruction. By Inspiration Divine. And now that Mother

Maurina had murdered Magdalena, she had to bring her back to life. And she *did*. She accomplished something no storyteller had ever done before or since: she brought she story to life in the black madonna. It was a story to top all others. Even the Biblical one.

We had all seen the miracle with we own eyes: the beautiful black madonna walking by sheself in the early-morning mist surrounding the swamp. True, she had stopped walking since Monsignor O'Connor had torched she carrotroof and moved her here to St Maggy Cathedral, but that mattered little. We had all seen that one enough times already. Now the black madonna gave we a new miracle every day: lifelong illnesses cured, birth defects repaired, disabilities wipe away clean clean. There were gifts of wealth, barren wives became fertile, unfaithful husbands returned, long estranged sons and daughters embraced they parents. But more than these innumerable personal miracles, the whole of Corpus Christi seemed miraculously transformed: racial tensions which had marred we entire history seemed suddenly to disappear. The many religions did more than accept they former rivals: they now sought to incorporate each other. Whatever class differences remaining after we long years of colonialism were finally torn down, dissolved without a trace. All of this happened almost at once, inescapably, uncontrollably, and almost imperceptibly. It was a single moment in history, a *rebirth*, not simply fa Mother Maurina's Magdalena in the black madonna, but fa Corpus Christi sheself. And at that moment – even before we could realize it had happened – the whole of Corpus Christi let loose a single, involuntary cry: *St Maggy!*

It was we first self-sustaining breath, and it became we very respiration: *St Maggy! St Maggy! St Maggy!* Of course the one to breathe it first was Mother Maurina. But she had said it so quickly – and we repeated it behind her with so little encouragement – we scarcely even noticed. But

Mother Maurina was in fact the first. The first to call fa Magdalena's canonization. She dictated it like everything else, not only to Monsignor O'Connor, but to all the Church and Government officials. The canonization of she own daughter. The same daughter she believed she had murdered, strangulated by Divine Inspiration and Instruction. So that now, not even ten years later – by Divine Inspiration too – she could make she daughter a saint. She *demanded* it: nothing short of sainthood could satisfy she need to bring Magdalena back to life. And son, whatever were she hidden motives – even if we could speculate about them with any degree of confidence, which of course we cannot – now became irrelevant. Because now Mother Maurina was more than the instrument of she own disguised unconsious, of she own unshakable will. More than the instrument of Divine Instruction or Inspiration or anything else. Now she was the instrument of *history*: Corpus Christi had to come back to life too.

She wrote to the Pope heself, Pius XI, requesting a Commission of Inquiry fa Magdalena's canonization. And when she got no response she picked up sheself and went to Rome, to the Vatican, making she demands in person. Son, I don't have to tell you that nobody never stops Mother Maurina once she makes up she head: not before she had this Bishop Sévère in *tow* behind her, did she step she foot outside those Vatican gates. And she towed he ass straight cross the sea, right back to this island of Corpus Christi. She put this Bishop Sévère to dig up Domingo Cemetery with Monsignor O'Connor and they three little Warrahoons, which they did every night fa fortnight in succession. Two weeks of molesting all the old jumbies sleeping peaceful enough since the last time Monsignor O'Connor and Mother Maurina and the same Gomez Chief of Police went digging them up, not even ten years before, looking fa Magdalena's corpsebody then too. Of course, they never found it. Not now or then. Because in

fact Magdalena is still alive. But son, before this Bishop
Sévère could open up this sainttrial official, he had to find
she body: he couldn't make a statue into a saint. And all he
could come up with after two weeks of digging, and
reburying, and mismolesting was a coffinbox containing
three good-sized chockstones, the same coffinbox with the
same chockstones which Barto had buried in front of the
whole of Corpus Christi ten years before – and Barto
made good and sure all of we were there watching him too
– because he had to convince us all Magdalena was *dead*. (A
deception you daddy heself completed five or six weeks
later without even intending to do so: he made that
pappyshow-mockfuneral to bury *another* coffinbox containing *another* three chockstones – right next to the one
Barto had buried fa Magdalena – this one supposedly
containing Barto heself.

So by the end of that frustrating fortnight of digging in
the cemetery this Bishop Sévère was near dead up heself.
By then he'd make up he head he ga hold this sainttrial fa
three *chockstones* if necessary. Which is precisely what he
did. Of course, he had to tell Mother Maurina he'd found
the body. But son, if you have a secret to sit on, you don't
tell Mother Maurina. You might as well headline it in the
Bomb, which is exactly what she *did*, two days later on the
morning of 17 April. Of course, this is Corpus Christi
Day. Almost too much fa we little island to bear. This
time we not only busted up the jailcage and the
horsechains to get we hands on Magdalena, we nearly
mashed down the whole *cathedral*. So the following morning, when Mother Maurina headlined the three official
witnesses fa Magdalena's sainttrial to be you daddy,
Evelina and sheself, this Bishop Sévère was so geegeeree
after the events he had seen on the previous day, all he
could think to do was to lock them up in the jail fa they
own protection. Of course, after seeing the events of the
previous day, there are two things this Bishop Sévère

should have realized: no jailcage could never hold back nobody on *this* island, and nobody on this island could never *stir* from out they bed the morning after Corpus Christi Day.

So this sainttrial was nothing more than a big pappyshow from its very beginning. But not even the Church could stop we now, not at this moment in history. We needed to believe Magdalena was we patron saint. And now we dared to defy even the Pope. We took he rejection of Magdalena as a rejection of Corpus Christi sheself, as a denial of we very existence, and this final outrage – after we history of half a millenium of Colonial and Church subjugation – we could not tolerate: we would sanctify Magdalena *weself*. Of course, Mother Maurina was the first again. The first to climb up an old rickety bamboo ladder with all she white veils flying up wild in the wind, a tin of black paint in she hand, to write out the name of St Mary Convent and write in another: *ST MAGGY CON-VENT OF THE CORPUS CHRISTI CARMELITES.* We all followed she lead: *ST MAGGY MUNICIPAL LIBRARY, ST MAGGY HOME OF THE AGED, ST MAGGY HOSPITAL, ST MAGGY TELECOM-MUNICATIONS, ST MAGGY GROCERS, ST MAG-GY MOTORCARS, ST MAGGY ROTI AND PALORI. ST MAGGY SALTPRUNES AND TOOLUUM.* It was nothing more than the change of two letters, two Gs, but it was like carving we initials in stone. Like naming weself fa the world. Because of course, all these establishments and we capital city sheself, had all been named after *St Mary*. Ever since that old Pañyol Antonio de Berrio had changed the name of we ancient Amerindian village of Coyaba to Santa María. But now we even wrote over the ancient navigators' maps. We ceremoniously smashed open the glass case in the museum, and we wrote over the first official map of Corpus Christi, drawn out in Barto's own hand.

Again Mother Maurina sheself performed the ultimate
profanation. She wrote over the name of St Mary Cathedral. With old Monsignor O'Connor standing there at the
bottom of the same rickety bamboo ladder, shitting he
drawers. Because of course, almost before these events
could take place, the Church officials got word. They
ordered Monsignor to end it all with a quick full-stop. But
there was nothing Monsignor nor anybody else could do
to hold back history, and now we had gone so far as to
write over the name of Papa God's own cathedral. But if
he couldn't stop the forward march of history, at least he
could lead it in a circle: Monsignor made up he head now
to move Magdalena from out the cathedral, to send her
back to she same stenching mudswamp. Of course, to
accomplish this he had to do more than build her a new
carrotroof. He knew we would never stand fa that
cacashit. But he couldn't give her nothing ostentatious
neither: he had the Church to contend with too. So he
built her she little chapel there beside the swamp, just in
front of the huge samaan tree, and he had the good sense to
invite Mother Maurina to write in the name: *CHURCH
OF MAGDALENA DIVINA*. That night, under cover of
darkness, he wrote back over the name of St Mary
Cathedral. Of course, cobo came back not only to shit on
he head, but to shit on he cathedral too. Because now it
was empty as a dry calabash. We all abandoned it in one,
every manjack-womanjill pelting to Maraval like picoplats
to a pan of pampalam. Now in order to celebrate Mass fa
more than heself, Monsignor had to hold it outdoors
beneath the samaan tree, since surely we'd have bust the
little church by its seams. Because of course, no sooner did
Monsignor send Magdalena back to Maraval, when she
started up she old habit of walking. This, of course, only
fired up we frenzy fresh too.

But son, by now you have come to realize exactly how
this statue is walking. I would have realized it myself

donkey's ages ago, had I even the slightest doubt Magdalena was anything but dead and buried beneath the
ground. I believed it as fervently as everybody else –
because that is what we *had* to believe – if only fa the
simple reason that we needed to bring Magdalena back to
life. But of course, she was not dead, any more than was
Barto. He was the one who revealed this to me – just as
Magdalena had revealed it to him – exactly seven days
after he had thought her dead. Exactly when she'd promised Barto she would be with him again. Magdalena came
to him right there beneath the same samaan tree, at the
very moment Barto put the butt of General Monagas' big
rifle inside he mouth, and he reached out to push the
trigger.

Because son, ever since that morning thirty-nine years
after we had all thought him dead, when Barto walked
through the front door of this house as easily as if he'd
been doing it every morning fa the previous thirty-nine
years. And he climbed the stairs and the ladder up here
onto this cobo roost where you and I sit at this very moment
– Barto finding me here in this same newspaper-padded
hammock, with him sitting there on that same railing
where you are sitting now – ever since the morning Barto
revealed to me that he was still alive, I have made the
pilgrimage to Maraval on many occasions to see him, both
of we passing the evening sitting there together beneath
the same almond tree, knocking back we tasas of punching
rum, talking we oldtalk. But of course, there were certain
things Barto explained to me which even Magdalena could
not have explained to him, such as the precise medical
details of how she could still be alive. That could only
come from the one who saved her, moments after you
daddy pronounced her dead, moments after he blew way
the snowstorm of feathers from in front he face and
crossed heself to deliver this child by Ceasarean section.
Moments before, in fact, you daddy raised up Magdalena's

dress to verify she postpartum virginity. Only the one
who saved her could provide these medical details, the
only *other* person in Corpus Christi besides Barto and Mrs
Salizar to know that Magdalena was still alive: Barto's
own grandfather-in-law, Dr Brito Salizar heself. Of
course, there was one thing which was so obvious now
nobody needed to explain it, neither you daddy, nor Brito
Salizar, nor Barto nor nobody else. Because son, Magdalena Divina may have given we innumerable miracles
over the years. And she continues to give we miracles still,
even to this day, which I would be the last man on this
green earth to begin to deny. But son, she never walked
the banks of Swamp Maraval. Not so a-tall. The only
black virgin ever to walk the banks of that swamp is
Magdalena Domingo, and she is far from dead.

SUDDENLY the horizon lit up: hard yellow above the
still dark wall of the sea, fire-orange above the yellow,
then red, pink, purple, brilliant blue. With the edge of the
flaming ball of the sun, so bright it pained my eyes to look
at it, floating slowly up out of the dark sea. As it floated
higher the water lit up too, but more gradually than the
sky, and soon it was glistening again, as the water had
glistened only moments before beneath the moon. But
now the sea was altogether changed. It was turbulent and
agitated: hot, visibly boiling, a path of bright sparks
stretching forth from the flaming sun, popping on the
water's surface. The lake of cool, silverblack pitch I had
looked out over the whole night, for uncountable hours,
for immemorial hours, for a lifetime; the cool, silverblack
lake which had been so soothing for me, so comforting for
me all night long, was now molten, visibly burning,
blueblackred, infused with the same fire and threat as the
sun.

    I closed my eyes to it: the quickest, most effortless

twinge of nerve endings and muscle fibres to eclipse the huge, menacing sun. To douse it again beneath the water. And at that moment I felt a surge of strength moving through my body. New energy, moving upward through my thighs and groin. Surging into my chest, arms, my cheeks warm and tingling now beneath the new light, which I perceived blackorange-mottled through my closed eyelids. I was awake! Somehow! Fully awake, though it had been the longest and most exhausting night I had known. Though I felt like the oldest man alive. Though in fact it was the day before my ninetieth birthday.

But I knew this was not the end. It was only the beginning of the end, now that it was day. Because now that it was day I would have to get up out of my chair, finally. To rise up out of my chair at last. But I could not get up until Papee Vince removed his hands from my shoulders. He had to release me first. To reach the end of his story.

THAT IS WHAT Barto said to me, sitting here on this very cobo roost: that only the week before both Magdalena and she child had died. That is what Barto believed. It is what I myself would believe fa thirty-five years, living there in the jungles of that Delta Orinoco. Because the old Domingo Estate was bust – bankrupt like all the others – and after twenty-two years I had come to resign my position as manager of the cultivation. A cultivation now dead. Dead as my wife Gertrude, dead as Magdalena and she child, dead as Barto heself would be in a few hours. Dead as I believed the world was dead. But the world was far from dead, though it would take me thirty-five years to realize it, thirty-five years hiding somewhere up in the bush behind God's back. Barto and I sat up here the whole night, and at this same moment, when the sun finally rose up out of the black sea, we climbed down from this cobo roost and Barto saw me aboard my ship, she bow already pointed at the open mouth of the great river.

It was a Sunday morning. Barto wanted to make one last pilgrimage to Maraval, to sit one last time beneath the samaan tree. And on he way he stopped at the house fa General Monagas' rifle. But just as he placed the butt of that rifle inside he mouth, just as he reached out he hand to push the trigger, Magdalena appeared before him. It was not an apparition: she was alive, breathing, in flesh and blood, though she could tell Barto little of this miracle of she own rebirth. She knew only that fa the previous seven days Dr Brito Salizar and he wife had cared fa her, there in they own home, nursing her back to health after this operation fa the delivery of she child. A child she had never seen – never had the privilege of looking into he face – but a child she knew would one day return to her. Barto did not understand. He had buried this child heself, only three days before, just as Magdalena sheself had instructed him. He would have buried *her* there beside she child too, had Brito Salizar not sworn to him he had already done so. Barto did not understand what Magdalena was telling him, but he vowed to remain with her until the day she child returned. Of course, this child which Magdalena spoke of, this child which would come back to her many years later, was *Corpus Christi* sheself. All of we together: we would return to her as Magdalena Divina.

But Barto would not understand this fa many years to come. And there were some things which Barto, no different from the rest of we, would never understand. Because of course Magdalena's rebirth could be explained easy enough. He own rebirth could be explained, since Magdalena had come back to life in order to save him, to prevent Barto from shooting heself. But certain things could never be explained. Because Barto *did* push the trigger of old General Monagas' rifle. It did in fact fire, though its bullet was not destined to take Barto's life. At that instant Magdalena had pushed the butt of the rifle from out he mouth, and the bullet found the mark fa which it was destined: the chest of Gomez, the same Chief of Police, sitting on he horse hidden by the bushes, just there behind him. He fell to the ground instantly dead, he own pistol drawn and ready to fire, still intertwined between he fingers. It was as though Fate, or Providence, or whatever you choose to call it, had decided that Gomez would be the one to die, so that Barto and Magdalena could go on living. They could live out the remainder of they long lives together.

Magdalena was still very weak, and Barto walked her to the little mudhut nearby, putting her to lie on the same copra mattress on which she had slept only a year before. He returned to St Maggy not only to bury Magdalena, but to bury Gomez too. The same Chief of Police who had spent the previous five days digging up in the same cemetery with Mother Maurina and Monsignor O'Connor, looking fa Magdalena's body. Because that is where Salizar swore it was. It was the only way he could think to save her: he knew perfectly well that the instant Gomez discovered that Magdalena was still alive, he could come to kill her. And Salizar, in he attempt to save her, swore so solemnly that Magdalena was dead and buried – that he heself was responsible for both – in the end Gomez had no choice but to lock him up with you daddy and Mother Maurina. Of course, all this time Magdalena was there hidden in he own home recovering sheself. But we all believed that Magdalena was dead, and now we were *sure*: we all stood there watching Barto cover her up. And as soon as he finished burying those two coffinboxes, he went straight to the jail to let loose you daddy, Mother Maurina and the same oldman Salizar. That evening Barto gathered Granny Myna, Evelina and Uncle Olly, you daddy and all he brothers round the big diningroom table. He pulled the cork from a bottle of rum and passed it round saying that he would be leaving them that night. They all thought he was going on another of he expeditions up the Orinoco, but in fact he was only returning to the same mudhut in Village Suparee. The following morning Dr Brito Salizar went to the mudhut too – just as Barto had requested him – and after he'd examined Magdalena and found her in good health, removed she sutures and bandaged she abdomen again, Barto took him outside and put him to lie down in the same hammock beneath the almond tree. He took he seat on the cratestool beside him, and Salizar explained the precise medical details of Magdalena's miraculous rebirth. This, of course, was no miraculous rebirth a-tall. Nothing more than another of he old Warrahoon cure-alls (administered while you daddy and Mother Maurina were busy in the next room, reading in he big black book and studying the child).

All of these things Barto explained in detail to me, sitting there beneath the same almond tree, just as I have explained them all to you. But there was one thing which Barto could not explain, nor Brito Salizar nor nobody else. Not even Magdalena could account for it, because Barto asked her heself on more than one occasion. Because of course, *I* have never seen this woman. She may very well have been sitting there in that mudhut only a few feet away from me sitting there in the hammock, all those innumerable hours I sat talking with Barto there on the cratestool beside me. But I never saw her. Not with my own eyes. Nor she child nor even she statue. Nor was I there to witness a single one of the events I am giving you now. Not a one: all this time I am living in another world altogether, there in the bush of Maracaibo. And by the time I arrived back here to this island, everything had returned to normal. Everything had quieted down fa the most part – and Corpus Christi was near dead again – just as we have always known her, just as she remains to this day. Because it turns out that Monsignor O'Connor was right in the end, though it certainly didn't appear so at the start: history *could* be led in a circle. It could be led in one circle after another, which has always been the fate of this island, if we only stand back far enough to see it clear. It is the fate of the whole Caribbean. Son, we frenzy fa Magdalena died down almost as quick as it fired itself up. True, she continued to grant favours, she even continued to walk the banks of Swamp Maraval, as she is seen occasionally to do to this day. But son, Corpus Christi had a much harder reality with which to contend, and not even Magdalena Divina could save her from that: the reality of poverty, of malnutrition, inadequate housing and medical care, lack of education. An all-pervasive lack of *hope*, of belief in weself. It was the end result of half a millennium of Colonial and Church subjugation. Still, we managed to come back to life every year fa one day. No one could put a stop to that. This day is of course 17 April, Corpus Christi Day. But eventually, most of we wouldn't even remember what we were celebrating.

We story had reached its end, or at least it had reached the beginning of another circle. Yet there was one thing nobody could explain. One piece of mystery remaining in this story – nothing profound, or dramatic, or of any apparent significance a-tall – but it was a mystery still, and I made up my head to solve it fa myself. Son, as you well know, every year fa longer than any of we can remember, a bouquet of white roses has appeared mysteriously on Magdalena's grave in the cemetery. Every year without fail on the first day of November All Saints' Day. It started appearing there years before any of we – even Mother Maurina sheself – ever thought to consider Magdalena's sanctity, and it continues appearing there to this day. Nobody could say who was responsible fa this bouquet of roses. Nobody much cared. But son, fa some peculiar reason I could never dismiss it so easily. And it persisted

humbugging me until I made up my head to find it out. I
hid myself behind Magdalena's own headstone, and I
waited there crouched down in the dark the whole night.
Son, of all the people in Corpus Christi I might have
guessed, I would not fa one instant have considered the
person I eventually saw: I looked up to find you own
Granny Myna coming, alone, just a few minutes before
dawn. I watched her kneel down to lay this bouquet of
white roses gently on the ground before Magdalena's
headstone. And the next minute she was gone.

Son, you may think of this silent gesture of you
granny's as nothing a-tall. Perhaps I am reading much
more into it than I should. Perhaps I am *mis*reading it
altogether. But son, I have considered it fa good many
years, and I have come to the conclusion that this gesture
of you granny's is as significant as any other ingredient of
this story. And in some way I cannot articulate precisely, it
is the culmination of everything else: the last word somehow belongs to you Granny Myna. Mother Maurina may
have been the first to tell this story – with all of we
following each in we turn behind her – but Granny Myna
must somehow be the last. You see son, it is not so much
the telling of this story. It is the *believing* in it. Because no
story told without faith is any kind of story a-tall. It is
windballs and airfritters, and anybody who takes even a
taste knows the difference. Even before they begin to
chew. But son, while the faith of the rest of we seems to
have exhausted itself over the years – to have smothered
itself out slowly but surely in the end – Granny Myna's
own continues as strong as ever. The proof, which I came
to understand many years later, is that same silent bouquet
of white roses: *that* is the gesture of faith. Because son, fa
you Granny Myna this belief came harder than fa any of
we, perhaps as hard as all of we together. Understand: fa
Granny Myna, Magdalena was she husband's mistress.
The woman who had given him an illegitimate child. But

more than any of that, fa her Magdalena was the woman
over whom Barto had taken he life. This Barto explained
to me: it is what he had told Granny Myna heself. (The
others, you daddy included, all believed he had left on
another expedition up the Orinoco. And even if they
suspected something else, they could never be sure.)
Granny Myna knew differently. It was the last thing Barto
did before leaving the house late that night: he slipped a
note quietly beneath Granny Myna's bedroom door
downstairs. It was a suicide note, explaining that he could
not go on living without Magdalena. Several hours before
it would have been true. Now it was a boldface lie, as
deceitful an untruth as any man ever told the woman who
loved him. The woman who had accepted he mistress.
The woman who had even accepted he mistress's child,
just as she had accepted Evelina and brought her here to
live in she own home. The woman he now left a widow at
the age of thirty-six, penniless, with nine sons to raise.

Barto never explained to me why he did it. I never asked
him. Perhaps he thought it would be easier fa Granny
Myna to think him dead, easier fa her to forget him.
Perhaps he did not want her to live out the rest of she life
faced with the uncertainty of she husband's death. I don't
know. I couldn't tell you. But son, there is one thing I *do*
know: as much as I admire you grandfather above all other
men – as much as he is closer to me than all others, living
or dead – I can never forgive him this deceit. Neither can
any of we. There is only *one* person who can possibly
forgive him, and she did. Not after years of struggle and
deliberation: she forgave him immediately and wholeheartedly. Because before Barto could manage even to
reach that front door, you Granny Myna came running
behind him. She fell on the ground at he feet fa the last
time, and she reached up to press in he palm a solid gold
rosary. A rosary she begged Barto to give to Magdalena
Divina when he met her in heaven.

Son, it has taken me years to understand the full
significance of this offering of Granny Myna's, an offer
re-enacted each year in that bouquet of white roses.
Understand: the moment Barto closed that door behind
him was the moment of you grandmother's death. *Worse*
than death, because Granny Myna had to go on living,
alone, living with the knowledge that she husband had
taken he life fa another woman. But son, Granny Myna
went on living. I sat here and I watched her. Living with
enough life fa three people. I watched her raise nine sons,
alone, and I watched her send them all to Medical School,
and they are all nine of them doctors today. Son, that is
when I began to slowly realize something about faith: it is
not fear of death. Faith is love fa life, even in the face of
death. But son, it would take many more years fa me to
accept it. To embrace it not only fa myself, but fa all of we
together. Many more years of telling myself over and over
again that if this woman, Granny Myna, you grandmother, could believe fervently enough to go on living *not*
fa the memory of she husband, but fa she husband's
mistress, what Corpus Christi is, fa Magdalena Divina,
then you can say it too: *Yes. I live.*

5

Granny Myna's Requiem

SHE WAS BORN a saint, but between she legs she chucha was hot like a whore. It happen so, because that bitch Maurina have the same pussy on fire, and beside she bed she used to keep the little altar with this same saintstatue that she would look up at it in all she moments of passion, and that is how the child come out so much the same with she skin black, and she hair beautiful, and those big eyes shining in the night always watching you just like the statue own, because Barto utilize the same principle to create a zebra from two donkeys by putting them to do they business in a room he have paint with stripes. So when he climb through the window Maurina legs are open already before she can even waste the time to put she beads on the bedstand, because Barto is the only man on the skin of Papa God earth that can hold on and singando steady for three days and three nights without even a pause for you to breathe a breath of air, but no even that is enough to satisfy the scratching inside this putanga pussy. And it is that saintstatue Maurina *must* have been looking the moment she conceive the child, because how else could she come out so much the same in every detail like the statue come to life, and who ever before hear of a child born with that red mark of a coolie already stamp right here in the middle of she forehead? You see how Papa God does do He work?

In this same way Maurina make this child with she chucha incendida just like she own, and with she beautiful face of a saint to save this island of Corpus Christi from sinking in the sea!

It is my own dollstatue Uncle Olly have paste out for me for my birthday of seven years. That is when we was living in Venezuela on the cattle ranch in Estado Monagas, and Uncle Olly make it to mimic the little statue negrita the Capuchins have there in they mission of Catacas, just by the mouth of the Orinoco River to try hopeless to tame all those wadjank Warrahoons. Of course that saintstatue is a proper one carve from a trunk of purple-of-heart wood, but my own is only paste out from little papier-mâché with she features paint on with paint, and Uncle Olly push in two big marbles to make the eyes. I tell him thank you very much, but what am I to do with this fisheye statue of a skeleton with she baldhead smooth like the shell of an egg? Uncle Olly say of course that I must dress her up in my own clothes and my lace churchveil on she head, because this is a *living* dollstatue as each year he will cut two new sticks for me on my birthday, that she can grow up beside me to wear all my clothes. So that night I dress her up in my new whitedress with the frills on it, and my lace petticoats beneath, and my little white gloves on she hands. But every time I put the veil on she head it slide off again straight way, that I get so vex I start to curse and I take up the scissors to chop off all my beautiful long hair that have never been cut since I am born reaching almost by my knees, and I call Uncle Olly to bring some laglee quick help me stick it on she egghead!

So I have grow up longside this dollstatue that I used to play with her every day. I would dress her up and carry her with me on the horse wherever I go, and sometimes she could sleep together with me in the bed, but when we marry Barto tell me I am too big now to play with dolls, even though I have only just reach my thirteen years. But before he can have a chance to take her way from me I make the little altar in the corner of my room, and I put her there to stand up that I can take her down to play with her again soon as he back is turn, and I tell him that now she is a saint like she mummy in the mission. So when we leave Venezuela to come here to this island of course my little saintstatue must come too, and I pack her up in three shoeboxes one for she head in the nest of hair and one for each of she hands. I have no even have time to unpack her yet when this bitch Maurina arrive to take over everything. She tell Barto the convent he build for her is very nice, but who ever hear of a sacrarium like that without even a statue in the vestibule or a crucifix hanging on the wall? Next thing I see Barto is ransacking all the suitcases and boxes and crates like if he have catch a vaps. Sweet heart of Jesus! I grab on to he cojones to tell him if he only try to give way my little dollstatue I will squeeze them so hard they will burst in the air like two naranjas de sangre, but Barto can't even hear, because he hand over the three shoeboxes straight way to this Maurina standing there with she face of a bobolee as if to say what the ass am I to do with these as I never wear nothing more then my old jesusboots like all the other nuns? but Barto answer her that what she holding beneath she chin is no oldboots a-tall, it is the *Patroness Saint* of this island of Corpus Christi!

Of course Maurina can never understand what he is saying as no even Barto can make a statue into a saint. She can only think that he must mean her to make this saint for him sheself, and she dress up the statue in one of she own nuncostumes beside she bed waiting for Barto to come. And this saintstatue have remain there so on the little altar quiet enough, until one night Maurina is waiting for him the whole night long that he don't arrive a-tall, and she loose she head viekeevie to take up the statue and pelt her out the window. Sweet heart of Jesus! Next morning the

three little nuns find her sitting there in the almond tree in
front the convent. They pull her down quick to fix back
on she head, and they run to Monsignor O'Connor only
to sell him my sweet little saintstatue for a scrunting five
coconut dollars! Monsignor say that he have see more of
these Black Virgins even though he never have the privilege before to own one heself, and the coolies and the
Warrahoons have another statue just the same beneath
they carrotroof there in they village of Suparee, but I
know that is impossible because this island could never be
big enough for two. Monsignor make the little chapel for
her in the cathedral with all the other saintstatues, that
now I am happy I can go there at night and take her down
secret to play with her again, and sometimes I carry her
home to change she clothes and my big white hat with the
flowers of crinoline on it, until one night I forget myself
and the next morning Barto find us sleeping together in
the bed. Sweet heart of Jesus! I have never see Barto so
upset as when he come to me that morning. He stand up
here just so at the end of this bed looking down on me
with he eyes only burning fire, and he tell me that I am
sixteen years now with two children of my own that I am
too big to play with dolls, and he crack the two sticks over
he knees *crick-crack*, demanding Evelina to take up this
bundle of papier-cacashat and carry it way. Of course
Evelina only turn round to carry her straight back to
Monsignor for another five coconut dollars, and she tell
him Uncle Olly will cut two new sticks for him if he want,
and Monsignor say yes and this time he will put her inside
the big jailcage that Myna will never again make a
pappyshow of he sacred Black Virgin!

When Maurina see this child coming out the little purple
cocoamonkey with she head the shape of a sucked mango
seed, she only want to push it back inside she pussy and
hide it from the rest of the world. Maurina could never
accept that she is the mother of this child ugly like sin,

because it take her only one look in the cocoaface to press the pillow against it and try she best to suffocate her. Maurina would have kill this child even before she navel-string can have a chance to cut, with all the little nuns pulling and tugging and tearing at the pillow that they can no loose it a-tall from out she hands, until one of them can think quick to konk her with the bottle of brandy kaponkle over she head. Feathers was gusting back and forth inside the convent bedroom like a blizzard. The little nun blow way the floating feathers from in front she face, she cross sheself, and she bend over to bite off the cordstring from the belly of this cocoachild to join the world of the dead with the living for the whole of we apocryphy!

The nuns didn't have no choice but to send for Barto to come take back he child, because Maurina only want to pelt her out the window. Of course Barto turn round straight way to hand her over to me, and I tell him I don't mind a-tall as I have already Barnabas sucking at my breast, but Papa God give me two so one could just as well go to feed he Magdalena, which is the name Barto pronounce on he cocoachild official with salt and water. Next thing Juanito and José come running to question Barto where do he find this little chimpanzee, and could they please take her in the tamarind to find out how good she swing. But Barto only have to put one cuteye on these boys for them to know he is no skylarking, and little Juanito and José take off running and we don't see them again until late in the night. Evelina start to beat she breast and shout one set of Creole-obeah bubball on the child, because she say nothing could bring mauvais-fortune on a house like two whorechildren under the roof, and she run to she room quick to bury sheself beneath the bed. After a time though everything have calm down again, and Barto give me he little Magdalena that I could take out my next tottot beside Barnabas to put it for her to drink. But something happen soon as that cocoachild begin to suck at my breast. Something happen, and I don't know what it is, because I drop Barnabas *boodoops* to take off running with my tottots flapping for that big pepperpot that is waiting for me boiling way in the kitchen, and before I can know what my hands are doing they are bury up to they elbows in this sludgethick cassareep-quenkstew slurging slurging like the red flames of hell!

Barto pull her from out the pot dripping like blood with bitter cassava, and he gone to sea for a bucket of water to bathe her off. When he have finish, and Magdalena is back beside Barnabas in the cradle sleeping peaceful enough, Barto turn to me and he say that if I don't care for the child proper he will carry her to oldman Salizar and he wife where they are living in Suparee with all the other Warrahoons, and he will tell them that this nasty little-negrita is they own great-grandchild that they must raise her up, because *I* am the mother and I don't want her. Sweet heart of Jesus! I grab on to he moustache and I put one cursing on him to say how everybody know this cocoachild belong to him and that putanga Maurina and *I* don't have nothing to do with her a-tall, and neither will I never have nothing to do with that pendejo Brito Salizar no even to give him up my own husband whorechild. No even until the *ends* of the earth!

Barto know good enough the hatred I bear in my heart for this oldman. Because it is ever since daddy is the Spanish Captain of ships that he have die so young to bury beneath the sea, that soon as I reach my menses this bushdoctor Salizar come to the ranch secret in the middle of the night, and he steal me way from my mummy and Uncle Olly just like all the other little Warrahoon girlchildren. How he can know I have reach my menses I couldn't tell you as I didn't even know myself, but here is he the same night and he grab me up to carry me deep in the forest with all those wadjank Warrahoons running behind, until they come to a clearing with only a hammock

between two maho trees and the fire burning beneath it for
my blood to drip inside. There with the drums beating and
the flames sweating and all these oldmen howling *oyo-oyo-
oyo* for two more nights until my dripping is done, that
now they can hold me down on the ground one after the
next to do they nastiness, and it is only the grace of Papa
God that send Barto inside that jungle to take me way
from these Warrahoons howling that this bushdoctor
Salizar can give me to him in marriage. Ay Dios mío hijo
María! Of course the next afternoon soon as the pepperpot
begin to boil it is the same thing again, and when darkness
fall Barto is back again on he horse, with poor little
Magdalena in he arms *ca-clap ca-clap* disappearing to the
same miserable blind fate!

FOR A MOMENT longer I considered the absurdity of
this miniature Windsor chair on which I sat. This ridiculous chair, carved ages ago according to a diagram Barto
had copied from the *Oxford Dictionary* – according to
Barto's own instructions given in a language nearly forgotten – by one of the same outrageous little Warrahoons.
Were it not for this chair, I thought, *for this desk of purpleheart,
the whole story might have been nothing but a figment of your
imagination.* I laid my palms flat on the exquisite wood,
feeling its solidity, its comforting inertia; and with some
spiritual trepidation and much physical relief, I strained to
get up finally out of my tortuous chair. The sun had risen
fully above the horizon. It stood huge and menacing in the
cloudless sky, master of the hot earth, of the boiling sea.
My eyes swept slowly across the water. But when I went
to turn my back to it I could not pick up my feet: they
were numb, unyielding, the circulation in my legs cut off
for hours by the ridiculous chair, for years and years by
my invincible old age. I was thinking: *It is not one leg you
have already in the grave but two. Two legs already in the grave,*

so how can you foot it all the way back to that swamp when you can't even manage the first step?

But thick blood returned grudgingly to my old legs, and I turned myself around with a series of short, laborious steps – just as I had manoeuvred my young legs stuck so long ago beneath the mud – as though I were back there in the swamp already. As though I had never left. I bent over and shoved the chair out of the way, rattling the wooden floorboards. There, in the corner of the room with its red-and-white label pressed against the wall, was Papee Vince's old Carnation sweetmilk tin: ragged-edged, *content*, impossible. I pretended not to see it. Then I stepped around the chair, took hold of its back with one hand to steady myself, and I crouched to pick up the tin. I placed it again on the desk, its contents still unspilled. Beside it lay the large medical journal – just as daddy had left it – open in halves like two yellow-white wings, the bulging eyes of that anencephalic child still staring out of the page. I looked at him for one last second, closed the book. But the journal was so heavy I could hardly pick it up (my task made more difficult by my awkward position as I reached over the chair) and I practically heaved the book into its slot on the shelf. I left the library, closing the door behind me.

In the bedroom I pulled a shortpants over my boxer drawers, tucked in my marino-vestshirt. Then I sat on the bed to rest for a few seconds. It had been Barto's own bed ages ago – the bed where my mother and father had slept and had conceived me – the same old mattress of stiff coconut-fibres on which I had slept with my own wife, on which we had conceived our three children. I leaned over to buckle on my jesusboots.

I closed the bedroom door and walked down the hall, stopping for a minute to look into the room I had once shared with my younger brother, the room where my own two sons had slept. The mattresses were bare, and a leg at the bottom of one bed had caved in. Its wooden headboard had warped in the opposite corner – twisted in a backward arch as though to compensate for the broken leg – as though straining to hold the bed up. They had not been slept in for over forty years. On the bureau in the corner stood the oscillating fan, its blades scarcely visible within its cobweb-covered cage.

But it was Evy's vacant bed in the second room which saddened me most of all – my sister's and Papee Vince's bed – and after a few seconds I turned and started down the stairs, my jesusboots slapping softly against the soles of my feet. I walked past Granny Myna's closed door, through the livingroom and around the big diningroom table, and I entered the kitchen. From the cupboard I took down a large teak case, its hinges nearly rusted shut. The utensil-shaped compartments were lined with worn navyblue velvet, a few tarnished pieces of silverware scattered on top. I selected a fishknife, its blade flat and unserrated (with a curved lobe on one side, an uneven V with a notch at the joint on the other) the entire blade bent upward at an angle from the handle like the scoop of a spade. I put the case away and took up the knife. I walked past Evelina's room, out the back door.

I got down on my knees beneath the tamarind tree, holding the fishknife lengthwise in both hands, scratching at the hard dirt with the V side of the blade. The yardfowl soon arrived, looking to see what I was doing: I took a swat behind them and they ran off in a burst of cackle. I held the knife by its handle and started digging.

After a minute I removed a small square tin, covered in a powder of bright orange rust. I brushed it off and slipped it into the pocket of my shortpants, jingling as though it contained a few coins. I smoothened the ground over with the curved side of the blade, then I wiped it on my shorts and slipped the knife into my pocket along with the tin. I got up and passed through the back door, through the house again and out the front.

As I pulled the front door shut I was frightened for a moment that the old house would come tumbling down behind me. It was the same fear I had fought off for years – every time I closed the door – but my fear at that moment was more acute than ever: I felt my sputtering heart skip a beat. The old house stood tall. It had been a construction of careful but vicariously placed cards – piled up enthusiastically and naïvely too high, too long ago – but it stood. I stepped off the frontstoop and turned around to look up at its aspiring two-and-a-half storeys. I leaned back to take them all in, complete, as though for the first time – half of the basement storey its foundation buried solid beneath the ground, which had withstood even the legendary explosions in Uncle Olly's laboratory – and I could not help but admire the old house. I felt confident that it would remain standing for another decade. It had seen the passing of four generations, had know the dreams and despairs of its great-grandchildren, but now it did not belong to any of them. And as I turned my back to it and passed though the front gate, I realized the old house no longer belonged to me either.

The sun was rising quickly behind me, rising with the dust stirred up by my hesitating feet. The contents of the tin in my pocket jingled annoyingly with each step. I shifted the knife to the other side, put my hand in my pocket and cupped my fingers around the tin, muffling its noise. St Maggy was deserted at this hour. Even the potcakes were still asleep, curled up in groups of two or three in the middle of the road. As I approached they opened their eyes and looked up at me without even bothering to raise their heads, not perturbed in the least by the soft familiar step-slap, step-slap of my jesusboots. I walked quietly around them. On my way through town I passed a parlour, its doors surprisingly open, even at this hour: I decided to stop for a drink.

It was dark inside. At the end of the bar there was a candle and some incense burning in a small brass bowl, a picture-postcard propped up against the wall beside it: the wise and gentle elephant Ganesha, patron of merchants and shopkeepers. A boy in his late teens stood behind the bar, a book open on the counter before him, reading with the light from the candle. As soon as I entered the parlour he snapped his book shut, the candle almost outing. I'd expected some religious title – *Upanishads* or the *Ramayana* – but I saw that it was a schoolbook, covered in brown papersack, POLYSCI printed carefully across the spine. There was another on a shelf behind the bar lined with bottles: ECON.

I nudged my nose at the book he'd been reading: 'You won't find anything inside this book to save you soul.' For some peculiar reason I spoke in a whisper.

The boy laughed out loud. 'No Doctor, nor in no other book neither. But prayers rise faster on a full belly!'

My brow furrowed at the hackneyed expression.

He laughed louder. 'Is hunger bring the devil's temptation!'

I waited for him to quiet himself. Asked for a whisky. Instead, the little East Indian made a pappyshow out of pouring me a rum.

'Birthpaper bun!' he said. 'Mummy's milk finish with boydays!'

I frowned and tasted the rum – like a coffee with too much sugar.

He laughed again: 'Dis is not altogether fool, boy!'

'Son, have you ever heard of an elderly fellow, used to call himself Oldtalk?'

He smiled. 'Dat oldman was me grandaddy, Doctor. Is after him dey does call me Frank.'

'I never knew his Christian name.'

'Christian name what! Is after him dey does call me Frank *Tedium*!'

Now it was me who smiled.

I drank down the rum as best I could, but when I
reached into my pockets I realized I had no money: only
the sardine tin, the fishknife. For a moment I even
considered giving him the knife, my left hand stuck in my
pocket. But the little fellow was already waving me off,
calling the rum a lagniappe, a petipak. 'Dee-ray, dee-ray!'
he shouted. 'Chirrip-chirrip!'

I protested: 'But I never even gave you grandfather
those medicine tablets!'

'Doctor, dey ain't no magic Yankee medicine could save
any of we. Few halfdollars in we shit would help, but de
only medicine could save we is we weself!' He patted his
small chest. 'Now go long before you arrive late fa you
own funeral!'

He opened the book again.

SO WHEN she fate like mine is finish this pendejo Salizar
send her back to Barto still wearing the stains of she first
adolescent blood. She have no even reach she thirteen
years yet, but when she appear kneeling before him at the
top of the cathedral steps she is the most *beautiful* woman
this island have ever see, like a photograph-copy of that
same saintstatue in she chapel inside. Of course everybody
start to bawl straight way milagro! milagro! the statue
have come to life, and as if the stains from she menses is no
dramatics enough the little Chief of Police have take out he
pistol to shoot her in the foot, because that is all he can
think to keep this statue from walking way. So one minute
Magdalena is the living saintstatue kneeling at the top of
the steps, and the next the martyrsaint cover in blood
sprawl out cross the bottom, with everybody shouting
already St Maggy! St Maggy! patrona who come to shed
she blood in we mancipation. Sweet heart of Jesus! Those
frizzlefowl love to dress theyself like guineahen, and the

queen of the frizzlefowls is that same bitch Maurina, because soon as Barto take up Magdalena in he arms she come running the next minute to grab her way, holding her upside-down with she legs throw over she shoulder dripping the trail of blood, down the stairs cross the square running like the cannibal Carib she hungry to cook inside the convent!

In truth Maurina was so hungry to make Magdalena a saint, she scarce even give her chance to dead sheself first. There isn't nothing could slow down Maurina once she make up she head, that it is a wonder how Magdalena survive in that convent even the year. Of course the rest of Corpus Christi never find time to tolerate a living Magdalena of flesh and blood *a-tall*, because for them the only Magdalena is the miraculous statue lock up in she cage inside the cathedral. In truth from the moment Maurina have disappear with her behind the barricades of that convent nobody never see Magdalena again, unless it is the apparition beneath the moonlight of one of those balconies sometimes on a Sunday evening you strolling in the square, and of course first thing every Sunday morning leading she pack of chupidees scampering long the trace, before they can commence as always trunging through the chourupa of that stenching mudswamp. Because all these chupidees are witness every Saturday night how the statue will disappear miraculous from out the darkness of she jailcage soon as nobody is watching, and at dawn the next morning sure enough here is she again walking long the trace, follow as always like the Pie Piper by she cloud of dust and jumping chupidees. In truth she never do appear on that trace wearing she nuncostume, so why should they even consider for a moment that she is a sister living inside the convent? Magdalena only appear to them dress in the same whitedress with the frills on it, and sometimes even my own big white hat with the flowers of crinoline, that every Monday morning Monsignor must open the pad-

locks again for Evelina to off the dress still dripping
chourupa, and she carry it home cursing again to wash it
out.

So this miracle of the walking saintstatue have continue
every Sunday after Sunday without release for these
chupidees, all dress in mud high as they chucha-cajones
and dead to they bones with exhaustion. Of course by the
end of six or five of these mudbaths they have all lose
interest, and the only two chupidees with perseverance
enough is Evelina and me hiding behind the mangrove
bush, because now when Magdalena go to Maraval it is
only to meet with Barto that they can watch the crapos
singando. And it is this same business of the walking
saintstatue and the frogs fucking that have continue almost
until the very end, because Magdalena is already haveen
seven months one Sunday evening that she have forget
sheself. When Barto climb through the window here is she
like two black twins sleeping together identical in the bed.
Oui fute papayo! Barto can no even decide who is who and
what is what. In truth it is this dollstatue and no the real
Magdalena Barto go to repremand first, because she is the
one wearing the dress and the doll the nuncostume!

Magdalena explain to Barto how Maurina is the one
give her this key to that jailcage hanging on the scapular
round she neck, and she is the one tell her to go to that
cathedral sometimes at night when she feel lonely and
make good and sure nobody is watching, that she can take
out this dollstatue and play with her again. Magdalena
explain too that she could never restrain sheself from this
beautiful white gown with the frills on it, just like the
princess fairy out the schoolbook, and neither could she
help sheself to wear it for him so beautiful every Sunday
and no that nasty nuncostume beneath the samaan tree.
Because all she ever know for all the long years of she
miserable childhood with those wild Warrahoons, is the
same old grassskirt scratching with she tottots flapping.

But Barto only pelt the bundle of papier-cacashat out the window *crick-crack*, and that is the end of my dollstatue beginnings.

'EH-EH WHITEBOY, tell me what you say!'

I stood staring, as if I were seeing a ghost: it was the same oldman wrapped up in the same costume of aluminium foil. Same angelic robot in the same Biblical rocket.

The oldman laughed. 'Boy, like you seeing de jabjab dancing he nabnab!'

I was still too astonished to speak.

He chupsed. 'Me ain't know where you going footing fa health, you long past the cemetery you should have lie down youself! Better climb up here rest you bones a space, let me carry you little bit down de trace!'

'Who you is, oldman? You, or you daddy's son?'

'Boy, is not me to play pappy on Papa God name. But all three in me one dead and born again: father, son, and holy ghost the same! And you best get you bamsee up here fore you drink you bane. You could dead up youself today fa true, but is not me ga take de blame!'

I considered the cart, each spoke of its wheels shining in silver paper; the colossal ox, its bluegrey hump shrouded in sticky mist. The rickety cart seemed about to self-destruct, the decrepit buffalo ready to drop.

'Oldman, you think this bisquanky oxcart could tote the two of us?'

He chupsed again. 'Dis St Michael chariot of fire you blaspheming so! Cross de heavens and back every day of life it go!'

I assumed he meant between St Maggy and Suparee Village. And if the ox and cart could manage the trip daily, they were at least as sturdy as my old legs. I climbed up with some difficulty onto the cart, sitting on the bench beside the oldman. He turned to study my face for several long seconds. His white lashes were beaded with perspiration, and I looked into his grey, old-people eyes, silver against his umber-burntblack skin: his eyes seemed part of his aluminium outfit. They seemed to belong to another world.

'Oldman,' I said, 'you think somebody could die with their eyes closed?'

'Boy, if you could pose me a question so, you done dead up long ago!' He sucked his teeth, exasperated. 'In truth me is de one to pose *you* de question: all dese years and you still walking de contrary direction, what you expect to find in dat swamp to give you revelations?'

I did not know the answer. We sat in silence for another minute, listening to the breeze in the branches of a tremendous immortelle tree, stretched out a brilliant orange above our heads: remnant of some long abandoned estate, hypertrophied symbol of exploitation and ruin. 'I am looking for nothing,' I said. 'There is nothing left.'

The oldman sucked his teeth. He raised his aluminium arms, crackling, and he gave the worn rope he had for reins a tug. The huge buffalo raised its widespread horns, shoofed loudly, took a step. Suddenly the cart lurched to my side – dropping as if into a hole – flinging me out face-first into the dust.

For an instant I was sure that I was dead. Then I heard the oldman laughing beside me. I took a deep breath, opened my eyes: something silver. I got up slowly, brushed myself off.

The wheel on my side had caved in – its wooden spokes snapping around the top half of the rim – and the cart rested on its broken wheel, like the caricature of a wounded spaceship. The oldman got down, laughing still: 'Boy, best watch what you said, boulderstone ga drop out de sky top you head!'

He was already removing a spare wheel from below the

cart, with admirable dexterity. In a minute he rolled it around beside me.

'De problem is only one thing, no tool to screw on dis spare-wing!'

The wheel was attached to the hub by five bolts, the nuts behind: he needed a wrench and a large screwdriver, at least one of them. Immediately I thought of the fishknife in my pocket.

The short side of the V (between the notch and the point at the top) fit the bolts exactly. The angle of the blade seemed to have been calculated for maximum leverage; it was as though the knife had been designed for just this purpose. In no time at all the oldman removed the bolts. He propped up the cart on a fishcrate left conveniently beneath the immortelle tree.

After bolting on the new wheel he took up a roll of aluminium foil from the back of the cart, and he began carefully wrapping each of its spokes – the most tedious part of the operation. When the wheel was complete and shining, he spent as much time repairing his own costume. I continued to marvel at this oldman – his agility, his boundless energy – and I was about to ask him his age, when suddenly I became confused about my own. I tried counting it out on my fingers, starting from thirteen: was it the day before my eighty-nineth birthday? or my ninetieth?

'Oldman,' I asked, 'what is the date of today?'

He chupsed. 'Don't play de fool fa me now! Everybody know today is de sixteen of April, Holy Thursday: Corpus Christi Day. It is de *happiest* day in heaven, and all we *happy* to be here!'

I shook my head: 'But the year? what is the year of all this?'

Now he seemed confused himself. He asked to borrow the fishknife again. The oldman crouched to sweep a neat square page in the dust. He made a few calculations, swept the page clean, and he wrote in large, clear figures: *6661*.

A shock ran down my legs to my toes. Then I turned my head upside down to read it correctly.

SO WHEN Barto arrive now with this crapochild inside the shoebox, and he tell me I have Amadao already sucking at my breast so the other can go to feed he Manuelito, I grab on to he moustache and I put one cursing on him to say that I have accept all he whorechildren like if they are my own, but I am no taking out my tottot to give it to no frog. *Never!* No even until the ends of the earth! You own daddy is the one trying to defend this crapochild saying that he is no a frog a-tall, but he have this *Anna-and-Cecily* disease that bring him to be born without a brain, and that is what cause him to *look* like a frog. But in truth you daddy is only the boobooloops schoolboy-doctor that he have learn everything from a book without ever seeing a sick person, and you only have to hear him talk to know the difference. Because it is you Uncle Olly who prove without any questions that this child *is* a frog, and he *do* have a brain, even though it is no bigger than the size of a prune. Uncle Olly only have to cut a little cut in the zabuca-head with the scissors, and he squeeze on the both sides, and the little brain pop out like a chenet out the shell. When Uncle Olly go to compare it with the brain of a frogbull they was so much the same, that soon as he have run outside for a quick weewee he forget who belong to who, and to this day Uncle Olly can never remember if it is the frogbrain he plant back inside the child or the child the frog. All he can know for certain is that when he return to Maraval to let loose this crapo grande, it is still singing *oy-yuga oy-yuga* happy as a jab molassi on jouvert morning!

By the time Uncle Olly have finish with that brain he was all excited, and he decide now he want to preserve this crapochild for more dissections. Uncle Olly explain to me how in this first stage of a crapo he can breathe water easier than air, and so long as he can remain inside he bottle except to come out every now and again for some new experiment to break the ground, there is nothing to prevent him from studying this crapochild forever without exhaustion. In truth Uncle Olly have dedicate the remainder of he life to studying what is the nature of this frogchild, and it is all these fruits that he have compile together with the pictures and tables and charts and so to prove it. Uncle Olly explain that of course nobody will consider to publish this book of a little tweettweet coming from some place like Corpus Christi lost somewhere in the sea, and that is why it is very important to choose the big fancify pseudoname with plenty blueblood in it that nobody can help to ignore, like SIR EARDLY HOLLAND. He say the second thing when you making a big blockbuster like this is the title with enough sensations in it, and don't mind it say nothing that is going on inside the book a-tall: *ENGLISH GYMNASTICS OF OLYMPICS PRACTICE.*

And you only have to look on the shelf to know that Uncle Olly is right. Because in truth this crapochild would have live happy forever after, there inside he bottle in Uncle Olly laboratory, if this story do no end the way it do. You see, when Evelina go to climb up on that big Vatican ship ready to cross the sea for we inquisition, and she say that it is up to me now to carry this crapochild back to Domingo Cemetery and make sure to bury him again between me and Barto where he belong, I answer her straight way smiling one ear to the next of course yes, but of course I am only lying between my teeth. Now I run home quick with my heart bursting to hand over this crapochild to Uncle Olly, and I give him five coconut dollars please to pelt him for me straight way in the swamp. Sweet heart of Jesus! I should have *never* trust

Uncle Olly with this thing, because of course as far as this crapochild can reach is right back inside he laboratory up on top the shelf. But after a time I begin to think that this is the best place for this crapochild to end, because now at least Uncle Olly can have him there for any new experiment he want to break the ground, and I will never again have to see him so long as I can restrain myself from that basement, and I forbid Evelina and me never to make another callaloo never again inside the house. But it is the Christmas Day many years later, when all the boys have return home from they Medical Schools in England and Canada and Venezuela and so, bawling and fighting each other and shouting down the place, that after a time I begin to feel so full up of nostalgia with all this confusion going on in the house, that I make the mistake to tempt my faith. Sweet heart of Jesus! Soon as those dasheen leaves begin to boil I take off running. Evelina scream but I can't feel nothing in my hands a-tall, because before I can pull them from out the pot he is already cooking!

It is the *biggest* callaloo anybody ever see, and anybody who taste it say it is the *best* they ever eat. We are all gather round the table for this big Christmas dinner, you daddy and José and Barnabas, Simon and Pablo and Tomás with he cokeeeyes, and Reggie and Paco and little Amadao, and when these boys start to eat they can never stop, that soon I begin to think this story will no finish a-tall before they burst. All you can hear in the house is *slup slup slup* with the spoons scraping the bowls, and pass some more of that callaloo please! and even Evelina can no help sheself to taste some. In no time a-tall Uncle Olly have have another of he brainstorms again, and he jump up to say the thing to do with this big pepperpot is make weself a fortune. So before you can catch you breath Uncle Olly is outside again on the soapbox with he big megaphone selling tickets, five cents for a cup and ten for a bowl, and the line up of chupidees is stretching far as Tunapuna, with

Evelina and me the two priests at the top dishing it out!

WE COULD HEAR the Divina Church band beating steeldrums in the distance long before we met them. There were no clouds in the sky, scarcely any breeze, and the oldman continued to sweat in his aluminium outfit. The band appeared suddenly, rising over a short hill in an expanse of ruined canefield. But the band had changed dramatically. Now they were *all* wearing silver costumes like the oldman – an army of fiery angels, of shining robots – all brilliant beneath the sun. Behind them dragged the cloud of hot dust.

There must have been fifty people in the band, and twice as many children – twice as many as I remembered from years past. The oldman steered his oxcart to the side of the road, and we watched the angels go by, waving to us as they passed. Most went on foot, but there were bicycles and a few donkeycarts, all wrapped up in bright tinpaper. A couple of the bicycles had been turned into papier-mâché rockets, and there was a spaceshuttle with a Chinese boy pedalling frantically inside, a red light blinking on its tail. The children were running back and forth, screaming, trailing long strips of aluminium foil, flapping their silver wings. Each of the angels carried a musical instrument of some sort – steeldrums, horns, quatros – but most consisted of nothing more than a pair of toktok sticks, a rumbottle and spoon, or a cocoacola can with a handful of pebbles shaking inside. The oldman began to sing, his lips flapping over his nearly toothless gums, spittle flying. He took hold of my hands and shook them up and down with the music, his aluminium arms crackling: 'Time to jubilate whiteson, open you mouthgate!'

I began to sing too:

Sal-ve Regina,
Regina Magda-lena!
Be-ne-dicimas te,
Glo-ri-ficamas te,
A-do-ramas te,
Regina Magda-lena!

When the band had passed I got down slowly from the oxcart. The oldman turned the cart around and waved, his costume flashing molten metal for an instant as it caught the light. I watched him disappear into the cloud of dust which followed his band of angels. And I continued looking after him for a long time, until the dust had settled and the steeldrums had been reduced to a rumble in the distance. I looked around and realized I was again alone. There was no one left on the road. I turned and continued walking.

I walked less than a mile before I neared the end of Divina Trace, but the short distance seemed to me interminable. The sun was high and hot. I was covered in dust, my vestshirt sticking to my back with sweat. The eight or ten houses of Suparee Village looked deserted, beaten down by the heat, not even a fowl or a potcake in the trace. I checked the mudhuts quickly for a hammock in one of the frontyards: I couldn't even find an almond tree.

At the end of the trace the Church of Magdalena Divina was small, hard white against a hard blue sky. It would be cool inside. The thick wooden doors were shut tight. I pressed against them: nothing. Pulled on the black metal rings: nothing.

Now I felt as though I had not slept in three days. All I could think of was the huge samaan tree behind the church, the shade beneath it, the plot of soft green grass. I walked around the side of the church, and I managed only three or four steps across the grass before I collapsed in a heap beneath the tree. I took a few deep breaths. No sooner had I closed my eyes when the words began to move past, spectres out of the darkness: *The bottle was big and obzockee. I was having a hard time toting it. It was the day before my thirteenth birthday, seventy-seven years ago: tomorrow I will be ninety years of age.*

I HAVE ALWAYS accept Magdalena. She is Papa God saint, and if she is a whore it must be of He will. Who am I to say she is wrong to be Barto mistress, and how can I hold it against her when she is a creature of Papa God, breathing of He own spirit, make of He own flesh, touch by He own hand? Magdalena and I are both born to the same fate, both given to the world with the same misery, and joy, and the same hope, so how can I help to share this love for my husband with her when she ask it of me? How can I help to sacrifice some of this love that is overflowing the cup, when I know it is *he* wish too. And so I embrace her. I embrace her with my open heart!

I have always accept Magdalena. I try my best never to listen to what people say, and let me tell you people can say some words to push like a knife in you chest. But I am always kind to Magdalena, and when I meet her in the church with all the other nuns I make a special point to wish her a pleasant todobien, and when she come running to me crying in the middle of the night, and she press in my palm this gold rosary, I tell her how I will cherish it very much. Even though in truth it is *burning* a hole in my hand! Because of course she can never know how that I am hiding with Evelina behind the mangrove bush, watching Barto make her a present of that same gold rosary only the Sunday previous. But I accept it even so, and I tell her that I will pray to her on it every night. And that is just what I have do. I pray to her on that rosary every night, even though my fingers are trembling with rage only to hold it. No wife have ever honour she husband mistress more, and

offer her more love and devotion then I give to her. I raise
Magdalena up on a pedestal, you hear? On a *pedestal!*

But I begin to suspect something soon as Barto
announce for he last supper that he is making another of he
expeditions up the Orinoco. I am lying in my bed later
that night praying the same beads, when I hear this paper
sliding beneath the door. I jump up quick to on the light
and I run to this letter grabbing it up, reading it now with
my fingers trembling and my back press hard against the
door sweating, with these words passing before my eyes
like the dream of my own death. I throw open that
bedroom door and I take off running, and before Barto can
even reach the front door I catch him up. I press these same
beads hot inside he hand, and I tell him how *everybody* in
the whole of Corpus Christi know Magdalena is no dead
a-tall. She is living good as ever hiding all this time in the
house of that same pendejo Brito Salizar, right there on
Rust Street beside the hospital, because *he* is the only
wadjank wicked enough to defy Papa God self by bringing
her back to life, even after He have pronounce her dead. So
you can take this rosary to her waiting for you there in that
same little mudhut where you leave her this afternoon, and
you can tell her if she want to be my husband whore that is
one thing, but if she want to take him from me that is
something else, and she can take this solid gold rosary the
same time and push it up she sacred black culo! And when
you finish with that, you can take this fakeyfake suicide-
prayerletter and push it up you own culo too!

I AWOKE feeling as though I'd been sleeping for days,
but in fact it had not been more than several hours: the sun
was just beginning to set on the horizon of the swamp.
The air was cool, still, quiet. I got up slowly. Without
thinking I went to the back door of the church: it was
open. I passed through the sanctuary and out onto the

altar. I walked slowly towards the chapel at the side, the smells of Creole incense and sweetoil growing stronger as I approached.

I stood in front of the chapel, but I could see nothing in the darkness within except the bright red flames. I climbed the steps, a line of calabash shells filled with sweetoil on either side, and I knelt at the chapel railing. She began to take shape slowly out of the darkness, reflections of the tiny red flames rising on her face, flashing through the clouds of rising incense: her gentle eyes, comforting lips, the crimson mark on her forehead, her burnt-sienna skin, long wig of black hair. Everything the same – exactly as I remembered it. But now in her arms she held a child!

I reached quickly into my pocket for the sardine tin, my fingers trembling. I placed the tin on the handrest and removed the lid. Carefully, I took hold of a bead, slowly lifting out the rosary, its length slowly uncoiling: the gold had tarnished to a milky green. I closed my eyes, breathing deeply, feeling the chalky bead between my fingers: *Hail* –

Hail who? Hail *who*? I could not remember the words. All I could do was open my eyes, stand again, reach out slowly to hang the rosary around her neck.

But I stopped with my hands in the air, a bead frozen between the thumb and forefinger of each: now I had to see the child. Now I had to look into his face. I bent over, still couldn't see – not because of the dark – I could not see his face because it was hidden in the folds of her arms. I let go of the two beads: the rosary dropped around her neck, over the child, its cross dangling, swinging gently back and forth.

With one hand I slipped the sleeve of her gown up her forearm. With the other I took hold of the child's leg. I pulled. But I could not take the child from her arms. I let the sleeve go and held on to the child's leg with both hands, pulling with all my strength. My hands slipped: I fell backwards as though I'd been shoved, tumbling down the steps, and someone threw a bowl of sweetoil in my face – like I'd been slapped. I wiped my eyes. Got up slowly.

I climbed the steps again, knelt again at the chapel railing. I closed my eyes again. Slowly, carefully, I reached out for the basin of holywater: wet the tip of my index finger. I touched it to the centre of my brow, my breast, to each of my bare shoulders, touched my lips.

I stood and turned to leave, walking slowly down the centre aisle, my jesusboots squeaking on the polished stone, each step-slap echoing through the church. When I reached the big doors I looked for a handle: there was none, only two black metal rings as on the outside. I pulled. Pushed. Then I panicked: *trapped! locked inside the church!* Immediately I reached for the fishknife in my pocket – ready to push it into the keyhole – determined somehow to pick the lock. Then I remembered the back door.

When I closed it behind me I still had the knife in my hand. I passed beneath the samaan tree, over the plot of grass. I made my way through the tall reeds, to the edge of the foul-smelling swamp, my jesusboots sinking an inch into the mud. The water was flat, greengrey, a light mist floating above it. On either side of me there was a clump of moss-covered banyans. On the horizon the huge sun was disappearing into the sea. I reached my hand back, flung the knife as far as I could flipping out over the water, *clup*.

I turned, passed around the side of the church, and I started along the trace again: an oldman, raising the dust, walking towards the darkness.

BARTO LOOK DOWN on me now, and I see that I have truly touch him. Because he reach down to press back in my hand the same beads, and he say that he is no worthy to take them for me to Magdalena. Neither he, nor no man is worthy to step between the pure hearts of two women as Magdalena and me. Barto say that only I can give her these beads. Only I can give them to her, as only I can ask her forgiveness for taking way she child. But that I can ask of her in heaven! I can give these gold beads to Magdalena myself when I arrive, and I can remain there with her happy forever after. Because that is a place that he will never reach. And with that Barto open the door, and he leave disappearing into the night.

But Barto do no leave me alone. He leave me here in this big house, in this big crazyhouse that is so full up with children it is ready to burst, and that is consolation enough. It is happiness greater than any of us can ask, and in truth it is a happiness Magdalena sheself never know. Because the one child Barto give to Magdalena, never mind he is the ugliest creature ever to crawl on the skin of Papa God earth, is the one child that I have take from her.

But I can never suffer any more for that. After ninety-six years I have no more strength left to go on. My eyes have dry up, and there is no more tears left to pass, and Magdalena have forgive me. She have forgive me, and today I will be with her in heaven! Magdalena have forgive me, and Barto must forgive me now after all these years of crying in the dark, and I am ready. I am ready to lie my bones down in peace, peace that I have earn with sweating blood cold in the hot night, but I will never know peace so long as I have to be bury with this rosary burning a hole in my hand. Never! But you will take it to her, Johnny. Here, let me reach, *ay!* good. Here Johnny, you will go for me today, and you will carry these gold beads I am pressing inside you hand, and you will give them to her. Now I am ready to lie down my bones in peace. I have receive my long life, and so it have pass away, but now I have the hope of all my children to carry on for me when I am gone, and you can no ask for much more than that in

the end. Now I am ready to die. Go and call you daddy
and mummy.

Freeport, Bahamas
1983–1990

Robert Antoni's background includes two hundred years of family history in Trinidad and Tobago. A recipient of a National Endowment for the Arts Grant and a James Michener Fellowship, he has published in numerous periodicals including *The Paris Review, Ploughshares,* and *Conjunctions.* He received his doctorate from the Writers' Workshop at the University of Iowa and a master's degree from Johns Hopkins University. He teaches creative writing and literature at The University of Miami.